PENGUIN BOOKS

A Lost Wife's Tale

MARION MCGILVARY lives in West London with her four children. *A Lost Wife's Tale* is her first novel.

A Lost Wife's Tale

MARION MCGILVARY

PENGUIN BOOKS

PENGUIN BOOKS

Published by the Penguin Group
Penguin Books Ltd, 80 Strand, London WC2R ORL, England
Penguin Group (USA) Inc., 375 Hudson Street, New York, New York 10014, USA
Penguin Group (Canada), 90 Eglinton Avenue East, Suite 700, Toronto, Ontario, Canada M4P 2Y3
(a division of Pearson Penguin Canada Inc.)
Penguin Ireland, 25 St Stephen's Green, Dublin 2, Ireland
(a division of Penguin Books Ltd)
Penguin Group (Australia), 250 Camberwell Road, Camberwell, Victoria 3124, Australia
(a division of Pearson Australia Group Pty Ltd)
Penguin Books India Pvt Ltd, 11 Community Centre, Panchsheel Park, New Delhi – 110 017, India
Penguin Group (NZ), 67 Apollo Drive, Rosedale, North Shore 0632, New Zealand
(a division of Pearson New Zealand Ltd)
Penguin Books (South Africa) (Pty) Ltd, 24 Sturdee Avenue, Rosebank, Johannesburg 2196, South Africa

Penguin Books Ltd, Registered Offices: 80 Strand, London WC2R ORL, England

www.penguin.com

First published 2009
1

Copyright © Marion McGilvary, 2009
All rights reserved

The moral right of the author has been asserted

Set in 11/13 pt Monotype Dante
Typeset by Rowland Phototypesetting Ltd, Bury St Edmunds, Suffolk
Printed in England by Clays Ltd, St Ives plc

Except in the United States of America, this book is sold subject
to the condition that it shall not, by way of trade or otherwise, be lent,
re-sold, hired out, or otherwise circulated without the publisher's
prior consent in any form of binding or cover other than that in
which it is published and without a similar condition including this
condition being imposed on the subsequent purchaser

PAPERBACK ISBN: 978-0-141-03623-6
TRADE PAPERBACK ISBN: 978-0-670-91789-1

www.greenpenguin.co.uk

Penguin Books is committed to a sustainable future
for our business, our readers and our planet.
The book in your hands is made from paper
certified by the Forest Stewardship Council.

To Mr K from Miss M in the Library

I

My name was Edith Lutz.

So – what do you think? Thin? Earnest? Maybe broad, stream-lined cheekbones flaring like wings from a sharp nose, and perhaps blue Slavic eyes cut like tribal scars into the tight, bare canvas of her face? Or are you seeing feral wariness, muddy skin and nondescript pale brown hair, yanked into a ragged ponytail with a rubber band? Or German, perhaps? A statuesque, Jane Mansfield blonde, with stout legs, an uncomplicated relationship with porn and a wardrobe full of accessorized Birkenstocks?

It was open to interpretation.

In fact, once that summer, I met an underdressed American on the bus who, despite the Boston Celtic vest that hung like slack-jawed chins from his moist, hairy armpits, introduced himself with a formal handshake and made me spell it out for him as he held my bony fingers in his sweaty palm.

'So, like in clumsy?' he asked.

'You know – Lutz, klutz,' he elaborated when I gave him the blank stare I used for idiots and men in shorts – which pretty much had my social life covered back then.

'In the "you-ess" it's a person who drops stuff all the time,' he explained.

Yep. Just what you need sitting next to you on the No. 88 to Trafalgar Square – a fucking poet. But, anyway, ineptness hadn't occurred to me at the time. On the contrary.

To me, the name was always German. She would be staid, practical, fiercely capable and a bit worn around the edges. The sort of person who favoured sensible shoes like the kind my mother had worn when she was nursing – with maybe a plain, knee-length, A-line skirt and white cotton underpants bought a size too big for comfort. Like the real me, she was in her late thirties – not quite yet middle aged but in training for it – slim, average height, pale and fairly uninteresting. She was a woman who did not care too much about appearances, who could fade easily into the background, like a thin wash of watercolour paint.

While I was not perfecting a goose-step or manufacturing an accent with lots of z's in it, to get fully into character I still had to dress the part. I went to a department store in the High Street and bought a simple, made-in-the-Philippines, polyester skirt with a liquorice-thin plastic belt looped through the narrow waistband and a cotton shirt in a sad shade of nursing-home lilac. The footwear wasn't much of a stretch, since I always wore flat heels, but nevertheless I felt my Indian leather flip-flops were too ethnic to pass muster. I sifted through the cast-off shoes in Oxfam and, since it was summer, picked out a pair of shabby sandals with crêpe soles and the ghosts of another person's toes imprinted on the insoles, like a Turin Shroud for feet. I thought about bleaching my fair hair several shades blonder, but, on the salary I expected to become accustomed to, I knew there was no way I could maintain roots. Of any sort. I did, however, thread my long hair into a plait and then wind it into an amateurish bun. All I needed to do was perch my glasses on the end of my long, straight nose and I would become the stereotype of the mousy clerk I had once been – except then I had been young. And I had looked absolutely nothing like this.

So, would you hire this woman, I asked myself as I pirouetted in front of the mirror in the women's bathroom at Paddington Station. Well, I supposed it would depend on how desperate you were for domestic help. I sincerely hoped the next name on my list would be frantic, because I was running out of time and options. I had not liked the couple at the last interview. Their main pile was inherited, somewhere in the Cotswolds, but in town they lived in a hushed mausoleum cradled in the smug arms of the Boltons. They already employed a cook, a nanny and a chauffeur but were now looking for someone to take sole charge of the wife's bedridden mother. I had told the agency that I was not interested in looking after children, but it had never even crossed my mind that I might be expected to nurse the old. Had I been struck by a sudden urge to transform myself into a Mother Theresa of the Aged, I had a demented mother of my own whom I could care for.

I left without even meeting the invalid.

By ruling out either end of the age spectrum, I'd whittled down both my options and the patience of the woman at the agency, and so far I'd been offered only one job: as a chambermaid in a small hotel in Earl's Court run by a cartel of Nigerians, one of whom hired me without his bloodshot eyes ever meeting mine. But it was too public, and the job sounded closer to slavery than to hard work. Also, the hotel was in the sort of street where you could earn more money by lying on top of a bed than by making it.

So, for the nineteenth time I checked the appointment in the letter from the agency. The short job description said only that Adam Davenport lived alone and wanted a full-time, live-in cook/housekeeper who would work weekends and housesit over the summer. He specified someone honest, reliable and organized.

Two out of three wasn't bad.

According to my pocket street finder it was almost a straight walk from Paddington across pages 59 and 60 to the house in Notting Hill Gate. I let my severe reading glasses dangle on the chain around my neck – sadly, a necessity, not a prop – and crossed my fingers. I headed west along Craven Road, through Queensway and along Westbourne Grove, past a parade of shops that started off flyblown and sordid, advertising cheap international calls and sex of a similar nature, and ended up showcasing antiques and doll-sized clothes in frighteningly smart boutiques. Holland Crescent stood, abruptly, at the end. Fortunately, the pre-worn, crêpe-soled sandals were comfortable.

It took me less than half an hour, and I arrived early. I perched my slippery polyester bottom on a ledge at a nearby bus stop and watched the front door. No one came out while I waited, which was, I told myself, surely a good sign. It meant he hadn't lined up a whole stream of interviews. The minutes sighed away in the heat, until, with a brisk step, I crossed the road and rang the doorbell. It responded with a distinct lack of enthusiasm and apparent silence. Then the door slid open on buttered hinges, and there he was.

I had been expecting a fussy sixty-something bachelor, with cats, halitosis and a sparse side parting, but the man who led me into what was either a boardroom or a formal dining room was younger, albeit in a fogeyish, Sunday-afternoon-at-the-Vicarage sort of way. He was, at most, fifty, with mad, barely tamed, Beethovenish, dark brown wavy hair and the kind of even, square-jawed, fair-skinned good looks you got on knitting patterns in the 1950s.

'So, Mrs Lutz,' Adam Davenport queried over the top of his black-framed Thunderbirds spectacles, the almost identical twin, separated-at-birth, of those on my own nose, 'where does your name come from? I presumed you must be East European when the agency sent your details – Polish, or perhaps Czech, but your accent' – he coughed – 'would suggest otherwise.'

He laughed wryly, so I joined in, as though I were used to this sort of reaction, which, in a way, I was. Though it still took all my self-control not to ram the gold cigar of his fountain pen up his aristocratic nose.

'Prague by way of Princes Street,' I said. He laughed again.

Ha, fucking ha, I thought.

So much for Germanic restraint.

I should have realized that the Scottish accent was going to be a bit of a problem for any would-be Fräulein. But, even after nearly twenty years of listening to RP on a daily basis and being surrounded by scholars who even spoke Spanish with an upper-class drawl, I couldn't banish the Scottish slang that slipped into my sentences like the neighbour's cat whenever the door swung open. Five minutes into the interview and I was off script and improvising, dropping *ochs* into my sentences the way a bad cook oversalts the stew. And now, dear God. Now, I was even doing stand-up.

You can see why, when I was sixteen and tried to pass myself off as English, calling myself Annabel, it wasn't a success. I said *ken* so often that people thought it was the name of my boyfriend. But the misunderstanding came in fairly useful under the circumstances.

Davenport was staring at the paper on his desk, reading and rereading my references with Talmudic concentration. It was as though someone had hit the pause button in the middle of a long Swedish film. My finger twitched to press Play.

'I think it may have originally been Lutzman,' I babbled, hurrying him along.

His eyes flicked up.

'But I'm not sure,' I continued, carefully trying not to trip up over the consonants, bouncing the *t*'s smartly off the back of my teeth. 'My husband, Frank – his family moved to America from Germany during the war, but they didn't like to dwell on the details.'

I was already evicting Francisco's father from his antique-stuffed brownstone in the East 80s, relocating him to a dusty Upper West Side apartment filled with bad modern art, wonky pots and macramé, and substituting his trophy wife for a septuagenarian with an untidy chignon and a part-time psychoanalytical practice conducted from the spare room. What can I tell you – too much Woody Allen at an early age.

In fact, apart from my old boyfriend Karl, the only German I had ever known was Henny, the greengrocer in the village where I lived in the Borders. He had acquired a Scottish accent thick enough to spread on toast but with a razor-sharp German edge to it. Apparently he had been rounded up during the war and had spent it interned somewhere in the Highlands. After it was

5

over he resumed his life selling cabbages and turnips to the local populace, who treated him as though he had just been away for a fortnight's holiday in a caravan at Saltcoats, instead of living as an enemy alien for five years. Not that anyone ever forgot he was a German. But they just called him 'Henny the Hun' and left it at that.

Anyway, as I had hoped, the merest mention of war and the whiff of a possibility that there might be a Jewish horror story hiding underneath my adopted family's reluctance to discuss the provenance of their name, and the subject was dropped. There was another painful pause while Adam, once again, scanned the papers spread across the table.

For fuck's sake, would he ever stop reading the references? There wasn't anything wrong with them. I knew that. I had written them myself.

I took the opportunity to glance at my surroundings. We were both poised awkwardly at one end of a long lacquer table running like a ruler down the length of a room whose walls were painted a deep shade of Wedgwood blue and trimmed with white cornicing. A huge chandelier dripped glass prisms from an ornate plaster ceiling rose; two long walnut cabinets, each containing an army of glasses lined up in ranks, ready to march out over the table, stood on either side of a chalk-white marble fireplace. A pair of tall French windows, which cut the light into squares, like a slice of Battenberg cake, across a faded wine-coloured Turkish carpet, revealed a lush communal garden the size of a small park at the back of the house. It was the kind of place God would live in if he cheated on his taxes, and it was by far the grandest I had ever been in, even taking into account Francisco's family's Colonial house overlooking the sea outside Cartagena. Francisco's summer home was vast and elaborate, but not oozing money like sap from the floorboards the way this was. I couldn't imagine living here. You could get lost simply by wearing Paisley and standing on the pattern of the rug.

A cough and the briefest glint of eye contact brought me back to attention. 'I see you've worked as a housekeeper only once before – in Oxford? Did you like living there?'

'Yes, it was fine. I was working for a Canadian couple, but their sabbatical is over and they've gone back to Vancouver.'

'Which college?' he barked.

'Balfour.' I held my breath, hoping that his mother's sister's vicar's dog-walker wasn't related to the warden in that peculiar way the upper classes have of networking. It was tricky sticking so close to the truth, but I couldn't risk a lie that took me too far from what I knew, and Balfour was a big, unfashionable graduate college whose members were international and varied. It would be difficult to pin anyone down there.

'I went to Cambridge, myself. Don't know Balfour very well.'

What a relief. I exhaled so loudly the papers that he had finally set down on his desk fluttered.

'What about before that? It says here you lived in New York. Oxford must have been a bit of a change?'

'It was, but my husband . . . well . . .' I faltered deliberately and counted to three slowly; I had practised this for hours. 'He was a Latin American expert, he was at the UN. But – I'm a widow – he died recently . . .' I let my voice trail off and waited long enough for the expected sympathy to wade into the space before continuing. 'When I came back to Britain I had nowhere to stay and no job – so a live-in situation seemed to be the best solution. I knew Oxford from before. Frank and I once spent a year there, so . . .'

Interrupt, damn it, I thought. I was running out of lines. Then on cue, Davenport mumbled: 'Oh, I am sorry, that must be have been difficult for you.'

I inclined my head to acknowledge the weight of grief and my stoic acceptance of it, twisted the sliver of gold on my wedding finger and smiled bravely.

'No children?' he asked.

I shook my head no. 'It never happened.' I shrugged again, going for the Oscar in understated tragedy. I could see that this was yet another topic that Adam would treat like an outbreak of herpes.

'Em, well, the main reason I need full-time help is that my own daughter will be spending a fair bit of time here after the summer vacation. She lives with her mother at the moment. She's fifteen. I don't think she takes *too* much looking after. Quite independent. I also have a son, but he's at boarding school and will come only for the odd weekend. That wouldn't be a problem for you, would it?'

'Of course not,' I lied, while silently damning the agency for not filling me in on all the details. I really had no interest in doing the whole Mary Poppins thing – especially not for a teenage girl. Panic gripped me as a store detective would a shoplifter. I wanted to get up out of the chair and leave, but I was held down by my collar.

'And your family – are they still in Scotland?'

'All dead now.' I didn't elaborate but stared at him, daring him to inquire further.

He looked as though he wished he could evaporate. He dropped his glazed eyes back to a re-examination of the loop in the *L* of my signature, which I had written over and over again, like a boy's name on a school textbook, until it had just the right flourish. He adjusted his glasses.

Poor soul, I almost felt sorry for him. He was interviewing Typhoid Mary in his dining room and I expected him to give me a job, hand over his keys and entrust me with both the care of his impressionable children and the smooth running of his household. In another culture they would burn me at the stake.

'Cooking,' he ventured, back on safe ground. 'Mrs McBride speaks highly of you?'

There seemed to be a question hiding in the statement, so I hastily attested to my skill in the kitchen: 'I can cope with most things. Mrs McBride used to entertain a lot, and I did all the cooking – mostly plain dishes, roasts, salads, but I can also do Spanish, Hispanic, Italian, French – I'm not a Cordon Bleu, though.'

'No German food?'

I couldn't think what he was talking about. Why would I be cooking sauerkraut and dumplings? And then I remembered the German in-laws.

'Ah, no,' I said, smiling politely. 'We spent a bit of time in Central and South America, so we got a taste for the food,' I explained.

He opened his mouth to inquire further, then thought better of it, doubtlessly fearing that curiosity would unearth an even more torturous past.

Nice lips, I thought, as he closed them. Being very English, he was too polite to pose any more personal questions, and, as I had hoped, too desperate for some household help to care. I was the ideal employee. I could speak English, or at least a recognizable version of it, I could cook, run a house and, according to the estimable Mrs McBride, was honest and efficient. I had no dependants, and I could start immediately.

And so, after a few token inquiries about my old life in New York, which I carefully dodged, I was hired on a month's trial, beginning on Monday, and given a set of keys to the street door in the basement, where I would have my own flat.

I accepted so quickly that I didn't even ask how much he was going to pay me.

We shook hands, and I went back to Oxford, where, to the creak and groan of naked floorboards and the hollow sighs of bare cupboards, I packed.

I dumped the contents of the freezer, put out the last of the rubbish in black bags, deleted all my computer files, turned off the gas and opened the door of the empty fridge. I wrote a note explaining how to turn on the hot-water heater and stuck it on the boiler. I left a spare set of keys to the house on the hook by the back door for the new tenant – a visiting professor who had arranged to rent the house for a few months in the autumn term – and on my way to the station I dropped my own in an envelope at the porter's lodge.

Before I'd had time to register my loss, it was done. I was back in London, letting myself into the basement flat at No. 22 Holland Crescent, which, though lined with statuesque Georgian houses like a shop window full of wedding cakes all iced with stucco, was in fact a short, blunt, fag end of a street, stubbed out halfway down Ladbroke Grove, and about as much a crescent as I was a German widow.

And, as neither of us was quite what we seemed, we suited each other just fine.

2

But that doesn't mean I liked it.

Downstairs in the basement, the house dropped its gracious manners. My bedroom was full of angry Victorian furniture that missed no opportunity to nip spitefully at my shins and elbows as I walked past. There was an overbearing mahogany wardrobe the size of a fat woman's coffin that tipped forwards whenever I opened the door further than a crack. The bed was a narrow single with a buckled frame like a giant oak yawn, showing the gaping teeth of a wrought-iron base; the mattress collapsed with exhaustion whenever I sat on it, which was often, since the room contained no chair. The single chest of chipped veneered drawers backed against the wall behind the door like a cornered fugitive and dropped dandruff flakes of sawdust over all my clothes. At night I could hear woodworm chewing through the wood.

Whenever I walked into the bedroom, a tight sensation of unease pinched me like a second-hand dress that had once belonged to someone much thinner. I couldn't help but long for the bright little room I had left behind, with its shaky brass bedstead and primary-coloured tribal rugs on the painted floorboards. We liked to pretend we'd found the carpets while trekking through Peru, but the only things I picked up in Peru were bedbugs. The rugs had arrived, sight unseen, from a mail-order firm in the back pages of a Sunday supplement.

I thought I had graduated with honours in solitude when I left home as a raw teenager, but in Holland Crescent I soon came to realize that I hadn't even made it out of primary school. In the cramped bedroom I sat hunched in the hollow of the mattress and stared at the curling Sellotape left by the posters of a previous tenant, listening to the rest of my life tick away on the bedside clock.

What had I done to myself? I looked at the dust felted on top of every surface in the room and choked on something halfway between despair and asthma. But I had to make the best of it. This was my life now.

At around about the time I realized that losing a husband spawned a corresponding need to make a living, fast, it also became blindingly clear that I didn't have employment opportunities ringing my bell like the Avon lady. Up until then, Francisco had supported us both on his modest but steady academic salary, supplemented by a small family trust fund that yielded enough to pay for travel during the summers.

I made pin money here and there by typing and editing students' doctoral theses, but obviously this wasn't going to be enough to sustain me in the big, wide, expensive world of independence. Outside of a university town, where could you hope to find a sufficiently large stash of Ph.D. students? My typing, never particularly accomplished at the best of times, was accurate but slow. I was used to paying more attention to syntax and accurate foreign spellings than to speed and spreadsheets. My office skills were hopelessly outdated, and even if I had wanted a job as only a shop assistant, I would need references and experience – neither of which I possessed.

I did a quick stocktake and decided to build on my existing skills. I had rusty Grade 5 piano, a Gold Medal for Life Saving and a Bronze Medal for Highland Dancing. I knew the Dewey Decimal System backwards, and I could speak enough Spanish to order food and communicate with the maids. I could cook, run a house and smile prettily while looking riveted at dinner parties when I was bored to the point of catatonia. I was good at pastry and proficient at sex, but, since I was probably too old for prostitution and not decorative enough for the escort business, it seemed as though I should concentrate on the pastry. If I found a job with cooking that let me live in, it would also solve the problem of accommodation. That settled it: instead of summoning the maid, I would become one myself.

I went to the Senior Common Room in the mid afternoon when even the dust was asleep and scanned *The Lady* and *Country Life* for agencies that specialized in supplying domestic help, choosing a small but respectable-looking company with a PO box that gave the impression of being run from someone's spare room in a London suburb. Then, posing as my own previous employer, I used Balfour College-headed notepaper to furnish myself with a glowing character reference. Those laborious word-processing skills finally came in handy.

When the recruiter at the agency rang the house to check me out, I adopted a vague North American drawl, playing accent keepie uppie for the few minutes I spoke to her, and praised my wonderful housekeeper highly.

And so I became Edith Lutz. The name took a bit of getting used to, especially since no one ever spoke it aloud.

At first, hoping to familiarize myself with the curt, sharp vowels, I began to recite it like a mantra, over and over again – a Buddhist chant echoing eerily around the rapidly emptying rooms, as painfully, picture by plate, I dismantled the traces of the years Francisco and I had spent together, packing my own belongings, and then his, into boxes; some for charity, some for storage. But I was still afraid that my new name would sneak up on me unannounced, hail me from across the street, and I would forget who I was.

Once installed in the basement of Holland Crescent, I was more or less living alone, with only fleeting glimpses of my employer, so it wasn't as though a whole host of people were calling out my name on a roll-call. The men on the market stalls where I shopped daily called me 'darlin'' or 'luv'; and the sari-swathed Asian woman in the chemist, embarrassingly, addressed me as 'ma'am', until I set her straight with an overfamiliar 'Edith', which only embarrassed us both even more.

Meanwhile, Adam Davenport, who seemed to find it as

awkward having me in the house as I felt being there, didn't call me much of anything at all. Mostly he assiduously avoided making eye contact. I began by calling him, deferentially, Mr Davenport, but, addressing a spot somewhere between my knees and my feet, he mumbled an unintelligible protest and insisted upon Adam, managing to make the name sound more like a curse than a plea for informality. I rarely saw more than the jacket of his linen suit, crumpled like a hankie at the bottom of the stairs, so it was a moot point.

At least it meant I could throw away the polyester skirt and forget the uniform of the East European drudge. There was no audience to dress the part for. Instead, I wore all the cotton dresses that I had intended to take with me to Colombia, where, in the life that had been so cruelly snatched from me, I had planned to spend most of the next six months sunning myself in a hammock on the beach. So, as July steamed into August, I was cool, at least, if not comfortable.

The days I could just about manage, but the nights were long exercises in barely suppressed terror. Like a good Stepford wife, I started work before seven and prepared breakfast for the master of the house. When he had gone to work, I polished and dusted and scoured and scrubbed the already spotless house until every piece of silver cutlery lay, untarnished, in a drawer, the tines of the forks and the cups of the spoons all facing East, cuddled against one another in sets of twelve, while the plates gleamed in graduated tiers like porcelain ziggurats.

I swept the stairs in shifts, although only Adam and I walked on them, and I dusted every unread book on every shelf. It was like being in my own self-inflicted Sisyphean hell, but with a toothbrush and a bottle of ammonia cream cleanser instead of an uphill struggle with a rock. I finally became the kind of housewife that my mother would have approved of.

Pity she wasn't around to clap.

In the swelter of the empty summer afternoons, I passed the time walking to distant supermarkets for only one item, or taking the stammering, traffic-choked bus ride to China Town for minute quantities of ginger and lemon grass when the Malaysian shop three streets away had everything displayed in a cloud of exhaust outside on the pavement. I wore a baseball cap and a hideous pair of rhinestone sunglasses, both bought from the Saturday flea market at the unfashionable end of Portobello Road, lest someone from my previous life should find and claim me, loitering in the produce aisle at the Hammersmith branch of Tesco's.

Naturally I avoided galleries and exhibitions where the chances of recognition were greatest, and imposed an exclusion zone around the British Library, where I might have encountered a stray academic who knew me from Oxford. To cool off, I swam in the local municipal pool until my hair, which I had decided I couldn't afford to lighten, became bleached a Midwich Cuckoos shade of green-blonde from the chemical combination of chlorine and sun, while my arms and shoulders grew good East European shot-putter's muscles. In the afternoons I lay under a tree in the communal garden until the cooing and crying of well-bred, overindulged babies drove me inside to the dim, welcome silence of my bedroom.

As long as I busied myself with unnecessary chores, I could keep my anxieties at bay. But they would circle round and round the edges of my mind like wolves round a campfire, waiting for that second of inactivity when I would drop my guard and they could slink right in and curl up at my feet, their teeth gleaming in the flames.

I'd be in the middle of choosing something to pretend to read in the local library, fighting the urge to reshelve misplaced books, when sorrow would catch me and tears would course helplessly down my cheeks. I'd find myself at a pedestrian crossing in a stunned trance while the scissor-legged man changed from red to green, and back to red again. Once or twice passers-by stopped and asked me if I was feeling all right, as though they thought I might be about to do an Anya Karenina and throw myself under a car. But that would have shown a lack of imagination and required better underwear than I possessed. In any case it would have taken too much effort. Or at least a sharp push from behind.

But, still, there weren't enough hours in the day to worry; I had to borrow them from the night instead. The enormity of what I had done would crouch at the end of my bed and pounce on my chest at 3 a.m. I would wake, already sweating in the stewing heat of the suffocatingly airless bedroom, my heart compressed with anxiety, blood drumming in my ears, and lie in bed frozen with terrors, both named and unthinkable.

I took St John's wort and Bach's Rescue Remedy, but both had as much effect on my anxiety as a deer pissing on a forest fire. For sleeplessness I tried a range of over-the-counter remedies from the Indian lady in the chemist, but they made me disorientated and fuzzy-headed, yet still wide awake. I drank a lot of herbal tea with names like SleepyHead and Nighteaze, then woke up from my precious few hours of slumber to go to the bathroom and pee. SleepyHead, my arse.

Eventually, I gave up and just got out of bed and paced. I listened to the tinny sound of the World Service, and middle-of-the-night Music to Slit Your Throat By on a powder-blue children's tape player that I found in one of the kids' bedrooms. I indulged in long washing-and-ironing sessions with anguish added to the final rinse instead of fabric conditioner. As my arm slid back and forth over heat-shimmering planes of rippled French linen, Leonard Cohen and I would groan in unison. At a whisper, in the flannel-lined silence of the otherwise silent house, we sang: 'It's four in the morning . . .' But by this point Leonard and I had been wretchedly harmonizing for long enough to tell the time.

In a fit of unaccustomed female intimacy, the wife of my friend Karl had once told me that this was her favourite song. She said that if any man had played it while he was trying to seduce her, she would have immediately succumbed. Who would have thought it? I didn't know what was stranger: tuneless moaning acting as an aphrodisiac or the notion of Karl's wife having a libido. I thought the song was too full of regret to be erotic. Anyway, I doubted whether Karl had ever got into her sterile underwear with any help from Cohen. He was more into Liebach when I slept with him – thankfully not as an accompaniment to sex but to shot glasses brimming with peach schnapps.

It was a novel concept: sexual discernment through song. I had always gone to bed with men regardless of their taste in music – regardless of their taste in anything, actually, as long as they had a liking for me. Even now I would have happily slept with the entire road crew of a Black Sabbath tribute band if afterwards I could do just that – sleep.

I wondered if I would infect the whole house with insomnia through the concertinas of crisp white bed sheets. But then everyone was just 'Damn' Davenport and myself, and he already had problems sleeping. I sometimes heard him walking about in the kitchen overhead, slow, light footsteps and then the tap running, the splash of water. With a little upswing of hope, I began listening out for him. I took to leaving a jug of iced tea in the fridge, with one of his errant wife's frigid white china plates bearing a couple of biscuits on the table, as if he were Santa Claus. But then, just like Santa, he stopped coming when I started to believe in him.

I missed his footsteps. I often felt as if I were the only person in the whole world awake. A sudden flare of light from a bathroom window the size of a postage stamp in the house on the opposite side of the garden square would fill me with optimism – or as close as I got to the feeling, which was maybe a slight lift in my heart, one floor up from desolate.

My flat was folded into one half of the basement, obscured by a block of granite stairs. The front door, by the dustbins, led to a room that, I assumed, had once been Adam's children's playroom. It had an old corduroy sofa, a wall of bereft shelves containing a few leftover kids' videos, tattered picture books and some very old classics that I remembered from my own childhood, and an ancient TV with a trailing aerial cable that ended in a tripod of coloured wires.

In theory this room was my sitting room – but it was like the waiting area in a children's hospital where all the kids were dead. I went in there only when I had run out of other places to clean; the spots on the carpet alone held at least a week's possibility of fruitless scrubbing and shampooing. I was saving it for a rainy day. In the middle of a July heatwave it was something to look forward to.

Next to the sitting room was a series of windowless rooms in a line like cereal boxes, used for storing wine, a washer and dryer, and a large chest freezer. My small sixties-decorated shower room came next, and finally, at the rear of the basement – with a view of eight broad, jagged, stone steps leading up to the garden above, and the briefest glimmer of blue sky and the attic rooms in the houses opposite – lay my bedroom. Next to it was a small galley kitchenette with French doors, and a boot room with a row of poignantly small wellingtons for children who had long outgrown them. When I could bear to look at them no longer, I hid them in a box behind a similarly incrementally sized pile of bikes.

We fell quickly into a routine, Adam Davenport and myself. He worked in publishing, and I worked in the kitchen. I made him coffee in the morning, which he drank wordlessly at the vast dining-room table where he'd interviewed me, marooned alone behind the *Daily Telegraph*. I offered him breakfast: wholegrain toast, eggs cooked in a Kama Sutra range of ways, home-made muesli. Each he declined, saying that he was happy with coffee, but I squeezed him juice and made a fruit salad anyway – then usually consumed most of it myself, standing up at the sink, before scraping his untouched leftovers into the Tupperware for tomorrow's juice.

He told me it was his custom to eat lunch and often dinner in a restaurant with writers and agents, and so he instructed me to make sure there was some bread and cheese in the fridge that he could take to his study if he was hungry, or leave sweating in its cling film wrapper if he wasn't. He usually wasn't. But this didn't deter me from leaving him beautifully arranged plates night after night in the hope that he would eat.

I gave up on the supermarket cheddar and experimented with tortilla stuffed with spinach, and pipérade with truffle oil, but apparently he didn't like cold eggs wherever they hailed from in continental Europe. I left out plates of grapes, a selection of charcuterie and olives with rosemary, but they lay there till the ham turned up its toes and the olives grew fish-eyed. Sometimes I'd rescue the plate buried under papers in his study, jubilantly empty but for crumbs and crusts; at others I'd find it on the draining board, with the plastic peeled back a few inches, the food missing only a few bites. But most often he didn't even open the kitchen door. The waste disposal ate very well.

My frustration finally got the better of me. One day, after I had found fat Sicilian figs almost bursting out of their dusky purple skins, I walked up to the top of Portobello Road to the Spanish deli and instructed the wall-eyed assistant to shave me some transparent slices of Serrano ham. That night, instead of closeting myself in my room, I sat upstairs pretending to attend to some unnecessary chore, like licking the chrome clean on the kettle, and waited until I heard him come in. Luckily it was not a dining-out night that he had forgotten to tell me about, and he arrived around eight thirty, a heavy exhalation and the rattle of his keys announcing his presence. The moment the street door swung closed behind him, I walked into the marble hall and held my hand out to take his jacket, which he usually threw like a drunk on to the gilt chair that sat daintily next to a table bearing a matching, monstrous clock, big enough to have its own hunchback.

I smoothed the linen of his jacket and hung it in the coat cupboard, feeling like a fifties housewife. I would be asking him if he had had a good day at the office next, except that I could tell from the dark circles under his eyes, and the slump of his shoulders as he bolted the door behind him, that he almost certainly hadn't.

'Edith,' he said, looking as shocked as if I had turned up wearing tassels on my nipples and barely restraining a man on a leash. 'You shouldn't be working this late. Is everything all right?' He spoke to the blue cheese veins in the marbled tiled floor and turned as though to climb the stairs.

'Mr Davenport . . . Adam,' I amended. 'I know that all you want me to do is leave you a plate of something in the fridge, but please, please, just for once, come and sit down and let me cook you a proper meal.'

'I'm really not . . .' he began, foot poised on the bottom step.

'I just hate throwing away all this uneaten food night after night, but if I don't prepare anything then I feel useless.' I noticed he was getting thin. He was wearing a rumpled white shirt with a loosened striped tie; his sleeves were rolled halfway up his forearms and the elbows poked out of them like a skinny schoolboy's.

He began to stammer excuses into his chest, his whole body twitching in eagerness to avoid me and get back to the business of climbing the stairs, but I wasn't letting him get away.

'Please, come into the kitchen and let me feed you,' I said, and, without another word, I walked through the hall towards the back of the house, hoping he would follow me.

In anticipation, I had set a place for him at the kitchen table. There was a tureen of iced gazpacho, salty Sardinian flatbread and a platter with the ham and the figs, torn apart and pursed up like the pouting lips of a silent screen star. Without asking, I opened a bottle of beer, poured it into a tall glass and handed it to him, pulling the chair out and indicating that he should sit.

'Really, it's unnecessary,' he stammered. 'You don't need to go to all this trouble. I don't have much of an appetite these days.'

'I can see. You're fading away. But it would be a kindness to me if you would sit down. I haven't spoken to a soul in three days, except to say two hundred grams of ham, thinly sliced, and even that was in Spanish. Bad Spanish. So, please, please, indulge me. Have a drink. Talk to me.' I smiled to show I was kidding, but I wasn't. I was pleading.

Francisco would have sighed, long-sufferingly, and rolled his eyes. He would have complained wearily, saying that he had been talking to people all day, and that now all he wanted to do was relax and be left in peace.

I had only the sketchiest idea what Adam did at his office. For all I knew he led corporate bonding sessions all day and was exhausted from standing at a white board with a flip chart, sick of the sound of his own voice. Maybe he was just like Francisco had been: keen to keep his own thoughts and withdraw into a distracted silence. But I didn't care. I had begun to strike up conversations with the cold callers who rang trying to sell financial services. I was only one 0800 number away from the Samaritans. I needed some company.

To my relief, Adam started to laugh. He took off his glasses, rubbed his eyes and took a long, long swallow of the beer. 'That sounds wonderful; you have no idea quite how wonderful. I'm going to need another one of these, though' – he gestured to the bottle of beer – 'and there's a condition,' he added, drawing out a chair and sitting down.

I looked at him. Actual eye contact. They were green, I noticed.

'Get a glass and a plate, and join me.'

I hate beer, but this wasn't the time to quibble. I snapped off a few shards of bread, cut some tomatoes, took out another bottle of Corona and sat opposite him.

'I didn't know you spoke Spanish,' he said.

'I don't, not really. But we travelled around South America a lot. Frank was . . .' I rummaged through the index cards in my head, which I had supposedly prepared for just this moment. They were blank. 'He loved South America. We spent some time there, with his job.'

Had I told him this? I couldn't remember. 'I picked up a bit;

21

just kitchen Spanish. And then in New York, you know, it's the second language.'

Was it? I just kept spitting out word after word, digging myself in deeper, instead of shutting up.

'Yes, New York. It must be a bit of a change being stuck here after the excitement of New York. Do you miss it,' he said more than asked.

I shook the question off casually. 'Not really. It's not such an easy place to live,' I answered.

'I'm always working when I'm there. Never any time to relax. Did you meet your husband there?' he asked.

Now, *this* I had thought about, and had a ready-made answer. 'I was working in a bar, sleeping on a friend's floor, and he was a grad student at NYU; he used to walk me to the subway at the end of my shift. Not very romantic, I'm afraid. What about you and your wife?' I asked, trying to deflect further curiosity.

'Who? Gay?' he asked as though he had a few wives stashed in a cupboard that he'd outgrown and wasn't quite sure which one I meant. 'Oh, Lord, that wasn't romance either. It was just sort of inevitable, I suppose. We were at Cambridge together. But I knew her before. Her sister went out with my brother Tim, and my parents knew hers. We used to go to the same children's parties when we were small.'

I murmured something encouraging, though I couldn't think of anything worse than marrying your childhood sweetheart.

'We started going out the first term we were there; she was at Girton, I was at King's; and when we graduated, getting married just seemed the next step. It was as if someone had filed the flight plan for my life when I was about six and I merely went ahead and followed it. It was all so predictable. I always saw that as a disadvantage, but I suppose for you predictability would have been something of a luxury.'

'What do you mean?'

'Well, I mean with your husband, em . . .' He wanted to say 'dying', but the word stuck in his throat like a piece of dry bread.

His face flushed with mortification. 'I am so sorry, what a tactless idiot I am.'

I shook my head wordlessly. I couldn't go there. Sirens were flashing, slow down, pull over, turn back.

'Gay always used to tell me I was the least sensitive man alive.' He grimaced as he bit off the last word.

'It's fine, really . . .' I said hoping to pre-empt yet another apology. 'Tell me about your work,' I said quickly, trying to steer him into safer waters.

'Only if you promise to shoot me first,' he said and laughed again. A joke. We were making progress.

'It's very boring: booksellers, budgets, keeping the shareholders happy, meeting targets. Believe me, it's not interesting. I'm very dull company, I'm afraid.'

I poured my beer inexpertly into a tall glass, wishing suddenly that I had made myself something other than a barmaid as I sipped my way through five inches of foam, wiped off my moustache, and listened while he talked about his house in Provence where he was planning to spend most of August and then, on his third beer, about how Gay had left him six months previously. It wasn't exactly easy listening to the catch in his voice as he described her sudden departure. By this point, rather than a beer, I could have done with a vodka myself. Preferably intravenously.

The subject of the kids seemed a better bet, though I really wasn't keen on getting into a doting discussion on the joys of parenthood. I did a hurried U-turn. 'Your children are cute.' Judging by the forests of photographs arranged throughout the house, they weren't, but I could hardly say, 'Your kids are a testament to the dangers of inbreeding.' 'You must miss them.'

'Yes. But of course it was better for them to go to live with Gay. What kind of mother would walk out on her children?'

I cringed inwardly. The sentence was like a knee in the groin, but I merely wrapped my arms tightly across my chest and nodded my agreement. I felt as though I had a broom handle welded to my spine.

'What are their names?' I asked, when I got enough breath.

'Ned, my son, is thirteen,' he replied, his face breaking into a smile. 'He's at Marlborough.'

I was glad he had his attention fixed on the last drops of gazpacho so that he didn't see the look of disbelief in my eyes. Ned, what kind of name was that? I had an imaginary donkey called Ned when I was about eight. But it's surely not something you would call a real-life, almost buck-toothed kid.

'And your daughter?' I prompted.

'Oh, Lennie – Leonora – she's fifteen going on thirty-five. You'll meet her soon. She'll come to stay when we get back from Provence. Her mother wasn't keen on her being here while I was alone. As you will have appreciated, I'm not home often enough to look after a child – I work such long hours.'

I smiled in vague agreement while thinking, my God – Ned and Lennie. What a pair. The middle classes never failed to amaze me with their capacity to inflict unnecessary handicaps on their otherwise privileged children. Poor girl. What sort of parent calls a baby girl Leonora? It sounded like fabric softener. I felt an unexpected surge of sympathy for the blonde, orthodonticized teenager whose latest school mugshot I had just that morning dusted in its square silver frame.

We had something in common after all – myself and this teenager, whose arrival I was already dreading. I may not have known much about kids, but I knew exactly what it was like to be saddled with a hideously awful name.

My own real name was Agnes.

3

But at least mine was inherited, not capriciously bestowed on me at birth by the bad-name fairy.

There's a whole dynasty of us – withered, mousy Protestant women – with two things in common: fragile complexions and the first name Agnes. My mother was called Agnes, and my grandmothers, coincidentally, on both sides, were called Agnes, then there was one great-grandmother, another even greater, two aunts, four cousins, a small niece and – well, you get the point. The women in my family either had remarkably little imagination or they considered Agnes to be their own particular brand-name – like Hoover is to vacuum cleaners.

But the Agnes was an unpopular brand. As a girl I couldn't understand why my mother hadn't chosen a modern name – like Michelle, Vanessa or Samantha (though in retrospect I can see that there are good reasons why no eight-year-old should be allowed to chose her own name). I wouldn't even have minded being one of the five girls in my Primary 5 class called Linda. At least they had something to bond over. But instead I was Agnes, pronounced with a Lowland snarl to sound something between a dry sneeze and the yip of a small, irascible dog just before it sinks its sharp little teeth into your leg.

However, I learned early that there was no point in complaining about having to bear the family mark of Cain. It could have been worse. In a moment of brief post-partum madness, my mother had toyed with the idea of bucking family tradition and calling me Bridget.

I rest my case.

So I spent the first part of my life as the uncompromisingly stern Agnes McBride. And, later, when I married Francisco and replaced the McBride like a pair of baggy old knickers with his much frillier, flouncier surname, I couldn't help but marvel at my lucky escape. I liked being Agnes Morales, but if I had been stuck with Bridie Morales I would have sounded like a can-can girl in a Wild West saloon, or a pet beautician who specializes in shampooing poodles.

Sometimes you have to be grateful for small mercies.

But even Agnes Morales wasn't great. From the mouth of my husband Francisco the harshness of Agnes was transformed into a sex-laden endearment. He swallowed the *g* like an oyster and sucked on the *s* till it swelled into a short breathy *a*. But on English lips I sounded like a Spanish maid, which, as things turned out, was ominously prescient. I grew into it, you might say, except that just as it began to fit me, I had to shrug it off and find another.

After much deliberation the first name I gave myself when job-seeking was Ruth. I had decided that this, finally, was my chance to have a gentle, feminine name that would soften my edges. Yet, when I began filling in application forms for the agency, I just couldn't think myself into it. I didn't know her. I tried it on, but it didn't fit. I found Ruth's meek, biblical prettiness too delicate and forgiving. A lifetime as Agnes had conditioned me to something with a snap at the end of it, like a rolled-up towel on a bare leg. So I chose another ugly name, to match my nature.

I picked Edith from the hatchet-profiled frontispiece in a beaten-up copy of a book on the Bloomsbury Group and added it to the Lutz I had already decided on. I went to the college library and looked myself up on LexisNexis and yes, my instincts had been right, there was an Edith Lutz living in Germany – a fiftysomething Freudian analyst, and the author of several long monographs with compound German titles, not a word of which I could understand.

Edith Lutz.

It settled on me like a hard-wearing, scratchy tweed suit, and soon it came to grace my artfully self-composed references and testimonials, my newly laminated Kensington and Chelsea library card, and the front of the envelope Adam left for me at the end of the month with my wages inside, in cash.

I couldn't do anything about a new bank account, driving licence or passport, but the possibility of foreign travel was unlikely to arise, at least for a while.

Working for Adam quickly appeared to be not unlike the day-to-day business of marriage to Francisco, right down to the absence of sex, which in our relationship had been slowly replaced by diffidently polite goodnight kisses and low-voltage his and hers bedside lamps that allowed each of us to read without disturbing the other. Granted, while married, neither had I ever done a great deal of housework, but then I hadn't realized that if it wasn't included in the package, you could actually get paid for it.

With Adam my duties were not onerous and mostly self-inflicted. He worked long hours and rarely returned home before 9 p.m., still eating only when I forced him. He travelled occasionally, a night or two here and there for which he packed himself. He told me that in the autumn he would go to Frankfurt for the book fair and to New York for meetings, and that around this time he planned to entertain occasionally, promising it would not be extravagantly and that I could hire extra help if necessary. He expected his shirts to be sent to the laundry, but I did them myself from choice. Yet, though I may have ironed his striped boxer shorts and made his bed, housekeeping still allowed for an element of mystery that marriage did not accommodate.

His estranged wife, Gay – who apparently wasn't, in either sense of the word – worked as an editor in a rival publishing house. His son, Ned, was happily ensconced at Marlborough, Adam's old public school, and his daughter, Lennie, lived with her mother in her smart, minimalist penthouse flat high above the river in Vauxhall. Since I had been installed in the basement and was able to function as a ready-made proxy house-mother, I knew it was only a matter of time before she began coming here

27

at weekends. A prospect that I anticipated with about as much relish as a root canal without anaesthetic.

So far I knew the rest of his family only from the two rows of silver-framed studio photographs on the top of Adam's grand piano, seemingly placed in the middle of the elegant drawing room for the sole purpose of displaying snapshots.

There was a speckled black-and-white one of his father, founder of both the fortune and the publishing business that accessorized it, posed beside a stout, boot-faced woman who was, unfortunately for everyone doomed to inherit her genes, his mother. I could see no resemblance between this stern, well-upholstered, moustachioed man and the slim, gaunt face of his son.

There were brothers, all stouter variations of Adam, like balloons with more air in them. I couldn't tell Tim from Stanley, but both were older.

In the back row there was a single glamorous professional portrait of Gay signed 'To Gaynor with best regards' by David Bailey, taken in the early eighties, judging by the ruffled neckline of her dress. But no wedding pictures. She was beautiful in a chubby, home counties, pony club sort of way, I grudgingly allowed, but the New Romantics did no one any fashion favours, least of all the plump.

At the front there was a chronological selection of each of his two children taken at various stages of their school careers, obviously chosen by a fond, if wilfully blind, parent. Certainly Adam's daughter would not thank him for displaying the picture of her, aged around nine, looking like a bespectacled Jack Russell terrier, while Ned's latest photograph in rugby kit could have graced a wanted poster.

Behind these ranged a great number of black-and-white publicity shots in which, treading perilously close to sub-vulgarity, Adam was flanked by famous authors, well-known broadcasters and even Salman Rushdie. A peculiar vanity, I thought – as if he were in danger of forgetting his place in the world without a photograph to remind him. But then he wasn't the one chanting his name out loud to cultivate an identity, so who was I to talk?

Sometimes, on a good day, I would go upstairs with my duster and footle around the room, adjusting paintings and straightening cushions, knocking them into shape with such military precision that even my mother would have saluted them. I would sit at the piano and play my Grade 5 examination pieces, plodding gracelessly through the Viennese Waltz, before carefully replacing the damask cloth and rearranging the photographs one by one, marvelling at Adam's ability to live so peacefully surrounded by all these people from his past.

In Scotland we kept our family photographs under lock and key – like the last strains of a deadly virus, isolated from the general population – crammed inside a battered tan leather suitcase that was, in turn, crammed at the back of my mother's wardrobe.

I am around nine or ten, and bored. Being an afterthought has its advantages, not least that arriving thirteen years after my closest sibling means that I am usually home alone. My mother works in the local pharmacy, counting Ponderax into smoked plastic bottles for the sleepless and Diazepam for the depressed. My father is the manager in the local bank, giving out Masonic handshakes and short-term loans. My sister Maisie has married a Catholic – her former ballroom dancing partner – and, whether to escape the Presbyterian censure heaped on Proddies who cross over to the Fenians, or in search of better opportunities, has emigrated to Australia. And my brother Geordie is at Strathclyde University being brainy.

I have already found and read the Christmas annuals hidden under the bed and trawled through my mother's dressing table looking for anything of interest. But, with my mother's obsession with hoarding, storing, secreting away, you can always find something to look at.

Nothing is thrown away; everything is neatly stored – as if the secret drawer police might make a dawn inspection without warning, cresting the mountain range of ludicrously large brassiere cups pointing up like the Alps. Most of the drawers contain piles of clothes being kept for best. We have whole rooms for best. A best front bedroom that no one ever sleeps in, a best front sitting room for visitors who never come, a best front door through which the visitors who never come can make their arrival. So naturally, best clothes for visits that never occur are absolutely necessary.

She also likes to keep some new clothes aside to be buried in just in case death should call unexpectedly, without ringing first. Not content with maybe a nice nightie and a clean set of underwear, my mother seems to regard death as a two-week trip to Blackpool and has several collections of burial clothes – a costume for every occasion. Whether at a cocktail party, an impromptu summons to afternoon tea with the Queen Mother in Balmoral or a walking tour of the Hebrides in particularly cold weather, she will be the best-dressed corpse in the graveyard. With a hat and gloves to match.

The suitcase is a rare prize. I shake it gingerly. I've learned the facts of life from a childbirth manual that I once found inside an ottoman, and I am not overeager for any more information. One twist and the locks on either side of the case spring back smartly to reveal a treasure trove of photographs: hundreds of them, held together by elastic bands shrivelled like souvenir umbilical cords. Some are in albums, others still in the yellow Kodak envelopes they were born in, but most are lying in untidy heaps amid a mess of loose negatives curling like fortune-telling fish.

Old people, seen as young people in old-fashioned surroundings. Photographs of my mother looking impossibly skinny and pretty and happy. My father tall and lanky, owning the same kind of body that in my adolescence I will have to learn to grow into. Baby Geordie, baby Maisie, baby me and even, I am sure, baby mother and father, though I can't recognize them. Instead there are grey-mottled strangers galore, dead people dripping through my fingers, colour prints already losing their definition and frozen smiles fading to dirty nicotine shadows.

When I at last brave my mother's admonishment not to poke my nose into things that don't concern me and ask her about them, she sits on the easy chair with me sprawled on the floor beside her, lights a fag and starts to pick through the contents.

She strokes my sister's ballroom dancing portrait. Deep, deep sighs from mother. Moving swiftly on. Maisie's wedding album. White embossed paper with tissue paper and professional photographs taken mostly in the chapel. The book hastily put aside. More and heavier sighs. Instead we sift through generations of Agneses until we hit on Maisie with an oversized bow in her hair. 'Aye, but she was a bonny wean.'

My mother's eyes grow all misty, for once not because of cigarette smoke. I am fed up with hearing about Maisie's superior childhood and adolescent beauty. Neither she nor my brother takes after my mother's side of the family in anything except height. They are both short. Petite, according to my mother; trolls according to anyone else. But in all other respects they resemble my father: glossy dark curls, brown eyes. Nature has reversed her gifts for me. I got the Agnesy wishy-washy complexion and the kinky fair hair, but am tall and thin like my dad. I have his nature too, my mother maintains. I don't really know what that means. Just that it isn't good.

So I tune out of my mother's soggy reminiscences and help myself to some of the pictures of Maisie when she was a teenager, posing with her head on one side and black sixties eyeliner curling at the corner of her eyes. She was very pretty, like a model. I wish I looked more like her. I wish she was closer. She seems to have been gone for so long that I can hardly remember what it feels like to have a sister.

Of course, it isn't to evade the past that my mother hides the suitcase at the back of the wardrobe in the best front bedroom. It is dust more than death, dirt, not disgrace, that my mother fears at this stage. Ornaments and picture frames attract it, she says, lying idly around wantonly beckoning to it like the Pamela

Anderson of the dust world. To combat this and thus wage her personal war against filth, everything is packed away in the name of hygiene. Cleanliness is not merely next to godliness but a whole cult of its own. But I didn't understand my mother's fetish for keeping things nice until we started hiding the real filth under the carpet.

Adam's house would give my mother a coronary if she wasn't already demented, half dead of Embassy Regal emphysema and so immobile in a nursing home that dust settles on her as if she were a Dresden shepherdess while she waits out her days. Here, in the drawing room, unlike the more modern starkness to be found elsewhere in his house, was a shrine to inherited consumerism. Everything was on display. Each surface came with its own particular sitting tenant : Staffordshire figures on the shoulder-high mantelpiece, silver candlesticks on the sideboard, clocks chiming different hours on different shelves as if the house had several time zones.

Worst of all was Adam's study at the top of the house, which had a whole metropolis of papers and manuscripts piled up around the floor, each topped with a yellow Post-it note giving coordinates for its successor so that he knew his way around. That, at least, was familiar to me. Francisco had a little room in our house that looked much the same. His props, he used to call them. The detritus of academia, which made him feel learned and secure. A man of letters and teeny bits of paper covered with indecipherable references.

My mother would have tidied both places in a matter of seconds with everything boxed up and locked in the cellar, where she would first have vacuumed the wine bottles, washed the labels and rearranged the bottles alphabetically. Damn it, she would probably even have thrown the oldest bottles out.

However, with Adam, the real horror would not have been the attraction of his dirt, but that I was working in service. Coming from a long line of women who had clawed their way out of other people's kitchens, my life as a maid would have been greeted with long looks and sharp intakes of breath.

But it didn't matter now. My mother had not spoken to, or even recognized, me for years.

Now, with Francisco gone, I was finally alone. It was terrifying. Enough time had gone past for me to have grown accustomed to his absence, but I still missed him as if he were an amputated limb that, every now and again, you try to use, to stand on, because you forget that it's gone. You can still feel pain in all the nerve endings, even though you're massaging the air.

Loneliness was a pillow pressed to my face. After the discovery of a black-and-white portable television in the room with the bikes, I switched my allegiance from the World Service to afternoon soap operas and late-night made-for-TV films in which the craggy, perma-tanned heroes kissed pretty, barely adolescent heroines, sure that no one would ever kiss me like that ever again. Over the years there had been the occasional lover to fill some of the white space left by Francisco's frequent foreign conferences and long field trips from which I was invariably excluded, but now it was all gone. I couldn't call on anyone for affection, and the only men I was likely to meet while in Adam's house sold fruit and vegetables for a living, or steam-cleaned the carpets.

In the small hours of the morning, after a few glasses of cheek-clenching wine and a film in which the hero – any hero – kissed the woman with just the right degree of raw desire, I would crumble like a cheap biscuit. Their mouths would come together as the culmination of 119 minutes of anticipation, and I would sigh, feeling the same longing as the heroine.

But it was momentary; so fleeting that I could almost believe I had imagined it. How was it possible to feel that kind of yearning? It was like remembering the burning desire I felt for a boy when I was fifteen, and the subsequent humiliation of rejection, but without being able to touch any remnant of the boy himself. Like the light you could see in the night skies of stars that had burned themselves out years before.

That kind of passion had been dead between Francisco and me for a long time. Since he stopped hoping for children, sex had dwindled to a celebratory obligation undertaken on birthdays and Christmas that we both pretended to enjoy, the way you do an unwanted gift. But it didn't mean that I stopped loving him. In bed I lay curled against his back like an animal sheltering from the wind, my palms pressed against his waist as though to brace myself against an imagined onslaught, knowing that he would cushion me. And, loyally, he had been my barrier against the world, even when disappointment had burrowed in between us and I hadn't been able to give him the family he longed for.

But now the bed was empty. As I lay, night after night, looking at the lightning bolt fracturing the plaster on the other side of the room, I just wanted to squeeze myself inside the crack and disappear. Francisco had been the witness to my life. He was all I had known, and now he was lost. All those years spent talking animatedly to the front of his newspaper each and every morning over coffee and toast, being stupidly annoyed when he didn't respond. What had it mattered? All the plans we had made for a life that seemed set to run before us plain and straight, like one of those roads in the Prairies, sometimes frighteningly so – now it was all over.

And so, long after I heard the hiss of the cistern flush on the third floor that heralded Adam's last visit to the bathroom before he slept, I would open the back door and pockmark my thighs on the top garden step overlooking the communal garden and stare at the black shadows of the dark terraced mansions opposite, watching as their illuminated windows were extinguished one by one.

I listened to the occasional stream of gentle laughter trickle out of a neighbour's open bedroom window, or to the ever-present music from the superannuated pop star on the other side of the gardens and probed, tentatively, at an even more distant past, wondering what Kirsty would think if she knew I was living one street away from her teenage heart-throb. She had queued for hours to see his concert in Glasgow when she was fifteen, while I, a year younger, was left behind at home to marvel jealously at the story of his every gyration. Now I saw him most days, sitting in the garden with his two daughters, his once luxuriant locks replaced by a shiny, silver-fringed tonsure. His real name was Brian Hogg. You could see why he had changed it.

I would think of the two of us, sitting giggling in her bedroom, the window open a crack so we could blow smoke out of it before leaping back from the memory, with a cattle prod of pain.

Then I'd hear the foxes in the middle of the garden square, screaming like molested women who just wouldn't give up and die already, on and on and on, and the piercing, unearthly sound would follow me back inside and ring shrilly in my ears, long through the night.

4

I am twelve.

Kirsty is a year older and she's ahead of me, running up the street, her yellow hair flapping in sheets across her face, when she turns to urge me to follow her. We stop to peer in wee Tam's shop window, past the pyramids of yellowing Tide boxes and the dead bluebottles. But it's his wife that's serving, leaning against the counter to take the weight off her feet. Her legs are all swollen and look like two glistening pork sausages underneath her shiny surgical stockings – the crease at her ankle just needs a bit of string. If we go in and say hello, wee Tam sometimes gives us an ice lolly to share, but not Mrs Tam. She always hunts us. We don't like her.

Kirsty goes skipping along the pavement, her legs wobbling like undercooked chips. 'Step on a crack and ye'll break yer mammy's back,' she shouts, pulling a string of hair out of the corner of her mouth.

But I don't like playing that game. My mother's back is bad enough already. She's always rubbing it and groaning, saying, 'Oh, I'm fair done. I'm fit for nothing,' and then asking me to get her two distalgesic and a cup of tea.

'Step on a crack and you break yer mammy's china,' I call instead. 'Look, that's her teapot away, and her sugar bowl.' But it's a bit of a boring game, because really it's easy to avoid the cracks, and if I broke my mother's china she'd kill me.

We stop at the bottom of the steps next to the Running Dog. Kirsty asks me if she should go up and get Margaret out to play, but I say no. My mother doesn't care for Margaret, not since that time she came to sleep the night and didn't wash her feet before going to bed. 'What can you expect with her folks downstairs in that pub all night?' she'd said. 'Dragged up, that wean is, no better than a gypsy.' But I wouldn't mind being dragged up. You always got lemonade and crisps at Margaret's house, any flavour you wanted. You just went down to the off licence at the Running Dog, knocked on the wee door and asked. Nuts too.

We run round the war memorial, cross the street and see Mrs Ponti from the café walking up towards the ironmongery. Her coat makes swishing noises as she marches up the road, a fan of black hair flattened by her tights running down the front of each leg. American tan, they are. A horrible orangey-brown colour.

When I got my first pair of tights to go to Kirsty's last birthday party, I asked my mother if there were other colours of tan. Was Scottish tan different? In the end I got golden-rose, and they turned my legs a funny red, as if I'd been sitting too near the fire; like the lazy tartan that Kirsty's mother has. She sits in the chair all day reading romances from the library and doing the *Daily Express* crossword. She never goes out. Kirsty even has to change her library books for her. She puts a little sign in the back of all the ones that she's read, so that Kirsty knows not to get the same ones out again. Kirsty says her mother is feart to go outside. But that's daft. It's because her dad is rich.

Mrs Cameron doesn't need to go to work or even do the cleaning. She has a woman who comes in and does it all – a home help like the old folk have. Mr Cameron is quite old. He has hair growing out of his nose. He is a funeral director, so he has a big black hearse and his own private petrol pump. When my mother started working at the chemist at the far end of the village, I used to ask her why she couldn't work for Mr Cameron instead and be just over the road, but she said those coffins in the back room gave her the creeps. Maybe they give Kirsty's mother the creeps too and that's what she's feart of. I asked Kirsty if they ever had dead bodies in the house, but she just gave me a look that would have curdled milk and told me I was ignorant. Kirsty can be a bit superior sometimes, but I like her mother. She always wears bright red lipstick, which people say isn't decent on the undertaker's wife, but I think it's nice. And anyway nobody sees it since she stays in all the time.

'Mrs Ponti . . . Hiya, Mrs Ponti,' calls Kirsty in a sing-song voice, running up beside her.

'Aye, Kirsty,' she answers, nodding as if she were headering a ball. 'How are you, hen – how's your mother?'

'Fine . . . she's in the house,' she adds, as if she'd be anywhere else. And besides it's me Mrs Ponti is talking to. She was pally with my mother when she was young, when she was still Cissie McLean. I'm going to answer but Kirsty butts in. 'What about your Dan – where's he today?' asks Kirsty. She's got a brass neck, that girl.

'He's away on his bike, hen – I think he went fishing.'

'Awe.' Kirsty's face falls. So he wouldn't be serving in the café. Sometimes, even when we don't have money, we go in and pretend we can't make up our mind what we want just so we can speak to him. He's gorgeous.

Mrs Ponti stops at the ironmongery and says cheerio, but Kirsty has already lost interest now that she won't be seeing Dan, so I wave an answer for her. She's dancing along the side of the road, heading up towards the church on the corner where we can see a crowd of people hanging around.

'Look,' she says. 'It might be a wedding.'

A wedding means a scramble. The best man throws bags of pennies and thruppennies out of the car window as the bride's car drives away. You can get quite a lot of money if you're lucky, especially if you wait for the bag of sixpences. We can't see any other children at the church, so we rush forward expectantly, thinking we'll get all the money, but the vestry door is shut. It isn't a wedding.

Kirsty pulls herself up on the railings and sits on the church wall, kicking her legs. I jump up beside her, my knees pressing forward on my bri-nylon slacks with their little stirrups tucked inside my shoes, pulling so tight that they start to drop away at the back, showing my bum. I stand up quickly, hitching them up to the place where my waist should be. The knees still stick out as if I've got two apples down the front of my trousers.

There's a faint skirling of pipes somewhere in the distance.

'It's a band,' says Kirsty.

I wish I could disappear. I hate parades. I know that every time there's a band, sooner or later the subject will get on to Kirsty being last year's Queen at the village fête, when she rode through the streets, waving at everyone, on top of a lorry covered with paper flowers made out of toilet paper.

'Do you remember when I was the Queen and there were three pipe bands walking behind me? I was nearly deaf from them.'

Like I said, the man with the big drum was hardly over the head of the brae and already it's Queen, Queen, Queen. I say nothing.

'And do you remember when they came to the house in the morning and stood outside in the road and played "Flower of Scotland"?'

I feel like one of the snails in the back garden when my mother throws salt on them and they just sizzle and dissolve into slime. I can remember only too well when she came down the front path with her wee white gloves and her long train.

'Do you know I can see right up your skirt?' I tell her. 'You've got flowery drawers on and your bum's hanging out of one side.'

'Well, they're clean and paid for,' she snaps at me, but she gets down off the wall anyway and shuts up about being the Queen.

She takes my hand, and we run off down the cutting to Ogilvie Crescent, across the back way, past the railway, and home. She lives in a huge house up the street from me – you could get lost in it. There's a sitting room and three bedrooms upstairs, all just for her. Her mum and dad sleep downstairs, where there're another two big sitting rooms. The mum and dad sleep in twin beds, like Rock Hudson and Doris Day; though Kirsty warned me not to tell anyone that. But anyway the woman who cleans it already told my mother when she was in at the chemist, so everybody knows. The cleaner also said that Mrs Cameron never lifts a finger or does a stroke of work. I don't know what she's complaining about. If Mrs Cameron did the washing and dusting herself, then the cleaner wouldnae have a job.

'I'm going in to see if I can get some money for ice cream. Wait here – I'll be back in a minute,' orders Kirsty as she squeezes herself through a hole in the fence.

I wait for ten minutes, but she doesn't appear, so I wander up to my own house. I know there's no point in asking my mother for money. She isn't working today and is sitting in the back kitchen, legs apart with her bum on the storage heater, even though it isn't on. Her arms are resting on each knee and she is puffing smoke into the carpet.

'What are you up to?' she asks, drawing her rapt attention away from the floor.

I see her eyeing the knees of my trousers.

'Have you been out dressed like that?'

'Aye,' I say, backing away out of reach of the pointed finger of her lit cigarette, which she turns and grinds out in a saucer. 'What's wrong?'

She shakes her head in despair. 'You're a disgrace. I don't know why you can't keep yourself looking clean and tidy like Kirsty.'

I sigh, fed up. Better to brush past this one.

'Can I get a drink?' I ask with a rush of optimism over experience, hoping for lemonade from the fridge.

'Aye – there's plenty of water in the tap.'

She sighs and resumes her examination of the carpet as though she were being paid by the hour to watch it.

In the back lobby, I sneak open the cupboard, pull off my old plimsolls and put on the shoes that are in the back, hidden inside the box the toaster came in, quietly, without my mother hearing. The shoes are leather slip-ons with straggly bows at the side. They're hand-me-downs from Kirsty, though I don't think she's ever had them on. They're too big for her, but her mother got them out of the catalogue and didn't bother to send them back. She doesn't like to go to the shops. They're a bit loose on me too, but I've stuck a fleecy insole inside to make them fit my long, thin feet. If my mother sees them, she'll make me give them back. We don't need their charity, she'll say, even though she's always moaning when things don't fit me. She says she can't keep me in shoes because I'm growing too fast.

Sometimes I get things from the youngest Agnes, and that's great because at least she's fashionable. That Agnes told me I could be a model, that I had the right cheekbones for it. I don't really know what she means – I'm just skinny. Anyway, everybody's got cheekbones, otherwise their face would collapse.

I stroll down to the front gate dragging my feet through the gravel, getting wee pebbles in my shoes and watching for Kirsty. She's lucky: she's cuddly, with dimples. Her hair is like a poker and it floats like a bride's veil when she walks. She doesn't have pointy hip bones and her legs aren't all gangly like mine. I don't know why I got made the wrong way, like scones without the bicarbonate of soda so nothing rises.

I see her coming back through the fence and I walk wearily towards her.

'I had to make my mother a cup of tea, but then she gave me a shilling,' she says, opening her hand lined with dirt across the palm and showing me the coin. Typical: I get cold water out the tap and she gets money. 'We can get ice cream at Ponti's.'

That cheers us both up. She's so lucky, that Kirsty – honest, if she fell in the Clyde she'd come out with a fish supper.

We walk along the grass verge by the side of the road and kick stones across the cracked tarmac that looks like a big sheet of liquorice that's been split down the middle.

Then Kirsty birls round, skirt billowing. 'Come on, Agnes,' she says. 'Maybe the band comes back down the street again and we can catch it going the other way.' And she links her arm through mine, hooking my elbow. 'COME ON!' she shouts. 'Or we'll miss it.'

My shoes are half falling off and make clapping noises, like slow applause, behind me on the pavement. But still, I run up the street. Behind her.

5

'So, how are you coping with all this, Edith?' asked Adam.

He cast his arm around twenty square feet of blank-faced oak cabinets as though worried that the dishwasher might lead a sudden revolt, bidding the German kitchen appliances to rise from the walls and overwhelm me, but I knew what he meant. I had been working for him for just over two months, much of that time spent all by myself running up and down in this teetering game of snakes and ladders that he called a home, with only a shifting gang of Croatian decorators providing a diversion.

I had been wrong about my prospects for meeting members of the opposite sex. I could have had my pick of squat, paint-splattered men in overalls.

'Oh, it's fine. No problems at all,' I said airily. 'The house runs like clockwork.'

'It must have been lonely here on your own.'

'Not at all. I like my own company,' I lied and smiled reassuringly.

Adam and Gay had a place in France that, despite their imminent separation, they continued to share: she took July and he got August. When he offered me the job, he had told me that he would be away for much of the summer and that all I would have to do was stay in the house and supervise the painters who were coming to redecorate the labyrinth of corridors and stairways.

'Let them in, make sure they don't steal the silver and keep on their backs all the time,' he instructed – unnecessarily, as it turned out. The men found the silver as ugly as I did and were so hard-working that I had to remind them to stop. The Croatians and I mostly communicated in mime, much of it me pointing at my watch or proffering refreshments with lots of agreeable nodding. We struck up a relationship using the international language of cake and beer, both of which they spoke fluently. Thankfully everything in the house was to be painted the same shade of corpse blue-white, so at least there was no discussion about colour swatches.

During August, Adam had spent only a few nights in the house, returning overnight for meetings and, once, to make a short trip to Dublin. At the end of the month he went to friends in the country to escape the Carnival and offered to put me up in a hotel for the few frenetic days when Red Stripe flowed in the streets just north of Holland Crescent. Carnival or not, despite the bass that seemed to shake the house to its foundations, it made no difference to me. For weeks, I had been barricaded in the basement with ear plugs, against the arthritic moans and groans of the old house.

However, since his return, at his insistence, we had fallen into the habit of sharing supper most evenings. By the time he came back from Provence, tanned and antsy with the forced suppression of all the energy he usually channelled into his work, I had begun to feel as if my mouth had been stapled closed. Now I waited for him to come home at night with the eagerness of a young bride.

I was frantic with excitement that there was another living, breathing, English speaker who actually responded to my voice. Francisco and I had fallen into the sort of non-speak that I supposed all couples did after a few decades together of happy enough married-dom. I chattered about anything that came into my head, and he pretended to hear me, grunting assent with an off-hand benevolence that faltered only with the challenge that he wasn't listening, which could rouse him to exasperation because it was true. I could have asked him for a toy-boy and he would probably just have nodded pleasantly and said: 'Of course, darling, whatever you like.'

'You know I'm no good at small talk,' he would protest,

giving my cheek a distracted pat, followed by a kiss on the top of the head that usually heralded his walking backwards into his study.

He had not always been so reticent. When we first met, we used to lie awake long into the night talking about our very different childhoods, each of us drawing pictures in the dark to entertain the other. I never tired of hearing his stories of growing up with his grandmother Olinda in Cartagena, all more colourful and exotic than my own grey, shadowy anecdotes, so that my past faded modestly into the background of his. But eventually the only thing we discussed in bed was who had locked the back door.

Of course in the early years of our marriage he didn't have tutorial groups and lecture halls to service with the sound of his voice, nor had he an ever-changing stream of students regurgitating the same essay topics term after term. I could occasionally engage him by feigning a sudden desire to debate the toothlessness of the United Nations, or Third World debt, but most of the time I let him be.

I was sure that some of his emotional reserve stemmed from losing his mother at a such a young age, but the years of childlessness hadn't helped. If we had had babies, I supposed we would have been infatuated with their every word and gesture, but we merely had the disappointment of their absence, and each other. My inability to have children was the great unspoken subject, never alluded to, never discussed. It was my failing. And so I simply resigned myself to the house being a talk-free zone, and got my fix of frivolity from his students.

But with Adam there was no taboo subject to carve a line across the dinner table, and, furthermore, I did my homework. I started scanning *The Times* so that I could do right-wing politics and bought the *Telegraph* for the crossword that, half finished, I left ostentatiously strewn across the kitchen table. I read up on his authors in the book pages in all the review sections, until I could have given him an essay on modern British poets. Well –

the price of strawberries and the brevity of the English asparagus season could take you only so far.

Adam, to my astonishment, couldn't give a damn about the latest economic crisis in Argentina. To my joy he was much more interested in discussing his authors' private lives than the plots of their novels. I discovered who was gay, impotent, alcoholic and illiterate. As the recipients of secrets, publishers, apparently, are just like priests – except not nearly so discreet.

We usually ate together on week nights while a heap of engraved stiffies inviting him to openings and book launches piled up, unopened and unanswered, stuffed into the drawer in the hall table. On weekends he went to dinner parties where, he complained, he was lined up with a series of well-groomed, blonde divorcees straight from desperation central casting, while I stayed home for my string of hot dates with Noel Edmonds or Inspector Morse. But tonight was a Sunday, and he was home – an unexpected bonus. I had been planning on watching *Prime Suspect*, but now I would be standing up Helen Mirren.

At first he had made the bold suggestion that we walk down Portobello Road to a restaurant, but I thought that this was taking good labour relations a step too far. How would he introduce me if we ran into one of the neighbours – oh, this is Edith . . . my char? And what if I saw someone I knew? It was safer to stay home.

And so I did what I did best. I cooked.

The remains of supper lay ravaged between us. Half a cold roast chicken with Persian apricot and pistachio stuffing splayed, legs akimbo, next to a bowl of curdling, garlicky paprika mayonnaise and a Greek salad. I cooked across cultures, influenced by years of homesick boyfriends who each had his own idea of what constituted comfort food. Even the German potato salad was a memory of beds gone by. It had been Karl's one culinary flourish, usually accompanied by roughly hewn salami and served between the sex and the cigarette, but I told Adam that the recipe came from my mutter-in-law Lutz.

46

Francisco's mother had been dead since he was seven and probably had not even know where her kitchen was. His grandmother lived with full maid service in a faded but beautiful Colonial house within salt spray of the sea and hadn't lifted more than a tea cup in her life. Back on the family's farm, there was a black mud-packed farmyard full of sinewy, coffee-coloured Colombian peasants hand-grinding corn for her tamales, while in New York his Manhattan stepmother thought cooking meant dialling for take-out. And generally, she had the houseboy do that.

I began rinsing the serving dishes, scraping the limp floury potatoes into the sink and covering the chicken carcass with foil. I would use it for stock tomorrow.

'Was your mother a good cook?' asked Adam. 'I suppose you must have taken it in with your mother's milk . . .'

I laughed so hard that I could hear myself begin to snort. 'My mother's milk. Are you mad? The only thing I inhaled from my mother was second-hand smoke and Ajax. God, no. My mother's twin contributions to world gastronomy were boiled mince and brisket. The main ingredient of everything she made was salt. Until I was fifteen I thought baked beans were a green vegetable, and I'm still strangely addicted to the smell of ammonia.'

'So what happened when you were fifteen?'

That brought my laughter quickly under control. I hesitated. 'Oh, then I was initiated into the dark satanic arts of broccoli and runner beans. I moved south and was corrupted by the English. Before that I thought red peppers came in packets, dried into flakes like fish food. Even the local Chinese restaurant had been corrupted. If you rang up for a take-away, Mrs Yang would say: "Aye, Taiwan Hoose, d'ye want chips with that?"'

'You moved to England when you went to university?'

'Erm, no, I came here, then I travelled. Europe, after that the States, met my husband and just never came back, really. Not until I had to.'

'So where did the interest in food come from?'

'Necessity, I suppose. France . . . I mean, Frank liked food that reminded him of home; he had to have rice at every meal, rice and beans, he even ate rice with potatoes. I guess baked beans *are* a vegetable in South America.' I made a face. 'Anyway, I suppose I started to learn to make the sort of things he liked.'

'I'm confused – France? South America? I thought your husband was German. Are beans and rice a big German thing?'

'Oh, no – of course not. I, he, Frank, studied in South America, not France.' I took a deep breath; I was getting this all wrong. I needed to shut up, but Adam was still looking at me attentively. I began to long for Francisco's indifference. 'And then later – you know, we spent time there because of his job. So the food sort of stuck. I'm not thinking straight – too much wine.' I tapped the side of the glass with my fingernail: it rang out like a division bell. Then I hurried on. 'We had to do a lot of entertaining in New York and couldn't always afford to take people to restaurants. So we had dinners. I wasn't really working, which made it easy to do – we had a nice apartment with a great view over the East River.'

'Didn't you want a job?'

'Well, there was a problem with my green card at first and then I got sidetracked into being a sort of career wife, moving around with . . . Frank.' I said the name somewhat over-deliberately, as though I were on a game show and had to be sure to get the right answer before the buzzer went off. 'Then it got too late and I didn't know where to start.'

I was losing it here. Time to stop drinking. My tongue didn't seem to have any connection to my brain.

'Actually, I worried about you here all alone for the summer.' He made it sound like a confession. 'It must have been very strange and lonely.'

'Noooo, it really was rather peaceful,' I said brightly as the waste disposal finished grinding its leftovers like a good child cleaning its plate. 'Really. It was probably just what I needed. Some recovery time.'

He protested when I bent to pick up his plate and cutlery, and told me to sit back down and relax. 'Just leave it, Edith, the washing up isn't going anywhere, and that bloody dishwasher sounds like Concorde taking off. I'll never be able to hear you if you turn it on.' He poured the last inch of Pinot Noir into my glass: a pink Venetian goblet that he had brought, together with the wine, from the elegant dining room next door.

The kitchen, though lavishly appointed with every glimmering example of German domestic engineering, was not stocked with any sort of luxury. Concealed behind the oak doors was enough stylishly uniform china to host a sit-down supper for twenty-four and three sizes of wafer-thin water glasses that threatened to shatter if you hit a high note singing over the washing up. But there was nothing frivolous or beautiful. Adam's ex-wife was obviously a woman who liked to keep everything in its proper place, for its proper function, including the hired help. My own tiny kitchenette in the basement had only two each of Wool-worths' finest soup bowls, side plates, dinner plates and earthen-ware coffee cups, as if they were marching together into a Soviet minimalist ark. She hadn't anticipated that the maid would be doing much entertaining.

'You didn't find the house intimidating, here all by yourself?' Adam persisted, in a tone that hinted he was not unfamiliar with the feeling.

I took a sip of the wine to delay answering. It tasted like soft fruit, with the fragile velvet fur of overripe raspberries slipping down my throat. My half-pint mugs of Tesco's Bulgarian Cabernet Sauvignon, chilled to the point of merciful tastelessness, were never going to hit the spot after this.

'Well, I did think I might be a wee bit scared, so I slept with that big Victorian chest of drawers pushed against my bedroom door.' I smiled, to show how ridiculous I knew this was, though the truth was that I had made one of the Croatian handymen screw new bolts on to every internal door inside the basement, and I kept the windows locked even when it was 95 degrees outside.

'I know how awful this house can feel when it's empty,' Adam said, playing with the blue-striped cuffs of a shirt that I knew from my laundering had tiny pink tips on the underside.

He had very elegant hands, which I noticed as he fiddled with his cuff links: clean, square fingernails and long, clever fingers, thin and tense like the rest of him, a dull gold wedding ring still worn on his left hand.

'When Gay first moved out, I hated coming back in the evening. The house was like a morgue, especially with Lennie gone. I told Gay that I would leave and she could stay – it is, was, her family home after all, but she said she hated the place. I don't know why, quite.' His eyes darted to the space beside the refrigerator where his children's heights, noted from the ages of three to fourteen, climbed the wall. He looked around the kitchen helplessly, as though the toaster might pop out an answer to his wife's discontentment. Poor man: I didn't know what Gay had found so oppressive about Holland Crescent, but I was in no position to judge what made a woman pack her bags and disappear. Nevertheless Adam's pain was palpable. I could hardly bear to examine it. He was holding a mirror up to my face.

'You didn't find it too quiet?' he asked.

'Oh, you get used to it.' I replied, as casually as if solitary confinement were a leisure activity you got on Club Med holidays as an alternative to scuba diving.

'Well, I'm back now, except for a few short business trips – the Frankfurt Book Fair, some meetings in New York, *again*, which is a bore. I don't know how you could stomach living there. It's so hectic and aggressive. I'm also hoping that the children will be spending some time with me at weekends and possibly at half-term, so it will be a little busier from now on. Lennie is going to come next week – you'll meet Gay too. I think she wants to check you out. She even asked about your references.' He laughed awkwardly, and my stomach somersaulted. 'I showed them to her; I hope you don't mind. Nervous mother and all that.'

I did mind, but I was in no position to say so. A cold feeling of unease ran through me at the idea of her scrutinizing my faked testimonials. Bloody cow. Nervous mother? I hoped she wasn't nervous enough to check with the agency.

'Do you want some dessert?' I asked. 'I have tarte tatin – or there's Armenian cheese from that deli on the corner.' We were like two strangers out on a first date.

He shook his head. 'Thank you, Edith, but I'll stick with the liquid sustenance.' He raised his glass in a mock toast. 'And anyway it's too hot to eat much.'

Even in September it was still stuffy enough at nine o'clock in the evening for us to be sitting with the French doors thrown open on to the wrought-iron balcony and the inky evening beyond. A few voices tumbled in from the communal garden, and some children, running around in the dark, yelled out excitedly in a game of hide-and-seek. We had the lights turned off so as not to attract moths, and at Adam's urging I had lit the candelabra that usually festooned the walnut table in the dining room. From the outside, we probably looked like just another happily married couple sitting in the dancing candlelight, but, inside, the awkwardness between us was almost a third presence at the table. I could have set it a place. After just a couple of weeks of a formal employer/employee relationship, it was still strange to be sitting sharing a meal with a stranger who paid my wages. Especially a stranger whom I looked forward to seeing and who had just admitted he had been worrying about me.

'It must have been great for your kids growing up here,' I said, as another skirl of second-hand excitement whipped through the doors and bounced around the room. 'All that space to play outside.'

'I suppose,' he said doubtfully. 'To tell the truth, I was never here. We had nannies; and Gay dealt with all that.'

'I would have loved it. When I was a kid in Scotland, we lived outside in the summer months – you didn't come home until you heard your mother calling for you. We used to pee in the bushes, because if you went home to use the loo and your mother noticed the time, she might keep you in; otherwise you could get away with playing outside until ten o'clock.'

I got a little carried away with my reminiscences.

'One summer, my friend Kirsty and I decided to camp out in the back garden and . . .'

'And?' Adam had a happy, go-on-and-entertain-me smile on his face, but my voice dried up. Where had that come from? 'Oh, nothing, really.' I shook my head.

'Do you still see her?'

'Who?' I asked, though I knew perfectly well whom he meant.

'Kirsty, your friend. Is she still in Scotland? I should have told you to invite her while I was in France. You must consider the house yours when I'm away.'

'Oh, no. Kirsty . . .' I began, but I didn't know what to say. 'I haven't seen her since we were teenagers. We don't keep in touch.'

'A shame,' said Adam. 'But if you want to ask any of your other friends?'

'There isn't anyone.'

'Surely there's *somebody*. You must have been bored out of your skull being cooped up in the heat and pollution of London for the summer. It can't have been much fun,' he insisted.

'Adam, you forget that I lived for fifteen years in New York,' I reminded him, keeping up the fiction I had invented for myself. 'You just said you couldn't understand how anyone lived there. You're right. If you want smog, humidity and boredom, try spending August in Manhattan.'

'What did you usually do for the holidays? Didn't you and your husband go away? Did you want to have a few days off yourself and go somewhere this summer?' he asked, no doubt overlooking the fact that people who worked as hired help probably weren't in the habit of weekending with the jet set on the French Riviera and that, in any case, the recently bereaved and penniless wouldn't have vacations at the top of their list of priorities.

'In the old days we used to spend most of our summers in Newport, with my husband's family.' This much was true – but I was hoping, nevertheless, that the words 'we' and 'used to' would be enough to kill the rest of the conversation as dead as the husband. But no.

'Newport – isn't that where they used to hold the America's Cup? I've been there once or twice. One of our American authors was a big sailing fanatic, and he took us out on his yacht. Very pretty, I remember. Do you sail?'

'No. No sailing. I took a few lessons, but I discovered, several miles into the Atlantic, that I'm scared of water.' I laughed. 'Franci . . . I mean Frank's family had a house in a little town just outside Newport, on the beach – but they, we, didn't socialize much, and they definitely didn't sail.' I hurried on before he could start to ask for details. I had probably met the author he had visited. Newport society was worryingly incestuous.

'Several times we went to Colombia – for Frank's research. Once to Guatemala, Peru, Argentina, Brazil.' This was also – more or less, give or take the odd cousin – quite true. I had allowed the fictional husband the same area of expertise as Francisco, as my powers of invention could only go so far. I couldn't conjure up a whole new specialist subject, so I gave Frank a minor job with a Latin American NGO and an unspecified lowly post at the UN. Then I threw in a few vague words such as aid and development, masquerading as details, and hoped Adam knew as little about it as I did. We all know the cardinal rule of a successful lie is to stick as close to the truth as possible, and not to elaborate.

'Erm, Colombia must be nice,' he ventured doubtfully.

So I elaborated: 'Oh, yes. What with drug cartels, the kidnapping, the crime, the mosquitoes bigger than cats – you know – it's not exactly Tuscany, Adam.'

He looked shocked, and I jumped in to correct myself. 'Actually, it's not nearly anything as bad as people say it is. As long as you stay in the big cities, life goes on pretty much as it does anywhere else. Very pleasantly.' I stopped myself from blabbing about the armed bodyguards that any trip to the country necessitated, and the fortress-like security surrounding granny in her isolated bubble of privilege and old money.

He laughed. For a long time, even as he walked into the dining room and came back with another, already open bottle of Pinot Noir.

The fortunate thing about Adam and his English correctness was that he was usually so afraid of prying into the circumstances of my widowhood that even the most oblique mention of it had him backing off like a vampire confronted with a crucifix. He was not alone in that. Most people shied away from the shroud of misery that was wrapped around me like a dress that summer; prêt-à-porter from the Bereaved Collection by Edith Lutz. I wore it well.

But tonight the alcohol had put Adam in touch with his warm and fuzzy side. He was intent on empathy. 'You must miss your husband, Frank.' He touched the name as though it were a poisonous spider, nudging it tentatively with a long stick. 'It must have been unbearable for you.'

I didn't respond, but he stuck at the subject, nervously but doggedly. 'I can only imagine how terrible it is to lose someone you love.'

'Yes.'

'Do you mind talking about him?'

After a pause, I shook my head no, but I waited until he had refilled my glass from the new bottle and took a long gulp before answering. 'Of course I miss him. But I talk to him all the time in my head, which is silly, really, because it's not as though he ever really listened to me when he was alive. But you know, it's that audience you have to your life; the one other person who applauds your victories and overlooks your mistakes. Then, suddenly – poof – it's gone. You're alone.'

I had another swallow of wine before continuing. 'And it doesn't get any better, it just persists, like a pain that only occasionally responds to morphine. He was my only family, my history. Being without him is like walking around without any skin, except that every morning I wake up and have it stripped off me afresh. Just before I open my eyes, I sometimes forget where I am. I think, for that moment just before I swim up into consciousness, that I'm still living my old life, and that he's going to be lying there on the other side of the bed; that I can reach my hand across the sheets and feel his chest, or the curl of his hair between my fingers. And then I remember he's gone – and lose him all over again.'

I swirled the purple liquid around the pink-tinged glass and took another long drink. Jesus fucking Christ. I closed my eyes and took a deep breath. First Kirsty and now Francisco. Let's do babies, and he can hit the jackpot. If I kept on talking, the tears that were filling my eyes would start cascading down my cheeks in torrents. And with half a bottle of wine inside me, once I started I could flood the basement.

He saw I was fighting for composure, and his green eyes clouded with concern. He pulled his long fingers through his rumpled hair. 'I'm a clumsy idiot. I should shut up. I didn't mean to upset you, Edith, I'm so sorry.' His thin fingers reached across the table and held mine in a surprisingly firm grip. I drew in my breath with a sudden gasp. It seemed like years since someone had touched me, and centuries since I had welcomed that touch. I closed my other hand over his.

'It's fine. I'm fine.' How many times had I said that this evening? I was like one of those dolls that repeated stock phrases every time you pulled a string in her neck.

'Too much to drink,' I said. I pulled my hands away and pushed the chair out, ready to start clearing up. I told him that it was getting late, that I should put things away because I had lots of chores to do and had to get up early. We both knew I was making excuses. The place shone like the show house on an OCD timeshare.

'Oh, leave the bloody housework, Edith, please sit down. I'm a stupid, insensitive fool. I shouldn't have said anything. It's just that I see you sitting there in the candlelight and you look so' – his voice dropped an octave – 'sad.' He paused. 'And, well, it seems so wrong that I've got you slaving away in my kitchen, keeping an old fool company when you should have a happy life with someone you care about. This shouldn't have happened to you.'

Now I felt like a worm. My self-pity evaporated into salty, crusty puddles of self-loathing.

'Please, Adam, leave it. It's not like that. It's really not what you think. No one knows what goes on inside another's marriage. Relationships are complicated. Ours certainly wasn't perfect. Far from it. I don't think Frank was always very happy with me, but, you know, when you look back, there's always a tendency to remember the good times, not the bad. Maybe it's self-preservation.'

'Tell me about it,' he sighed. He leaned across the table and put both hands on my shoulders, guiding me gently back towards the chair. 'Here, have another drink. Please. Look, I know you must be lonely, because I'm lonely myself. I've spent three weeks in an idyllic villa overlooking the Mediterranean, surrounded by olive groves, with two teenagers who barely took their eyes away from MTV, entertaining so-called friends to whom I had nothing to say, buying meals for authors to whom I already pay a great deal of money, telling them how wonderful they are when they are mostly sociopaths with massive egos, wishing I could just sit quietly, like this, with someone who made me feel comfortable. So don't let me chase you away with my loutish prying. I hate drinking alone about as much as I hate eating alone. It makes me feel like the sort of sad old git whose wife has tired of him and left him rattling round in a too-large house with no one to talk to . . .' He grinned weakly, and I felt yet another twinge of guilt strong enough to make my throat burn.

He looked so defeated, so solemn and vulnerable, slumped in the kitchen chair, rubbing the edge of his fist against the grain of the wood as though he could polish up his sorrow and make it more palatable. I couldn't help myself. I stood up, seeing a fleeting glimmer of anxiety in his eyes as I walked around the table towards him. Maybe he thought I was going to slap him, but nothing could have been further from my mind. I wanted to gather him up and do to him what I longed for someone to do to me. I curled my hands over his balled-up fists, bent over and kissed him on the forehead. His unruly hair snaked across my face and stuck to my lips. I smoothed it back over his temples, but it sprang through my fingers.

He was the first person I had touched for months. His skin felt cool, like the underside of a pillow on a hot night.

'Mad hair. It was the first thing I noticed about you.'

He pushed his chair back, the sound a scream of alarm in the otherwise silent house, drew me down into his arms, until I was crouching on the floor between his knees, and kissed my mouth.

'You probably didn't want me to do that,' he said. In answer I tilted my head up towards him and kissed him back. He pressed his thumb against the corner of my lips. 'You have a smile,' he said. 'From the wine.' His fingers traced the curl of the wine across my cheek and slipped into my mouth – and maybe two, or twenty, minutes later, with my loose cotton embroidered shirt unbuttoned, hanging from my bare shoulders, I stopped to wonder, briefly, if the kiss had been one of my better ideas.

My body said yes.

My head said get the fuck out of there and push that chest of drawers in front of your body so it doesn't swing open for the first intruder who walks past.

'Adam, this is a bad idea. We don't really know each other. You have no idea what you're getting yourself into,' I murmured, as he began to peel off the rest of my clothes. But he wasn't listening, and, in truth, I didn't say it very loudly.

For once I really didn't want to be heard.

6

Even before I slept with Adam, I had already fallen in love with his bedroom. On my first tour around the house I managed only the briefest glimpse of a thick, palate-knife nude with nipples the size of small planets swirling in a constellation of flesh on a canvas above the bed. Adam was embarrassed and closed the door almost as soon as he had opened it, then led me past the empty guest bedroom to the mournfully abandoned children's rooms upstairs. But I went back later, after he had gone to work.

The room was large enough to contain the whole floor plan of the house I used to live in. There were slim, shuttered casement windows, floor to ceiling, overlooking the street, and a pair of dressing rooms opposite, side by side, like two sentry boxes, each leading into its own separate bathroom. Unlike the rest of the overstuffed house, it was sparse and modern with several impressions in the carpet where large objects had once stood and left behind their indelible footprints.

As the Croatians worked their way methodically around the house, obliterating golden-yellow from the drawing room and Wedgwood blue from the dining room, I waited expectantly for the bedroom's transformation. It was such a peaceful, anonymous place, like the best suite in a well-appointed lunatic asylum. Maybe that's why it so appealed to me.

The nude was bubble-wrapped and relegated to the wine cellar, and the grimy ghosts of other, departed paintings were covered with the same brittle shade of blue-white as the rest of the house. Now the surfaces gleamed like mother of pearl – or polished snow. You would swear they would melt if you turned up the heating.

The whole house resembled a Breughel winter scene without

the tiny people. It reminded me of the Scotland of my childhood, when you woke up in the morning after a big storm and looked outside to see everything fresh and clean, with a blindingly white covering of snow; when Kirsty and I knew there would be no bus to transport us the five miles to school in the next village and that a day of tea and toast and fireside Scrabble lay ahead of us.

Gay's bathroom, however, was more or less as she had left it, with assorted toiletries arranged around the marble sink and stored inside her medicine cabinet with the precision of a department-store stock cupboard. These were, presumably, the products she had no use for in her new *Architectural Digest* loft in Vauxhall. Inquisitively, I sifted through her shelves, smelling the towers of expensive French and Italian soap still in their pristine wrappers. From the boxes of unopened cosmetics in shiny black Chanel packaging, I saw she wore sheer pink lipstick and pale, fragile porcelain face powder – and contact lenses, judging by the numerous products for cleaning them.

There was also a row of perfume bottles arranged by height, each almost full: Guerlain, Chanel and Dior – heavy floral, middle-aged French scents that would make my throat itch and my eyes water. I can wear only one or two fragrances without turning into a walking asthma attack, which is a nuisance, as I used to have a similar row of perfume bottles in the small bathroom back home whose names more or less spelled out the emotional trajectory of my sex life. Young men, I had discovered from experience, could not resist the cliché of perfume as the furtive gift of choice. Over the years I had been given the whole Calvin Klein range from Obsession to Eternity, each of these from a student who had a crush on me that lasted about as long as the flu, and on our wedding day Francisco gave me a huge flagon of Joy, which was probably the closest I really ever came to experiencing it. As far as I know there isn't a scent called Contentment or Security, but, if there had been, it would have been more apt.

Ironically, the most recent addition to the snaking conga line on my bathroom shelf was a bottle of Escape that had been slipped shyly into my handbag by a vertically challenged Rhodes Scholar after I had finished typing his thesis. A year on, and Escape was still in its cellophane when I packed my belongings. I threw it into a bin bag, where it chattered fretfully to the rest of the bottles. I didn't want to leave any trace of my previous selves behind.

Gay had had no such compunction. There was still a flannel nightgown hanging in the dressing room and some lightweight cashmere sweaters wrapped in tissue paper in one of the drawers. Several pairs of dated but unworn shoes and sandals listed forlornly on the cedar racks, artfully constructed especially for the purpose. What did she do with all this footwear, I wondered? Alone of all the women I knew, I had no affinity with high heels and girly shoes. I had outgrown dressing up long ago. I hated shoes I couldn't walk in; I liked shoes built for speed. But Gay didn't share my Presbyterian foot fetish. Some of her underwear remained folded into neat triangles in a line in one drawer, and some bras in another. I opened them and inspected the size. 36DD. I felt inadequate.

It was as if she were the one who had died, and Adam the bereaved husband, leaving her untouched belongings as some sort of shrine to her memory. It was only a pair of monogrammed silver hairbrushes short of being sinister. Every time I walked through the dressing room to her bathroom beyond I felt like the second Mrs de Winter, pressing my nose against the glass of Rebecca's impeccably preserved territory, dreaming of bathing in her tub and wrapping myself in her monogrammed towels.

Of course, Rebecca was the wrong comparison. I had been expected to play the Mrs Danvers character, with my hoop of keys and access-all-areas pass, not that of the new bride. It had been up to me to change and smooth Adam's virgin white sheets, to knead the dumplings of his goose-feather pillows into fluffy perfection every morning and to shake out the cumulus clouds of his duvet. I had picked up his book, face down, from the carpet beside his bed and, after adding a book mark, replaced it, but until now I hadn't as much as brushed against him as I passed him at the breakfast table.

And now I was waking up with his lips on my shoulder and his long tapering fingers laying possessively across my stomach.

Dear God. What have you done, you silly cow? I thought, as I gently edged myself out of Adam's grip. So what if he was upset? So what if you felt sorry for him? Wouldn't a sympathetic pat on the back have been enough?

I felt Adam breathe softly against my skin. He smelled of wine and lemons and sex. I tried to extricate myself gently, slithering out from underneath his arms. The clock beside him seemed to say two thirty, or at the very least, half past something unreasonably early in the morning. I needed to pee. I needed to go back to my own room.

I crept out of bed, trying to gather up my clothes, which, illuminated by the streetlights flooding in through the unshuttered windows, lay in a trail scattered across the silvery carpet and out into the gloomy cavern of the hall. My shoes were agape, surprised, by the door, my plain, schoolgirl bra dropped on the threshold inside the puddle of my skirt. The rest of my underwear I would no doubt find when I made the bed the next morning.

As I tiptoed, almost crawling, across the white rectangles on the carpet, disentangling my garments from Adam's, I wondered anxiously how awkward it would be serving him coffee in the morning when his mouth, surprisingly soft and yet pliable, had spent most of the last three hours between my legs.

I had almost reached the door, painfully aware of the whiteness of my backside picking up the glow from the streetlights behind me, when I felt his skinny but muscled forearm snake around my waist.

'Edie, where are you going?' The *th*, I noted, had been dropped at about the same time as my knickers. 'Don't leave. Come back to bed,' he whispered sleepily into my neck. 'Shall I get you something – water, tea, wine?'

'Don't you think it would be better if I went downstairs to my own room?' I answered, with as much dignity as it was possible to muster while floodlit and stark naked before my etiolated shadow, a bra and a crumpled skirt hooked over my arm.

Even my nipples looked embarrassed and hangdog.

In answer, he gently took the clothes from me, dropped them back on to the floor and tugged me inside the white blur of his sheets.

'It would be wonderful to wake up with you,' he murmured. 'As long as that doesn't make you feel uncomfortable. I know it might be hard for you after what you said earlier.'

'It would be lovely not to wake up alone, Adam, but to wake up,' I reminded him as his hands slid across my body, 'you first have to get to sleep. You have things to do tomorrow, as do I.'

'Take the day off,' he whispered. 'As your employer, I insist. Hell, as my employer I insist I take the day off with you.'

I was surprised by his ardency. To be honest, though my lovers have been many and varied, on the whole they had been consistently inept. College boys of the kind I was once attracted to were inexperienced and shy, but, since on the whole it wasn't their sexual skill I was really interested in, it didn't matter. I liked the attention – and the penis, swaying slightly under its own weight because of a desire, totally, for me. Oh, yes, I knew that this was a delusion, it wasn't *really* me. The penis is its own master and shows the same appreciation for a pair of twin blow-up balloons flickering on a computer screen as it does for any available orifice, but when you are in the room with it, ask not for whom the bell tolls, it tolls for you.

I wasn't looking for love or tenderness. Sex for me was often just an exercise in self-loathing carried out by proxy. I wanted the fucking, the purely mindless fucking and the chance to check out of my body and float to the rhythm of their thrusts while they filled me up inside. But staying power wasn't every student's strong point, and they usually came quicker than wasps to a picnic, and then wouldn't go away again until you swatted them.

Adam, however – though nervous, or perhaps because of the nerves – had amazing stamina, and the potential for recovery of a man half his age. He acted as though he had been put on earth for the single purpose of devoting himself slavishly to my body. I was, frankly, astounded. Francisco had always been a utilitarian lover. He ticked all the boxes, in the same order every time, patted my back, kissed my cheek and fell asleep facing in whichever direction I wasn't. I used to see him slap the flank of his horse on the farm with the same offhand affection he showed when he rubbed my shoulder blades. He wasn't much for the touchy-feely, unless it was ritualized foreplay. His after-game consisted mostly of handing me a towel to blot my body.

But Adam lost all his emotional reserve in bed. He kissed and stroked and petted me like an expensive, long-haired lapdog, and in return I almost begged like one. He kissed the back of my neck while I was sleeping, and, when he was inside me, I opened my eyes to find him just looking at me, as though I had been specially ordered from a celestial mail-order catalogue and arrived before I was expected, looking even nicer than I had in the picture. I felt like Cinderella – risen from rags and transformed into a sex goddess.

I liked looking at him too. The irises of his eyes swelled with the rest of him when he watched me, and whereas Francisco, who made love with his eyes closed, had been small and compact, Adam was long and lithe. He had only a scattering of dark hairs on his chest, and was otherwise smooth and sinewy. His chest and upper arms were broad and knotted from tennis; his penis thick and heavy in my hands. When I bent over to kiss him we banged noses.

'I have such a big nose,' he whispered, running his finger ruefully down the length of his profile.

I laughed, before drawing my tongue down to its tip. 'It's absolutely perfect, Adam. You have no sense of spatial awareness,' I told him. 'And that's supposed to be a woman's failing.'

He pulled me towards him and kissed me, then I laid my head

against his chest, drinking in the scent of skin, closed my eyes and fell into a thick, padded sleep – the first I had enjoyed in months.

7

Gay dropped Lennie off at around seven the following Friday. I was hiding downstairs in my bedroom, almost the first time in days that I had been in the room for longer than it took to change my clothes.

The previous week Adam had begun to dally in the morning, eating the breakfast he had resisted for so long, never leaving for the office before ten thirty. He arrived home by six every evening, once with flowers that he left, wordlessly, on the kitchen table – whether they were a gift or a housekeeping chore, to be arranged and displayed, was never quite spelled out. Dinner took on less and less significance, and each night, before the food had time to cool on the plate, I abandoned the table and let Adam lead me back upstairs to his bedroom.

I counted the seconds until he took my hand.

I was sleeping better, but, because my demons now had less time to drive me, they began to hunt me throughout the day, hunching behind doors, ready to spring out the minute I found myself alone. With no night shift, I had less time for the house-work, and sped through the rooms in a flurry of activity, but this only made the guilt all the hungrier to consume me whenever the chance presented itself. I stopped looking in the mirror. I didn't like the bright gold leaf flecks in my eyes. I didn't like the way my skin, tanned after months of forced marches through the scorched London streets, suddenly glowed, as though the sun were rising within.

So Lennie's imminent arrival, in some ways, was a relief. I would sleep in my own bed and get back to the kitchen sink where I belonged.

I heard the front door slam shut. Gay obviously still had her keys. Heels tapped across the marble floor overhead, followed by some indeterminate scuffing and dragging. The word 'Adam', pronounced with an imperious upswing, sliced the silence. He was upstairs in his study, but he had also been listening for her, and within seconds, amid a muddle of voices, I heard the muffled sound of numerous footsteps on the stairs.

My stomach tied itself into elaborate macramé knots of tension. I could have fashioned pot holders out of it. Should I go upstairs and offer tea? Or maybe I should open a bottle of wine? Adam had not given me any pointers, and it seemed presumptuous to put myself in the role of hostess, proffering drinks in what had been, in fact still was, the woman's own house.

I tried to make myself look calm and distracted. I grabbed one of the paperback proof copies that Adam had given me to read, stuck my glasses on the end of my nose and curled up on the cord sofa in the old playroom. I put on the radio to drown out any threads of second-hand conversation. I fixed my eyes on the large print until it danced around the page like ants, and read not a word. There was a clatter on the basement stairs. Adam poked his head round the door.

'Edith, would you mind coming up and meeting Gay?' I noticed my *th* had reappeared at the same time as the wife. I jumped up ready to follow him, hurriedly folded my glasses inside the book and jammed it down the side of the sofa. My hands were shaking, but Adam was standing in the middle of the room, looking at the scabby walls and the stained carpet that no amount of shampoo had shifted.

'Good grief, has it been like this since you arrived?' he asked, then shook himself, muttering under his breath. 'How stupid, of course it has. I haven't been in here for years. What a dump.'

I couldn't agree more, but nevertheless I felt slightly defensive about the shortcomings of my personal space, though at the same time relieved that he had not seen my bedroom. He thought this room was bad – at least it had natural light. The bedroom was the sort of place in which you locked up your mad aunt and pushed dog food under the door.

'It's not so bad,' I began, but he cut me off with an expression that I had not seen before, somewhere between anger and disgust. I wondered how much of it was directed towards me. Instinctively I crossed my arms protectively across my breasts and stuffed my hands under my armpits like a street urchin, trying to keep warm. This was not looking good. I followed him upstairs to the first floor.

Gay was sprawled elegantly on one of the cream sofas in the drawing room, her arms spread across the back of the cushions, her oversized bust pushed upwards as though she were sitting in a showroom modelling yachts. Apart from the waterwings, she was pin-thin but with an underfed, too-many-cigarettes, too-much-coffee pallor. No trace of the chubby pony club girl of her early studio portrait remained – unless you counted the pearls round her throat. She was slimmer than I was, but with an unhealthy pinch to her cheeks, and a scrawniness to her neck. She looked as if she hadn't had a good meal in her life. But those amazingly prominent breasts. They seemed too cushioned to be fake. I could see the faint outline of peach lace through her shirt. I immediately felt defensive. He must be a big-tit man. What did he see in me? Convenience, I suspected.

Her hair was a mix of blonde and white that I thought probably owed more to the hairdresser than to nature, and was cut in a short, ruler-straight, Mary Quant-style page-boy that fell a millimetre under her ears. She blinked a lot, I noticed, as she gave me the once-over, as though she couldn't quite believe her eyes and was trying to clear her vision. I had thought she wore contact lenses, but today she had on very serious half-frame spectacles. She looked like a late-model Andy Warhol in drag, if Andy Warhol's mother had been Garbo and had worn good lingerie.

She didn't get up. I prised my right hand from its clenched

position, hoping that it wasn't covered in sweat, and shook the limp tips of her little manicured fingers. She looked at me over her headmistress glasses, blinked and said nothing. I wish I had kept on my own specs, just to provide some competition. I felt as though she were going to give me a detention.

'Edith – Gay, Gay – Edith,' snapped Adam. A slight narrowing in the other woman's eyes told me that she had been expecting to be introduced formally, with her surname and probably some forelock tugging. Years of inherited chippiness rose in my throat.

Adam scowled at her. 'I can't imagine how you let this house get into such a state. That flat of Edie's downstairs is a disgrace – it's a hovel. You can't expect anyone to live in it.'

Apparently I wasn't the only one who was mightily pissed off. And Edie was back in town.

'I beg your pardon, Adam, but "I" don't expect anyone to live in it. The state of "your" house is entirely "your" affair. You can organize your own life – that's why it's called Do It Yourself. Anyway,' said Gay, her eyes studiously avoiding me, 'isn't that what you have the housekeeper for – to keep house? Shouldn't she clean it?'

Bitch. I was very near slapping her ugly specs right off her nose.

' "She" does clean it, Mrs Davenport,' I replied with ice in my voice.

She blinked again, several times.

I blinked back, hard, for emphasis.

Gay looked flustered, and for a second I could see that she was as nervous as I was and merely trying to bully her way out of an awkward situation.

'The house does look well taken care of,' she allowed tersely, her lips barely moving. 'You've obviously been doing a good job. Adam let it go to rack and ruin after I left.'

Adam poured himself half a tumbler-full of whisky and threw himself into an armchair.

'Well, to be fair, Gay, you did take the cleaner with you.'

I hovered uncomfortably, Gay and I both quivering like a pair of scorpions facing up for a fight.

'What are you standing up for, Edie? Sit down, for God's sake. You're not on trial.'

I sat on the opposite armchair as Gay compulsively smoothed down the legs of her trouser suit, and then opened her Louis Vuitton handbag with a loud snap. She took out a small Cartier diary from inside the leather cover and extracted a business card. She handed it to me. Her perfect pink fingernails gleamed like opals. I took the card and tucked my rough unkempt hands back under my arms, suddenly remembering another reason why I had absolutely no women friends. They were too bloody hard to live up to.

'This has all my numbers on it. Anything, and I mean *anything* that Lennie needs, check with me, whatever time it is, day or night.' Her eyes blinked on every other word. She bit her lip, and I could see the signs of strain on her face. 'It's the first time she and I have been away from each other, and she's at a difficult age at the moment.'

'Don't worry, Gay. Edie will take care of her as though she were her own child,' said Adam.

'Do you have children?' she asked, almost hopefully.

'No,' I said and looked away. I couldn't meet her eyes. I just couldn't take any more of that blinking.

'I know, I'm being a bit overanxious, but she's asthmatic and you have to be careful that she doesn't exert herself too much in this heat, or that her hay fever doesn't get worse. This is her medication; I've had a list of it typed out. Make sure you read it.' She handed me a small washbag together with a folded A4 sheet of paper. 'You can speak English, can't you?'

'I can just about manage it,' I replied stiffly.

'You do have a very strong accent,' she said, as though I might not have noticed it had she not taken the time to point it out.

'I'm Scottish originally.'

'Quite,' she said.

I looked at Adam. He rolled his eyes, then winked. I couldn't stop myself from laughing, but Gay went on as though I had opened my mouth merely to let my teeth air. 'She's allergic to dairy produce, feathers and wheat, and she shouldn't have sugar because she's becoming far too porky.'

I thought it was a bit harsh of her to refer to her daughter as porky, but just then the door opened and Porky herself stood before me.

Actually, Gay had a point.

She was a plump sunflower-blonde with the sort of pink skin that looked as though it had been scrubbed with a nail brush. She was also rather spotty around the chin, which didn't help, nor did the purple train tracks adhering to both upper and lower teeth. She had on a scruffy school uniform and an expression of abject misery, both of which looked as though they had been worn for a very long time.

'Hi, you must be Edith,' she said, brightening when she saw her mother and father were not alone. Her face lit up as she gave me a handshake and a full three grand's worth of purple plastic and metal smile. 'I like what you did to my room.' She walked across and perched one cheek of her bottom on the armchair occupied by Adam, but she addressed her mother. 'Mummy, the room's all been painted and I have a new bed with a pretty quilt, and there's a proper desk and all my old things have been arranged on shelves. It's wicked.' She kissed her father's head and toppled on to his lap like a sack of tennis balls. A heavy sack of tennis balls.

'Thanks,' she said again to me, as though I had paid for the bed myself. She didn't mention the box of wheat, sugar and dairy biscuits I had left on her bedside table.

'And I love your hair,' she said.

She had to be kidding. I had cut it with the poultry scissors halfway through August and instead of straggling down my back it now tangled around my shoulders, twenty-six different shades of chlorine-bleached blonde with jade-green highlights, and ends like an untrimmed hedge. But no.

'It'th really cool,' she enthused, lisping slightly through the metal. Getting her tongue round Edith Lutz was going to be something of a problem for her.

Getting my head round Lennie Davenport was going to be an even bigger problem for me. Yes, she was overweight, and had pimples and braces, but the girl was heart-stoppingly beautiful. She had Adam's direct green eyes but with the addition of startling little orange flecks and full cupid's bow lips.

She looked like a blonde, pedigree cat.

She sucked the ends of her buttery-yellow hair and all the doors in the rickety house of lies I had built for myself swung wide open. The ghosts of my past walked out of the shadows, drew out the chairs, sat down and drummed their fingers on their rattling skeleton legs, waiting for an audience. I would have to get to them one by one. But absolutely the last one I wanted to deal with was the teenage girl.

Some women would probably turn into mushy, maternal Mrs Friendly Bigheart at this point, rapidly taking the tubby teenager under their wing and into their squishy big hearts. But that wasn't going to happen here. She wrapped her soft arms around her father's neck and kissed his cheek, laughingly complaining about the scratchiness of his face.

And I loathed her on sight.

8

I am fourteen.

Kirsty was fifteen last week. She got her own television in her room and a gold locket. This Saturday she is going to her first dance in the Welfare Hall. I beg to go with her, but I am too young, my mother tells me brusquely, as though I had asked for something obscene, like red stilettos and a bondage mask instead of fifty pence for the entrance fee.

'I am not too young,' I protest, but she won't even entertain the idea.

'You are not going, and that's that.'

There is no point in persevering – my mother is like quick-drying cement when she makes a decision – but her refusal is not going to cause me much of a problem. Kirsty and I simply initiate the first in a long string of successful scams – I say I am staying at her house and go to the dance anyway. By this point, Kirsty's mother not only never leaves the house but rarely ventures out of her bedroom. She stays in bed most of the day in a pink satin dressing gown and reads with the blinds down.

'It's her nerves,' says Kirsty.

'She's a lazy trollop,' says my mother. Either way, she is never going to tell on us because no one ever sees her. Kirsty's dad isn't much better. He only speaks to you if you have a corpse that needs to be buried, and even then you have to snuff it before the nine o'clock news. Any later and he's well into his whisky.

As we grow older the scam becomes more complex: we each claim we are staying with the other and spend the night with whichever schoolfriend has the most lenient or neglectful parents. We are confident that we will never be found out, and, until the policeman arrives on my parents' doorstep in the middle of the night a little over a year later, we never are. And by that time it doesn't really matter, because Kirsty isn't speaking to me any more.

And so we're squeezing through the swinging saloon doors of the Welfare Hall to a fanfare of strobe lights and Alice Cooper banging out of the speakers. Kirsty's eyes flash white in the stuttering darkness, mad with excitement. Her halter top is fluorescent. Her teeth gleam. She tucks her perfect honey-blonde hair behind her perfect small ears with their perfect silver heart-shaped earrings and grabs my hand.

'Come on and dance,' she urges, but I shake my head, suddenly shy. I want to go to the bathroom. I want to go home. I feel useless and awkward and gangly – like a lighthouse with a big yellow beacon on my head that flashes on and off telling every-body that I'm at my first disco and don't know what to do. But worse is yet to come.

Kirsty ignores my protests and drags me to the centre of the crowded floor and there, to an enthusiastic chorus of 'School's Out', I learn something new and totally unexpected about myself. While Kirsty's breasts bounce like they're being tumble dried under her Persil-white halter top and draw the attention of every pair of male eyes in the room, I discover I can't fucking dance.

How come no? I ask myself in a flurry of panic and flailing arms as I try, in vain, to move my limbs in time to the beat of the record that is pulsing out across the dance floor. I stumble, I trip, I slap someone standing close to me, who doesn't even blink. His eyes are so intent on the orbs threatening to escape from Kirsty's shirt that I could probably have taken his wallet. My legs feel as though the circulation is just returning to them after four years in a coma. They wobble and drag themselves across the floor five seconds after my brain gives them the instruction to move. I am shaking like someone with cerebral palsy.

I still can't understand why this is happening. Don't I know the song? Yes – I've danced to it in my bedroom at home. I've sung to it with the electric plug of the Hoover as my microphone. I can feel the bass thudding in my chest like slow hiccups, but I just can't find it with my feet.

Kirsty is standing next to me, her hair swishing back in front of her face as if she is in some kind of manic shampoo advert, her feet tapping in tall heels, her smooth arms waving to and fro, her breasts swaying. How is she doing it? I slow everything down until I am barely moving. I shake my shoulders and shuffle my feet from side to side. This is better. At least I am not hitting anybody, but you can hardly call it dancing. It's more like when you're dying to go to the toilet, but there's a queue.

Mercifully, the record plays out, and in the brief pause before the next song starts I edge through the sweating bodies to the fringes of the hall. Feigning fatigue, I plonk myself on to the row of folding chairs, linked together in an unruly conga line around the perimeter of the room like wee schoolgirls on a class outing, and contemplate the collapse of any hope I may have had of a normal adolescence.

What happened to my feet? Hadn't I spent years drilling my heels and toes into the rough planks of the floor of this very same hall? Didn't my Highland Fling send the Johnny Walker ashtrays into wide glass o's of astonishment? And hadn't my Sword Dance dazzled the disco ball – if not the judges – at the youth county finals in Selkirk last year, when I had failed to win a medal but had come home, nevertheless, with a Highly Commended Ribbon?

I suddenly realize, as I listen to Haircut 100 singing 'Fantastic Day', that the reason Miss Mathieson had repeatedly clapped out the beat, calling one-two-three-four when I heel-toed it across the boards, was because otherwise I couldn't keep time to the music. I had not, in fact, learned to dance; I had learned to count, and to move in formation like a hen-toed shire horse doing dressage.

'Why are you sitting down there?' yelps Kirsty. 'You canny be tired already?' she moans, looking around the room to be sure she isn't missing anything. Fifty pairs of eyes stare back at her for exactly the same reason. She shoulders me out of the seat and yanks me back on to the floor.

'But, Kirsty, I canny dance,' I hiss in her ear. 'I look glaekit.'

'Just jiggle about. Nobody's even looking at you,' she says, immediately beginning to rock from the waist, the male population of the room swaying with her as though they were watching Wimbledon.

She is right: absolutely nobody is looking at me. I am invisible.

At least she has a waist, I think to myself, watching her shimmy about, and good legs. Not only does her chest spray across the room like a volley of automatic gunfire whenever she turns around, but, having seen her put her trousers on a hundred times, I know that her legs meet at strategic points all the way down from the top of her thighs to the bones of her ankles. This, my mother told me, is how you know you have a perfect figure. My hip bones stick out at angles. I have a washboard chest. I don't need my mother to outline my limitations. I am nothing compared to Kirsty. I mean, all that blonde hair, never out of place but hanging straight down her back like a knife. While my hair is short and of an indeterminate colour somewhere between boring and fucking boring, which no amount of shine-enhancing shampoo will enliven. And, since my mother works in the local chemist, I have tried every single brand.

Thankfully, the next song spins into silence with final guitar chorus and a diminishing drum solo. 'Move,' says Kirsty, pushing me towards the stage, where a row of boys holding bottles of Coke sit hunched and draped over the edge, like vultures waiting for road kill.

'Where are we going?' I whisper.

'Peter Nelson is sitting over there. Let's go and stand in front of him; maybe he'll ask me to dance.'

Kirsty knows that Peter, the doctor's son, has a monumental crush on her. If they start going out, it'll be a match made in Women's Guild Heaven, where your daughter kisses only boys of her own social class. In our village there is a very small pool in which to dip. Because my dad is the bank manager, I get to be in it, but I'm down at the muddy end, owing to being skinny. Then, apart from Kirsty, there's Peter, Derek, the pharmacist's son, and Dan Ponti, whose parents have the café. I have already been warned off him because Kirsty likes him, and anyway he's what my mother calls 'wild', which is just another way of saying Italian and Catholic and to be avoided. Fat chance. He'd never look at me. I am a head and a half taller than everyone my own age, but I am still hoping that some of the other boys will grow. I also hope I'll wake up one morning and find I have turned into Britt Ekland or that I'm in the *Partridge Family* and David Cassidy's my brother.

I follow Kirsty to the back of the hall, feeling ridiculous. I wish I had worn my new shoes, which have a stacked heel and a little crossover strap with a pearl, but Kirsty wouldn't let me. She said they made me too tall.

So she's wearing them, the toes padded with cotton wool so they fit her.

She drags me on to the floor. I do what's expected.

I came, I saw, I danced to Glam Rock.

Older boys ask us to dance, but I can see them arguing before they walk over and tap our shoulders about who gets Kirsty. I am the spare. I wish I could slip through the jaggy cracks in the planks, or maybe hide in the bathroom, where girls draw lines around their eyes and lips as though they needed to find their own edges before they could colour themselves in.

The girls say 'hiya' and tell her they like her shoes. Everybody always smiles at Kirsty; even Dan Ponti, who is gorgeous, no matter what my mother says, always hangs around Kirsty whenever he sees her on the street. He has tanned skin and dark curly hair. He looks like David Essex.

Peter Nelson jumps off the stage and holds a long conversation with the front of her shirt. A slow song comes on and the two of them start dancing as I stand there like a pint of milk left to sour on the step. It's just like being back at school, practising for the Christmas party, and everyone gets picked except me and I have to dance with the laddie from the dairy farm who always smells of cow. I look around and see Dan Ponti watching Kirsty and Peter with a bitter expression on his face, his jaw dropping like a bottle opener.

He glances over at me, looks me up and down, and then turns away. I make a show of rummaging through my handbag, but there's nothing in there except a purple lipstick and a safety pin. I slip away to the bathroom and hide in a stall. I hate this dance. I wish I could go home, but I'm spending the night at Kirsty's and I can hardly go to her place without her. I feel like crying, but if I do all my mascara and eyeliner will run down my face. I only put it on because Kirsty told me to. I look like a boiled egg with a face painted on it for Easter.

I stay in the stall even when someone starts banging on the door. I don't care. But eventually I have to come out and go to look for Kirsty. She is standing in a corner with Peter and a couple of other girls who are in her class at school. I wonder why she didn't go to the dance with them instead of me. She's really popular. I wave at her. She waves back but doesn't move. I wiggle my fingers and make for the door. I think I would rather wait outside her house than hang around here like a bad smell. She runs after me.

'You canny go home now.'

'I'm fed up.'

'But I'm not ready – we just got here.'

'I'll wait for you round the back – in your summerhouse,' I say, pretending a casualness that I don't feel. 'You've got your other pals.'

'Okay.' She looks at her watch. 'We have to be home by ten o'clock, but it's not even nine yet.' I realize I have been hiding in the loo for nearly an hour.

'Peter is going to walk me home.' She smiles conspiratorially. I smile back, even though I think that the skin around my mouth is going to crack like the leather on her dad's car seats.

She dances away. I am dismissed.

Outside, it is nearly dark. It's been raining and it's cold. I shiver as I run quickly down the short road, past the war memorial, past the Running Dog, and round the corner to Kirsty's house. I have to be careful just in case I see my dad out for a walk, but the street is deserted. I splash through the black clouds shining up at me from the puddled street, then, just when I get to the side passage near her house, I hear the swoosh of a bike on the wet asphalt. I turn and am surprised when I see that it's Dan Ponti, his bicycle cutting the street into twin fountains of water. He's always running up and down our street on his bike, mostly looking for Kirsty, I think.

He pedals the bike round in a circle, spraying water everywhere.

'Agnes,' he shouts, making a hissing sound on the *s*, as though he's trying to charm a snake, or calling a cat. I didn't think he even knew my name. It's Kirsty that he always pays attention to. He never speaks to me; even when I go into the café where he often works after school and buy cups of coffee, he looks right through me. He's a couple of years ahead of us – at the Catholic school – and he'll be leaving in the summer. He told Kirsty that when he turns eighteen, he's going to take over the café and newsagent's full time.

'Ssh,' I say back. 'I'm not supposed to be here until later on.'

'Where's your pal?' he asks.

'She's still at the dance – with Peter,' I add, mostly out of spite, really. Just to rub it in. 'But I'm staying with her the night, so I have to wait here until she comes home.'

'I saw you leaving the hall; I thought she'd be with you,' he says, getting off the bike and standing awfully close to me.

'Nah.' I shake my head. I'm nervous. I haven't spoken to any boy for this long, ever – not unless I am doing a project with him or we are related or something.

'Do you want to come for a walk with me?' he asks.

I am stunned. 'Who, me?' I ask. My mouth is open, rain drops fall into it. I forget to close it.

He nods, shrugs his shoulder and scans the street. 'I can leave my bike, and we can walk along by the railway bridge.'

'No.' I find myself shaking my head vigorously, though inside I'm digging my elbow deep into my ribs and saying, go, go, go, Agnes – for God's sake. It's Dan Ponti. 'I said I'd wait for her round the back in the summerhouse, and I better watch that my dad doesn't see me. I live just over there.' I point over at the square sandstone house on the other side of the road with the lime-green paint trim that my colour-blind dad insists is maroon.

'Nice house,' Dan says. 'So did yer dad rob that bank he works in?'

'No, he did not,' I say indignantly. But he's not really listening. He lights a cigarette.

'I'll wait and keep you company, then,' he says, and with a final look over his shoulder he follows me up the side path, through the creaky back gate, and along the side of Kirsty's overgrown garden to the rotting gazebo at the far end of what would be her lawn if anyone ever cut the waist-high grass.

It's pitch black except for the light coming from her mother's bedroom window. I put my fingers to my lips and point. 'Shhh,' I say.

'It's a tip round here,' he says when we get to the end of the garden. There's smoke curling out of his mouth that makes him look like a dragon. 'Where do they keep the stiffs?'

I point to the yard on the left, where a long shiny hearse sits outside a building with small blacked-out window panes.

'It gives me the creeps,' he says.

I agree. 'But there's nobody there the now,' I tell him confidently. I wouldn't spend the night in the house if there were any dead bodies waiting to be embalmed.

'It's a funny thing to do for a job, burying dead people. I'd rather serve chips to the living any day,' says Dan, settling himself down next to me on the green mossy slats of the bench in the summerhouse.

'Your jacket is lovely,' I gush inanely.

Dan is wearing a leather jacket and a pair of Levis that fit his long legs like sticky-back plastic. He puts out his cigarette on the concrete and gives me another look like the one he ran over me at the dance. It makes me squirm.

'Do you smoke?'

I shake my head.

'Drink?'

Again, another no.

'You're a good wee girl, then.'

'I'm not so wee,' I reply.

He grabs my arm and pulls me closer to him, and I realize with a half-excited sort of dread that he's going to kiss me. I've been practising, on the inside of my elbow, and on my pillow, and Kirsty showed me how you move your mouth, though to be honest she looked like a complete divvy, gaping away like a guppy looking for fish food. But Dan's mouth, when it lands on mine, is nothing like what I expect. He tastes sour and smoky, and before I can even think what to do he's stuffing his tongue into my mouth. I nearly gag.

He cracks up laughing. 'Did nobody ever kiss you before?' he says, snorting through his nose. The smell of stale cigarettes blasts across my face.

He kisses me again, and this time he puts his hand on top of my chest. I try to pull back, but he keeps hold of me. 'You can open your mouth a bit,' he says. 'And maybe breathe or you'll be in one of those boxes over there in the hearse.'

Tears are jabbing at my eyes. I don't know what I should do. First I can't dance and now I can't kiss either. And I don't think he should be squeezing me and touching me like this.

'You have to stop,' I say, but not too loudly, as I'm scared that someone will hear me.

'I don't have to do anything I don't want to,' he says. 'You should be begging me for it. How old are you anyway – fifteen, sixteen?'

'I'm fourteen,' I whisper.

'Jeez, I'm baby snatching.' He pulls back like he's been burned, stands up, lights another cigarette and starts to walk away. 'I'll see you,' he says without meeting my eye. 'Tell Kirsty I said hiya.'

I hear the gate slam behind him. The bolt tinkles as it hits the catch, then the night blots up the noise and it all goes quiet.

Kirsty doesn't turn up till half past ten, and she has a soppy expression on her face and no lipstick. Her chin is red and scurvy-looking.

'Oh, Peter Nelson kissed me,' she crows in a sing-song voice, shutting her bedroom door behind me after she's wheedled her mother into not caring that we are late. 'He kissed me loads,' she shrieks, throwing herself into a starfish on her frilly eiderdown and kicking off my shoes, which are all scuffed.

'Well, Dan Ponti kissed me too,' I shoot back, aiming right for her back.

'What?' she says, sitting up and looking at me with disbelief. You'd think I told her there were Martians in her kitchen helping themselves to the Gypsy Creams.

'I'm telling you – he came down on his bike and sat with me in your summerhouse, where he kissed me. Twice. With tongues.' I want to say that he even tried to get his hand into my bra. I might have let him if it hadn't been for the toilet paper already there, but I realize that this might make me into a slag, so I shut my mouth.

'You're havering,' she says.

'I am not. It happened.'

Kirsty's almond eyes, hard with navy-blue eyeshadow, narrow into nasty little slits. 'Oh, Agnes, you are so jealous. You're just making it up.'

I am so annoyed I could slap her fat face. 'I am not making it up,' I sob. 'He sat with me round the back. You'll see his fag end stamped out on the ground if you look.'

She is sceptical. 'Aye, aye, and the band played believe it if you like,' she snorts. 'Everybody knows that Dan Ponti likes me; he's not going to bother with a wee lassie like you.' She struts along the hall and slams the bathroom door shut.

'He did, Kirsty.' I am crying now. But she isn't listening. She's back out of the bathroom with her nightdress on and is getting into her bed, pointedly putting the light off. I have to get changed in the dark, and when I get in beside her she slips right over to the other side of the bed. She ignores me, and then I hear soft snores coming from her pillow. I get up and wipe my nose on a bit of toilet paper, but it has lipstick on it that I don't see in the dark, so when I wake up I have a purple stripe on my face.

Next morning I am going back to my house. Kirsty is annoyed, but her mother has told her to walk me home. We are just crossing the road when I see Dan Ponti speeding along the pavement on his bike, and I wave at him. He ignores me.

'What did I tell you?' says Kirsty, her mouth twisted and her voice snide with satisfaction.

'Look, he did so kiss me,' I insist.

'Hey, Dan,' she shouts really loudly, right across the middle of the street for everybody to hear. 'Agnes says you and her were snogging round the back of my house last night.'

'Aye, that'll be right,' Dan shouts back. My heart swoops up through the cloud and does a flip.

'See.' I look at her for an apology, but Dan is still talking. 'Who do you think you're kidding? What would I be doing sitting fiddling with a wee lassie? I'd need to be desperate. But I'll take you round there any time you're ready,' he says, with a big smug grin.

'You're a liar, Dan Ponti,' I gasp.

'Have you been telling stories, hen?' he tuts loudly.

'You know I haven't,' I say, but he's already cycling off up the hill, his bum wiggling in the air, ugly laughter trailing after him, rancid, like the smell of tobacco.

'You're rotten with jealousy, that's what it is, Agnes,' says Kirsty, flouncing back into her house and leaving me by myself on the pavement.

I tuck my nightdress under my arm and drag my feet as I walk along the street. Even on a Sunday there's nobody in when I open the back door. The house is cold and, as usual, the fire isn't lit.

9

Lennie began to come every single weekend, arriving straight from school on Friday afternoon and leaving late Sunday night when her mother collected her, usually without ever taking her expensively shod foot off the accelerator. Slowing to a crawl, she'd sound the horn, and Lennie would run out to the car. The whack of the front door slamming behind her was the high spot in my week.

While she was in the house she stuck to me like cling film. Whenever I turned around she seemed to be behind me. I'd go up to the kitchen to start dinner and there she would be, leaning against one of the worktops, peering into the fridge or sitting on the edge of one of the pine chairs pulled out from the table, waiting expectantly for me – as though I were going to start doing magic tricks or handstands across the floor. Mooching, my mother used to call it. It made me edgy and irritable. I couldn't shake her off.

What are you cooking? What are you making? What's that? Where does this go? What was your husband's name? What was it like in New York? Did you go to Bloomingdale's? Have you been to Central Park? Do you know Jennifer Aniston? She had an insatiable curiosity about my previous life and no compunction about indulging it. The questions went on and on – and, yes, I could manage the ones about the cast members of *Friends* and explain the finer points of bread making when I was up to my elbows in dough, but I started to struggle when she wanted me to give her a virtual tour of Bergdorf Goodman. It was like being interrogated by the shopping Gestapo.

I thought it couldn't get worse, but occasionally, such as when Adam went to Frankfurt, I was left to entertain her alone. Entertaining? It most certainly was not.

I just couldn't cope with her constant presence. She rarely left the house unless I walked down to the market, when she invariably accompanied me. In the evenings I often found her snuggled under a blanket in the sitting room that was supposed to be mine, immediately reclaimed as hers, watching the television that had miraculously grown a working plug and acquired a matching video recorder. But whenever she heard my footsteps on the stairs she would follow me, almost to my bedroom door, asking me if I wanted to watch a film with her.

I didn't.

I had hopes of some respite when I learned she had a friend living next door, but Leila's mother worked most weekends, and, instead of on parole, I found myself under virtual house arrest with two fifteen-year-old inmates, who lolled around the kitchen asking for sandwiches and then didn't eat them.

If this was motherhood, I hadn't missed much, I thought, as giggles and shrieks filled up the space in the house and CDs, crisp packets, magazines, open bottles of nail varnish, soiled towels and squished sachets of face packs bred indiscriminately in the downstairs sitting room, which also acquired new posters, a bead curtain and a lava lamp. I didn't see any point in having the painters come back to redecorate it, as Adam had instructed, since I had effectively been banished to the three square yards of my bedroom. All it meant was more work, more upheaval and less privacy.

I came to long for the time when my weekend activity consisted of watching the dust motes drift through the air.

In the midst of it, Adam retreated to his study with the cheerful resignation of a man who knows when he's beaten and eagerly hands you the cane so you can whack him some more. He loved Lennie's noisy presence, and when she wasn't pestering me with questions about Central Park, she was cupped in the tiny sofa opposite his desk, surrounded by displaced manuscripts and papers, chattering to him about her teachers, or her friends, with whom, I'm afraid to say, I was also on first-name terms. I dreaded the imminent arrival of his son at half-term. I didn't know how much more of this middle-class sitcom I could take.

Lennie, for once, was upstairs in her bedroom, doing homework. Her preferred location was the kitchen table, but I had tried to drive her out by colonizing it with sheets of pasta. I knew it would take me nearly an hour to crank out enough tagliatelli for the four of us – Leila was staying to supper – when I could have opened a packet in three seconds, but I thought that this was one way to get rid of her. I should have known better. The minute I dragged the pasta machine out of the cupboard, she sprang up like a weed from behind the fridge door, her eyes bright with curiosity. Before I had the dough mixed, she was aimlessly turning the handle, asking for instructions, and the chore that should have been accomplished in peaceful Zen-like silence took all morning and acquainted me with twenty-seven things I never wanted to know about Mariah Carey.

Did you know she was born in Huntington, Long Island?

I'm sure you are as thrilled as I was with that information.

The pasta should really have been moved to an airtight container by now, but, having finally levered Lennie out of the room by leading her upstairs with a trail of chocolate brownies, I covered it with damp tea towels and left it hanging over the back of every available chair. I decided I'd run the risk of salmonella and was even willing to chuck the whole lot out and use dried spaghetti if it would keep Lennie away from me. I made tea, put two cups on a tray and tiptoed up to Adam's study. I poked my head round the corner of the door and was greeted by a smile on his face that made the new paintwork look dingy.

'Can I come in?' I whispered.

'Yes,' he mouthed back, rising to help me with the tray. He closed the door behind me and turned the key in the lock.

'Where's Lennie?' he asked, still whispering.

I pointed my finger upwards. 'Homework and carbohydrates,' I said wryly.

'Is she driving you mad? She really likes you, you know. She was in here singing your praises earlier.'

I shrugged. The feeling wasn't mutual, but I didn't have to write that out in capitals. I poured each of us a cup of tea and nursed mine, leaning on the edge of Adam's desk.

'I think she likes having a woman around the house. Gay always worked and the au pairs were never much use in the kitchen. It's good for her to have proper meals. I think that Gay just nags her all the time for eating too much.'

I made no reply, but Adam didn't notice: he was too happily wrapped up in his little domestic dream of the woman barefoot in the kitchen, and the child fat and rosy and fast asleep in a crib by the hearth. Okay, we didn't have a fireplace, and the woman in the kitchen was his mistress, but who was I to spoil the fantasy?

'It's a pity you never had children, Edie,' he said. 'You're so good with Lennie. She wants to stay longer. She asked if she could stay here during the week. It's so much closer to her school than Gay's flat.'

I nearly choked. The Earl Grey burned my throat like arsenic.

'But Gay won't agree. She wants her home. We compromised by letting her stay till Monday morning. Can you drive her to school? I never asked whether you had a licence. You could take my car.'

'I don't drive. I haven't got a British licence, and I'm sure my American one isn't legal,' I lied. I didn't want to get into the sticky question of insurance details.

'Don't worry about it. I'll go in late and take her myself.' Then he ran his hands up the inside of my thigh. 'I'll be glad to have you to myself again,' he said, smiling, his eyes narrowing with concentration as his fingers rose higher. I felt myself begin to melt, almost sliding off the desk, the cup clattering in its saucer. He just had to look at me and I wanted to tear my clothes off. He pulled me on to his knee and began kissing me, the skirt pulled up around my waist. In seconds I would be fucking him on the chair, but I drew away, tugged down the fabric of my skirt and wriggled from his grip.

'Mr Davenport,' I protested. 'You must learn to keep your hands out of the help's underwear. Lennie will hear.' And, as though my voice were connected directly to God, her shoes clattered downstairs and ran past his door. A few minutes later I heard Leila's voice join hers in the kitchen.

I gave a resigned sigh, as I knew I should go to clear up the pasta.

When I went back downstairs, both girls were hunched over the dining table, flicking through a magazine.

I shut the kitchen door, but Lennie opened it again.

'Edie, you speak Spanish, don't you?'

She turned to me for confirmation, before dropping her eyes back to the magazine when I protested that I knew only a few words.

'She lived all over Spain and Brazil, my dad told me,' she announced, glaring at me as though daring me to contradict her.

'I spent a couple of months in Latin America, is all, not Spain. And they speak Portuguese in Brazil,' I said insistently, but she merely shrugged as though this were an unimportant detail.

'Latino men are so fit. Look at . . .' Her mouth moved and words tumbled out, as her squat fingernail, half of it painted with green polish, pressed into the glossy face of a muscled man dressed in a wife-beater.

'But he's gay,' said Leila, turning the paper idly.

'He's not; he's going out with some model.'

'I was telling Leila that you could help her with her Spanish if she was stuck, couldn't you, Edie?'

'I can speak only a little bit. I have no idea about the grammar, sorry,' I said tersely. Bloody, bloody hell – what was I – the homework elf?

I started to gather up the flat ribbons of pasta and drop them into a Tupperware box. I wiped the table, clearing the flour into little white peaks, then swept them into my hand. The moment

88

I made my final swipe with the cloth, the girls swooped across the surface. *Vogue* and *Elle* lay spreadeagled on the table, their pages already wrinkled and dog-eared.

Lennie was smearing a free sample of face cream over her cheeks.

'Did you ever see Madonna when you lived in New York?' she asked. 'It must have been really glamorous having an apartment in Manhattan. Where did you live exactly? In the Village or near Fifth Avenue?'

I froze.

Good question – where the hell had I lived? Francisco's dad lived on 81st and 2nd, but during the six months we spent at NYU we had lived in the West 150s. I think that's where I told Adam we'd lived. I couldn't remember. Maybe I should have kept crib notes. It had been five years since we had been on the Upper West Side. I hardly remembered how to take the subway.

'I've been to New York lots of times,' said Leila. 'My mother has friends there. We stay on Madison Avenue. But my dad always drags us to all the museums – it's really boring. I just like Barneys. Did you go to Barneys?'

What was Barneys? A kid's restaurant, a circus? A store? Yes, it was a store. But where? Madison, Fifth – Third, or was that Bloomingdale's? And which museums were near Madison Avenue? My mind went as blank as the white board on the front of the fridge. All I could think about was that we needed eggs and sea salt.

'I don't really like to talk about New York much,' I eventually stammered.

'But it's so exciting. I want to go there when I'm older. I want to live by myself, and be thin, and have lots of boyfriends – just like her.' She caressed the page in the magazine lovingly where a tastefully nude model unfolded to reveal a perfume sample.

'Well, I hope you would be wearing more clothes, and have a bit more flesh on your bones. You would have to be anorexic to look like that, Lennie. It's not real life.'

'No, I wouldn't. You're thin. You've got a great figure.'

'No, and neither am I lying across a page, naked, making come-hither eyes at the camera. I'm a woman with a dead husband standing at your sink washing your plates, making your bed and cooking your supper. That might be your idea of a fucking fairy tale, but it's not mine.'

Lennie and Leila both looked at me as though waiting for my head to spin.

I might just as well have vomited across the waxed oak floorboards. That sort of mess would have been easier to clean up. Instead my words sat and steamed, the 'fucking' buzzing round and round in my ears like a fly.

Lennie had tears in her eyes that she hastily wiped into a snail's trail across one of her newly moisturized cheeks. Leila dropped her gaze and stared avidly at the magazine, as if it held the secrets of the universe and not just of how to get really great skin in three weeks.

'I'm sorry, I didn't mean to upset you,' stammered Lennie, her voice teetering like a glass on the edge of a table, ready to fall and shatter into a thousand pieces.

'I know you didn't. I'm sorry. I shouldn't have snapped,' I replied, already hearing the story being repeated to Gay. Or, even worse, Adam. I shuddered. I felt bad, but, as I dried my hands hurriedly on the tea towel and ran downstairs to my bedroom, I knew only a sense of relief, the way you do when you've been banging your head for ages on a brick wall and suddenly you stop. Or at least how I imagined that would feel.

All too soon I was back to butting the wall with my forehead.

I didn't go up for supper. I said I had a lot of letters to write. I returned to the kitchen just long enough to throw out the pasta and leave them a salad and cold cuts. Then I sat on the edge of my bed and bit my knuckles, wondering how long I could keep this big sister charade going.

After two and a half months of insomnia, I had finally managed to fall asleep when I spent the night upstairs with Adam. Even better, the hours before sleep passed in mostly mindless, adolescent sex – or at least the kind of sex I should have had when I was an adolescent. We seemed to fall asleep having sex and wake up in mid thrust, ready to take up where we had left off.

The return to the dank room in the basement every Friday night brought the sexual idyll to an abrupt end. It was like being banished to subterranean Siberia, and I usually spent the time staring into the dark, thinking about the future as though it were a lump in my breast that I was frightened to acknowledge.

So, of course I had no letters to write. There wasn't one single person in the world who knew where I was. I hadn't seen my mother in years. I had hardly spoken to my sister in twenty years. My cousin Agnes, the only person from home whom I vaguely kept in touch with, thought I was abroad, and I communicated with my brother Geordie in Singapore only when necessary, and then only in pounds and pence. He paid all of my mother's nursing-home bills but queried every last packet of cough sweets she sucked. I had no girlfriends. I couldn't contact Karl. I couldn't seek out any of Francisco's old students, and his family were as dead to me as he was. It was frightening how small your life could suddenly become – no more than a tiny soot stain that a wet finger could erase. Just like that.

Now all I had was a second-hand name, a second-hand bed and a second-hand husband, and only then until my contract expired.

Which, after tonight's neurotic outburst, might be sooner than I had imagined.

I did my mental arithmetic. I had saved almost every penny I had earned. I had accumulated a couple of thousand pounds, which I had stuffed into an envelope inside a pillowslip at the back of the linen cupboard upstairs. The share of the money I had taken from our joint current account was hidden in bank-fresh bundles of twenty-pound notes in the downstairs freezer, inside a Tupperware box marked 'Chicken Stock'. I had something saved from my previous life in a building-society account, also untouched. If I had to leave in a hurry I could live for six frugal months without working. The thought made me retch. I needed air.

I opened the back door and crept to the top of the garden steps, where I wrapped my jacket around my shoulders and looked out across the garden square. It was almost the end of October. I had been here for nearly four months. Summer was over. The leaves from the fig tree next door had curled up and died, the unripe fruits scattered like dog turds across the York stone patio. I could see into the kitchens of the houses opposite, my neighbours popping occasionally into view. How much longer would I be here to watch them?

The kitchen light upstairs went out, plunging me into darkness and sending me back indoors. As I negotiated the dark cavern of the stairs, I heard the dishwasher kick into action overhead. There were heavy footsteps and the clicking of interior light switches. Lennie's voice danced across the ceiling, out into the hall and up the stairs like Tinkerbell. I lay on my bed with the jacket still draped over my shoulders and listened to the house settling down for sleep. I closed my eyes.

I woke up to feel the jacket being tugged off my face.

'What the fuck,' I screamed, but nothing came out of my mouth. I grappled with the hands that were round my throat and drew myself into a ball in the corner of the bed.

My vocal chords would not work, billiard balls of panic ricocheting around in my brain.

'Don't,' I finally whimpered. Great – after eventually getting the words out, all I could manage was 'don't', and even that sounded like it was coming from a long way away – like Jeanette MacDonald calling out for Nelson Eddy from out across the valley.

My heart was beating so loudly it muffled everything. I focused my eyes and saw the outline of a body hunched over me, and heavy-framed glasses revealing eyes that looked even more shocked than I felt.

'Edie, you had it wrapped round your neck,' he said. It was Adam; his hands held out my jacket, twisted into a cloth croissant.

For a second I couldn't think who he was, or who he was talking to.

'Edie, Edie, it's okay – it's me,' he murmured.

'What in the name of holy fuck are you doing creeping round my bedroom in the middle of the fucking night?' I half coughed, half cried, swatting him away, even though he was only trying to calm me. I started rifling for the serrated bread knife that I had hidden under my pillow and yanked it out, waving it in the air. 'I could have fucking killed you. Are you off your fucking head?'

Too late I remembered that I was brandishing a knife at the man who was paying my wages. Adam carefully took the knife and laid it on the floor, giving it a kick underneath the bed, and I started to sob, noisily and with an unattractive amount of snot. It was not my finest moment.

'I'm so sorry.' He patted my hair, smoothing it down. 'I didn't mean to scare you. I just wanted to see if you were all right. Lennie told me you were a bit tense this afternoon, and then you didn't come up for supper. I told her to apologize, but when she came down she said you weren't here. And now I seem to have done a pretty good job of upsetting you myself,' he added.

Tense. Does threatening to knife your boss make you seem tense?

'Adam, I-am-not-your-fucking-wife.' I enunciated the words precisely, as if I had been taking elocution lessons for Pissed Off 101. 'I'm the housekeeper. I'm supposed to clean up your crap and do your laundry, not sit at the top of your table dispensing food and womanly wisdom like I live here with a little bell that I ring for the servants. I-am-the-fucking-servant. I don't come to supper; I fucking cook it. I can't deal with this. You seem to have some kind of *Brady Bunch* thing going on in your head and to have forgotten that I only work here. We're not a couple.'

It was a good speech, but, except for the cursing, most of it was unintelligible.

'Oh, ssh,' said Adam, his face white and aghast. 'You must know you mean more to me than that?' he said and began to kiss me, stopping to wipe my face tenderly with the corner of his shirt, then kissing me again. He kissed my eyes, my cheeks, the corners of my lips and, open-mouthed, I wound my arms around his neck and pulled him closer. He began to drag my clothes off, but I stopped him and just tugged them aside. My head was crushed between his shoulders and the rickety headboard, the springs of the geriatric mattress wheezing like an old man, as I pulled him into me and he pushed me hard against the wall until my cheek slapping the plaster made him stop.

'Shit, this is no good.' He looked at the red mark spreading up one side of my face, which had an imprint of the wallpaper embossed into it, as though in shock. 'What the hell am I doing?'

I didn't care, I just hoped he would keep on doing it.

'Here I am trying to tell you I care about you and I'm hurting you.' Hurriedly, he stood up and fastened his belt over his still gaping jeans, before gathering me into his arms. He looked around the bedroom. 'Look, get up and come upstairs. Let's get out of here. This place is depressing. I had no idea.' He surveyed the tattered wallpaper, the bare walls, the barred windows, as though he'd opened his eyes and found himself in a Bangkok prison cell.

'I know, it's fucking awful, isn't it?' I started to laugh through the tears. And I couldn't stop: it suddenly all seemed so ridiculous.

'It's a wonder Amnesty International haven't started a letter-writing campaign for you. You should have told me how bad it was,' Adam said, pulling me up the stairs behind him.

'I've been in worse,' I replied, without elaborating.

Upstairs, he brought me a brandy and a sleeping pill, dressed me in one of his t-shirts, and put me into his bed.

I never even felt him get in beside me, nor, in the morning, did I hear him get up. When I woke it was already eight o'clock. My head felt like birds had been nesting in it, and my eyes looked as though they had been pecked out of their puffy sockets.

I crept into Gay's bathroom to look for something from her pharmacopoeia for my headache but the bathroom cabinet was empty. It took me a second to realize that the perfume had also gone, as had the soap and the bath oil. There was nothing except a lone white towel with a little seashell embroidered on the corner.

I went into her dressing room and found it had been similarly ransacked. A pair of black bin bags lay sprawled on the floor like drunks. I was just peering into their depths when Adam walked up behind me.

He folded me inside his arms. I could smell his lemony cologne and feel the wiriness of him underneath the crisp cotton of his shirt. He looked like the captain of cricket, ready to go in and bat for the game.

'I was just coming to get these,' he said, kissing my ear. 'I left you a cup of coffee beside the bed. Stay there. I mean it,' he added forcefully. 'We're going out to dinner tonight, and if you cook something, I promise, I'm going to throw it into the dustbin myself.'

He picked up the bags. 'I'm going to stick these in the basement and drop them off with Lennie when I next take her back to Gay's.' I peered over his bent shoulder and looked inside the first bag. The heel of one of Gay's Prada sandals pointed right up at me like an insult from a passing car.

'I'm driving Lennie to school, but I'll call you later from the office to see how you are.'

'I'll be fine. I'm sorry about my meltdown last night. It was just a big fuss about nothi . . .' He put his fingers on my lips, then kissed them.

'I'm the one who should be sorry. I've been a fool. I should have realized that I was putting you in an awful position and that you would be feeling insecure. Things will be different, I promise, but I have to go now. Rest and we'll talk later.'

'What have you done with all of Gay's stuff?'

'I moved it out,' he answered. 'So that there's enough room for your clothes. I want you to bring them upstairs today.'

It was the most direct order he had ever given me.

'I can't move up here. I can't. I can't use her bathroom.'

'Well, we'll swap if you like: you can have mine. Whatever you like, just put things where you want them.'

'What about Lennie?' I asked.

'What about her?' he replied, holding my eyes in an unwavering gaze. 'Last time I checked Lennie didn't decide where people slept in this house. She'll just have to deal with it.'

If we'd been wrestling, I would have been pinned to the floor in a shoulder lock, and panting.

As it was, I was just panting.

'I'm not moving into your bedroom, Adam. It doesn't seem right,' I said.

'Suit yourself. Take the guest room, then. But you are not going back into that fetid hole in the basement, and we are not going to sneak around like a pair of kids any more.' He grabbed the bags, kissed me again, inaccurately, on the lips and left.

I ran my fingers lovingly across the marble edge of the sink. There was nothing I would have liked more than to run myself a bath and languish in it like Cleopatra, but I couldn't.

I walked back into the bedroom and lifted the coffee cup to my lips. Adam's shirt swivelled around my hips. I sat on the edge of the bed, spread my legs and examined my toes. I would wait for them to leave and then go downstairs and have a shower.

A second too late I noticed the bedroom door was still open and Lennie was standing on the landing watching me, her eyes taking in the indelicate amount of flesh I was displaying.

'Hi,' she said.

'Hi, Lennie,' I replied, as though I were Delia Smith with a bowl of pancake batter in my hand, not the hired help sitting on her father's bed with no knickers on. I tugged the corner of the shirt in an attempt to cover my knees but only got as far as the top of my thigh.

'You're wearing my dad's shirt,' she said unnecessarily, since it had the name of his tennis club emblazoned on the front.

I couldn't think of any explanation that would sound convincing, even to myself.

Adam's voice called out, urging her to hurry or they'd be late. She didn't move but just stood watching me.

'But what are you doing here?' she asked, sounding suddenly like a little girl who has just lost her favourite doll.

Adam called out again.

Her expression changed from disbelief to faint disgust, as though the implications of finding me sitting on her father's bed had just begun so sink in.

'Did you sleep here?' she gasped in a tiny voice.

I wanted to say 'no' and tell her that it wasn't what it looked like. But I couldn't. Because it was. In fact it was even worse than it looked.

But thankfully nobody knew that but me.

'So, what? Are you and my dad, like, shacking up now?' Lennie said the following weekend, giving me a sly look from underneath her long curling lashes.

The painters had finally come back and were in the process of turning the basement into an ice palace, and I had moved into the upstairs guest room – right across the hall from her – but the girl wasn't stupid. Or particularly forgiving. There was a sneer in her voice.

I wasn't sure what Adam had told her. He could do really interesting things with his tongue, but dissimulation wasn't one of them.

But, however he had explained my half-naked presence, it hadn't made Lennie any less interested in pursuing me. If I thought she had stuck to me like static before, I was now discovering a whole new meaning to the word 'attachment'. It was like having a chaperone, a blind chaperone, to whom everything had to be explained, step by step. I felt as if I were in a fly-on-the-wall documentary and providing my own running commentary. Even when I hid in the bathroom, she knocked on the door asking me for everything from nail-varnish remover to advice on period pains.

'What about your husband, have you got over him? I thought you were going to be, like, tragic for ever. Are you going to marry my dad? Will you be my stepmother? I hope you don't think you can shove me out of the way if you get married.'

I didn't know which question to rebut first, so I made a list and worked my way through them.

'Well, we're definitely not getting married, so you can forget that, and where you live is nothing to do with me – that's up to your father and mother, and always will be. I know you saw me in his room, but that has nothing to do with the fact that I still just work here. I'm not going to be making any decisions beyond whether I buy Ariel or Daz. I'm not going to interfere in your life. I would not and never shall presume to make decisions for you. That's the last thing I have any interest in. As for getting over my husband – that's my business.'

She looked disappointed that there was not more drama to be milked from the situation. 'It's weird, Dad having a girlfriend. In some ways it's kind of gross, but Leila says you're cool, so I shouldn't really mind. I mean, I liked you before, so what's the biggie now?'

I sighed – so now the neighbours knew about my sleeping arrangements.

'I mean, as long as you don't move to, like, the country or anything. Or have babies – jeez, I'm not interested in the whole stepsister thing.'

'I'm not his girlfriend, Lennie. And I'm definitely not in the baby-making business. However, you shouldn't be discussing your dad's private life. Not without talking to him first.'

'But I did talk to him first.' She cast me another sly look. I felt like a teenager gossiping about boys: my friend fancies your friend. Not that anyone had ever fancied me when I was that age.

'I don't know why you have to be so sneaky about it, is all . . .'

'Oh, please, Lennie,' I remonstrated, 'I don't want to talk about it.'

'Whatever, anyway – it's not me that you have to worry about – it's my mum. She's going to freak when she finds out. It was bad enough when Dad was on holiday in France without her, and he had all their friends staying there. She didn't like that at all. She kept ringing us up all the time. I think she was waiting for Dad to ask her over. But this – ha, this is going to turn her into queen psycho bitch, big time.'

And the girl wasn't far wrong.

It was not pretty.

On Sunday evening Adam drove Lennie home with Gay's clothes and toiletries packed into two suitcases, my having persuaded him that the bin bags did not send the right kind of message.

He didn't arrive back until 2 a.m., tight-lipped and rigid with anger. I was sitting up in his bed, where I had been reading the same sentence for the previous hour, when he walked in.

He began to undress, pacing in and out of his bathroom, punctuating his sentences with his toothbrush, and appearing each time wearing successively fewer clothes, until he stood only in his boxers.

'You know,' he railed, 'I thought that my wife had walked out on me but apparently not,' he said. 'Suddenly we're still married and she has a right to determine how I live my life, who I live with, and when and where I see my children.

'She won't let Ned come for half-term, and she wants me to sell the house.' He laughed without humour.

'Will you? Lennie says she doesn't want you to move.'

'Oh, she can't touch the house. It's not even mine. It's all tied up in some kind of family trust. We only came to live here because none of the brothers wanted it. She's probably entitled to about a tenth of the value – I can buy her out. She can have the house in Mougins if she wants. What she can't have is the last word about my private life.'

He climbed in beside me and gave me a spearmint-flavoured kiss, sliding his hand across my stomach and knocking the book from its resting place to the floor.

'Adam, you mustn't let this get in the way of your family – it's not worth it.'

'Oh, don't be ridiculous. In the first place, I want you here – in my bed, in my life – and everyone will just have to suck it up and get used to it. And in the second place, it's not about you, it's about Gay wanting to control everything. It would be the same whoever I started to see; it just gives her a particular pain in the neck that I've replaced her so easily – I think her exact words were my "own live-in kitchen whore".'

I flinched as though he had slapped me.

'Sorry, that was harsh, but you might as well know what you're dealing with. I think she thought that my life would just stay on hold while she was the one having all the new beginnings.'

He reached across me and turned out the light, pulling me against him as he lay down.

'But why did you have to tell her? Why is it anything to do with her?' I asked the hollow of his neck. 'As you said – she left you.'

'I didn't want to put Lennie in the position of having to keep secrets. It's better to get it out in the open. I hate subterfuge. So you might as well move in here with me – there's no point in keeping up the fiction that we're not a couple. Whatever you say, we are a couple, and it makes me very happy.'

'I don't feel right about it, Adam. I can't sleep with you when your daughter's in the house. You're right about not wanting her to keep secrets. She can't. She's already told Leila and God knows who else.'

He shrugged. 'If Gay gets her way, Lennie's not going to be a problem. She doesn't want her to set foot inside the house again.'

'All I seem to be doing is causing trouble for you. What will you do?'

'Don't worry about it. I'm not going to give in to her.'

But I did worry, and for the first time in months it wasn't about myself.

Long after Adam had fallen asleep, I lay awake, sobered with that awful 3 a.m. clarity in which, despite the gloom, everything is illuminated, and you get brutal truth, straight up, without a twist.

I was making Adam's life worse, and for what? There was no future for me here, and I knew that I should be extricating myself before he got even more comfortable with the idea of me as a benign Mrs Suzy Homemaker. I would have to leave, and soon, but how? Where? I turned to look at him, at his face, half covered by his left hand, where the wedding band still gleamed on his ring finger. He slept with a child's fierce concentration, his eyes squeezed shut as though unconsciousness was a serious business that demanded all his energy.

His features had none of Francisco's angelic sensuousness: the lips were narrower, the cheeks thinner, and, of course, he was older. The eyes, without Francisco's thick, fringed lashes, radiated lines across his pale cheek like a five-year-old's drawing of the sun. But when he smiled, his whole appearance transformed: his cheeks fell into merry folds like one of those funny dogs with the pleated faces. It entranced me, that change, which I could bring about with only a word or a gesture or a touch. I loved it.

Comparisons are odious, my mother used to say, before making them anyway, always to my detriment. And I made them too, measuring Francisco against Adam, then hastily wiping out the differences I found. But, inside, the two men were a lot alike. Both had the same relaxed kindness, which they offered generously, even casually, although Adam was a lighter soul and much less self-contained and detached than Francisco had been. He had more ardency, more intent – at least where I was concerned. He saw me. Or at least he saw who he thought I was.

I stroked his already roughening cheek, resisting the urge to kiss him awake. I promised myself that I would find some way out of this mess. I owed it to him.

But, no matter what people say about the cold light of morning, it's still a lot warmer than the stark, surgical chill of the night, and as usual, when I finally woke, a little after seven, I reneged on all the deals I had brokered with myself four hours earlier. I rose, brushed my teeth, made Adam coffee and kicked my good intentions to the side with the rest of the lies, then shoved them in the hamper for another day.

But I was tired.

I couldn't get moving. Adam sprang out of the door soon after eight, bristling with purpose. I watched him go with the same wistfulness I had always felt when Francisco rushed off to his office in college, leaving me dangling, cut adrift, looking at a long, formless morning until he came back and pulled me in to shore. I needed something to do, but instead I dallied. I drank several cups of coffee until my ears sang with static. I stripped Lennie's bed, washed her sheets and practically breathed on them until they were dry enough to iron. It was almost a relief when I heard Adam's key in the door just after lunch. I wasn't expecting him home in the middle of the day, but the chance to stop working, stop thinking, stop agonizing, was welcome. I set the iron down on the ironing board, snorting steam like a dragon above the duvet cover I had been ironing creases into for the previous half-hour, and walked out to meet him, a smile ready on my face like that of a chat-show host, waiting to cue in my next guest.

It faded when I saw Gay standing in the hall.

'Ah, Mrs Mop,' she said, swinging her keys round manicured fingernails. They were painted pale lilac today, I noticed, and the glasses had been banished.

'I hear your job description has been expanded somewhat.' She was wearing a dark suit with heather-coloured cashmere underneath. She tapped her high heel on the marble floor, though she still only came up to my chin, and blinked several times. 'I thought we should have a little chat. Set a few things straight.'

I stood and looked at her for a long time, then tossed my head haughtily and strolled slowly back into the kitchen. Rat's tails coiled around my neck, but I acted as though I had just spent three hours at the hairdresser's. Fuck her, I thought. If she was expecting a cowed little Victorian scullery maid, she was in for a surprise.

'I'm talking to you,' she piped after me.

I ignored her and unplugged the iron. I hoped she didn't see my hands shaking.

'Don't walk away from me when I'm talking to you.'

'You're not talking to me; you're yelling at someone you think you can order around, and that definitely isn't me. What-ever you seem to think is or isn't part of my job description, Mrs

103

Davenport, doing what you say certainly isn't on the list.' I spoke without looking at her, calmly winding the flex round and round the handle of the iron, so tightly that I strapped my hand to the handle and had to undo it.

'But fucking the boss is?'

'No, fucking the boss I do in my spare time. For fun. I don't get paid overtime for it. It's a pleasure, not a duty. Though, obviously, you approached the task rather differently when it was part of your job description,' I added, turning now to face her and being confronted with more of that bloody blinking. 'You didn't give me much of an act to follow.'

'You've got a nerve. Who do you think you are, you slutty little gold-digger? You're forgetting that you're an employee, and that this is still my house. And that' – she pointed her thin index finger upwards – 'is still my bedroom, so don't get too comfortable up there.'

'For your information, I'm sleeping in the guest room. When I spend the night in your bed, I don't actually sleep.'

I paused for effect, as her eyes fluttered.

'Much.'

All this, delivered in my best Edinburgh accent. Miss Jean Brodie couldn't have done it better herself.

I understood a little more about Gay than she realized. Whether by accident or design, she had left the blue paper innards of last year's Cartier diary in the drawer of her bedside table. Naturally, I had read it. There was little of interest. It was mostly lunches, dinners, meetings, dentists, functions at both children's schools and a series of appointments for her varicose veins. I noticed the last with a little thrill of spite that only a woman who cannot see into her future would feel.

Adam hardly got a name check, but the initials RF next to lunch appeared with notable frequency, and even blocked out a few weekends that coincided with Adam's visits to Sydney and Rome. I wondered if there was more behind her decision to leave than boredom with marital bliss.

'If you think Adam's going to choose you over his children, then you're even more stupid than you seem. Obviously, he's not going to be influenced by the sort of person who gives free blow jobs and scrubs lavatories for a living.'

I wanted to push the iron into her face and hold it there until her hair singed.

'Well, *obviously*,' I parroted, 'you don't know just how good I am at blow jobs.'

Her pale face flushed, and for once the eyes widened – yes, I thought, remembering my earlier comparison, she did look exactly like Andy Warhol, screen printed crimson. I wondered if there were another three copies of her elsewhere in yellow, blue and green.

'I don't expect to influence Adam. As you say, I just scrub toilets for a living. But if I'm no threat to you, why are you here? Why did you walk out in the first place if you're in such a hurry to come back and mark out your territory? Remind me – didn't you *choose* to leave?'

I folded the ironing board, jammed it back like a gangling skeleton into a cupboard, pulled out a kitchen chair, sat down and crossed my legs as elegantly as you can when you're wearing old plimsolls, cut-offs and a man's Ralph Lauren shirt that is several sizes too big for you. By sitting I had lost the height advantage, but my legs were shaking so much I was afraid they would collapse like the ironing board.

'And since you've done it once, I'm sure you can manage to find the door again. I'll let you see yourself out.'

She opened her mouth to answer but was interrupted by the rumbling of several men in overalls, lumbering up from the basement. A stepladder appeared from the small stairwell like a rabbit being pulled from a magician's hat.

The Croatians had been replaced by a team from Ecuador, shy, grinning, gap-toothed men who worshipped the empanadas I made especially for them.

'*Disculpe. ¿Que hago ahorra, señora? Hemos acabado de pintar el cuarto de frente. ¿Comienso a preparar su cuarto de baño?*' asked Jesus, the shortest, squattest, smiliest of them.

'*Sí, Sí, pero primero, tengo que librarme de esta perra,*' I responded. Then, without pause, I launched into a long and unnecessary barrage of Spanish, none of which had anything to do with their chore of redecorating Gay's bathroom upstairs, but had a lot to do with Shakira's last album. In my previous life I had never directed workmen; I only knew how to order food, thank maids, ask about children, husbands and wives, and talk dirty. I thought that fulsome congratulations on their *pingas grandes* might have taken them, somewhat, by surprise, so instead I rattled on about the weather and their grandmothers, recited a few song lyrics and asked them if they wanted to drink something, using all the wrong tenses.

Gay's thin pink mouth quivered with uncertainty. The painters looked perplexed. They were used to my being friendly, but until now I hadn't been quite so effusive. Or personal.

'Was there anything else, Mrs Davenport?' I asked her. 'The men want to get started on *your* bathroom.' I hoped she would leave soon because my well of Spanish was rapidly running dry.

I led the painters up two flights of stairs and heard the door slam. I had just enough time to tell the men where to go before I sprinted next door and vomited into Adam's sink.

I could talk a good talk. Those many mid-afternoon reruns of *Dynasty* had obviously had some subliminal influence on my inner bitch, but the outer coward was still sick to her stomach. All these bloody locks in the house, and who could have known that the first bogeyman would arrive in the daylight and have her own key.

I came out of the bathroom and lay down on the bed. One of the Ecuadorians peeped out of the door with a roller in his hand and asked me if I needed anything. I said no.

Nothing that yet another new identity wouldn't fix, anyway.

I hoped I hadn't just made sure that the next time Adam saw his children would be when they graduated from university.

I hoped he had a good lawyer.

I hoped I wouldn't be looking for a bed and breakfast.

But Adam only laughed in rather delighted disbelief when he heard what I had said to his wife. He laughed even harder when the painters began nodding at him and smiling, while patting imaginary bumps on the front of their stomachs.

'Are they hungry?' he asked me.

'No, they heard me throwing up. Now they obviously think I'm pregnant. They're congratulating you.'

'You're not, are you?'

'I already told you: I can't have kids.'

'I know. I know. Bad joke. It's a shame. You would have beautiful children.' He sounded almost sad.

'Yeah, yeah.' I pushed him away with a shrug of pretend amusement; I had already been through this with one man and wasn't looking to reprise the role.

Adam had already been to his solicitors', and, while I had been lying on the bed mentally counting out my running-away money, Gay had obviously been doing her own accounts.

Most of his money was locked up in a family trust. His kids were taken care of well into their dotage, but his personal fortune was tiny and tightly entailed. Gay could afford to retain the lifestyle she had grown accustomed to only if she toed the line in the Manolos that her husband's generous allowance subsidized.

Lennie threw a tantrum when her mother refused to let her come back to Holland Crescent and jubilantly returned for the weekend, after spending half-term on a school trip to Florence.

Ned, poor soul, went to a golf clinic, but turned up the following Saturday afternoon with two friends, three sets of filthy rugby kit and a small ecosystem of head lice that were harder to get rid of than Gay.

Meanwhile Adam's lawyers quickly arranged a formal custody agreement. He would have both kids for alternate holidays. This year he got Christmas and Easter. Gay got New Year, half-term, an undisclosed lump sum, all her living expenses paid, and the deeds to the house in Provence as a sweetener.

However, she also kept her front-door keys.

Adam immediately changed the locks.

And suddenly, just like that, I was a stepmistress.

II

'I used to live in Oxford.'

As soon as the words jumped out of my mouth and across the table like unruly toads, I realized that I had made a mistake. Adam had invited over his oldest friend, Baxter, with his family to watch the annual fireworks display in the garden square, but I was the one being smoked out.

Baxter swivelled in his chair and looked at me curiously.

'Really? Which part?'

'Woodstock Road,' I added quietly.

'Oh, yes?' He waited for me to say more, but I merely concurred, wishing that he would drop it.

'I know Oxford quite well. My brother went there. Keble? Do you know it?'

'Well, I know where it is, if that's what you mean.'

'Where were you exactly?'

I felt as if I were being cross-examined under oath. I wished I had kept my mouth shut, but it was too late: Baxter had his teeth into me now and wasn't letting go.

'I wasn't at the university.'

'I mean, where did you live?'

'Near South Parade.'

'Ah, yes, there was a pub there, what was it called – the Carpenter's Arms?'

I shrugged non-committally. 'I don't know. I didn't really go out much.'

'Didn't go out much?' he parroted, as though I had just confessed to being a member of the Ku Klux Klan. 'Good God, that sounds very dull. What did you do with yourself? No cinemas, no concerts, no restaurants? Oxford's such an interesting place. You must have done *something*, surely?'

'This from Mr Culture himself. When was the last time you went to a concert? You haven't seen a film since you took the girls to Disney's *Pocahontas*,' said his wife, Jenny, a sloe-eyed Canadian with Brillo-pad hair that made you think of only one thing: conditioner. She wore lots of layered vintage clothes in velvet and lace, and had a permanent smile pasted on her face that was impossible to resist.

'You'll have to excuse him, Edith; he's obviously been doing some sort of Stasi interrogation course in his lunch hour.' She turned to her husband. 'I wish you were half as interested in anything I tell you . . .'

But Baxter persisted: 'So what were you doing there?'

'Working.'

'Goodness, you don't have a lot to say for yourself, do you?'

'Not everyone has your charming way with words, darling,' Jenny laughed. 'Really, I do apologize. I don't know what's got into him.'

'Red wine,' said Caroline, the other woman, a literary agent who looked like a young, already fat Elizabeth Taylor with high colouring and obscenely red lips. 'Have another glass and leave the poor woman alone,' she said, lighting a cigarette.

'I'm only saying that it sounds like a very dull life,' Baxter said, shaking his head in a bewildered schoolmasterly fashion, as you might if one of your pupils told you that John Lewis used to be the prime minister.

'I was working as a housekeeper, so I didn't have a lot of free time,' I mumbled by way of explanation. I felt as though I had shown myself to be only one notch up the evolutionary ladder from a talking chimp in a tea advert.

Baxter did not look convinced. He had long furrows etched into his cheeks like the creases on a pair of cheap trousers, and his teeth were stained purple from Adam's good burgundy.

Adam leaned over and took my hand. 'Baxter doesn't understand that some people have to work for a living. For him being a dick is a full-time occupation.' He gave him a hard look as though to say that the subject was closed.

I smiled. I was drinking white wine, so I had the Chardonnay ring of confidence, and anyway my tolerance had been honed by years of being addressed as 'my dear girl' by a range of patronizing elderly professors.

'Someone put the blanket over his cage, please.' Jenny sighed wearily and flapped him with her napkin. 'Ignore him, Edith; he's professionally bitter. You're lucky – I have to take the wretch home with me and hope that he doesn't infect any of the children.'

Baxter threw his hands up in mock surrender, while Caroline, mercifully, changed the subject and began enthusing about her latest find: an American biochemist from Harvard who was going to popularize bacteria for the masses. He could start with Baxter, I thought sourly.

'He's going to be the David Attenborough of germs,' she protested enthusiastically, above the hoots of cheerful derision. 'I'm telling you, Adam, you really should get him to do a book. I've already got him signed up for a series on BBC 2.'

But Adam paid her scant attention. He was too busy watching me.

I caught his eye and the rest of the room vanished. He smiled. I smiled back. I couldn't wait for them all to leave and for it to be just the two of us.

I rose and began to clear the last of the plates. Jenny heaved her ruffled bulk out of the dining chair and followed me into the kitchen.

'I hope you don't take my pig of a husband seriously, Edith. His abrasive personality is part of his charm,' she said archly, 'or so he keeps telling me. If it's any comfort, he warms on further acquaintance. And he really couldn't stand Gay, even after all those years.' She chuckled.

In reply, I kicked open the dishwasher. Caroline appeared with a pile of cups and saucers teetering Pisa-like in her plump, varnish-tipped fingers. 'I know it's a cheek after all that lovely food, but I don't suppose you've got any chocolate?'

I produced a bar of dark chocolate from the back of the fridge, where I had hidden it inside an empty egg box to keep the kids from eating it. Caroline accepted it gleefully. 'Fan-bloody-tastic. Gay wouldn't have sweets in the house. I used to have to stop at the petrol station on the way home and buy a Snickers bar.'

Jenny reached her hands out and snapped her fingers, demanding a piece. 'Caroline, I was just telling Edith that Baxter never got on with Gay.'

'God, no. He used to call her Gary. Behind her back, obviously,' said Caroline through a mouthful of chocolate.

I wondered fleetingly what names he would be calling me.

'So how long have you two known each other?' Caroline asked, a little slyly, breaking off a square of chocolate and putting it into her smiling mouth. 'I must say, Adam's kept you very secret. We hadn't a clue until Adam told Baxter that he'd met this "amazing woman". Gay is spitting, apparently.'

I stuck my face into the dishwasher to avoid answering and got a blast of hot damp air left over from the last batch of plates. My glasses steamed up.

'Everyone says she's livid. I think she thought she could swan back whenever she felt like it. Have you met her? You haven't turned to stone, so I assume not.' The two women sniggered.

'Oh, she dropped by,' I muttered, piling clean crockery into a space in the nearest cupboard. It wasn't where they went, but I rammed the door shut, sending the mugs rattling to the back of the cupboard as if they'd just been confronted by a fat man in a crowded lift, knowing that I'd be sneaking back to rearrange them later.

'Well, the food has certainly improved since you arrived – not to mention Adam's mood. I don't know what you're putting in his tea, darling, but it's done wonders for him. He looks really happy for the first time in years.' Caroline patted my arm.

'You should give me some for Baxter; he could do with a bit of tenderizing,' Jenny added.

'Darling, don't you thump meat with a mallet to tenderize it?' said Caroline.

'Oh, poor love, he can be such a pain in the arse.' She rolled the r as though it was going to unfurl from her mouth like a party streamer. 'The truth is that he's just being stupidly protective of Adam, who is obviously completely besotted with you. I think Baxter just wanted to make sure you weren't a Gay 2, the sequel, which you're obviously not. He'll be eating out of your hand like a pampered pug by the next time you meet. I promise.'

It was kind of the women to try to reassure me, but I sincerely doubted that Baxter and I would ever bond.

Furthermore, he had been absolutely right about Oxford. My life in the droopy, dilapidated house in Plantation Road, pigeon-chested with ornate wrought-iron balconies and squeezed like a sharp intake of breath between a block of mansion flats and the Carpenter's Arms, had indeed been dull and uneventful.

And that's exactly why I had loved it.

12

I crunched up the gravel path to the porter's lodge. The entrance hall, normally milling with bodies, was almost deserted. As you would expect in early June with term almost officially over, everyone was sleeping off hangovers after the major social event of the year. A lone girl in a lilac dress with a dazed, still drunk, sleep-creased face was drifting across the college lawn like a crushed flower, carrying her shoes in her hands.

Not one of our students, I decided, examining her face, the remains of last night's mascara lying in a grubby crescent under her eyes; probably a casualty from the college ball going back to her own halls after waking up in the wrong bed.

I watched as she approached, lost in her own dreamy thoughts, bending to unchain a bicycle from the tangle of others crammed into the rack. As she left, I saw myself almost two decades earlier, winding back to my bed-sit in Summertown with blisters on my feet, the morning after another ball in another college.

A couple of inadequately pinned papers and posters fluttered as the door swung closed behind me, sucking the air out of the already stifling corridor. The main college building had once been a convent before a reverence for books and learning overtook that which was held for God, but a respectful hush still pressed its palm over the place, making loud conversation an affront.

Even my flip-flops, slapping the flagstone floor, seemed intrusively noisy, attracting the attention of James, the porter, who manned the ancient switchboard in the corner of what was once the Mother Superior's office, and was now walled with pigeon holes and filled with ozone and boxes of photocopier paper.

'Ah, Mrs Dean,' he wheezed, dragging his eyes away from the

Daily Express. 'Lovely morning, is it not? Did you enjoy the ball last night?'

I explained that, with Francisco already in Colombia, I hadn't gone. Instead, I spent the night at home with Ray Charles, Jonathan Coe and Jack Daniels. I think he thought these were the names of three college students, but, either way, he couldn't have been less interested in my activities if I'd started reciting the chord sequences from 'Georgia on My Mind'. His rheumy eyes glazed over. If he had been fifty years younger, he would have said, 'Whatever.'

As the dean's wife, I had no function or identity of my own. I seriously doubted whether anyone in the college had ever even known my own surname. I was merely a plus one to Francisco, and without him I became a virtual nobody; a minister without portfolio.

The porter and I exchanged pleasantries, forgoing the usual weather chat in favour of college gossip: how many complaints about noise the lodge had received last night; how many students had been sick in the flower beds; and the discovery of a syringe in the changing room of the squash court. One of the students had been taken to the John Radcliffe suffering from drug-induced hallucinations, but, thank goodness, that was not currently my problem. As Francisco was taking a sabbatical next term, the odious John Willis had taken over as acting dean until Christmas.

When the Freshers arrived in the autumn, it would be John's long-faced wife, Sylvia, who would be decanting the Sainsbury's wine boxes and hosting the welcome parties, in between explaining the concept of the meter-fed gas fire to a whole new generation of confused Japanese kids, and taking the shivering Africans to buy coats. It would be she who reassured the Muslim students that the pork cocktail sausages were a hundred per cent halal beef, at the same time as telling the vegetarians they were tofu. If I didn't have to endure one more meet-and-mingle lunch while reigning my Scottish accent into slow sentences with all the syllables fully articulated, I'd be a happy woman.

This would almost make up for the fact that I would be stuck in Oxford until term started, but it was a very, very small consolation. The original plan had been that we would both go to Colombia until December, but at the last minute Francisco had announced that he would go alone. His grandmother had died, and, instead of concentrating on his book, he would have to devote himself to sorting out her estate as well as the farm, which she had left him in her will. He claimed he needed some time 'to think' and that he would have his hands full with business. In short: I would be in the way.

He suggested that I wait until the end of September and join him in Bogotá when he started teaching, which was a bit like winning a weekend on Alcatraz instead of a Caribbean cruise, but I bowed to the inevitable. With Francisco, I was so used to bowing to the inevitable I had calluses on my knees.

I gathered up the bundle of post jammed into the dean's pigeon hole and reminded James to forward the dean's mail on to Dr Willis. Then, as usual, I flicked through the 'M' slot, where some of our mail invariably ended up. Milligan, Monroe, Mahboubi, Mohammad, Matsuko, but nothing for Morales.

And then my fingers froze on a long pale blue envelope, tucked away at the back, addressed to Ms Agnes McBride, c/o Balfour College.

Damn it. What now? I didn't have to look at the postmark to know it was from Edinburgh. My heart plummeted like a suicide off a bridge. What did they want? More money, probably. They usually contacted the lawyer or Geordie about the financial stuff. Geordie was the family cash cow these days, but if there had been any other problem, surely they would have got in touch with Maisie, who would then have rung me. The envelope bulged, pregnant with unknown dread. Whatever was inside, it couldn't be good. I glanced over my shoulder to see if James was watching, but he was engrossed in a crossword puzzle. Quickly I slipped the envelope into the middle of the rest of my mail and turned swiftly back into the hallway, calling goodbye over my shoulder. My voice shook as if it were walking in heels.

Outside in the street the sun smacked me flat in the face like a flashbulb. I crossed over to the shade on the other side of Woodstock Road and looked up into the blank windows of the glowering, double-fronted houses set back from the street. At No. 56 there was a heavily laden flowering almond, hunched underneath the weight of its pink crêpe blossoms.

Karl had lived there while he was studying comparative literature. He was now a professor at a small liberal arts college in rural Pennsylvania, where he lived with his wife, a diminutive, overexercised jockess with perfect teeth and a surgically enhanced nose.

We still kept in touch through the odd postcard or letter, and he visited the college every couple of years, often, mercifully, without his competitively skinny wife. The only thing she and I had in common was Karl. Certainly she wasn't the kind of woman you asked along to your next Tupperware party, even if I had been the kind of woman who held them. Whenever I walked by his old house, I could almost summon him from the past. I looked up at his room and expected to see him through the open window, which today was inhaling a pair of dirty net curtains, like a panting dog. But he wasn't there.

Across the hall from him there had been an Italian economist who once wanted to marry me. Unfortunately his mother had other ideas. At No. 60 had been Bruce Grossman, a pretty-boy Canadian whom I went out with until he left for a job in Washington, and then, finally, at No. 62, there was Francisco – Francisco Eduardo Alvaro Morales, all the way from Colombia by way of East 57th Street. I slept with them all, serially and concurrently. I did them like declining verbs. What can I tell you? I was a regular one-woman United Nations of sex.

Francisco was just another scruffy student with too much facial hair when we met. I was working as a two-fingered typist at the Centre for Latin American Studies, and he was writing a thesis on some obscure Latin American border dispute. Well, I say obscure, but back then I thought Colombia was a TV detective and Honduras a small Japanese car, so it probably wasn't quite as rarefied as it seemed.

We met in the Centre for Latin American Studies. This, in itself, was not unusual: I met everyone in my office, since it was merely a desk with a sit-up-and-beg manual typewriter right in the middle of the main reading room, like an aid package dropped on to a desert island. Here I drank coffee, smoked cigarettes, made change for the photocopy machine, typed letters heavy with correction fluid and chatted to students as they arrived for their tutorials.

He was not tall, only a little taller than myself, with a halo of dark, luxuriant curls. The first thing that struck me was that he had the coldest, bluest eyes I'd ever seen. The second thing was his voice. Though he'd lived in America since he was a teenager, he had retained the lilting cadence of an accent that, at will, he could sprinkle through his speech like the cinnamon on a cappuccino. There was something sinfully furtive and intimate about the way he spoke, and within half an hour I was totally hooked.

I discovered that he had done his undergraduate degree at Brown and that he had a black-eyed brunette with an overbite back home, to whom he was practically engaged. I couldn't have cared less – I was concerned only with the long-distance part of the story, not with the relationship. I had already time-shared Karl with his high-school liebchen and the woman who would eventually be his wife, so what difference did a girlfriend 3,000 miles away make to me? I had a vacancy. And weekends to fill. And, most importantly, no central heating.

I was always cold in those days. Oxford was a damp place in the winter. I often wished I had chosen somewhere warmer to live, but then I hadn't really chosen Oxford in the first place. It had chosen me.

I was sixteen and wretched beyond words. I had been back home for the last of several brief and deeply uncomfortable meetings with my parents and the lawyer, and had not been encouraged to linger. I wasn't eager to return to my aunt's boarding house in Scarborough, which, by now, was perpetually full of pensioners on bus tours who had me running up and down the stairs like a demented bluebottle. So whether it was chance or subconscious design that I got on the wrong train in York, fell asleep and ended up chugging my way to Oxford, I'm not sure. But when I arrived, instead of crossing to Platform 2 and retracing my steps, I was washed out of the station in the flood of young people gushing through the open arms of the doors, each dashing off in their own purposeful direction. For the first time in almost a year, I felt a wonderful invisibility fit over me like a well-tailored coat. No one noticed me, no one looked at me; I felt like a wartime evacuee whose label had fallen off.

On impulse, I stopped a taxi driver and asked him if there was a youth hostel near by, and he drove me to the bottom end of the Abingdon Road, where I moved into a dormitory in the YWCA. It was five days before I thought to let my aunt know I intended to stay there.

I had done a typing course over the winter in Scarborough until the scrutiny of the other girls became unbearable, and, though slow, I managed to get an interview at a temp agency in the High Street. The first job they sent me to was that of a temporary receptionist in the Admissions Office at Balfour College, but, with my accent requiring subtitles, it was decided that I would be much better suited to a post where vocal interaction wasn't essential. When a position came up as a typist in the Centre for Latin American Studies, I carried my coffee cup three doors north, set it down at another desk and began a perfectly calm, quiet and anonymous life.

My living arrangements were less comfortable. I couldn't wait to get away from the intrusive oestrogen of the dormitory, where the presence of so many meddlesome and opinionated girls made me feel claustrophobic. The minute I found something I could afford on my meagre wages, I moved into a bed-sit in the inaptly named Summertown, where it always seemed to be damp.

Privacy was all well and good, but my room was freezing, with only an electric blanket between me and hypothermia. In common with all the men I made a habit of dating since I arrived in Oxford, Francisco lived in college and had radiators that were always on – even in June – a scout who vacuumed once a week and a laundrette in his basement. I'm not altogether sure if the warm feeling I got whenever I thought of him had to do with his personality or his access to constant hot water. He used to joke that I had only married him for his central heating, but he was only half wrong. He also had a full-time teaching post.

By the time we had swapped small talk and tea in the Centre for Latin American Studies common room, I was already pencilling Francisco into my life. He was shy and low key, and, though his eyes were icy sharp, he exuded a calm unruffledness, and an irresistible I-can't-believe-you're-really-flirting-with-me modesty.

By the end of the year I was his unofficial room-mate. And by January the girlfriend was an ex. When he finished his thesis, he accepted a junior teaching post at the college.

Francisco's job not only gave him full dining privileges and a fat pension plan. It also came with its own accommodation and a front door that I could lock behind me at night.

And that's when I married him.

13

At the beginning of December I had been presented with Francisco's dead mother's extremely old-fashioned engagement ring. He sneaked into my office before I arrived in the morning and, in a sentimental gesture not since repeated, typed out in uneven, one-fingered Courier 'Will you marry me?' on a sheet of headed Balfour College paper, and left the ring on the space bar of my typewriter. I was halfway through my first cigarette before I noticed it glinting on its Bakelite ledge and, when I reached for it, knocked it tumbling into the tinny, clawing levers of x,c,v,b. By the time I slipped it on to my finger, the index card was matted with overtyping.

It was a square emerald set in gold the colour of oranges in syrup, with sharp-faceted diamonds on either side. I couldn't quite believe how big it was, nor could my mother. Her small blotting-paper eyes darted towards my finger as I lifted a cigarette to my mouth.

'Is it no heavy?' she asked. Relations, though strained, had been maintained over the years by painful three-day visits at Christmas, mostly made because students also had a tendency to go home at that time of year, and even I didn't have the stomach for Plumrose turkey roll in a bed-sit by myself. But this pre-seasonal trip had been taken to break the news that I was getting married, and my mother, in her own restrained, lugubrious and critical way, was delighted. Finally, I had done something right. In the place of bunting, balloons and family celebrations, we had shop-bought cake and mother-and-daughter smoking sessions. She even shared her Embassy Regal.

'There's a bit of money in that ring. Unlucky, though – green,' she added. 'Green for envy.'

'Well, I don't think I'll have much trouble with that, will I?'

She lifted her chin in disagreement, offended. 'I don't know. You've got a good job, a good life. Things turned out all right for you.'

I kept my mouth shut. I didn't really want to pursue this subject.

'Are you planning on bringing him up to meet us at Christmas?'

'No. We're going to see his family. You'll see him at the wedding. He's very nice,' I mumbled inadequately.

'But you're not planning on getting married here, are you?' Her eyes snapped open like poppers.

'No, we'll do it in Oxford.'

'That's good, because I told you at the time, that was your wedding money all spent. There would be nothing left, and we're living on a pension now.'

'We'll pay for it ourselves. We're not planning anything grand.'

'As long as you're sure he'll be good to you,' she said, then, satisfied that he wasn't going to cost her anything, she asked for another look at the photograph I had brought.

'Touch of the tar brush about him, though.'

'Mum, he's tanned. He's from South America.'

'Aye, whatever you say. Still – your bairns will look like darkies.'

'There won't be bairns,' I said.

'Away, Agnes, you say that now.'

I didn't waste my breath contradicting her; I saved it for the smoke. She gave her scruffy slippers with the sheepskin trim a minute inspection, turning her heel as though she were trying on a pair of dancing shoes. 'Does he know about your wee bit of trouble?'

'No.'

'That's right. He doesn't need to know. Don't bother saying anything.'

Eventually I rose. I didn't want to listen to this. I headed for the kitchen, hoping to escape, but, wincing and groaning, she inched herself out of her chair and hobbled after me.

'Agnes, it's not too late to have children of your own. Life is long. You've got every chance.' She slid her words like a knife through butter.

'No, Mum. Don't go on about it.'

'You did the right thing at the time.'

'I didn't get a choice, if you remember,' I snapped, lifting my eyes to stare at her, daring her to contradict me.

She didn't.

I filled up the kettle, plugged it in and spooned Nescafé into a couple of mugs. My mother leaned against the washing machine, her hip indenting on the Formica worktop as she settled herself to wait for the water to boil. There was a long silence as the kettle cleared its throat and whined into life.

I pretended to be interested in the row of frozen cabbages in the back garden, while my mother tapped her cigarette into the sink. The hot ash made a satisfyingly spiteful hiss as it landed in the plug hole. I couldn't think why I had ever thought it was a good idea to come home. I could have done this on the phone for ten pence, but I had wanted to show my mother that I could make a success of my life my own way. I should have known she wouldn't be happy until I had two point four Protestant children, one of whom was called Agnes. That, alone, was a sufficient excuse for birth control.

To my relief, when it came to the actual wedding my parents declined to attend, and I convinced Francisco that their reasons were those of health rather than indifference, and he didn't press the matter.

We were married in a register office with only Francisco's closest friend from college as best man and my ex-lover Karl who, in the absence of anyone more qualified for the job, stood in as the bridesmaid.

Though we tried to convince ourselves it was an impulsive, romantic event, the register office was situated on the upper levels of a brutal concrete shopping centre in the middle of Oxford and the event was about as close to a picture-book wedding as I was to a virgin bride. A damp caul of fog hung over the city, and it rained, expressively, all day long. I wore a long black lace skirt that I had bought on a market stall, and had my bicycle waterproofs draped over my head like a veil for the dash from the car to the ceremony. In the afternoon we ate sausage rolls and chocolate eclairs at an informal party in the Centre for Latin American Studies. The toast to the bride was an enthusiastic one, especially among the seventy-five per cent of the guests who had slept with her. It was more like a stag party than a wedding. The next evening we boarded a flight to New York, where we played the final date on the Francisco and Agnes let's-get-hitched tour. Unfortunately, the Manhattan audience was lukewarm and less inclined to celebrate with high-calorie snacks.

Over on the other side of the pond, Señor Morales embraced his new daughter-in-law with slightly less warmth than you might show to a three-days-dead fish. The banishing of Miss Preppy Princess, Francisco's original intended, had been the first punch to land on the elder Morales's shoulders. The sudden appearance on the scene of Miss Scotland, with the family heirloom already wedged on her finger, was the final knockout. But in his stilted Spanish accent he managed to formally welcome me to the family. He did the honourable thing and swallowed his objections like a piece of gristle he was too polite to spit into his napkin, praying that I would be merely the practice wife. He himself had rehearsed at length, finally getting it right with number four, Herminia. There was every hope that Francisco would follow suit. I was so far away from his idea of a match for his brilliant son that he didn't even know where to begin his protest – and anyway it was too late, since the ring was on my finger. So he summoned a bottle of Krug, hijacked from another, more warmly anticipated occasion, and we drank ourselves catatonically drunk in close to ten minutes.

So that was meet-the-folks, done and dusted. The family, such as it was, consisted of Señor Morales, *madrastra* Herminia – who had a fulfilling career visiting the hairdresser, the dermatologist and the manicurist – and a matching pair of ever-changing Hispanic housemaids who were always called Maria something. It saved Herminia, bless her, the bother of having to learn new names. She had something in common with my family after all.

For my part, my sister Maisie had put herself into voluntary exile by emigrating to a suburb outside Adelaide, while my brother Geordie, the success of the family, was off playing poker with other people's money in an investment bank in the Far East. He had never married, but, according to the annual Christmas card, now had a girlfriend who worked in the same department and worshipped the same stocks and bonds. My mother and father saw no need to hang banners in the hallway for the new husband. We would communicate by phone and photograph until they felt like braving British Rail and visiting us. They had already limited their physical contact with me, and were happy to extend the same courtesy to Francisco.

So, as far as I was concerned, it was really just me and Francisco, the house in Plantation Road and this brand-new surname that I could adopt and disappear into. Finally, I could rise from the ashes into a brand-new life, and bury the incinerated remains of the old one.

14

Until chance raked them up again.

In Holland Crescent, autumn chewed up the months, until Christmas itched only a few weeks away. It wasn't my favourite time of year, but, despite everything, I couldn't help being infected by the frenzied excitement that quivered around Lennie's increasingly elevated heels as the holy festival of consumerism approached. It was something of a novelty.

Francisco and I had usually stayed quietly in Oxford for Christmas. We never had a tree and made do with one simple gift exchanged on Christmas Eve, which was usually a book for Francisco and a scarf for me. I didn't wear scarves, but that fact didn't concern Francisco, who obviously thought he was married to a different kind of woman; which also accounted for the several pairs of earrings I had accumulated, all of which were for pierced ears, while my lobes remained smooth and unpunctured.

In London a cheerfully uncomplicated Ned had been coming home every couple of weeks accompanied by a series of shape-shifting friends with voices as shrill as Windolene on glass, who ate their way through the fridge like locusts in rugby shirts.

The phone rang constantly for Lennie, while plans for parties and sleepovers and a list of must-have presents appeared on the fridge, with items crossed off and reinstated according to whichever magazine was most recent on the newsstand.

Outside in the market, fairy lights glittered atop the pyramids of satsumas and pomegranates, flaming poinsettias lined the stalls, and conifers leaned against the walls on street corners like unemployed migrant workers waiting for a pick-up. The windows of the gift shops on Elgin Crescent sparkled silver and gold, crammed with stuff I didn't want and certainly didn't need, but which nevertheless entranced me. I had a wonderful, heady feeling of happy anticipation – a sense that everything was possible and attainable.

The children were going to New York with Gay for New Year, and Lennie had already extracted from me a whole list of things she should see while there, all of which I had cribbed from a guide book I found in the Travel Bookstore. This left Adam and me blissfully alone and checking in to the Halkin Hotel, where he had booked a suite for three nights. 'It will be our new start for the new year,' he maintained.

I squashed the voice in my head screaming at me from across the desk in the headmistress's study where I had been dragged to account for myself: what new start, McBride? Just let me have this, I pleaded. Just this, and then I promise, cross my heart, swear, that I'll get back on track. The headmistress was unimpressed. I told her to fuck off. I was so excited that my stomach filled with butterflies and my toes curled. Ankle-deep carpeting that I didn't have to hoover, adolescent sex, eyeshades, a tub big enough to swim in and 24-hour room service. The prospect hung there in the future like the star on top of my own personal Christmas tree, the last unopened door on my advent calendar.

However, until then I still had to deal with the hormones that hit you in the face like a blast of Teen Spirit in the perfume hall at Selfridges. Lennie had had her braces removed after half-term and most of her brain at the same time. Her school uniform was rapidly modified. The skirts got shorter, the socks became tights, the shoes, bought after much wheedling, with my help and grave misgivings, grew several inches higher, the pretty hair was expensively cut and gelled into jagged peaks, and her green eyes acquired rings of black eyeliner that leaked down her cheeks as if she were going to tour with a Kiss tribute band.

She came and went through the house as it suited her. She and Leila, often in a clump of similarly scantily clad girls with sullen, underfed expressions and high-pitched overdramatic voices, trailed back from school later and later, until I found myself lingering by the window in the dining room, waiting anxiously for her to get back. On Saturdays she wanted to hang around on the High Street and come home late, unaccompanied, on the night bus. I nearly choked on the prospect.

Adam had no idea who her friends were or who she was with, but he was happy as long as she was out enjoying herself. Boys' names fell from her newly glossed lips as if she had Tourette's, her neckline plunged with her mood, and what had once been a bovine, sweetly agreeable nature became full-scale attitude.

'You're not my mother,' she said, when I suggested she should wear something a bit less revealing than a cropped t-shirt to stalk the aisles of Top Shop.

I was torn. There was nothing I wanted more than to back off, but I couldn't. It was stirring up too many uncomfortable memories. In spite of myself, I kept after her.

'But doesn't Gay mind your going out in a vest in the middle of winter?' I was being kind calling the two pieces of string and the hankie Lennie was wearing a vest.

'She doesn't care, nor does my dad, so I don't see that it's any of your business. You're hardly one to talk about looking cheap.'

I swallowed my terrier urge to rip her throat out. Calmly, I said: 'Lennie, I'm not saying anything about looking cheap; I just think you have to be aware of the kind of message you're sending out. You're only fifteen. You look twenty. Men will think you're more experienced than you are. You don't know how their brains work.'

'Yeah, but you do. You must know how men think, since it didn't take you long to get your hooks into my dad. Maybe you should be giving me lessons.'

'I just don't want you to make the same mistakes I did,' I stammered, but the words were difficult to say; dragging them out of my mouth felt like pulling a cork with my teeth.

'What?'

'I just wish you'd be more careful about attracting the wrong kind of attention. I do know what I'm talking about. Believe me. I had to learn the hard way.'

'Whatever. Leave me alone – it's none of your bloody business.'

'Len . . . .' I remonstrated, but she was gone.

I took hold of my temper with both hands and held it down till it surrendered. Otherwise I would have kicked her legs out from under her and asked her who the hell she thought she was talking to. When dealing with Lennie for those difficult weeks, I regularly informed the God I didn't believe in that he ought to be cancelling out some of my sins for having enough self-restraint not to wallop the stroppy little cow.

I got no further when I tried to reason with Adam.

'She's young – she'll grow out of it. Weren't you the same when you were a teenager?'

'Exactly the same,' I agreed.

'Well,' he said, shrugging in a helpless what's-the-biggie sort of way.

'But I didn't grow out of it; it just got to be a habit,' I muttered.

'What do you mean?'

But I pretended not to hear. I could still turn a teenager's deaf ear when the mood took me.

'She looks like a slag,' added Ned from inside the cupboard where he was looking for biscuits. I had found an unexpected ally in the anti-sluttification of his sister. 'I told her she was turning into a shazzer, but she just told me to eff off.'

'Don't swear.'

'*She* did.'

'She really swore at you?'

'Oh, Edie, you're so naive,' said Ned, with all the world-weariness of a fourteen-year-old who has toast crumbs around his mouth and is wearing a shrunken Spider-Man t-shirt.

I gave him a wry look. 'I'm not the naive one; it's your father who needs convincing. Hasn't Gay said anything to you about it, Adam?'

'Mum thinks it's all your fault, Edie,' Ned supplied matter-offactly. '"What can you expect when he's living with Slutsky and Bitch?"' he repeated in a reedy voice that was apparently supposed to mimic Gay's plummy accent.

'Ned . . .' cautioned Adam, but Ned shrugged, a fistful of cashew nuts in each hand. 'S' not my fault – I'm just telling you what she says. I don't call you that.'

Adam looked as though he were trying not to laugh as Ned disappeared back into the basement. 'Ah, well, Gay . . .' He blew out his lips. 'I haven't heard that one – I'm usually privy to the less witty epithets – but, yes, now that you mention it, there have been mutterings that your presence has been inciting the craven use of eyeliner. But bear in mind that Gay was still wearing navy-blue school knickers – with name tapes – when I first met her – and it was the third year of university before I got near them.'

'But it's not me, or Gay, we're talking about here: it's Lennie. You should always be sure you know where she is, Adam. Speak to Gay – make sure you both have some idea what she's up to. At least make her leave the telephone number of where she's going – and if she's supposed to be spending the night somewhere, speak to the parents and check it out.'

'She has a pager.'

'And it's never switched on.'

'I don't know why you're so worried. She's not duplicitous enough to actually lie, surely?'

'I was.'

'I can't believe that,' he said, smiling and grabbing me round the waist and dancing me round. 'Not my sensible, goodie-two-shoes Edith. I bet you rescued kittens and helped old ladies cross the street. You couldn't tell a lie if you tried. You're an angel. Sent from heaven to make me – what are we having tonight?' He stopped and sniffed the air.

'Roast lamb,' I supplied.

'See – practically perfect in every way.'

I scoffed. Men. Feed them, fuck them, they think you walk on water. Thank God.

Eventually, he did agree to be more attentive, but I could tell it was only to please me, and not because he thought it was necessary. However, I had to drop the subject for the time being because I had other things to fret about. We were having people for supper – with the emphasis on the 'we'. I was now fully installed as Mistress of the house – in all senses of the word.

Baxter was coming with his horsehair wife. He had warmed to me a little over the past weeks, but he still had a tendency to snipe every now and again from up there in the control tower of Bastardtown. Adam insisted that it was merely an affectation and that Baxter had a heart of gold. The two had gone to Cambridge together, and Adam maintained a stubborn fondness for Baxter that couldn't be shaken, and, to be honest, I didn't try. He was a loyal friend, if not a particularly sweet-natured one, so I gave him the benefit of the doubt.

I had yet to meet the other guests. They had been Gay's friends, but had defected to Adam after the break-up. The man was a banker, but I didn't know what the woman did. It didn't matter; I hardly expected her to be president of the housewives' union. We'd probably get stuck on theatre and cinema. I hadn't been to either in living memory, but I read the reviews so I could manage to sound knowledgeable.

With Baxter in mind I had decided to forgo 'that foreign muck', as he had so winningly referred to some of my past offerings, while nevertheless having several helpings of everything. So we were having a traditional roast, and a boarding-school steamed pudding made with persimmons, which, just like Baxter, had a tendency to dry the mouth if not ripe.

The kitchen I could manage. Even the prospect of entertaining with a smile I positively embraced. What I couldn't deal with, increasingly, was Lennie. Every decision I made about the day-to-day running of the house was questioned and contradicted.

First it was the food fads, then it was the mess – the careless flotsam left strewn in her wake. I didn't want to give Gay the satisfaction of knowing her daughter had me on the ropes,

131

begging for mercy. So I bore it as best I could. Nevertheless, the girl drove me so high up the fucking newly painted walls that I was surprised to see there weren't claw marks on the ceiling. Truly, there weren't enough orgasms in the world to make this teenage crap worth shovelling.

I had thought Lennie was staying in for the evening, but she suddenly declared that she had plans. She came downstairs at five o'clock wearing jeans, for which I got down on my knees and personally thanked the patron saint of denim. I was less delighted with the divinity in charge of the low-cut sparkly dress that clung, barely, to her chest.

I eyed a pair of pushed-up breasts that would have put a Thanksgiving turkey to shame. She was definitely her mother's daughter. I made wide eyes at Adam, who was faffing around in the dining room, putting water glasses on the table and trying to look like a man who knew which side of the plate they went on. I moved behind him and transferred them to the right.

'I'm going out,' she announced, swinging her handbag. 'I need money.'

'Darling, don't you think that's a bit too much?' Adam protested, looking at her neckline and wincing.

I coughed, pointedly.

'Where exactly are you going?' he added.

'To Doug's place in Richmond.' Doug – I hadn't heard this name before. I willed him to ask questions.

'And Doug would be . . .' inquired Adam.

'From school.'

He seemed to accept that.

'But, Lennie, you go to an all-girls school,' I added.

'I know.' She gave me a look of annoyance. 'But – I – met – him – on – the – way – home – *from* – school, didn't I? He goes to St Paul's. A group of us are going to his house.'

What group? I screamed silently.

'How are you getting there?' Adam asked.

'Underground.'

'You are not going on the tube like that.'

'I'll have my coat on, Dad.'

'And how are you getting back?'

'We're all spending the night.'

Adam looked at me for guidance. I shook my head, trying to disguise it as a crick in the neck, and failing.

'It's got nothing to do with you, Edie, so butt out.'

'Leonora – you will not talk to Edith like that. And anyway, it's not Edith you have to convince; it's me. I would like you to come home. By midnight. We don't even know this boy. Give me the address, and I'll have the car service pick you up.' Adam began to pat his pockets for a pen.

Lennie looked thunderous. 'That's so lame.'

'You either come home or you don't go'

Lennie seemed to know she was beaten. A few further half-hearted protests followed before, finally, she flounced out, fighting tears. Adam and I exchanged glances, both feeling as though we had narrowly missed being hit by a speeding car.

'Will you talk to her?' Adam asked.

'Not me; you should go. I never seem to say the right thing.'

I wasn't overeager to step into the Lion's Den. I was fed up getting my hand bitten off. Let her do what she wanted. What did I care? She wasn't my responsibility.

'Please, Edie, I'm out of my depth here.'

Okay, so it *was* my responsibility . . .

I waited a second and followed her. By the time I got to her gaping bedroom door, her face was already smudged with eyeliner, spilled like ink all across her face.

She looked up at me pitifully. 'All I want to do is go out and see my friends,' she said in a broken voice. 'What's so bad about that?'

I sat on the bed and waited for her to stop emptying the contents of her handbag, theatrically, over the floor. There was a cigarette packet among the lipstick and crumpled tissues, one of which she wadded into her fist and used to dab her eyes.

133

I knew that I had to say something, but I didn't know what. I had no experience of dealing with teenage girls. I didn't even have any girlfriends. The silence stewed. And then it occurred to me: just try being Mrs Dean. When Francisco's students came to me crying, claiming they needed essay extensions because their boyfriend had dumped them, or worrying about pregnancies and parental expectations, I knew just what was needed: briskness and common sense.

'Look, Lennie, it's not that bad . . . Your dad is just worried about you.'

She sniffed and glared at me as though I'd just ripped the leg off a baby and stuck it on a spit.

Empathy, then, I thought.

'I do know how you feel. When I was a kid, my parents were so strict that I could hardly move. Once my father even came and dragged me out of a youth-club dance because I was ten minutes late.'

'I'm not a kid.'

'Okay, point taken.'

I tried again. Sincerity this time.

'Nobody wants to spoil your fun, but when I was about your age I got myself into shedloads of trouble, and it makes me a bit nervous watching you – oh, I don't know – being young, I suppose. I'm sorry – I can't help it.'

'What kind of trouble?' She stopped kicking clothes around and sat next to me on the bed.

'Bad, bad trouble . . .' I made a dismissive gesture, but, at last, I had her attention.

'No, tell me.'

'Well . . .' I hesitated, ready, even now, to just smooth it over, but I went on. 'One night my friend Kirsty and I sneaked off to a party that my parents had told me I couldn't go to, and while I was there, a fight broke out and I was hit on the head with a chair.'

'No! Really? What happened?'

She had swapped bags and was cramming make-up into the

new one. The cigarettes, hidden inside a purse, were quickly concealed in its depths. I pretended not to notice. You have to pick your battles.

'Well, the chair knocked me out, and I came to on the floor with blood on my face and everybody looking at me.'

'Cool,' she said.

'No, it wasn't. It was ugly. Really ugly.' In spite of myself, I shuddered.

She relaxed and threw herself back on her pillows, waiting for the rest of the story.

'So there I was, legs in the air, black eye, flat on my back on the floor, covered in blood, and the next thing the police were called, and I found I'd lost all my money, and we were about six miles from home. It was a really long walk – you know, deserted country lanes – middle of the night? My parents hadn't a clue where I was, so I could hardly call them up from a phone box and say come and get me.'

Lennie laughed but nervously.

'I was too scared to go to hospital, because then they would have found out what I'd done.'

'What did you do?'

'Walked it.'

'Walked home in the middle of the night? You must have had rocks in your head. Weren't you scared?'

'No, that's the point. I wasn't, and I should have been, but it just never occurred to me at the time. I was so innocent, I just didn't think it through.'

'But I'd never do anything like that.'

'I'm not saying you would. I'm just saying that not every mistake you make seems like a bad idea at the time. You have to be sensible. Your dad isn't saying don't go; just let him send a taxi for you.'

'But I'm not going to get bashed on the head. I'm only going to my friend's house – it's hardly running around with scissors, is it?' She started picking the nail varnish off her fingers. I could have put on flamenco shoes and tapped it out in Morse code for all the impact I had made. I gave in.

'Okay, go and enjoy yourself, but come home afterwards and don't let – whatsisname?'

'Doug.'

'Don't let Doug get too much of a preview. You've got a great figure. You're gorgeous – you're too pretty to be that obvious.' I nodded at her cleavage.

'Can I come home at two?'

'Midnight.'

'One o'clock?'

Since I figured there was a good chance that Baxter and wife would still be sitting around slugging liqueurs at one in the morning, I agreed. 'Let me help you clean your face up.'

I soaked a cotton pad in cleanser and carefully wiped off the black gloop.

'Models are supposed to put haemorrhoid cream on their eyes to stop the puffiness,' I volunteered.

'What's haemorrhoid cream?'

I explained.

'Yuck – I think I'll keep the bags. Look, I'm sorry for being such a bitch, Ede,' she muttered hastily. 'You're okay, really.'

'Don't be daft; it's in the teenage job description.' I gave her the stiff pat on the back that was my closest approximation to a maternal hug.

'Watch my hair,' she said, giving me an equally pro forma hug back.

I gazed at the jagged fright of rigid mousse that stuck out in seven directions from her scalp. 'It looks good,' I said.

She pulled a skimpy silk cardigan over her dress and gently rearranged the fronds of her hair until they looked like the leaves on an aspidistra.

I don't know why I was so worried about her. Any male would have had his eye poked out if he went within six inches of her face.

'I need to ring my mum,' she said, grabbing a quick look at her watch. 'Did I tell you she's going to take me to a spa next week? She's going to take a day off work, and we're going to have manicures and facials.' She named a frighteningly expensive hotel in Knightsbridge that even a style-challenged shut-in like myself had heard of. I left the room as she dialled the number.

'Hey, Mummy,' she crowed, 'you'll never guess what. Remember that guy Doug I told you about? He actually rang me – can you believe it? And Dad's letting me go to the party . . . I know!' She laughed delightedly.

My shoulders slumped as I closed her bedroom door and headed reluctantly back downstairs to the kitchen.

The smell of roasting meat and garlic assailed me, and this, I reminded myself, was really all I should have been concerning myself with.

It was just that sometimes – well, sometimes I forgot my place.

15

It was housewife heaven. The dishwasher was running, the table was set, the candles were lit, and the oven would be pinging within the next half-hour to signal that it was time to begin roasting the potatoes. It was really the simplest of meals. I had left myself only the task of soft polenta, which was unnecessary but would give me the excuse to hide in the kitchen between the butternut squash velouté and the roast.

Adam was wearing a cream shirt and a pair of jeans. I didn't have to dress up; I couldn't, in fact, dress up, since I didn't actually own a winter dress. But I thought I should change so that the first impression I made wasn't that of singed meat.

My few clothes hung somewhat forlornly in Gay's vacated closet. I almost wished Herminia would spring out of the shoe rack and invite me on a shopping trip. I had brought only my summer things, most of which were useless as winter engulfed me. I teamed a few of the skirts with tights and two of Lennie's cast-off cardigans. I also wore a coat that had once been hers. It protected me from the elements, but it also swamped me. She was at least two sizes larger. But I was grateful for her sudden interest in fashion, as without those items she rejected I would have had nothing to wear.

As it was, my choices were few: I could wear the black skirt with the white shirt or the clean jeans and the shrunken cashmere sweater with the snags at the cuffs that I had a horrible feeling had once belonged to Gay even before it had been gnawed upon by Lennie. I rejected the first choice as too utilitarian. I would look like a waiter. So, by default, it was the cashmere jumper and the clean jeans. I pushed up the sleeves to hide the frayed edges, rubbed my hair with a wet flannel to flatten down the wisps that were flying around my face, fizzing dementedly with static electricity, and smiled at myself in the mirror.

'How nice to meet you,' I said, several times, in several keys. 'How-kind-of-you-to-let-me-come,' I hummed, transported briefly to the Fourth Form school production of *My Fair Lady*, in which I had played, in turn, a dustman, a street urchin and, because of my height, a non-speaking male consort. Kirsty, of course, had been Eliza. I learned every one of her lines with her. 'Now once again, where does it rain?' I trilled. 'On the plain. On the plain.'

I bowed and curtsied. I wiggled my bottom. I sprayed myself with one of the least noxious of Lennie's perfumes to rid myself of Eau de Scullery, and waited with trepidation to see if it would make me sneeze. Miraculously it didn't; I hadn't had even the slightest wheeze in months. I looped the legs of my specs behind my ears and wore them like a Sloane Ranger's hairband, then slapped some colour into my cheeks that I didn't really need. The kitchen was like a furnace, and my face was already flushed and slightly damp. I hoped I wouldn't be too hot in the sweater.

The doorbell rang. I looked at my watch. Quarter to eight. It would be the Baxters. They were always early.

Sure enough, downstairs Jenny was removing her voluminous crushed-velvet coat. I held out my hand for it. Baxter was wearing a Burberry that smelled of cigarettes and damp and a misplaced belief that his own status could be elevated by a beige check raincoat. It was pouring outside.

'Edith,' he grunted, dropping his coat on the chair and giving me a frosty air kiss before walking straight upstairs to the drawing room. Jenny, however, her ubiquitous smile stretched from ear to ear on her broad, pixie face, raised her neck out of a roll of silk crêpe ruffles and touched her cold cheek to mine, handed me a bottle of wine and gave my arm a squeeze.

'Edie, you look incredibly well. Life must be agreeing with you. Something smells wonderful – what are you cooking? Is there anything I can do?'

I declined her offer of help and sent her upstairs, where Adam was undoubtedly already tipping his good whisky into Baxter's eager gullet.

'I'll be up in a second; I just have to get something from the kitchen,' I said to her broad backside.

Inside I peered into the oven, poured myself a few inches of vodka, iced from the freezer, and knocked it back. I lifted a tray laden with canapés – tiny blinis with smoked salmon, each with a limp sprig of dill draped over it backwards like an exhausted contortionist – and carried it upstairs.

The doorbell rang again as I reached the hallway. This time it was an extremely tall man with a tiny, black-clad wraith of a wife with too many, too white teeth and not enough skin, so slim that she could have slipped into her husband's breast pocket in place of the three-cornered pochette it currently held. These would be the old friends. I didn't catch their names, as I was juggling coats, dripping umbrellas, a cellophane-wrapped bouquet and the tray of canapés, but I led them up to the drawing room and busied myself rearranging plates and napkins on the low table while further introductions were made. Hands were gripped in turn, flaccidly and then bone-crunchingly, and careful kisses were bestowed. A distant ding-ding-ding reverberated below in the kitchen. I whispered in Adam's ear that I had to go tend to supper – and fled gratefully to the safety and delightful dearth of polite, social discourse than can be found in a tray of roast potatoes.

I had just shut the crossword in a drawer and was stirring the soup when Adam poked his head round the door some twenty minutes later. 'Is everything okay? Aren't you going to come up and have a drink?'

'In a second – I have to finish a few things here.'

He made a kissy face and, satisfied, disappeared bearing a bottle of Evian and another of champagne.

I stirred the soup again. But I hadn't even turned on the gas.

Ned sidled upstairs from the basement, where he was beating

up hookers and drug dealers on a games console, and started to forage for peanut butter, as you do when you're a fourteen-year-old drug lord in Miami. I made him a sandwich and sat at the table, watching him eat, until the timer sounded again. I couldn't delay things any longer. I had to take the meat out of the oven.

I sent Ned to tell Adam that dinner was served, splashed some truffle oil into the soup, ladled it into bowls and carried it out to the dining room.

Lights, camera, action. 'How-kind-of-you-to-let-me-come': I was on.

I sat on Adam's right. Jenny was opposite. Baxter, damn it, plonked himself next to me before I could direct him elsewhere. I smiled companionably at the other guests at the nether reaches of the table, the way you do when your train breaks down in a tunnel, or you're stuck in some unforeseen situation that requires stoic good nature. Behind them, a lopsided, half-dressed Christmas tree that Adam had brought in that morning from the market hunched apologetically in the window like a handicapped flunky. All it needed was a tea towel draped over one of its branches.

Jenny began to tell us, in almost forensic detail, about her family's plans for Christmas. Baxter grudgingly complimented me on the soup, which set off a round of appreciative sounds.

'It's delicious,' said the small dark woman – Sadie, Sandy, Saffy? I never did learn her name. 'I love truffle oil. I would put it on my muesli if I could.'

One look at the woman was enough to reveal that she hadn't ever eaten muesli in her life. The oat flakes would have overwhelmed her.

Baxter had begun a long conversation about an earnest pop group whose latest CD he had just bought. I heard him say: 'Yes, they're astonishing, quite astonishing.'

Twat, I thought, as I nodded in agreement.

Jenny, meanwhile, had got to the day after Boxing Day and was halfway to her sister's in Cork. It was like listening to the speaking clock: On the third stroke I will lose – *beep* – my fucking

– *beep* – mind. I tuned her out and immersed myself in pleasurable thoughts of the forthcoming carnal feast at the Halkin. Adam had promised there would be no enforced outings. We could spend as much time as we wanted, alone, in the room. I could have anything I wanted, he told me, as long as it began with C. 'Champagne, caviar, crab, chocolate,' he recited. 'Or cornichons, chutney, cold chips, and cheese and onion crisps,' I teased. The possibilities were endless. I amused myself with mental pictures of a huge, old-fashioned bathroom with marble fittings, a steamed-up mirror, little candles, ice buckets, crumbs in the bed and blindfolded sex.

But, even with room service on New Year's Eve, there would still be at least two formal dinners to be eaten in a restaurant. I would, occasionally, have to get dressed. With only one pilled sweater and a maître d's outfit in my wardrobe, this would be difficult. I would have to buy clothes, I realized.

The dark-haired woman was claiming my attention. 'Edith, you used to live in New York, Adam tells us. We spent eighteen months there – Charles' – she motioned to her husband – 'was with Morgan Stanley for a while.'

'Oh, really?' I said, trying to look interested. I was guessing that this was a bank, but I couldn't be sure. It could be their children. She chattered on about where they lived and where their kids went to school: no Morgan, no Stanley, so I was probably right about the bank. I smiled energetically and made a few general remarks about New York being busy, crowded, great for shopping, wonderful museums. Hell, if she'd slipped in that they had been involved in a drive-by gang shooting, I would have probably enthused about that too. New York, New York, it's a wonderful town – why hadn't I put myself somewhere like fucking Idaho where they only grew potatoes?

The moment there was a lapse in the conversation I stood up and excused myself.

The phone rang while I was beating a vat of boiling polenta that hissed and bubbled like a hell mouth. I heard Adam pick up the extension in the dining room, but I was too busy evading spitting globs of corn meal to hear what he said. It was probably Lennie, petitioning for a later curfew.

But no, it was Caroline, the literary agent who had also been a regular visitor over the past weeks. She said she had been having a drink with some new author she wanted Adam to meet – could she bring him round?

'We have enough food, don't we, darling?' he asked, kissing my flushed cheek. 'I told her it would be fine. We'll just set another couple of places.'

I agreed, only really hearing the 'darling' – darling – an endearment. A public endearment. He sometimes whispered this sort of thing when we were in bed together, and I saved them up, like a miser hoarding coins, and got them out when I was alone to gloat over without ever believing they were really mine. This was a first: a 'darling' in plain hearing without being prefaced or accompanied by an erection. Or at least, not visibly so.

'It's not the germ-man, is it?' I asked idly, still silently stroking the darling and tucking it into my back pocket for later examination.

'German?' He looked blank.

'No, germ-man. You know, the person she was talking about last month; the microbiologist who's going to be big in bacteria? I hope he won't regale us all night about viruses and spores.'

'Could be. I'm not sure. She mentioned his name, but I can only listen to Caroline for about five minutes before I get worried she's going to eat me up with those big red lips of hers.'

'You wish.'

'I prefer yours,' he said, as he drew me towards him for a long kiss, which I broke off with difficulty.

I left him to carve the lamb while I put another pair of plates on the table. I moved myself down to the end and stuck the germ-man next to Baxter. Serves him right, I thought.

I put the rest of the food on serving platters and followed as Adam hefted it on to the table.

The doorbell rang again. I was dizzy from the noise of buzzers.

It was like being on a quiz show and not knowing any of the answers.

And your starter for ten is: where are Jenny and Baxter planning to spend Christmas Eve and what will Jenny be wearing – the blue velvet or the pink?

'That'll be Caroline,' Adam announced and rose to let her in.

My God, that was quick; where had she been calling from – a taxi outside the front door? I hadn't even managed to put a forkful of lamb into my mouth. Wearily, I noticed that I hadn't brought any extra wine glasses. Damn it. I had polished them and left them sitting on the kitchen worktop. I went back to get them.

In the dining room I could hear Caroline kissing and hugging and being brightly effusive. 'Brilliant', 'clever', 'interesting', I heard her gush at intervals. Heck, just the sound of her voice exhausted me. I pushed open the swinging doors carrying the two goblets ahead of me like weapons.

Charles was halfway out of his seat with his hand outstretched, Caroline had her fat little arm, resplendent with twenty or so gold bracelets, circled around Jenny's shoulder and was singing her praises to the germ-man. Lucky bastard – he hasn't had to listen to her recite her life like a railway timetable, I thought.

And then my feet bolted themselves on to the floorboards. My heart stopped its steady beat and began struggling to climb out through my ribcage. Someone pulled a drawer out of my stomach.

The man she had brought was standing on the threshold. He looked ill at ease, dragging his hand out of the pocket of his tweed jacket and grimacing tersely in lieu of smiling. His hair was cropped close to his scalp, with tightly clipped curls flattened by the rain, his eyes were like little bird tracks on his face, which, though tanned, had an unhealthy waxiness to it. I noticed his beard was also trimmed very short – no more than a shadow on his chin, which had a little dimple carved into it. Why hadn't I ever known he had a dimple?

He was speaking very quietly, something about Caroline insisting – being sorry to intrude – very rude, terribly kind. I could barely hear him above Caroline's babbling. Poor thing. His eyes seemed reddened, as though he had spent too long staring at a computer screen, although now it was me he was staring at, but with disbelief. His face collapsed like a condemned building being hit by a demolition ball.

'Ah, and this is . . .' Adam began, drawing me forward.

'Ag-nes,' gasped the man, the two syllables the sort of sigh you might make after a long climb uphill. His fists fell uselessly to his sides and hung there like plumb lines from the sleeves of the jacket we had bought together at the university tailor's in the High Street in Oxford, back when he was happy.

'Francisco,' I replied bleakly. It had been so long since I had spoken his name aloud that the fudge of it stuck in my mouth.

I watched Adam's face drain to the same blank shade as his shirt. He turned to me apprehensively. 'You two already know each other?' he asked.

'Adam, I'm so so so so sorry,' I whispered, as though I were soothing a baby. Then I took a deep ragged breath before plunging into the icy depths of the next sentence.

'This is Frank. Francisco Morales.'

There was a long, yawning, echoing, screaming silence.

'My husband,' I explained, just in case he was confused and thought there were any other walking corpses in the room.

And then I dropped the glasses.

Francisco's fist struck the side of my face and knocked me backwards into the door frame. Around me, shards of glass chimed all across the polished floor.

'You fucking bitch. What have you done to your hair?' he whispered, as I slid down the dining-room wall.

16

In Plantation Road, ice cubes snapped like gunshots in the freshly brewed mint tea cooling on the gas stove. I only needed to drop the needle on to the waiting record to hear Ray croon that Georgia was, once again, on his mind; but I was more concerned with the pale blue envelope I had found in the porter's lodge. It was still lurking in the buried depths of the manila circulars and foolscap conference invitations that I had dumped on the kitchen table.

I tried to ignore it, but the body was beginning to smell. There was no way to avoid the fact that, soon, I would have to exhume it. Why on earth was the nursing home writing to me? My mother had lived alone for several years after my father had died, becoming more and more isolated and disorientated until she began calling me in the middle of the night asking where the fridge was, or why God had turned all the lights off. After she almost blew herself up trying to put the milk inside the central-heating boiler, I was forced to make my second visit to Scotland in two decades.

With Maisie in Australia and Geordie sleeping under his desk in Singapore, it was left to me to make all the arrangements. I emptied my childhood out of the cabin trunk, filled it with some of my mother's clothes and ornaments, and moved her into a nursing home I found in Edinburgh, where she had remained ever since, slipping ever more surely into the milky waters of her own dementia.

She passed her time in a high-backed chair, staring into the middle distance under the illusion, on her good days, that she was sitting on a runway in Jakarta, waiting to take off on a long-haul flight to Adelaide. The nurses told me she was rarely lucid and hardly spoke, but then who would she speak to? Nobody visited her.

Since the money from the sale of her house had run out, Geordie was the only one of us who had the means to take care of the bills, but he usually dealt directly with the lawyer, and Maisie, though too far away to be of much use, made all the major decisions about her general care. If there had been a medical emergency, the nursing home would have telephoned to let me know, but otherwise there was absolutely no need for them to get in touch; all of which only made the letter addressed to me from the Bluebell Rest Home even more disturbing.

I poured myself a glass of tepid tea, turned on the record, which coughed out static until the scratchy bars of the first track kicked in, and then, unable to put the dreaded moment off any longer, I reached for the envelope.

I sliced it open with a vegetable knife and shook out the contents. To my surprise there was just a compliments slip from the Matron's Office with a couple of lines scrawled across it in biro, and another pale blue envelope that had been opened and inexpertly resealed with Sellotape.

'Dear Agnes,' said the loopy black handwriting on the compliments slip with the corny little bluebell on the right-hand corner, 'I am sorry that this letter has been opened, but we thought it was for your mother. Obviously there was some mistake – many apologies.'

I picked up the cheap envelope hidden inside like a Russian doll. Sure enough, it was addressed to Agnes McBride and had been forwarded on to my parents' address from our old house in the village. From here it had been sent on to the nursing home. There was no return address, but the postmark said Yorkshire. It had covered a lot of miles to get here. I took a long swallow of tea with hands suddenly clumsy and trembling, and turned the envelope over and over as though it would reveal its secrets through touch. To hell with the tea. I looked first at the empty bottle of Jack Daniel's, then scrabbled through the cupboards under the sink, pulling out three tins of chickpeas, until I found some apple schnapps that Karl had brought as a hostess present on one of his visits. I poured a huge slug into the grassy, green-coloured tea and took a tentative sip. It burned like creosote and tasted like shit – mint flavoured shit.

I took another swig anyway, sat down on a kitchen chair and carefully peeled back the long ribbon of Sellotape. Two sheets of lined Basildon Bond notepaper, rolled over on themselves several times, sprang out of the opening. The paper was so thin I could see scars like Braille that the pressure of the pen had made on the blank side. I smoothed the pages out on the table.

'Dear Agnes,' I read for the second time that morning. This time the handwriting was round and careful, as if it had been copied out several times to ensure it was word perfect. I suppose I knew who had sent it even before I opened the envelope, but I didn't want to admit that I could possibility be right. I read the address at the top left-hand corner. It had come, as the postmark had forewarned, from a town in Yorkshire.

Unable to delay a moment longer, I turned straight to the signature at the bottom of the last page.

I read the name, repeating it a few times under my breath. How in hell had they come up with that, I wondered. A few words were added in brackets – both as unnecessary as screaming at a deaf man.

Hurriedly, I read the nine neatly blocked paragraphs in between, before rolling the sheets into a long cigar and placing them on the table, where I watched them curl to and fro, as though waiting for them to burst into flames.

Oh God, oh God, oh God, I thought. In the background, Ray crackled into silence, the record whirring round and round until it swung into the next track. The orchestra struck up and soared into the chorus. 'Hit the road, Jack,' Ray sang. 'Don't you come back, no more, no more, no more.' The words snagged in my brain. I didn't usually take advice from song lyrics, but this time Ray had a point.

All these years, and now this. I was at a loss about what to do. I had an overwhelming urge to just get the fuck out of there as fast as I could, but where should I go? I couldn't join Francisco in Colombia until September, and I certainly couldn't hang around here for the summer. Not now. Perhaps not ever. The idea of having to face Francisco overwhelmed me. I couldn't do it. I had to leave. I had to leave quickly.

And so I did.

It took me two weeks, a couple of phone calls and two short letters to vanish. Not much to wind up twenty years of your life, but I was too numb to grieve for my own dispensability.

The first phone call was to Geordie.

'What have you done this time, Aggie?' His smooth, transatlantic accent immediately dropped down an octave and a hokey Scottish drawl kicked in. 'Have you started smuggling in prostitutes from Eastern Europe? Formed a drug cartel? Robbed a bank?'

Geordie had always been impatient with anything that threatened his tightly budgeted, balance sheet of a life.

'Don't be a dickhead, Geordie.' I explained what had happened; there was no point in beating about the bush. I wanted him on side and silenced.

'But what's the problem? Wouldn't it be simpler for you to just tell him about it? It's not a hanging offence. Not outside of Scotland anyway.' He laughed at his own wit.

'I can't. He doesn't know a thing.'

'Fair enough, Ag,' he said. 'I just hope he doesn't start pestering me – I don't need it, I'm in the middle of a big merger and I can't spare the energy for your domestics. Are you okay for money? Tell me where you are and I'll wire you some.'

I promised I would, but I never did get around to giving him my address.

Next I called Maisie and told her I needed to disappear. I knew Francisco would call her, so I gave no details of where I intended to go. She would have told him in a heartbeat. The past, however, was mine alone to divulge. She promised that she wouldn't say a word.

The first letter was to the nursing home, saying that I was now living abroad. I asked them to forward all further correspondence to my sister in Australia until I had a fixed address. I would have told them I had spontaneously combusted if I thought it would stop them sending anything else to Balfour. But, sooner or later, there was a strong possibility that someone might come looking for me, and I certainly didn't want to be found.

Finally I wrote to Francisco. It was a short note, to the point and only four lines long.

Four lines for almost twenty years together.

Poor soul.

No wonder he hit me.

17

For a split second I had been almost joyfully pleased to see him, but a smack in the face has the knack of clearing the head, as well as emptying it of any misplaced sentimentality.

Over the preceding months, I had often wondered what I would do if I ever ran into him somewhere. At first, before sex and sentiment stupefied me, I'd be daydreaming, dawdling by the flower stand or idling at a market stall squeezing a mango, and I'd suddenly think of him. I'd look behind me, imagining that he could be there, somewhere in the crowd. I'd conjure him up, and see him distracted, rummaging around in his jean pockets for loose change before glancing up and catching sight of me, delighted to find me again.

So, yes, I overplayed the wishful thinking, forgetting the reality.

Before Francisco left for Colombia, things between us had cooled, but, with his absence, I retreated to an idealized version of our life together that belonged to the far-distant past. I wanted the old Francisco to come back, eager and happy at the sight of me, not the disappointed man I had made him into. I toyed with the memory of him as he used to be, dangling it in front of my eyes the way you do a ball of wool to an old cat that is too sophisticated to chase after snaking yarn, but which, nevertheless, pounces. As would I. I'd resurrect his curly head in the crowd and run after him, calling his name.

But then there was Adam, and, in the messy hole I had dug myself into, Francisco was better off dead. As far as I was concerned, he was fulfilling his contract as a visiting professor at the University of Bogotá and the house in Plantation Road was occupied by some Professor Prim from a boondocks university in Wilderness, Wisconsin. I knew that he would be back in

January, but I had put it out of my mind, like everything else that happened outside the cosy little fantasy I had found for myself.

The punch was a wake-up call.

It was also déjà vu, of a sort. Though this time round I didn't actually lose consciousness: I just slithered down the wall, banged against the speed bump of the dado rail and crumpled into a heap by the skirting board.

But, once again, there was blood in my teeth and, more surprisingly, blood dripping from my ear. More seeped up between the fingers of my right hand from landing on the broken glass, and my left leg was bent like a tick on the lined page of the floor.

It took me a while to realize that I was speechless because I couldn't open my mouth, and that this and the screeching pain were related.

What a shame I had dropped those wonderful goblets – now there would only be ten, I thought vaguely, trying to remove a splinter of burgundy crystal from my palm and finding myself unable to make my fingers work. Kaleidoscopic faces peered down at me in fragments: Adam, his face so white that only his concerned and confused eyes seemed to loom out of the starkness of the paintwork; Baxter, red-cheeked with the exertion of struggling up from the table, gently holding my shoulders, attempting to pull me upright; Jenny, uselessly trying to wrap my hands in a napkin soaked in water from the jug on the table, which only diluted it and spread it further. I had put several slices of lemon in the jug, and it stung like the bejezuz. Tears oozed from my eyes. The other two faces came and went. Charles half carried me to a chair. His wife patted the hand that wasn't bleeding.

'Shall we take her up to the drawing room and lay her down?' fussed Jenny. No, I thought, but didn't say. I'll bleed all over the white carpet. It'll never come out.

Adam was screaming at Francisco. 'You maniac. What in the name of God do you think you're doing? You can't go around hitting people.'

Don't shout. Remember Ned . . . I murmured mutely in my head. I didn't want the child to hear and come upstairs to see this.

'You should leave.' Adam turned to Caroline. 'Get him out of here. Now.'

But Francisco just stood there, stunned, immobile, behind the group of kneeling figures crouching around me like a nativity scene. He clenched and unclenched his fist as though waiting for another chance to take a swing at me.

'So this is what you mean by "needing to get away" – this!' He spat out the word like dirt from his mouth. 'You didn't even have the decency to tell me the truth. What kind of person are you? You fucking bloody disgusting lying bitch,' he said, all in a rush without even bothering with the commas.

I couldn't have explained even if my mouth had worked, but it wasn't until months later that I told him to go and stuff that 'need to get away' up his arse, right after he'd removed his own 'there's really no point in your coming to Colombia with me because you'll just get in the way' to make room for it. Just then I had no room for self-righteousness. I merely hung my head in shame and dripped blood into the black cashmere, which accommodatingly absorbed it.

Caroline, looking as though her crocodile handbag had turned round and taken a bite out of her face, put her arm around his shoulders, trying to usher him into the hallway, but he shrugged her off. He reached into his inside pocket, wrote something on a piece of paper with harsh jabs of his pen and threw it on to the table.

'You had a visitor,' he said, then, without another word, he turned and walked out the door.

I felt like the sort of creature that just moves through life leaving a long trail of slime.

The front door swung open on its hinges until Caroline bustled out, closing it gently behind her. The women began gathering plates and glasses. Baxter had found a dustpan and brush, and was sweeping up glass. Charles disappeared into the kitchen. I heard water splutter into the sink.

'You might need stitches in that,' said Adam, gesturing to my hand, where Marimekko poppies of blood were blooming on the napkin. 'Come on. I'll drive you to Casualty.'

'Adam . . .' I began, then cried out in agony, which only made the pain worse.

His face was rigid. 'Let's just get the wounds dressed.'

'But . . .' It came out as blood.

'Save it,' he said, turning his face away from my gory attempts at speech. 'What do you think you could say to me now that I might possibly want to hear?'

I closed my eyes. I couldn't bring myself to look at him.

He drove me the seven blocks to the A & E department, where I struggled unaided out of the car and then watched it disappear from sight.

After waiting for what seemed like a century with the Paddington homeless, drunk and junkies' club, a male nurse cleaned up my face and sent me for an X-ray, where they told me I was lucky. I would have laughed if it hadn't hurt so much. A doctor plugged me full of local anaesthetic and told me to use ice to stop the swelling. The nurse then checked my various cuts and abrasions for glass, glued my skin together, and handed me a leaflet for a women's refuge and another for Alcoholics Anonymous.

'It's not like that,' I protested. 'I fell against a door.'

I might as well have been saying wah, wah, wah, for all the notice the doctor took of me, but that was hardly surprising. I *was* saying wah, wah, wah.

'You don't have to put up with it,' counselled the nurse. He was about twenty-five, with long dyed-blond hair showing several inches of dark roots, tied back and folded over on itself until it looked like a knot at the back of his neck.

'Ring them.' He gestured to the number that had been rubber stamped on to the bottom of the women's refuge leaflet.

I shook my head, briefly. It hurt too much to argue further. Let me take advice from a boy with his hair tied up into a bun.

I had a few butterfly stitches on my hand, and another on a gash behind my knee. He checked me for concussion, handed me a care sheet for head injuries and warned me to call an ambulance if I started to feel dizzy or sick. As though it were possible to feel any more nauseated than I already did.

I was exhausted, but I walked home. It wasn't far. The hospital was right next to the station where I had arrived six months earlier. I passed a drunken couple at a bus stop, wrapped around each other and oblivious to the car that skimmed the pavement, heading for the hookers on the corner of Sussex Gardens. I gave them a wide berth and stayed on the main street, with only my long-legged shadow splayed out like a sixties cartoon in front of me, leading the way. But I wasn't afraid. Where's a passing psychopath when you need one? If anyone had tried to cut me into freezer joints and pack me into his trunk, I'd have opened the boot myself and climbed right on in. Anything was better than going home.

Wherever that was.

18

When I was fifteen, there was no broken glass. Only an orange-moulded kitchen chair, dimpled with cellulite and radiating four heavy steel legs at unforgiving angles, one of which caught me on the side of the temple and knocked me out and over, taking the tip of my left incisor with it.

My lip split open, my cheek was grazed and bleeding, and by the next morning the whole left side of my face was swollen and my eye was purple.

As I fell, the world seemed to slow. The coil of kicking, punching bodies rolling towards me seemed to stop and start, jerking forward in slow increments like a child's flick book. There were screams, though the music played on in the background: Elton John singing 'Saturday Night's All Right for Fighting'.

He was right on the money.

The lights had just dimmed, and couples were everywhere, lying on the sofas, curled up in the chairs, while the dancers were clinging to each other and kissing like washing machines on a fast spin. Kirsty was already gripped in the vice-like arms of Dan Ponti, her blonde hair in a long ponytail, swishing indolently to and fro as they rocked, off beat, heedless of the music.

That was my cue. As usual, I was heading upstairs for the bathroom to sit out the smoochy records. If nobody had barricaded themselves inside, I would smoke a cigarette and wait for it to be time to go home.

The fight broke out as I crossed the sitting-room floor, and I intercepted the chair just as I walked past the open door to the kitchen, where it was kicking off.

Kirsty was embarrassed – annoyed that I had the bad taste to allow myself to be knocked unconscious, especially when somebody switched the lights back on and the full wreckage was revealed. Cans of beer were spilled and crushed on the floor, and the offending chair now lay on its back like an upturned turtle.

'What a sight you look, lying there like an eedgit – get up and stop making a show of yourself. Thank God nobody knows us,' she hissed, glancing across the room trying to catch sight of Dan, who, in common with almost every other male in the room, had scarpered like a cockroach the minute the lights came up, while their abandoned girlfriends hung around dazed and crying. She couldn't see him, and was furious that she had to link arms with me and shoulder me up off the carpet and out into the freezing night, rather than being able to go to look for him.

Outside, we could see our breath, little puffs of ectoplasm drifting through the air. Ferns of frost bloomed across the roofs and glittered on fences, crunching underfoot like sandpaper. We walked out of the cul-de-sac and up the main road as the windows of the houses slowly went dark, one by one, until only the acid-yellow pus of the streetlights remained, glowing like sores in the night sky. We sat on the wall by the deserted bus stop and shivered, our bums turning cold and clammy on the icy granite. A taxi idled at the kerb, but we waved it away. We hadn't enough money: the fiver that was supposed to get us home had disappeared from my pocket. A police siren wailed in the distance and then the car appeared at the end of the road. Kirsty dragged me behind the shelter so they wouldn't see us.

'Where has Dan gone?' she said, looking up and down. He was supposed to get us a lift back to the village with one of his friends, but he had vanished. He had been in some trouble with the cops the year before, when he had hit a drunk in the café, so he wouldn't be hanging around to be picked up again.

'Maybe he'll come back and look for you when it's quieter?' I suggested.

'I'll kill him if he does,' she said. 'Imagine just going off and dumping us.' She was offended, and there was a nasty glint in her eye. Kirsty wasn't used to boys letting her down.

'Can't you reverse call for your dad to come and get us?'

'As if – with you looking like that? He'll never let me out the house again. I'll be keeping my mother company by the fire for the rest of my life. Anyway, he's not there. He's away golfing this weekend.'

'Golfing? In the snow?'

'Maybe it's not snowing in Aviemore?'

'It's where people go skiing – where else would there be snow?' She narrowed her eyes, the way my mother did, just before she swatted me with the back of her hand. 'You're a right know-it-all. But if you're that bloody clever, why didn't you duck?' she scolded, giving me a disdainful glance. 'You looked a complete spastic spread out on the floor. And how could you have lost all the money? You're hopeless, Aggie.'

'I didn't do it on purpose,' I snapped, but half-heartedly, because it hurt to speak. I had a wad of paper towel in my hand, which, despite all claims to the contrary, was not absorbent, and blood was beginning to congeal on my cheek. My lip throbbed; my tongue hurt where I had bitten it; my leg ached from the fall.

She clicked her tongue, not exactly accusing me of attention-seeking, but letting it be known that she considered I had been.

'It's a rotten shame, I was looking forward to that party for ages. It's the first time Dan's ever taken me anywhere out of the village.' I resisted the urge to remind her that we had actually gone ourselves on the bus and met him there after he had been to the pub. The distinction would have been lost on her, but now it was too late. 'Trust you. And now we're stuck here with no money – and no fags.' She shook out her empty packet and tossed it into the gutter. 'We'll have to walk home.'

I was annoyed. We were in a little town several miles distant from our own village, all because Dan Ponti had wanted to go there, and frankly, even without the fight, it hadn't been worth the bus fare.

'I only came because you asked me to – do you think this is

the way I want to spend my Friday night – knocked out at a stupid, lame party in a stupid house, in the middle of nowhere? I'm not that desperate for a half-pint of cider. I've got better things to do.'

'Aye, like what?'

'Well, for a start I'm going training tomorrow afternoon.'

'Och, training,' she huffed. 'No wonder you fell over – it must have been the excitement getting too much for you!'

'I didn't fall over, I got hit on the head.'

'I don't know how you can be bothered, up and down, up and down – what's the point? It's that boring.'

I had recently joined the school swim team, but Kirsty didn't think much of it. Swimming was the only sport I had ever been any good at, and there was a big competition coming up the following weekend. I needed to keep up my times. How was I going to manage with my leg hurting like this?

'I like it,' I said stubbornly.

It was okay for Kirsty, who seemed to drift through life, good enough at everything to keep her bobbing like a perky little cork, but I had few opportunities to shine. On dry land and dance floors, I possessed neither skill nor grace, but with the opening of a pool in the school sports centre the previous year I had discovered that in the water I was sleek and fast. Amazingly, I had won race after race in the Annual Swimming Gala and had recently been asked to join the county swimming team. It meant training three nights a week after school and at weekends, but it wasn't as though I had any other commitments in my social diary.

My face felt as though it had been hit by a tennis racket, but I wasn't worrying about that. Instead, I rubbed my bruised thigh anxiously. My new white trousers were covered in blood and dirt. Not only had I lost my taxi money, but now I didn't have enough to get the bus to school on Monday. And there were still miles and miles to walk home. I hoped the walk wouldn't make my leg seize up and stiffen. I flexed and pointed my ankle, and groaned at the pain. The flesh was swelling through the straps of my sandals. My toes were blue.

'I'd hate to have to do all that swimming. You'll get shoulders like a man if you don't watch out. Mind you, I like Mr Anderson. I wouldn't mind seeing him in his swimming trunks.' She gave me a sly look, but she wasn't telling me anything I didn't know.

Mr Anderson was gorgeous. A wee bit odd, the way he kind of looked through you without really seeing you, but really good-looking and muscled, with white teeth and broad shoulders. He was a sports teacher at school and trained us for track, field and swimming. Even Kirsty, who didn't like running because of her big boobs, started turning up for gym in tiny little shorts. I knew she was envious that I got to spend so much extra time with him.

Not that he so much as glanced in my direction when she was around. At fifteen I still had no bust. I had stopped stuffing toilet paper down my bra since Kirsty had thoughtfully pointed out at the crowded bus stop that there was a roll of perforated white paper snaking out of my jumper. I tried pretending that I had stuck it up my sleeve like a hankie, and it had got lost. But nobody was fooled, and the boys had all sniggered. It's a shame I hadn't persevered. It would have come in useful now, I thought, spitting up blood on to the pavement and dabbing my lip with peaks of paper towel that only stabbed more pain into the cut.

In a swimsuit, however, there was no shape to stuff. I had nothing but a skinny sausage of lycra to hide behind. When I had my cap on, I looked like a Spanish exclamation point – as long and slim as an eel with a tiny black spot for a head. My bones shone through the thin nylon of the Speedo suit, and my hips jutted out like single quotation marks on either side of the full stop of my navel. 'Good child-bearing hips,' my mother, erroneously, informed me, when I complained. I sucked everything in but the bones remained en guard – pointing out at twenty past eight like a Dalek. I will exterminate you, they called to anyone who came close.

I longed for Kirsty's curves. Sometimes she would come to the swimming sessions with me, just to flaunt herself in front of Mr Anderson. She'd get into her pretty blue polka-dot suit with the frill round the neckline that she sent away for from *Jackie*, and dangle her round pink feet in the pool, looking exactly like the girl in the mail-order advert. I wished she would let me have just this one thing for myself, especially as Mr Anderson ignored me and sat next to her instead, chatting away to her with that glazed, slack expression on his face, oblivious to my laps. Eventually I'd stand up at the end of the lane and remind him that I'd finished, but he'd just look at his stop watch as if he were wondering why it was in his hands and absent-mindedly tell me to get dressed. Once he even called me Alice.

But Kirsty would be leaving school in the summer, and I would have my life to myself. She was going to get a job in an office in Edinburgh and live in her own flat. I couldn't leave school until I'd finished my exams next year, and by that time I knew Kirsty, with a whole new set of smart friends and new clothes, would have left me behind. But it didn't matter. I wasn't in a hurry to go anywhere. I had swimming to look forward to, and next weekend we were going to Glasgow for the competition. Just Mr Anderson and the swim team – me, a couple of girls from the Third Year and two boys in the Sixth Form.

One of the boys, Jamie, was as skinny as me, but quite nice. His dad was a milkman, and he had red hair. Hardly the catch of the century, but neither was I. He always congratulated me when I won, and sometimes, after training, we got the bus back home together and went and had a coffee at Ponti's. Dan Ponti had left school and was always there behind the counter in his white overall with his name embroidered in red on the pocket, smirking at me, calling Jamie 'Carrots'. Dan wasn't quite as good-looking any more now that he spent all day making soapy coffee and slinging chips, but Kirsty liked him. Jamie was cheery, always smiling, and he always bought the coffees. Mind you, Kirsty thought he was pot ugly and gleakit, so I never mentioned him to her; and when she started going out with Dan, she was always hanging around the café, so I stopped taking him there. Not that I would ever have gone on a date with him, even if he asked. No matter how nice he was, there was no way I would commit social suicide with a ginger nut.

I just hoped that my leg didn't stop me swimming.

'Your face is all mashed up, you know.'

I knew.

'Your eye looks like raw mince.' She laughed a bit, but then gave my hand a squeeze to show she was sorry.

'Thanks.'

'Is it sore?'

It stung like hell, and my tooth was thumping to the beat of an hour in a dentist's chair. I felt like crying, but when I had come round after the fight, bawling like a wee baby, Kirsty had warned me to shut up in case somebody rang for an ambulance.

'How are we going to explain it to your mother and mine if the hospital rings them? When you see her tomorrow, you can just tell her you fell. Nothing's broken, is it?'

'No,' I agreed. I clutched vainly at the hollow of my throat, where the locket I had got for my birthday just the week before had nestled earlier in the evening. It must have fallen off somewhere. It was exactly like Kirsty's. My mother would be livid that I had lost it, but I didn't say anything. I licked the missing tip of my tooth, swallowed the tears and the bloody saliva, and did as I was told.

But now it was really cold outside, and my Teddy Bear jacket, though it looked like sheepskin, was polyester fake fur. I was freezing, and my fingers were numb. I was wearing strappy sandals, and my feet, in tights, were slipping up and down on the silver platform soles. I didn't want my muscles to get too cold or I'd definitely get a sprain. We should move, I suggested.

'Aye, come on,' she agreed; 'we can hitch a lift, but we'll have to walk for a while first.' She managed to both drag me along the street and poke me with her elbow at the same time. 'The police might still come, and they'll pick us up if they see us hitching. They all know my dad from when he comes to get the bodies after there's been an accident. We'll have to wait till we're right outside on the road.'

I stumbled forward as though on stilts. Kirsty, in brand-new black leather boots, strode out like an officer in the SS. I looked at them enviously – it was me who had pointed them out to her in Timpson's in Galashiels the week before. I loved them and had tried them on, but I couldn't afford them. Not so Kirsty – her purse was padded out with cash like it was on display in a department store. She was into the shop beside me and had them bought before I could even peel the zip down. And now there she was, strutting about in the stacked heels with her piggy-wee legs while I was getting frostbite.

'For God's sake – come awn,' she shrieked, snapping me out of my jealousy. 'Move! We'll be here all night if you don't give yourself a shake.'

She had one cigarette left, tucked behind her ear, and we shared it; mine had been squashed in the packet when I fell. We took two draws each until the filter tip was soggy.

'Yeuch, you've got it all bloody,' she said, throwing it away into the dark hedges that cowered furtively on either side of the country lane. Outside the town the string of streetlights came to an abrupt end, but the crescent moon hung low in the sky and lit our way, making the frost shimmer like glitter on a Christmas card. No cars passed us until we reached the crossroads with the main road going off to Selkirk, but even then the first thing to pass was a lorry. It rumbled past us, making the road shake. Neither of us stuck up our thumbs. We weren't that daft; we would never get into a lorry with a stranger.

My feet in the high heels were killing me. I was dying to take them off, but it was too cold to walk on the frozen tarmac in just tights. Kirsty was humming away to herself, an Abba song, the metal tacks in the heels of her boots keeping time to the music, my feet staggering in semiquavers. I would normally have joined in, the two of us linking arms and singing together, but my mouth was sore and my tongue swollen. I didn't want it to start bleeding again.

We heard the swish and crunch of another car coming along the road. Its headlights made the white of my trousers seem like two long, skinny flags waving in the blackness, and threw my etiolated shadow across the tarmac. It was a little Ford Escort. Kirsty held out her thumb and turned to face the glare of the lights as the car drew closer. It slowed a bit, but it was a young couple inside who probably didn't want a pair of battered teenagers in their back seat. The car looped around us and accelerated away.

'Oh, fuck you,' shouted Kirsty after them, giving them the finger.

'Don't do that; they might get mad at us,' I warned.

'So what if they do? It's not as if they can kick us out of the car since they never bothered to let us into it in the first place.'

She stuck her hands in her pockets and trudged ahead, leaving me limping behind.

The next car didn't stop either, though Kirsty was practically dancing in front of it. It swerved and continued to speed off into the distance.

'They probably think we're drunk, watching you falling all over the place. Can you not walk straight – what's the matter with you?'

'My leg is really sore,' I complained, 'and my ankle is swollen.'

'Oh, Agnes, you're such a greeting face – stop moaning – if it wasn't for you, we wouldn't be in this mess.'

I couldn't work out how it had all got around to being my fault: it had been Kirsty's idea to go to the bloody party, and then we had stayed late waiting for Dan when I wanted to go home.

She had been the one who convinced me to lie to my mother when I had been told I couldn't go out. I would rather have stayed in and watched the television. But it was too late to carry on about it. Now I just had to concentrate on putting one foot in front of the other.

'Will your mam not miss us and be worried?' I wondered hesitantly, half hoping that her father's dark green Humber would appear and whisk us off home to the sweet purgatory of scoldings.

'Nah, she'll have had her cherry brandy, a valium and a Ponderax chaser. She'll be out for the count until twelve o'clock tomorrow. Not that she'll tell my dad that.'

It was true. Her mother ate pills like sweets. I knew this because my mother was the one who filled her prescriptions at the chemist. Sleeping pills, tranquillizers, water pills and laxatives. 'It's no wonder she doesn't go out; she would rattle like a tube of Smarties,' my mother had said.

We had turned off the main road where a back lane cut through the fields and wound over the hills to the first village on the necklace that led to ours. There was another lone bus stop at the crossroads. I sat on the frame of the shelter where the glass had been kicked out, complaining of being tired. I told Kirsty I needed a rest.

She joined me, shivering, when we heard another car. Kirsty darted out on to the road and put her thumb in the air. I leaned out of the bus shelter and did the same. 'Watch out,' I called out nervously, thinking that maybe we should be more cautious, but she just kept thumbing.

The car slowed to a crawl. I couldn't see through the windscreen; the headlights dazzled me. I shielded my eyes as I waited for the car to stop, but Kirsty was already walking towards it, pulling her short, squat shadow behind her until it pooled around her feet.

'Oh,' she laughed, leaning over to peer into the open window, her hair where it had escaped from her ponytail falling across her face until she pushed it back behind her ear in a showy gesture.

'Hiya, sir. What are you doing here?' she asked, all casual, leaning one hand against the bodywork. It was a shiny red Volkswagen.

'Look, Aggie – it's Mr Anderson.' She flicked her eyes towards me and raised her eyebrows in a can-you-believe-it expression of delight.

I came up beside her, reluctant. Bugger, damn, I was thinking – this was going to land me right in the shite. Why did it have to be him?

'I should be asking you two the same thing. Agnes McBride – I wouldn't have expected to see you out at this time of night. Do your mothers know you're trailing around the countryside?'

'No,' I muttered, trying to keep the bad side of my face hidden. If he saw me all bashed to bits, he would be sure to force me to go home. And what if he knew about my leg? He definitely wouldn't let me compete. I wished we had stuck to the main road. This was bad news for me, but Kirsty was almost squealing with giddy joy.

'Are you giving us a lift, then?' She was sliding from one leather-shod foot to the other, her heels crunching as she undulated like a genie let out of a bottle. 'Will you run us back to my house? Please . . . please,' she wheedled, all fake sweetness and light.

He had already opened the passenger door, and Kirsty was skipping round to get into the car. But then it was my turn for his full attention. 'What happened to you, Agnes? Are you all right?' He had seen my bruises.

'She got in a fight,' Kirsty supplied, climbing into the front seat and leaving me to clamber into the back.

'You were fighting?' He was shocked and beckoned for me to come on.

I wasn't sure about getting a lift from a teacher. Maybe we would get into trouble at school for hitch-hiking, but Kirsty's face was set in a sullen expression and brooked no argument. She told me to stop hanging about and get in. I turned towards the window, trying to keep the bad side of my face hidden.

'You're a life saver, sir,' said Kirsty. 'We were at a party, but this gleakit idiot here got in that fight, and lost all our money, so we ended up having to walk.'

'What are you doing getting yourself involved in fights for? It doesn't seem like you.' I caught his eyes in the rear-view mirror.

See that, Kirsty. 'I wasn't fighting, honest, sir, I wasn't. I got caught in the *middle* of a fight at the party, then her cretin of a boyfriend went off and left us, and I'd lost all my money, so we had to walk home.'

'Well, at least I've *got* a boyfriend . . .' Kirsty was chattering away. 'You should have seen her – all over the floor, but you won't tell, will you? Her mother will go off her head if she finds out.'

I saw Anderson's peculiar glassy eyes watching me. 'You look pale, Agnes. Are you sure you're all right, hen? Maybe you need a doctor. Poor thing, you've had a bit of a battering.'

'Oh, Agnes is all right. She'll do anything to be the star of the show, won't you, Aggie?' She laughed. I shut my eyes.

Mr Anderson said something else, but I wasn't really listening. He was being nice, and his kind voice was coming and going like bad radio reception. My stomach began to lurch.

'I think I'm going to be sick,' I managed weakly, before I started to retch.

Mr Anderson hurriedly stopped the car, and I toppled out and threw up into the frozen ditch by the side of the road. My knees gave way. I couldn't stand up again.

'God, now she's spewing – and she's staying at my house. I can't take her back like this.' Kirsty was almost in tears, legs and arms both crossed, her composure cracking now that the script wasn't reading the way she'd written it.

I felt Mr Anderson lift me under the arms, then gently half carry me on to the back seat. 'Lie down, hen,' he said, 'you're not well.'

Like that was breaking news.

Kirsty was chuntering on, her voice trembling, telling him where we lived, but I couldn't keep my eyes open. I was melting, giving in to the desire to close my eyes. The car was rocking me as if I were an infant in a pram. All I wanted to do was sleep.

My eyes drooped until I just let go and drifted off into the black. I heard Kirsty's voice bubbling away in my head, on and on and on in her usual Kirsty-World sort of way, until I woke up with pain chiselling into my jaw. The car had rumbled to a standstill. Thank God, I thought, we're home. Kirsty grinned at me from the front seat. We were back in the village.

'Mr Anderson says you can sort yourself out here first.'

'What?' I gaped at her. What was she talking about? I rubbed the condensation away from the back window and through the water, trickling in rivulets down the glass, I saw we had drawn up outside a whitewashed little cottage with darkened windows and a high hedge huddled around it, all dusted with frost. It looked like something from a fairy tale, like Hansel and Gretel, but made of chunks of iced limestone instead of gingerbread.

'But, Kirsty, where are we?' I croaked.

I was talking to her back, she was already picking her way over icy puddles to the front door.

Mr Anderson disappeared into the porch and switched the light on. Then he stood on the step and beckoned me forward with a wave.

I breathed on the window and watched his face mist over.

But he was still there when the glass cleared.

19

I half expected my bags to be packed and dumped on the pavement when I arrived back at Holland Crescent, but only a dustbin that I had forgotten to take downstairs welcomed me, its lid askew in a rakish salute.

It was 4 a.m., and all the lights were out except for the orange glow of the desk lamp in Adam's study. I hoped he wasn't still sitting up there waiting for me, but I supposed I would have to face him sooner or later.

A toy town of clean crockery lined the kitchen table. I sent a silent thank you to Jenny as I relocated everything as carefully and quietly as I could with one hand, knowing I wouldn't get a chance to tell her myself.

The piece of paper that Francisco had left on the table remained propped up on the sideboard. I picked it up and read it. You don't think things can get any worse and then they do. I crumpled it inside the pocket of Lennie's old coat, which I supposed I would have to take with me as I didn't have another one to wear.

I took my Tupperware box out of the freezer in the basement, then wearily climbed the stairs, listening for footsteps that didn't come.

On the third flight, I crept up and peered cautiously into Lennie's room, where, to my relief, a dark lump was visible underneath the covers. Across the landing Ned was asleep with his bottom in the air and his cheek jammed against the mattress as though he had been dropped from space at a great height. I pulled the duvet over his shoulders and stooped to pick up the glass of water on the carpet that he always kicked over in the morning. Outside his room, I opened the linen cupboard and slid my good hand underneath the folded pillowcases until I found the fat envelope concealed at the bottom. Inside, I had managed to accumulate about five and a half thousand pounds. My passport was also there, taped into a little parcel together with the bank card and cheque book for my old building society account, and, wrapped in cotton wadding, Francisco's mother's engagement ring.

I tiptoed downstairs to Adam's bedroom. The door was closed and I hesitated, but I needed to get my clothes, so there was no alternative but to enter. However, when I turned the handle and went inside, as I had half expected, the bed was empty and hadn't been slept in. I dragged my eyes away from the pillows I had smoothed that morning, a lifetime ago, then went into Gay's dressing room and rewound my life back into the same suitcase I had arrived with, plus a brace of larger shopping bags for the few extra things I had acquired since my arrival.

Adam appeared, his face ravaged and his eyes bloodshot, leaning against the door frame as I rummaged through the laundry basket for my few items of unwashed clothing. I pretended I didn't know he was standing behind me until he spoke.

'You're leaving already,' he announced more than asked.

I nodded my agreement, rolling up a pair of pants and jamming them into one of the shopping bags.

'Where will you go?' he said, trying to sound as though he didn't really care about the answer. His words were a little slurred. He had been drinking.

'I don't know – Oxford, maybe?' I spoke the words with difficulty, only to realize the foolishness of that idea and the downright stupidity of voicing it.

'You'll go back to him?'

'No. Absolutely not. I doubt he'd have me in any case.' Damn it, another wrong thing to say. 'I just mean I suppose I will try to talk to him. Eventually.'

He sat on the bed, following me as I gathered up my things with hard eyes, the pupils hammered into his head like steel nails. 'Do you want to go back to him?' he asked aggressively.

'No, but, even if I did, I think it's gone a bit past what I want, don't you?'

'How's your face?'

'It's fine; just bruised.'

His mouth opened and closed soundlessly. 'I just can't fucking believe you. What the hell kind of game have you been playing with me these last months?'

'It wasn't a game.' I shook my head How to begin? 'I'm sorry, Adam, I . . .'

He slapped the words away with an expression of repugnance. 'He called you Agnes . . . ?'

I lifted the suitcase and hooked the carrier bags carefully over my bad hand, to avoid touching the stitches.

'Yes, that's my name,' I said simply.

'Who the fuck have I been living with all this time? What kind of a person are you?'

I started to cry, but I kept my voice even. 'If it's any consolation, I liked being Edith a lot better than I ever liked being Agnes.'

His mouth looked as though it had been sewn shut, and the thread pulled tightly at one end. I could practically smell the stench of my own lies. I wanted to crawl across the carpet on my knees and beg him to listen to me, to look at me, to believe me, but what would be the point? What could I say?

I walked towards the door. The silence spread across the floor between us like sealing wax, hard and brittle, until Adam broke it. 'Just tell me one thing,' he called after me, with a little lilt of hope in his voice. 'Was he violent? Did he threaten you? Is that why you left him?'

Until that moment I think he was still willing me to give him some sort of justification that he could have accepted. He was longing for me to say something, anything, that would redeem me. What was one more lie after so many?

But I didn't have any more energy left for fiction, so I kicked the corpse one more time. 'No, nothing like that. You can't judge him on this evening; he's a tremendously sweet, gentle man.

I don't think I ever saw him lose his temper, not once. He never even raised his voice. That was part of the problem. It was as if he faded away. Tonight was just a shock, his seeing me here.'

'Then why did you leave him?' he asked, his eyes imploring me to give him an answer that he could make sense of. I wished I had one.

I put down the suitcase and fumbled in my pocket for the piece of paper that I knew bore an alien name and telephone number written out in Francisco's jagged, elegant script.

'Did you see the note that Francisco left behind?'

'No. Why, what is it?' He was too drunk even to register the significance of the question.

I opened it and closed it again. 'Oh, just some contact details. It's not important.'

I stared at Adam. He looked like a man who had walked across the Antarctic without his overcoat and had his skin flayed off by the elements.

I screwed it up into a ball the size of my heart and walked to the bathroom, where it fell eagerly into the tangled embrace of a skein of dental floss at the bottom of the bin.

But when I came back to the bedroom, he had gone. There was only the hollow of his body on the bed. I took the nightdress that I kept, for show, underneath the pillow and winced as a door upstairs slammed and bounced on its hinges.

20

Adam had said that there was no need for me to leave immediately, which seemed almost insultingly decent of him. However, I knew that I couldn't be there when the children woke up in the morning, so I sat downstairs alone on the hard hump of the Victorian sofa in the dining room in my too big, borrowed coat, surrounded by my collection of orphaned bags and waited for morning to call my name.

At seven o'clock, before it was properly light, I let myself out as quietly and efficiently as I had arrived. I went around the house and emptied the dustbins, put out the trash, set the breakfast table for the children and left the house keys beside the clock in the hall. It was still chiming as I closed the door.

In a little greasy-spoon café next to the taxi rank, I drank polystyrene coffee looking like the homeless person I had just become, and examined the leaflet the nurse had given me about the women's refuge in Hammersmith. I wasn't so sure that I deserved a 'non-judgemental safe environment', though, technically, I could have made a case for being a battered wife. Maybe I ought to go there long enough to decide what I should do next? But then, as I flicked through the *A–Z* looking for the address, I remembered the shabby hotel where I had once been offered a job. It was still marked on page 68 with a red asterisk on a street with only consonants in its name.

It seemed like the obvious answer. Nobody would ask me any awkward questions and, more importantly, I wouldn't have to make up any more lies.

Twenty minutes later a sleepy Nigerian was showing me into a room with barely a foot of pub carpet on either side of a large double bed. But it had tea- and coffee-making facilities, a television screwed to the wall and its own bathroom with two towels the size of a facecloth. The window opened. The sheets looked clean. It was perfect. I paid a week in advance and settled down to lick my wounds, or at least to leave them to heal.

By the end of the week my stitches had dissolved, the swelling in my jaw had gone down, and the bruise had faded to the same shade of dark disappointment as the shadows under my eyes. With the help of Nude Beige concealer from Boots, I ventured into the back office and renegotiated with the manager, an impassive African who had three scars on each cheek, as though his face had been marked up by an editor attempting to capitalize his yellow-rimmed eyes. Deal struck, I moved into the staff annexe, above a garage in the skip-lined mews behind the hotel, and changed bed linen between ten and three. In the evenings I worked on the front desk from six until midnight, and let rooms to Antipodeans with rucksacks the size of compact cars, or mismatched couples who rarely stayed longer than an hour and who always paid in cash.

I volunteered to do all the Christmas shifts, though at first the manager was upset that I didn't have plans to go to church. He spent ten dutiful minutes telling me about making room for Jesus in my life before I told him I was Jewish, and then gracefully conceded that I could work for the minimum wage on Christmas Day while he and his extended family went to a Pentecostal temple in south London.

I saw in the New Year on reception, reading a tattered *Cosmo* from June 1993 with a cheeseburger and Coke that Adi, one of the lesser Nigerian cousins, brought me from McDonald's. A drunken Australian called me a cunt when I told him we didn't have a dunny, public or otherwise, he could use. So, one way or another, I got all the *c*'s Adam had promised me.

I stayed there through January, until I saw a job advertised in a local paper for a receptionist in a holistic medicine practice in Acton. My Oxford credentials impressed the two men who interviewed me, and they hired me on the spot. When I mentioned that I would also need to find somewhere to live, they had the perfect solution. Within a week I found myself employed and installed as a lodger in the house of one of the practitioners: a divorced homoeopath who had a dusty spare room and a blind cat, both of which revived, rather spectacularly, my latent asthma. I gave the hotel manager, Adam and the bursar of Balfour College as my referees. As far as I am aware, not one of them was ever contacted. People are surprisingly slack about these things.

I took another job cleaning the surgery of a dentist in Turnham Green between seven and nine every morning, and worked for the socks-and-sandals brigade, answering the telephone and making appointments, between two and eight in the evening, Monday to Saturday. The rest of the time, I waited.

Do you know that feeling when you're longing for a letter, when you're almost itching for it to arrive? When, every morning, you find a dozen reasons to dart out into the hallway just to check to see if there's anything lying on the floor that isn't a pizza-delivery leaflet?

This was the vigil I kept, two postal districts west from Adam's house, for the first long, slow months after I left.

The moment I was settled, I had written to him giving him my address and telephone number, 'just in case I get any mail', I said.

I knew there would be no mail to forward, and in any case the only person I wanted to hear from was him.

Every morning, I took a widow's walk, to and fro across the window of the homoeopath's bedroom at the front of the house where, naturally, I should not have intruded. But I wasn't interested in her pots of arnica and rosewater face creams, or in the tapestry pillows of cats and dogs that she rearranged meticulously every morning on top of her bed. I was only interested in the street, willing the postman to jog along the pavement, pushing his trolley ahead of him while his skinny, mandarin pigtail flapped in the breeze behind.

Officially, I could use the kitchen only between certain

prescribed hours, as detailed on a typed three-page sheet of rules and regulations. These included: no use of the phone except in emergencies (it was in her private sitting room); no television in my room (the noise disturbed her); no using the waste disposal (apparently it encouraged rats); no using the microwave (negative rays and carcinogens); no kicking the cat (this last being the only one I broke with any regularity). Nevertheless, I dallied there like a man outside a sex shop, pretending to read the parts of the newspaper that contained jobs I was unqualified for. I turned the pages, concentrating on the type, seeing nothing, and all the time my ears strained for the clatter of the letterbox, longing to hear a bundle of envelopes being squeezed through the slot, followed by the soft papery thud as the letters landed on the tiles, splayed out like a peacock's tail.

Every afternoon I put on my increasingly oversized coat and left for the twenty-minute walk to work with the same sinking feeling of defeat as I realized that, once again, the postman had been and gone, passing me by with his treasure of low-cost insurance for the possessions I didn't own, and a life I didn't care about, all addressed to people who didn't even live here any more.

My landlady was as postally bereft as I, but at least she existed in the shadowy world of manila-encased copies of *Homoeopathy Today*, and *Reader's Digest* book clubs with their promises of large cash prizes if only she would tick the box and return the envelope within fourteen days.

I daydreamed at my desk, counting off the days in my head since I had written to Adam, and extending the deadline for a reply by another twenty-four hours. I booked in clients for cranial osteopathy and acupuncture, and felt dejected and deflated as I wondered how I would pass the interminable chasm of time until the next morning, when I would wake up and plead with the fates again, ah, yes – maybe today.

Then, as two weeks turned into four, it became: maybe next week, maybe next month, maybe never, almost certainly never, and then just never.

Francisco had always been a lax correspondent, even when we had been on good terms. Once, when he had gone home to Colombia for Christmas, I received a two-page missive on a lined yellow legal pad that arrived in Oxford three weeks after he did. The paper alone should have told me everything I needed to know about the future trajectory of our relationship. I have it now, folded into a precise triptych, the thick, spiky-black handwriting soaring up the page like the New York skyline or lines of Modigliani figures waiting for a bus. It reads like the travelogue of Dulles McDull and is a description of the view from his grandmother's balcony. It's New Year's Eve, and the night sky is ablaze with fireworks being set off from hundreds of craft in the harbour, the barrage of explosions punctuated with the odd round of gunfire. 'Every year', he writes, 'some poor bastard gets shot by a drunk who forgets to aim upwards.' I skimmed over the words, searching for something personal and found it, at last, on the line before he signed his name. It said: 'Take care, Francisco.' Hardly a love sonnet; no mention of love at all, in fact.

But then there were greeting cards for birthdays and Valentine's Day, some of which survived the years and nestle with the letter, still in their envelopes with a bite out of each corner where I had torn them open as they arrived, one by one, propped on the breakfast table, the mantelshelf or accompanying an ill-wrapped gift.

He brought all this redundant love with him when we met to pick over the ruins of our marriage. I sat opposite him like a failed Ph.D. student, with the papers he had found in his file cabinet and brought with him tossed on the butler's table in front of me.

I had arranged the meeting soon after I moved to Acton. I expected that he would have moved back into Plantation Road when our tenants left at the end of term, so I called him one evening, long after everyone at work had gone home and I had the office to myself. A woman with a heavily aspirated foreign accent answered the phone on the first ring. He must have been sitting close by, as, one wordless second later, he came on the line, his few curt words sounding more Spanish than usual, as though language were a sexually transmitted disease and he had caught it from the woman beside him. He didn't mention who she was, and I didn't need to ask. She was probably me, but fifteen years younger and with a graduate degree. By mutual consent we agreed that I shouldn't go up to Oxford. He didn't want me in the house, and, since it sounded like somebody was already sleeping in my bed, nor was I eager to return.

Instead, we met in the dining room of the Cumberland Hotel on a rain-sodden Sunday in the third week of February, the surrounding drab gold-brocade wallpaper and colour-blind, patterned carpet even more incandescently angry than Francisco. It was a place better suited to taking tea with an aunt of whom you weren't very fond than to cauterizing a runaway wife.

We ordered a pot of Earl Grey that we poured with great ceremony and crippling solicitousness, and then, with none of the care that had been lavished on the tea, he emptied out the contents of his briefcase.

He laid out the details of my college pension plan – my few years of employment at Balfour's Centre for Latin American Studies would entitle me to the princely sum of £3.05 a week when I retired; a letter that my father had sent me before he died, the sight of which stung me as much as it had the first time I read it, when he had congratulated me on what he considered to be the single shining achievement of my life – marrying Francisco. Then there were reams of building society statements addressed to Mrs A. Morales, which had continued to arrive at monthly intervals after I left. Francisco had opened them and stapled them together in chronological order.

'You didn't take any money out of your account,' he said bitterly. 'I thought you must be dead,' he said; 'otherwise what were you living on? The couple of hundred that you withdrew from the bank wouldn't have lasted long. Of course I jumped to the wrong conclusion. I should have wondered "who" you were living on.'

'It wasn't like that.' I started to tell him that I could explain, but, as I couldn't, I just winced, mutely, while he threw paper darts at me.

Underneath the statements were three powder-blue envelopes identical to the one that had been forwarded from the nursing home, but addressed this time to Agnes Morales at Balfour College. Each one had been opened. The floor lurched as though I had hit a sudden belt of turbulence. I wanted to vomit.

'You know what these are. Obviously,' he said, as he threw them on the table.

Oh my God. I braced myself. The plane was hurtling towards a pencil-line runway two thousand feet below me.

I scanned his face. It was hard to imagine that he could be more livid than he was, but I was sure it was feasible. However, he dropped the envelopes without further comment, his jaw clenched, as though being silent under torture.

I felt as though I had been strip-searched.

The last letter he produced like a flick knife, waving it under my nose before handing it over. It was a faded cream envelope in a square hand with a pre-printed violet Queen's head embossed on the front.

Jamie. I smiled in spite of myself, taking it from him and caressing the crown with my thumb.

'You bitch, you sit there and smile?' Francisco was watching me, the way you watch a rat in a corner.

'It was quite illuminating going through your letters,' he said, spelling it out in little chips of ice.

'You've read them all?' I covered the envelopes with my hands, as though I could still keep everything inside unknown.

'Agnes, you disappeared for six months without a word. Of course I read them. I went through your boxes and read every piece of paper I could find. I called your mother's nursing home, where the matron – the fucking matron – told me they'd *heard* you'd "gone away for a while". I spent hours trying to track down your brother, hoping you'd be there with him, but when I finally got through he wouldn't tell me a thing. Then he just wouldn't even take my calls, the shit. And as for Maisie' – he pronounced the z like a razor – 'you know, you used to complain about Herminia, but your family make the fucking Vietcong seem gracious. She just put her oaf of a husband on the phone, who treated me as though I were an insect.' He spat the word into my face.

I jumped back. I wouldn't blame him if he beat me to a bloody pulp.

'But not one of them would tell me a thing.'

I closed my eyes.

'Not one of them would tell me a thing about you and the bloody little bastard you told me you couldn't have . . . the bastard you've been hiding from me for twenty years.'

And then the plane hit the ground, but, unfortunately, I was still alive.

Where are all the bloody trigger-happy Colombians when you need them?

21

My mother sent me off to an Agnes who ran a boarding house in Scarborough when I was four and a half months pregnant. Spending ten minutes with my feet up in stirrups would have solved the problem easily, but my mother wouldn't even say the word 'abortion', let alone discuss it with me. It didn't help that I was already three months gone before I plucked up the courage to tell her, so time was short.

She was outraged. 'It's murder,' she had hissed when I meekly suggested that maybe I didn't have to have the baby. Stapling me with her eyes, she paused for a long breath and then said, in a whisper like vapour escaping from an ice box: 'Do you think you would be here if I believed in abortion? Two grown-up children and you think I wanted another bairn at my time of life? But I had to knuckle down to it, and so will you.'

I felt as though I'd just trudged home through a snowstorm without my skin. I couldn't feel my fingers; the saliva on my tongue froze.

'There have already been too many people hurt with all this . . .' She looked at me meaningfully, leaving me to fill in the blanks, which I did.

All of them.

And I didn't mention it again.

She brought home a test she had smuggled out of the chemist where she worked, but she wouldn't take me to the doctor. In a village the size of ours, she was worried that everybody would know. Everyone already knew far too much about me, and my family had been shamed enough. I was more talked about than Patty Hearst. My face and name had even made it on to the pages of a national paper. A school photograph with my head circled to single me out from my classmates had been shown on *Reporting Scotland*. Jean Rook had mentioned me, dismissively, in the *Scottish Daily Express*. My mother couldn't take any more gossip and wanted rid of both of us, but fortunately there was an even more convenient way to deal with the problem. After a few hurried trunk calls, it was decided to have the baby, and me, removed geographically.

After she recovered from the sight of the blue spot in the test tube and the flame of her handprint had faded to a palm-shaped blush on my jaw, she made plans for my exile. 'Don't tell another soul,' she warned, her mouth a thick pencil scribble of dislike. Who would I tell? Nobody was talking to me.

'They think you're enough of a hoor as it is, without this.' For several weeks all but obligatory public appearances were suspended, then, as soon as circumstances would allow, my mother put on her black Mussolini mohair cape and her Fair Isle tea-cosy hat, and marched into action with Fascistic zeal. Like a general leading her troops into battle, she goosestepped me along the railway platform with the tip of her furled umbrella and deposited me on a train in Carlisle. Finally, she had something she could control.

I put up my hands and surrendered. I had nowhere else to go. I didn't pack much on the basis that most of my clothes soon wouldn't fit me. I had a couple of pairs of nylon trousers with elasticated waists and a few jumpers in the brown leather case. A trunk full of schoolbooks, which I would be expected to study on my own, was to follow. I wouldn't need much else. 'Agnes is stout,' said my mother; 'you can borrow something of hers as you get bigger. You'll not be giving any fashion shows.'

I helped out a bit with the boarding house, though there wasn't too much work to do. It was off-season, and there were only a few paying guests. I washed up, helped with the beds, wrestled the wet sheets on to the washing line and ironed the ice out of them when they had frozen solid. Otherwise, Agnes took pity on me and let me rest.

I spent most of my time pretending to study, earnestly poring over Chapter 3 in *Bienvenue*, which involved asking people in small Provençal villages where I could find the nearest dentist, while really reading Westerns and romances set in the Australian outback that I found on the shelves in the boarders' sitting room. When not wishing myself wooed by a sheep farmer or rustling cattle in Oregon, I walked by the sea, watching the waves roll in and smash themselves into exasperated spit on the beach, while seagulls screamed furiously overhead. The vast North Sea terrified me. If I stood too close to the shore, I was afraid of the wrath of the water – that it would sweep in, swallow me up and drag me away. But sometimes I went right up to the water's edge in my Woolworths' gumboots and stood there anyway. I'd listen to the gulp of the hungry waves, and feel the sand collapse beneath my heels as the tide curled over my toes and sucked on them, coaxing me further. Come on; come on; just another step more. It made me think of Kirsty.

And then I stepped back.

I called Agnes 'aunt', but she was one of my mother's distant cousins in one of those twice-removed, elongated family relationships that I had never understood. Her kindness, though brusque and often baffled, was a balm after my mother's steel-knuckled scorn. She rarely sat still and was always tired, worn down as she was by hard work and taciturn men, but she gave me an easy ride, plying me with greasy bacon sandwiches, to 'keep my strength up', and the sweet, milky tea that I've never been able to drink since. Her own children were grown and married off to sensible Northerners, or at least sensible enough not to let any of their kids be called Agnes. Until she was saddled with me, she hadn't ever had to deal with a wayward teenager, let alone one who was also pregnant.

Occasionally we talked about the baby, but only as though it were some rather unwieldy ornament that, one day, when I went back home, could be shoved into the back of the cupboard under the stairs when visitors came.

We both knew it would never be on show.

It was she who arranged for me to take classes at the secretarial college, a room above a bakery that was redolent with the scent of custard slices and the casual spite of slow-witted girls with fast fingers.

'Don't mither yourself, lovey. Just ignore the silly mares. You're a smart girl. Life goes on,' she assured me. 'You'll put all this behind you, and the typing will be just the thing to fall back on after it's all passed,' she told me.

There was no question of my ever returning to school. I did my O-Levels as a moderately pregnant external student amid rows of schoolchildren at the local comprehensive in Scarborough. I looked as if I had a beach ball stuck up the front of my blouse, and none of the other kids spoke to me. I hoped to do just well enough to scrape a pass in maths and English but was so woolly-headed that I couldn't concentrate on anything: I could spend hours lying on my bed watching feathers fly through the air, but I couldn't get information to stick in my brain.

'Never mind, pet,' Agnes said. 'That's how it goes when you're expecting. You should be sitting quietly, thinking lovely thoughts so that you have a happy baby.'

That was a novel concept. I didn't have room in my mind for any sort of thought. I had closed off all the doors and windows, so that there was no space for French verbs, no space for Hamlet's soliloquy, no space for bovine reverie, and certainly no space for happy babies.

But the typing proved to be therapeutic, so I tapped out lines and lines of senseless gibberish, and week after week I squeezed my stomach behind the desk above the bakery until my fingers could hardly reach the keyboard. Then I practised blind on the breakfast table, clattering away on a copy of the *Yorkshire Post*: *sadly hasty kid is there; sadly hasty kid is there; sadly hasty kid is there.*

Yep: sometimes the gibberish was uncannily apt.

22

'She looks just like you, you know.'

'You've met her?'

'Oh, yes, walked up to the front door and rang the bell. A lot more forthcoming than you.'

'Oh, God, I . . .'

'She got your address from the matron of the home. She had been on quite the voyage of discovery. She had been up there too, visiting your mother.'

If my shoulders had buckled any more, they would have been on the table.

'She thought I was her father, but I soon disabused her of that notion.'

'I'm –'

'So who is?'

I looked at Francisco in a daze.

'Was it him? I can't find anything else from a man, and the dates fit. The girl says she's nearly twenty-one now,' he added.

I couldn't follow. 'Who are you talking about?'

'The – man – in – the – letter. Are you being deliberately obtuse? Because, if so, it's not going to work.'

Oh, the mists cleared, the man in the letter. I caressed the envelope tenderly. 'No, Francisco, he was just a boy at school. I hardly knew him.'

'You hardly knew the father of your own child?' His voice grew so loud the teaspoons shook in their saucers and moved pointedly away from us. 'A child I didn't know existed; a child you denied me?' He rubbed his hands on the legs of his jeans, as though he were trying to wipe them clean.

I didn't know how to begin to tell him. I didn't want it to

get any uglier than it was, but we were talking at cross-purposes.

'No, Francisco – I hardly knew Jamie, the person who sent the letter. He was a couple of years older than me. He wasn't the father. He wasn't even my boyfriend. He just wrote to me . . . well, to be kind, I suppose.'

'So who was the father?'

'It was someone who didn't want anything to do with me or the baby.'

'And why didn't you tell me about him – about the baby? I mean, didn't it occur to you at any of those times we talked about having a family?'

'It wasn't anything to do with you and me.'

I addressed the sugar bowl. It seemed to take the statement quite well.

Not so Francisco.

'How can you dare sit there and say that?' The teaspoons quaked again.

I squirmed like a kid caught stealing sweets.

The letter I now held in my hand had arrived before I left for Scarborough, when the scare had turned to scandal and my life had exploded like the dust bag on an overstuffed vacuum cleaner. Just seeing the handwriting made the past rise up like the smell of camphor in a long-undisturbed pile of clothes.

We were still living in the village, in the big house, before shame downsized us. It was a shrine devoted to starched anti-macassars and Dralon furniture, with three sitting rooms, each used according to the status of the visitor. The hierarchy was mostly untested – generally people sat by the kitchen fire and flicked their fag ash into the grate. It saved dirtying an ash-tray. As I may have mentioned, we didn't get many visitors. Especially then.

I was upstairs with the curtains closed, listening to Radio One on a black transistor held together with brittle, yellowing Sellotape. The sound faded and crackled, sometimes disappearing altogether until I gave it a sharp kick with my foot, when it would surge back to life with a sudden increase of volume. 'Why don't you write me/I'm out in the jungle/I'm hungry to hear you . . .' I tapped my toes encased in my father's thick fisherman's socks in time to the music, surprised to learn from Simon and Garfunkel that men too sat around alone, longing for comfort and solace.

I had thought it was just me.

I was a leper. Agneses came and went through the kitchen but fell into embarrassed silence if I entered the room. My father hadn't addressed a word to me in weeks other than to instruct me to change the channel on the television set, usually to avoid the local news. My mother pushed pills on me from her own secret stash: Librium broken into microscopic pieces to calm me down, iron for my wan face, cod liver oil to pad my bones, and alternately slivers of Mogadon to send me to sleep when she found me reading on her 3 a.m. bathroom run and Dexedrine to wake me up when I couldn't be roused from my bed until the afternoon. If I had stayed at home much longer, the happy baby my aunt would later anticipate would have had every chance of being born a junkie.

My mother spoke to me in plates of lumps of mashed potato and ground meat in oceans of cooling gravy, thumped on a tray on the ottoman at the foot of my bed, whose inevitable and rapid regurgitation, we had not yet realized, was caused by something more than merely the stress of public humiliation. I had no friends. Kirsty had been moved to a special hospital in Glasgow, but no one suggested I visit her. I hadn't so much as walked up to the village shops for weeks.

So I listened to the radio and sat shiva for the death of Disco, gorging myself on golden oldies. I sequestered myself with the *Children of the New Forest* and reread *Heidi* and *Jane Eyre*, wondering, not for the first time, what she saw in the miserable old bastard married to the lunatic in the attic, and how being saddled with a blind geriatric could possibly constitute a happy ending.

I counted the weeks on my fingers and got to August with a horrible chill that had nothing to do with the freezing fog hanging over the village like a giant net curtain.

Sprawled across my rumpled bed, surrounded by pop posters and fashion-magazine cut-outs, I pulled the eiderdown up to my chin and wished there was someone I could talk to. My few schoolfriends had deserted me. The cousin Agnes nearest my age wasn't allowed in the house lest she catch slack morals from the toilet seat. I could write to Maisie, but my mother had told me not to, and the solicitor had warned me against putting anything down on paper. Anyway – she was so far away. What could she do? I lit a cigarette from my secret hoard, stolen earlier from my mother's open packet, and blew the smoke through a crack in the skylight window so she wouldn't smell it. Despite doping me with every pharmaceutical she could persuade the doctor to prescribe for her, she baulked at allowing me cigarettes.

I closed my eyes against the biting wind blowing the smoke back into my face, trying to clear my mind of unwelcome thoughts with every exhalation, relaxing my limbs, just as the psychiatrist at the hospital had taught me. The sweet combination of nicotine and hyperventilation had just begun to make my head swim when my mother's voice snaked into the room like a whip. She rasped over the static of the radio: 'Ag-nes, there's a letter here for you.'

I jumped up, sending the ashtray ricocheting under the bed, spilling bent fingers of fag ends among the dust balls. I flailed at the smoke that hung lazily in the air before running downstairs. There it was, standing against the clock on the lace-topped sideboard, this nondescript cream envelope. I turned it over, while my mother hovered.

'Should I open it, hen?' she asked. Pregnancy had not yet turned her totally against me, and I was still treated to the odd chicken endearment.

'It might not be nice.' Not nice was my mother's way of saying that it might be from a raving fucking lunatic. We had received a handful of hostile anonymous letters over the previous month. We had been instructed to hand them all over to the police.

'And if it's from him, don't even touch it.'

'It's not going to be from him, Mum, all his mail gets read before he sends it,' I said, responding with more conviction than actual knowledge.

She pulled at her lip and smoked, meaning both hands were in her mouth at the same time.

I held the envelope out to her. 'You open it, then.'

She balanced her cigarette on the edge of the fireplace and peeled back the envelope as though she planned on reusing it at Christmas.

'Looks like a bairn's writing,' she said doubtfully, which was not reassuring. A lot of the crazy letters had the appearance of having been written by people who could hardly form their letters and often resorted to capitals.

'Oh,' she sighed in surprise. 'It's from Jamie somebody? There's no second name.'

I grabbed the paper out of her hands. 'Jamie Frazer?'

'Just says Jamie. I don't even know if it's a laddie or a lassie. Awfy neat writing for a laddie. Crawfoot Drive's the address.'

'Och, it's nobody. A boy at school with me. In swimming,' I said, before she started doing a census of Crawfoot Drive so as to discover his pedigree. My mother knew the stud line of the entire village.

'Dinnae read it if it bothers you, hen,' she called after me.

I dashed back upstairs and threw myself down on the bed. Wintery sunlight filtered through the almost opaque glass of the skylight as I began to read.

He was doing his Highers and bogged down in revision. He wondered if I would be going back to school. He said that I shouldn't worry about what people were saying. He knew it wasn't true. He asked if I was all right, and if I would write back to him and let him know. Maybe he could come and visit?

He was the first person who had expressed any interest in

seeing me, but, even without a precedent, I knew I wasn't allowed visitors. Neither could I send anything through the post without censorship from either my mother or the solicitor. I may not have been the one in jail, but I still couldn't get bail.

I replied to my mother's subsequent twenty questions with shrugs and monosyllables, and left the letter lying around in triplicate on my kidney-shaped dressing table with its wrap-around mirrors, so she could read it and reassure herself that he was a harmless schoolboy. But when the house was deserted – my mother at work; my father in his greenhouse; whichever Agnes left to guard me, gone up the street getting milk – I rang the telephone number he had printed underneath his address. I kept hanging up at the sound of his mother's voice until, at last, he answered.

We managed a couple of snatched calls over the next month or so. When I told him I was leaving for Scarborough, he thought it was for the sea air. But, after I arrived at my aunt's house, there was no more need for secrecy. He began writing again, and this time I could answer.

I don't think we ever discussed anything more personal than musical preferences or books. I remembered he was a big Pink Floyd and early Bowie fan, whereas I liked Carole King and Roberta Flack. He was reading *Catcher in the Rye*, and I was spending most of my time in a parallel universe dipping sheep and being rescued by a man in a slouch hat called Tex. Well, that and flicking, reluctantly, through the pages of *Mother and Baby* – ironically, the twin aspects of my condition that I would never experience.

I failed to mention either.

He complained about his exams. I complained about my solitary revision, which was so dull it would bore the fillings out of your teeth. I never referred to the expanding waistband on my skirt, or the check-ups at the ante-natal clinic.

His father, the milkman, was proud of, and eagerly ambitious for, his clever son. Jamie was planning to go to Strathclyde

University to train as an engineer. I was planning to go to a home for unmarried mothers run by some sort of religious organization in York. In my mind the future was a picture, frozen like a film still, with me forever clutching a cardboard suitcase on the threshold of an imagined convent, like Maria in *The Sound of Music*.

He wanted to come to see me when school finished in July, but I knew that by then I would already be living with the sisters of perpetual disapproval. I couldn't let him see me swollen and pregnant, wearing my uncle's shirt like a smock. I therefore had to perfect the first of my unaided disappearing acts.

So I stopped writing.

Undaunted, he continued to send the letters every two or three days for a while. Then they dwindled to once a week, hitting the mat every Saturday, as regular as married sex.

But, even though I never replied, I couldn't resist reading them. In later years, I found it easier to give up smoking than it had been to ignore Jamie's letters.

And still, even as I packed the matinée jacket I had painstakingly knitted and a doll-sized nightdress supplied by my aunt into an Army and Navy holdall, they kept on coming. Finally, dread engulfed me every time my aunt passed me another pale cream envelope and they lay, unopened, collecting like grime, under my bed.

At the end of June I gathered the whole bundle of letters, both those I had read and those that remained sealed, all with the same embossed stamps and Jamie's clumsy cursive handwriting, ripped them in two and sent everything back in a jiffy bag – and of course, I never heard from him again.

He deserved better, so I gave it to him. I thought I was doing him a favour, but I don't suppose he saw it that way at the time. If I'd known then the torture of waiting for a letter like the postscript at the bottom of someone else's life, maybe I would have been kinder.

I often wondered what happened to him. He could be building

bridges with giant Meccano sets, or whatever it was that engineers did. He could have a bungalow in a scenic spot and a second home in Spain where he plays golf in the winter with his wife. Or maybe he's a tired, disillusioned man with a beer belly, his red hair bleached prematurely white, counting out his days in bubble packs of Atenalol and Amlidopine.

All I had left was the letter in my hands, the sole survivor of the purge, hidden, as it was, inside the copy of *Lorna Doone* in the cabin trunk in my mother's attic, and rescued when I put my mother into the home.

'So who was he – or is that information given out only on a need-to-know basis?' Francisco persisted sarcastically.

I groaned, feeling like a ping-pong ball, batted to and fro between the past and the present.

'Who?'

'The father of this prodigal child who's been trying to smoke you out for the past year? Damn it, do I have to screw this out of you? Agnes, can you even begin to imagine what I felt like when I found out?'

'I didn't want you to find out,' I said weakly. 'That's why I left.'

'Well, how kind of you to spare me. Am I to feel grateful? Should I congratulate you for your thoughtful consideration? Now I know. So cut the crap and tell me the rest.'

I took a deep breath. 'I got pregnant, I had a baby, it happens. What's to tell?'

'But you must have been very young, impossibly young.'

'I was fifteen.'

'Fifteen? But Agnes, you were still a child yourself. You were only a schoolgirl.' He didn't seem to be able to bring himself to believe it. 'And what about the father, who was he?'

Okay, I thought, you asked for it, you can have it: 'He was my teacher.'

'Your teacher?'

I thought I knew what shock looked like, but it had even more manifestations than I had imagined. Francisco's face went blank. It was like watching one of those toy slates that you draw on and then pull across to make the picture clear.

'In the name of God, Agnes.' Shock had kicked a Spanish cadence into his sentence. 'You were a child and you had an affair with your teacher?' I heard disgust mix with disbelief.

'I didn't have an affair with him.'

Francisco tapped his fingers and his knee jiggled, as if he were on edge, waiting for a starter's pistol to urge him into flight.

'But what happened?'

'You want the whole story, chapter and verse? You insist on knowing absolutely everything.' My words crested on a wave of annoyance. 'Fine, here it is. We were hitch-hiking home from a dance and he picked us up. He gave my friend and me a lift back home, except that he didn't take us home, he drove us to this place in the countryside, and he kept us there. And yes, I was a bloody schoolgirl.'

He cradled his head in his hands. The sudden weight on his elbow clattered a saucer aside and spilled an oil slick of tea across the bottom of one of my building society statements. I noticed he was wearing the same tattered jacket with the frayed sleeves he had on the last time I saw him. Both the shirt and the sweater he wore underneath were things I had bought for him, washed for him, folded for him, packed in a suitcase, laid in his dresser.

He gasped and almost reached for my hand before he thought better of it. He kneaded the stubble on his chin instead.

'And that's how I got pregnant.'

There was a moment after I had told the story that I could have had him back. I had his sympathy, and his horror, and of course the element of surprise. He softened. His eyes melted. His shoulders lost their rigidity. If I had stretched out and touched him, I believe, I think, I could have turned it all around, poured my heart out, put my coat on and gone straight back home to displace the girl from my bed in Plantation Road.

He was contrite, ashamed even, as though he were the one who had done something wrong, who had abandoned me in my time of need.

'But, Agnes, fuck, why didn't you tell me? All the time that we've been together. You never mentioned a word. Nobody did.'

I could see him roll back the years and reinterpret my family's distance, their reluctance to visit, their reticence, the silences, my disinterest in home, all of it seen through different eyes.

'Did everyone know?'

'I didn't tell anyone, Francisco. My mother didn't even tell my sister and brother until the baby was born. It was hushed up. You have no idea how much worse it would have made things. I haven't spoken to a soul about it, not a single person. I just wanted to forget it all.'

'But what about the baby? That isn't over and done with. The "baby" is six feet tall and eager to track you down. Don't you want to meet her? It must have been terrible giving up a child. Didn't you want to keep her?'

I checked his face for signs of insanity.

'Why would I? Of course I didn't want to keep it. I didn't want any memories of what had happened. I gave it away. That was the end of the story. Then suddenly, out of the blue, there's this person trying to claim me, wanting to come to see me, wanting to drag it all up again. But I don't want to be seen. Why do you think I took off when I did? I loved my wonderful, quiet, anonymous, nobody little life – our life, Francisco. I didn't walk out on it because I got out on the wrong side of the bed one day and fancied a change of scenery. I didn't want to tell you any of this. Things between us were bad enough.'

He began to protest: 'They weren't that bad . . .'

'Oh, come on, ple . . . ase, let's not pretend. It was awful. You hardly spoke to me. If I had set fire to myself, you would only have asked me to turn the heating down. You arranged your whole sabbatical without ever consulting me once. You went away to Colombia for three fucking months and left me behind

194

by myself because I was surplus to requirements. Tell me which part of this comes out of the happy marriage handbook? I knew that a long-lost kid turning up out of the blue would be the final straw. I panicked.'

'Yeah . . . you looked like you were panicking,' he scoffed, disbelievingly.

My eyes began to tear up: 'You don't know how much I missed you. When I first left, there wasn't a day that went past that I didn't wish I could turn back time and go home, do things differently. But I was scared. When the letter came, I just flipped. I could not go back over all that again. Not even with you. Especially not with you.'

'I thought you had left me for the man in London.'

I raised my eyebrows. 'I never met the man in London until I started working in his kitchen, and he was away most of the time. He thought I was a widow.'

Francisco recoiled.

'I had to say something to explain why I was walking around like a zombie. In the beginning, it was just a job.'

'In the beginning? And in the end?'

'In the end it wasn't just a job,' I admitted.

'Did you love him? Caroline described the two of you as a couple.'

'Oh, Christ, Francisco, I used him, okay? I used him to hide away, to stop being me for a while. I lied to him about everything. He didn't even know my real name.'

Even then, I still had him, just a fingertip away.

'But, Agnes' – Francisco's voice grew tender, the subject of Adam swept aside like old confetti on the steps of a church – 'why run away? You could have told me this. How much of a bastard do you think I am? Surely you knew that I would support you. I would have understood that you wanted to see your only child. We could never have any. This was your only chance.'

I ducked that one. There were other reasons for not being able to have children than the mere physical inability to conceive. I couldn't contemplate another pregnancy. Ever. Francisco hadn't begun to make vague noises about parenthood until I was in my early thirties but then, when nothing happened, we didn't discuss it. He never asked for a definition, I never spelled it out for him.

'I can't believe you didn't want to meet her,' he prodded again.

I closed my eyes and drew air into my lungs as if I were about to make a deep dive into a cold pool. He just wasn't getting it. As usual, he wasn't listening to a single word I said. It was like trying to explain algebra to a polar bear.

'But you aren't hearing me. I did not and still *don't* want to meet my only child. To say what? Hello, dear, ehm, your father was a dangerous nutter, and you were a horrible mistake. Nobody wanted you – not your grandparents, not me. I didn't even bother to give her a name. Do you think it's going to be three verses and a chorus of "The Mother and Child Reunion" with a full gospel choir and three-part harmony?'

He fell silent, thoughtful. 'I know it won't be easy,' he faltered.

Under-fucking-statement.

'Not only will it not be easy, but it won't be happening.'

'You could explain things.'

I gave him an impatient look. As though I hadn't gone over it in my mind a million times. 'There is no explanation. The whole point is that I can't explain . . . It's not only my secret to tell. Other people are involved. The adoptive parents, for instance . . . The real father. His new family.' I broke off. I was growing impatient. I knew what I knew. He didn't have all the details. 'It's not an academic treatise, you know. You can't just lay it out rationally in paragraphs and say – discuss. It's a mess.'

'I know, you want to spare the child's feelings . . .'

'No, I wanted to spare my own. It was my pregnancy, my baby, my child and my decision. Can't you accept that, just for once, this is about me?'

'But the girl . . . You don't want to upset her, I can see that.'

'Oh, the fucking girl, it's not about her. People got *damaged* here. I damaged them,' I said in a small voice.

'I understand. It must have been awful, unthinkable. But, Agnes, you couldn't help being . . .' He searched around for the right word, settling finally for the wrong one. He dropped his voice. 'It's not your fault you were raped.'

'Oh, Francisco.' I shook my head wearily, my own words a corresponding whisper. 'Who said he raped me?'

And that was the end of it. I saw the brief flicker of light in his eyes disappear. His grip loosened, and let go. Almost twenty years of my life slipped away, downstream on a fast current. The moment for reconciliation had passed. I could have grabbed it, but I didn't want to. The life I wanted back wasn't this one.

I collected up my papers and rolled them into the carrier bag I was still using as a holdall. I pleaded with him not to tell the girl where I was if she turned up looking for me and, eventually, he agreed. In any case, as he pointed out, he didn't know where I was. I hadn't told him.

He said he would get his lawyer to draw up a settlement of our property. I wasn't aware we had any. Lawyers or property. The house in Plantation Road was rented from the college, and everything else – the flat in Bogotá, the villa near Cartagena, the farm, the Manhattan townhouse, the Newport saltbox by the sea – belonged to him and his family. But he insisted I should have something to live on. I told him I had a new job and a flat, without mentioning that it was a back bedroom with an Ikea wardrobe and a single futon that dug its lumpy elbows into the small of my back, but he said it was only fair that I had half the assets. He asked if I wanted any of the furniture. I said no. He could give me whatever he thought was fair, or not. I was easy. 'Apparently,' he said.

'Are you still seeing that man – the one you were living with?' he asked.

'No, that's over.' I was proud of myself. I managed to get the words out evenly, without the crack in my heart rending the short sentence apart.

He nodded as if it was no less than he expected or I deserved, wrapped his scarf round his neck and clicked the lock on his now empty briefcase.

'I know that you've made it patently clear that it's none of my business, but I think you should definitely meet *your* child. You can't keep avoiding it just because it's uncomfortable. It will give you some sort of closure.'

Closure. What psychobabble planet was he on? Where was the self-help stuff coming from?

I didn't need any more closure. I just needed to be left the fuck alone.

He said goodbye, but disguised it in legal speak: 'I don't have your address, so get a lawyer – you will need one – and tell him to get in touch with mine.' He gave me a card with the name of a legal firm on Queen Street. 'How should I address you these days? Are you still Morales or McBride, or what was it you were calling yourself in that house? Loost? Liszt? Wagner? I can't keep up.'

'It was Lutz, but no – McBride will be fine.'

'Lutz. Where the hell did you come up with that?' He shook his head.

'I made it up,' I said to the nape of his neck, as he walked away.

'Ah, well, you're good at that,' he said to the carpet. His tired shoulders buckled inside the tweed jacket. I hoped the girl in Plantation Road would take better care of him than I had.

I sat for a second after he'd gone, trying to look calm, stirring the scum in a cup of cold tea as though I were two thoughts away from working out the rate at which the universe was expanding. But, inside, I felt like one of those characters in the computer game that Ned used to play, with a big bubble over my head that, instead of 'tired' or 'hungry', just said 'fucked' and flashed on and off, visible to anyone who cared to look.

23

By the end of February there was still no response to the letter I had sent Adam when I moved into homoeopathy hell in Acton. I couldn't use the phone in the house, and had no privacy at work. Too late it occurred to me do what the rest of the modern world did and get an email address. I was a little behind when it came to technology. Thank goodness the people in the practice were Luddites: their computer was almost as outdated as I was, their accounting program only a little more sophisticated than carving notches on a stick, and their appointment system a highly innovative method consisting of a large date book and a pencil.

Still, I was in no position to feel superior. I could use a word processor, but when it came to the information superhighway I was still trying to find the slip road out of the car park. I read manuals. I made mistakes. I spent more time making back-ups of my back-ups than I did originals. Eventually I compiled a database and mastered a simple layout in a desk-top publishing program in order to put together basic information sheets for our customers on each treatment. In time, I even managed a monthly newsletter that I sent to every client.

I discovered that what one of the younger partners (shiatsu and Swedish sports massage) called 'all that office bitchwork' was much more mind numbingly absorbing than cleaning had ever been, but, just like an anaesthetic, it wore off when you stopped topping it up. And for that there was vodka. I found the predictability of my daily routine to be comfortingly reliable. I was surrounded by people, but they stood off at a safe distance.

Jocelyn, my landlady, a quiet microscopic speck, not unlike the much distilled remedies she prescribed for her clients, crept quietly around the edges of my life. She ate tiny meals of boiled eggs and quartered tofu-paste sandwiches on flax-seed bread. She bought goat's milk in miniature cartons, and single-portion chicken breasts that lasted her two days and that she accompanied with a solitary boiled potato or one tomato sliced into four lewdly grinning quarters. She insistently invited me to join her at suppertime, until I had no choice but to surrender my allotted time in the kitchen and stop cooking altogether. I subsisted on bananas, instant noodles and chocolate. Only the crudeness of the sugar and salt cut through my indifference to flavour. I weighed no more than I had when I was a teenager. The muscles I had cut when swimming lengths mushed into marshmallows on my arms; the toned thighs, tensed from months of fucking, turned into string cheese; and then the fat melted away.

'You're getting terribly thin, Agnes,' she said one day when I passed her on my way to the kettle, where I meant to add hot water to my supper – Chinese noodles with extra monosodium glutamate and pink rinds the size of toenail parings that were supposed to be prawns. 'Are you feeling all right? You don't eat enough, you know,' she said, peering though her Eleanor Bron Jewfro. Ring, ring, I said to myself, as I smiled benignly in response. Pot here, is that you, kettle? Look, sorry, but I was just calling to tell you that you're black.

'I've never had much of an appetite,' I replied, when the answerphone in my head clicked off.

'Your asthma seems to be getting worse too.' She had noticed that I walked round with an inhaler more or less permanently attached to either my hand or my mouth, like a Sambutol chain smoker, but it didn't seem to have occurred to her that this had anything to do with the patina of cat hair and dust, not to mention her own free-flowing locks, that covered everything in the house.

'Allergies,' I explained.

'Well, you know, homoeopathy is ideal for that. I'll give you a free consultation if you want.'

Hmm, I thought, before declining, cleaning the house more

than once a decade might also be quite effective. I had enough of the belladonna inside me without adding to it in tincture.

But then Graham, the putty-faced nutritionist, joined the balanced-diet refrain and proffered several jars of supplements that he urged me to take with meals. I didn't ask 'what meals' as I thanked him profusely, and later I deposited them in the dustbins outside Kentucky Fried Chicken on Acton High Street while I was waiting for the bus home.

I resisted all further interference until Krishna, the Indian acupuncturist, newly arrived back from a five-year apprenticeship in Mumbai, took me aside after the Saturday-evening surgery and told me there was concern in the practice.

He was slender, brown and incredibly pretty, with dark-fringed eyes as rich as Nutella. I could imagine him naked – small and smooth and perfectly formed – but that was as far as I got: imagining. There was, I knew, no Mrs Krishna. He was single and lived alone. He had even asked me out to dinner once, but I refused. I didn't do dinner, and I didn't do Krishna. I looked, but I didn't touch. I kept my eyes on my appointment book and called out patients' names.

Until one night, as I was laying all my sharpened pencils out in nice straight lines, he drew a chair in front of my desk and sat on it expectantly. 'You work like a Trojan, Agnes, and we all appreciate it, but, you see, you're really not taking care of yourself.' His voice had a hypnotic rick-rack cadence to it. It made me feel like a child being bounced on someone's knee.

'Let me treat you,' he urged. I thought he meant another offer of chicken korma and poppadoms up at the Last Days of the Raj in Shepherd's Bush, and I was already shaking my head, but he went on. 'We'll get your Chi back in balance in no time, open your passages, get you breathing properly.' He gestured to the inhaler lying on my desk. 'One session, and then you see how you feel.'

I said that my Chi was just dandy and my passages best left closed, but nevertheless, at six o'clock the following Monday, when his last patient, Mrs Soloman (migraines), had left in a cloud of Chanel, I found myself lying on his couch like a cadaver waiting for an autopsy, wearing a pair of paper knickers and a white sheet while he took my pulse.

Well. What the hell, I figured. I'd already had the amalgam stripped from my fillings free of charge by an alarmed Jim Goldmann in the dental surgery when he gave me a complimentary check-up; what was the biggie about having Krishna acupuncture me?

He examined my tongue and told me I had too much heat, muttered something about spleen and liver, then he casually stuck needles into my scalp, my forehead, my earlobes and my kneecaps, until I felt as if I should be wearing white make-up and standing outside some teenage babysitter's window on Elm Street wearing a trilby and carrying an axe in my hand.

He lit a bunch of herbs that looked like a large joint and started heating the needles. Acrid white smoke billowed around me. I half expected him to start making wa-wa-wa war-cry sounds, and dance, keening around the table.

'Is this supposed to do anything?' I asked, the movement of my jaw making the pins in my scalp and brow wiggle. That hurt.

'Ssh,' he said, stroking my hand and giving it a squeeze, my skin the milk on his coffee-coloured fingers. He smelled of cedar and cinnamon. It sounds more romantic than it was. My only previous exposure to cedar had been in the form of moth balls in Gay's closet, and the wood in her shoe rack, but it was both compelling and awkward to be so close to a male body after such a long while.

'You relax,' he said, sitting down beside me and holding my hand. It was the unaccustomed intimacy that did it. Tears slid sideways out of my eyes and ran in channels through the crows' feet into a reservoir in each ear.

'Agnes, ah, yes – you're crying. Don't worry. You see, it's releasing all the negative energy. It will cleanse you.'

It'll take more than waving a large Silk Cut at a few hat pins to cleanse me, I thought. There's not enough Surf in the world. I didn't need someone torturing me by sticking needles into my flesh; I could manage that perfectly well by myself. But I didn't speak. I just let Lake Victoria bleed itself out while I lay flat on my back on a plastic massage table looking at the magnolia paint on the Artex-stippled ceiling. We would need to do something about that, I decided. You couldn't expect patients to feel positive when they were forced to look into the impasto of swirling bas-relief.

I can't say it did me any good. It just put me in touch with my inner misery, whose address I had been quite pleased to have misplaced. But I said thank you very much like a good girl who has been given a piece of birthday cake at a party, even though she doesn't like marzipan, and took heart from the fact that the other practitioners in the surgery seemed to heave a collective sigh of relief. Each stopped proffering his or her own particular brand of snake oil and backed off, satisfied that I had been taken in hand.

And, still, the postman never rang twice.

Yes, Francisco was as good as his word and sent me an offer via my newly acquired solicitor, a cousin of Krishna whom I had never met but who had an office in Southall. A foolscap envelope arrived by registered post containing a full inventory of our joint possessions, which I was required to sign in order to waive any further claim on our estate. An estate – huh. We had a three-bedroom terrace with a basement that belonged to Balfour College, hardly an estate. The document listed every painting, every print, every chair in the house on Plantation Road, which, in total, couldn't have amounted to more than £5,000 pounds, and that was taking into account the new washer-dryer I had bought the previous spring.

I felt enormously sad reading the inventory. I could still close my eyes and walk through each room in the house, from the basement to the garret. I could recite from memory the shop in which we had bought each cushion and document the strata of the wallpaper on the bedroom wall; I knew the history of every single chipped plate, dragged back from various corners of the globe, set out on the dresser. I could plot the story of my marriage in the lines and checks of Francisco's flannel shirts hanging up in his wardrobe. And now I had the final page of the story, with everything drawn up into a balance sheet, and its very small sum underlined.

But if our possessions were worth nothing, I also discovered that Francisco had invested more than half his salary ever since we met, and that, furthermore, his trust fund was more generous than I had realized. I knew we had savings, but nothing had prepared me for this. Apparently Francisco had kept some secrets of his own: he was, to be blunt, rolling in money like a pig in shit. I was stunned by the figure at the bottom of the printout. My share of the spoils would be £500,000, payable whenever I wanted it. He had started the ball rolling on that too: irreconcilable differences. Fair enough – better than pathological liar and serial adultery. Once again, I was urged to indicate my acceptance and to have it witnessed and notarized before returning it in the enclosed stamped self-addressed envelope. He hadn't planned this overnight, I realized. The settlement had been in the pipeline for quite some time.

With half a million pounds in my bank account, I knew I would be free. I didn't have to stay in London, living in a threesome with a chest of drawers called Narks and a bedside table called Fluck.

I could go . . . well, anywhere.

I could retrain, go to college, study animal husbandry or move to Brighton. I could even travel the world. I could visit Maisie.

Or Geordie.

I could go to the States and visit Karl.

This time I could disappear properly.

But what about Adam?

Of course he never contacted me. He never responded to my letter, never called and never turned up, either on a white charger or in a black cab. I suppose I hadn't really expected that he would, but that frail hope that he might, just, one day, might be there in the Volvo, sitting outside the house when I turned the corner, kept me going until the anguish of waiting, longing, dreaming and continual disappointment obliterated it like Domestos does germs.

Why would he bother? I knew he had been in love with me, but we had no history, no family, no past, nothing but sex and hastily eaten pot roasts to hold us together – just a relationship built on lies and Marigold Bouillon Mix.

I rang his house from a call box once, but got only a mechanized voice on an answering machine that had obviously moved in when I moved out. I wondered if perhaps he and Gay had reconciled, and so I telephoned her flat in Vauxhall at 7 a.m. from the dental surgery courtesy of Mr Goldmann. Her voice, as sharp and fruity as fermenting pears, piped down the line. I hung up.

Easter was early that year. The practice closed. Mr Goldmann went windsurfing – I know, I was surprised too. You wouldn't think it to look at him, weedy little thing that he was. The divorcee went home to her widowed mother in Dorset. The cat was, thank you, God, placed in a carrying case and transported with her on the back seat of her 2CV. Touchingly, she invited me along, having twigged, by this point in my sad and lonely life, that I had no family and no friends. Krishna wondered if I wanted to go with him to visit another of his tribe of cousins in Wolverhampton, Graham told me that he and his wife would be delighted if I would join them for a vegan lunch on Easter Sunday. To each I said I had plans, which I did. I was happy to have the first weekend off in months and also to have the house, or, more importantly, the bathroom, to myself. In view of my soon-to-arrive riches, I had splurged on some bubble bath from Superdrug, and had decided to push the boat out and buy my food at three times the price from Marks & Spencer. I then planned to heat it up in the verboten microwave that my landlady used to keep her bread in.

Whoooo hooo, spring break.

On Friday I sat in the garden to soak up the first few consumptive rays of sun that the year had just coughed up, and ate luxury-recipe baked beans straight from the can (low salt – defeats the fucking object, I say). On Saturday I had toast and peanut butter and, thus fortified, put on the by now grossly bloated black nylon skin of Lennie's coat and went to Notting Hill Gate, where I mingled with the tourists in the market on Portobello Road. It was strange being back. Strange and not altogether comfortable. The same frenetic mix of glitz and sleaze, garbage in the gutters, tarnished silver on the stalls. I felt as though I were having the hair repeatedly waxed off my chest as I walked through the familiar streets. Everything was the same, except for me. I wasn't here any more.

I forced myself to wait through three cups of watery black tea in a ludicrously expensive café before I allowed myself a ten-minute detour along Holland Crescent, past the house. I stood at the bus stop, a few hundred yards away from No. 22, wishing Adam would walk out of the door. Even Lennie would have been a welcome sight. But the door remained closed, the house glassy-eyed and withdrawn, like something that had long been abandoned, and not loved much when it had been occupied. Even the evergreen plants in the window box had withered and died and not even a dandelion shoot reached for the light through the littered soil. The shutters on the dining room were pulled together. The lids on the dustbins outside the basement flat were upturned and pooled with water and dead leaves.

I toyed with the idea of knocking on the door. I even crossed the road and went as far as to put my foot on the bottom step, but then retreated. Gay might *once* have answered the phone in her flat, but that didn't mean she wasn't here now, or that he didn't have another woman who spent the night and shared his breakfast. If Francisco could manage to install an Agnes 2 before the interval, then it was certainly possible for Adam to have his own sequel during the second act.

The bus heaved itself up the hill. I let three go past before I had to admit defeat and board one. It was Easter after all. I couldn't see Adam's car parked near by. He was probably away, somewhere warm, with the children, or his new girlfriend, or even Gay. The thought made me ill.

To fight the nausea, I went home and ate a family-sized bar of Cadbury's Whole Nut; I nibbled around all the hazelnuts and threw them into the waste disposal to feed the rats rules be damned. Mr Goldmann had warned me about crunching down on anything too hard with my new white fillings. It was a pity he hadn't given me a similar warning about men.

What a fool I was. I was behaving just like a lovesick teenager, hanging around outside the house of the boy du jour, hoping for a glimpse. Just like Kirsty and I had done with Dan Ponti, the bastard. The Lucky Bastard. I bet he was still running the café – almost forty now, married to some harridan, with a couple of kids with Italian names and Scottish accents, serving Parmesan and pesto with his chips and tiramisu-flavoured ice cream.

I went to bed, giving the futon the kick I usually reserved for the cat, which insisted on sleeping on my bed, and tossed and turned on the flimsy Scandinavian pine bed long into the night.

That was it. Exactly. A lovesick teenager. It had taken me long enough – one illegitimate child, two getaways, one husband and too many bad bedfellows – before finally I scored my first proper fully reciprocated boyfriend. Pity it had taken me thirty-seven years to get there. Pity I had to fuck it up.

By Monday I was longing for Tuesday, and the welcome siren call of two hours spent vacuuming and swabbing floors in the dental surgery. It was almost enough to make me roll up my sleeves and tackle the hallway at home. Almost but not quite. I didn't want to send myself into anaphylactic shock.

I checked the paper and decided to go to the Tate. I had no interest in any of the exhibits but the journey alone would take the best part of two hours there and back. I took the bus from

Acton down to Hammersmith but was in no hurry to catch the tube. I window shopped as I ambled down the street towards the Broadway and made a loop through the backstreets, looking in other people's windows, imagining their lives the way I had once done when I first moved to Oxford and coveted coupledom as though it were a kingdom for ever denied me.

I crossed the street to avoid a group of people standing on the pavement beside a large streamlined coach that was just pulling away from the kerb. It was full of girls waving hysterically at their parents, who waved back with determined cheerfulness. Even as they drifted back to the empty stomachs of their Range Rovers and SUVs, their eyes still followed the back of the disappearing bus.

I could see a pair of open gates with a red-brick gabled building behind. A school trip, I decided. Lucky girls. Some of the women hung around chatting animatedly to each other, toddlers forked against their hips. The women were all so well groomed and beautiful, backlit by money. Lucky them. I stepped out into the road, and looked to the right to see if it was clear to cross, but traffic streamed out of the school gates. I stepped back and pressed the button at the traffic lights and waited for the green man to clear my path.

A dark blue boxy estate car drew out of a driveway and nosed towards the junction. I waited for it to slow and stop as the signal beeped peremptorily, impatient for me to cross. Then I looked again, and hastily clutched around in the depths of my pocket, reaching for my inhaler while my lungs clenched like fat girl's thighs around my windpipe. It was Adam's car. And there was Adam, alone at the wheel, staring at the traffic lights, his fingernails tapping out a tattoo on the dashboard.

Every time I walked home from work and turned the corner of my street, I held my breath and imagined this car parked outside my house. And every day I turned the corner and saw the driveway empty. But finally, here it was. In Hammersmith, where, I suddenly remembered, Lennie went to school. This school? It must be. She had taken the tube every morning from Ladbroke Grove. Maybe she had been on that bus.

His eyes flickered away from the light and caught mine. Without thinking I lifted my fingers in a feeble greeting. But, when he saw me, his expression told me everything I needed to know. Alarm, distaste, embarrassment, fear even. And yet, still I stood there, not believing the sworn evidence of my own eyes. I might have said his name. I heard something come out of my mouth, several times; my two hands joined in an ineffectual wave until my palms pressed together beseechingly like one of those gypsy women who pull at your sleeve and beg for money on the tube.

His lips moved mutely, his head shook from side to side. His skin looked patchy, like marbled paper in sickly colours; he had bags under his eyes. His hair was rumpled and unkempt. Rain coursed down across the windscreen, the glass misted from the inside, his silent words hitting the window. I could see the shape of 'no' through the beads of water.

The insistent beeping of the pedestrian crossing rang in my ears like the engaged tone on a colossal telephone and then stopped abruptly. The lights changed from red to orange to green, but he sat with his hands clenched on the wheel, looking at me, until a car behind sounded its horn, and hastily he put the car into gear and drove off.

I turned and watched him. He slowed beside the group of mothers on the pavement. My heart bounced and stuttered against my chest like pennies dropped from a great height. He was going to stop. He was going to come back. I took one step forward until I saw a waving figure detach itself from the crowd. Gay's metallic white head bent and opened the car door, her compact body jackknifed inside, and the last of my hope slipped away like water down the drain.

Stupid, stupid, stupid, I berated myself. He probably thought I had followed him there, that I had been waiting for him, that I was stalking him. I remembered sitting for twenty minutes on a ledge at the bus stop two days earlier. He might have seen me there, hanging around like a bad smell that you just can't air out.

I felt drab and grubby and pathetic – wheedling for scraps like a refugee with a baby in a bundle of rags.

I didn't go to the gallery. I turned and went home. It was only when I let myself into the house that I realized my coat was dry. There were no damp footprints on the sea grass carpeting. My hair wasn't wet. It hadn't been raining. I had only imagined it.

I finished my Easter egg and heated up some solidified sodium that claimed to be luxury beef consommé with sherry. I drank three inches of the Smirnoff with flat Diet Coke, and another inch straight up with an ice cube. When my landlady arrived home with the feline Helen Keller and offered me a piece of her mother's lemon pound cake, I pleaded a headache and went to my room with William Boyd.

The next morning I didn't go in to work. I stayed in bed and pretended to sleep. I didn't bother watching out for the postman.

He wasn't coming.

Nobody was ever coming.

24

And that's how I ended up here. Sitting in a black leather chair that looks like a chess piece and makes me feel like No. 6 in *The Prisoner*, while No. 2 sits across from me trying to look impassive, but not always managing. I can usually get a laugh out of him if I try, but I can't be fagged most of the time. I don't feel that funny.

His name is Irshad, and, unlikely as it seems, given that they have nothing in common except skin colour, he comes highly recommended by Krishna, who arranged the appointments. I would have expected to have had my nervous breakdown subcontracted out to another member of his extended family, but, being all dry lawyers and accountants, here the Indian mafia failed him. Instead he had to resort to that good old standby: word of mouth. One of his patients had taken her daughter to Irshad for treatment for anorexia, and so, when they realized I obviously wasn't eating but hadn't a clue what the root of my problem was, Irshad seemed as good a starting point as any.

I could have told them I didn't have an eating disorder. I had a waking disorder. I was finally cashing in on my sleep debt and had retreated to a semiconscious world where life ticked over nicely without me, and I slept.

I called in sick for the whole week after I saw Adam in the street, most of which was spent in bed with the yellow blinds casting a jaundiced light on the walls, while I floated in the shadows being visited by hybrids of the longed for and the long dead. I simply didn't want to wake up.

I knew Adam was gone, but I dreamed of him, sometimes entreating me to go back, at other times screaming at me to go away. Both left me weeping when sleep departed.

I had a photograph of him, cut from a copy of the *Bookseller* when one of his authors won the Booker Prize. Every now and again I took it out and looked at it, but it wasn't the same as the one in my head, with his crumpled smile, his generosity, his nervous laugh and the smell of his skin all mixed up together. It was his Adamness that I summoned forth to comfort and taunt me.

But still I knew he was gone, as I had known from the beginning he would be. I had just nursed the hope that he might return, like a sleeping baby in a spare arm, while I got on with the business of life.

When I dreamed of him, though, he came back. I saw him as he was in life, and heard his voice, and felt his touch, and had another chance to make things right.

So, no, I didn't want to wake up.

But Krishna and Jocelyn had other ideas. They called a doctor, a real one, then dragged me off to Harley Street and threatened me with needles and potions in eye-droppers and boiled Chinese herbs that smelled of halitosis and wet dogs. I was touched by how much they cared, but I really agreed only because the effort of moving out of Jocelyn's house and finding another place where I could pine in peace was beyond me.

But Irshad is okay, I suppose. I see him twice a week, every week, whether I like it or not. Krishna claims he's very good. I take his word for it and hope his judgement with shrinks is better than with hat pins. I do feel a bit better, though, and it can't be the happy pills my GP gave me because I flush them down the lavatory every morning with the homoeopathic tea.

Irshad's a rather solemn, low-key man, like a professional mourner at a funeral with no corpse who's very, very sorry all the time. He does this steeple thing with his hands, and I feel he might try to sell me a casket or ask me to pick out a floral arrangement. He's also big and broad, with the physique of a rugby player. His hair is a slippery sort of Grecian 2000 black, and he has blindingly white teeth that jump out of his ash-brown face. He always wears grey cords and either a charcoal-coloured jumper or another in the shade of something that was once beige but put in the dark wash by mistake. No wedding ring. I asked him once why his clothes look like a uniform, but he just said, 'What makes you think it's a uniform? Is that what you do, 'gnes – wear a uniform?'

He does that a lot – hits the ball right back at you, leaving you stumbling, wrong-footed, trying to pick it up. I've never been much good at ball games. Anyway, I suspect it's to keep the 'space', as he calls it, contiguous and neutral, so his patients remain calm.

'Analysand, not patient,' he corrects. Sounds like something you put in your hair to keep your fringe out of your face. That's one of the things that gets a smile, but then he asks, 'Do you always use humour in a difficult situation?'

He speaks with a clipped S'th 'fricken accent, that is, when he speaks at all, which isn't often. He mostly lets me ramble Vogonically on and on about the past. If I go quiet for too long, he asks me if I've had any dreams, so I usually keep talking. I don't want to talk about Adam, and anyway, now that he has stopped his nocturnal visits, my dreams are so dull that I answer emails in them. Sometimes I write stuff on my hand to prompt my memory, just to keep things rolling. If he's noticed, he hasn't said. I can't believe he's interested in listening to people recount the second most boring thing in the world, but I suppose he thinks I'm going to let something revealing slip on the royal road to the unconscious. But I'm not.

Irshad always manages to make me feel as though I'm walking around with my dress tucked into my pants, an awkwardness caused by the fact that he is really quite good-looking in a Bollywood sort of way. He has this slightly superior expression, as if he's indulging you, but is willing to be patient until you stop messing around. It's as if he knows what you're thinking. Well, hell, he does: you pay him to listen while you *tell* him what you're thinking. He's not as pretty as Krishna, but he has more of a presence, despite his attempt to seem ordinary so as to put us pathetic, drooling patients at our ease. He has the body of someone who's been enlarged to the point of distortion, so that the line of his nearly square jaw and the angle of his almost straight nose are just a little bit off. In my other life I would probably have slept with him by now. Oh, I know it's unprofessional, but when did I ever let that stop me? In fact I would probably have slept with both of them, he and Krisha; hell, I'd have thrown in Mr Goldmann, the dentist, on a three-for-two special offer.

I might have told him this in one of the sessions if it hadn't sounded a bit presumptuous, as if it were a boast of my powers of attraction rather than just my default setting. But what I would have done in the old days isn't relevant any more. Times have changed.

There had only been one man since I left Adam. A one-night stand when I was working at the hotel, a surfer on his way to the west coast of Scotland where, unbelievably, he was going to brave the waves. I thought that I could take a small maintenance dose of him, to get me through the night, but the minute he touched me I started to cry – always an effective libido booster, I find. Poor soul lost his erection and jumped off me as though I'd put a rat on his back. But it wasn't what he had done that made me weep, or who he was. It was who he wasn't. For the first time I found I couldn't just wipe out the memory of the last man with the next one. So why bother?

Now I don't even take all my clothes off to go to bed, I feel so cold all the time. I think sex must be one of those things that requires your inner thermostat to be set on high. My boiler just doesn't fire any more.

This is my fifth visit. Krishna drops me right at the door, then I take the tube back. It's fucking expensive: falling to pieces doesn't come cheap. He's giving me a discount because of my low earnings – he doesn't know I'm half a millionaire – and the practice picks up a small percentage of the cost. I should add that my attendance was a collective, not elective, decision. The partners said it was a condition of my continued employment. It's not good for the image of the Wellness Industry if the receptionist is barking and hasn't changed her clothes for a week. But I don't mind. It's like going to the hairdresser's but not having to talk about your holidays. It's not too bad.

However, the pockmarked anaglyphic wallpaper: now that *is* bad. And I'm not keen on the furniture, which is bulky and dark and has a lot of straight lines and corners, with nothing soft to rest your eyes on. Even the couch looks as hard as a ship's biscuit. You can just see the faint indentation on the pillow where the last person laid their head. But I don't lie. Well, not on the bed. I sit on the chair and try to look him in the eye.

The first time I came he said he thought he should probably refer me on to a woman. He said he had a colleague who might suit me, but I told him, no thanks, and that I didn't get on with women.

'That's precisely why you should see one,' he replied. But I had already resigned myself to him. So I stayed.

I think we're more or less up to date on My Life So Far. We've covered the absolute basics in the teenage pregnancy scandal – broad strokes, I think you'd say. I haven't told him any details, just that the father was a teacher at my school. Then we did Francisco, Adam, Mother, Geordie, and inked in the background of Gideon, Silvano, Karl, Ali and the other member of the International Brigade of Bedfellows, at least enough for him to get the idea. Some of their names I can't quite remember. I started to make a list, but it appalled me. Especially when I began writing things like 'boy from the King's Arms'.

'Why do you think you've been involved with so many men?' he asked today.

I was startled. There was a cobweb in the corner above the door. It had been there since my first visit. Didn't anyone ever clean in here? His certificates were in frames on the wall behind his head. A spider plant sprouted untidily on a shelf.

'I don't know,' I replied. 'It just happened. They were there.'

'You seem to think that you don't play any part at all in the progress of your own life, 'gnes,' he said, snipping off the first syllable off my name as if it were the dead bloom on an ugly flower. 'You don't take responsibility for the outcome. It all "just happens".'

I was rather taken aback. First, by the unaccustomed speech, which was more than I had heard him say in weeks; and secondly by the criticism.

'But it does. I didn't ask to get pregnant at fifteen; you can hardly blame me for that.'

He spoke softly, but his words fell on me like concrete dominoes, one after the other. 'Of course not. I'm not blaming you for anything; I'm asking you to see how your own actions impact on your life. Yes, you had a child when you were still a child yourself in some ways, and the father was someone who was in a position of trust, who should have protected you, not taken advantage of you. I know the circumstances were very painful, but you have to remember that you didn't do anything bad or shameful. Teenagers have been having babies since time began. In some cultures children are married at this age. I know, I know' – he waved away my objections – 'it's not something to condone, but there is no shame attached to the act of giving birth to a child. You can't let it inform every single thing that happens for the rest of your days.'

I tried very hard to keep my face impassive.

'What I'm asking you to consider is that after your child was born, you ran. When your daughter came looking for you, you ran. When your husband came looking for you, you ran. When things became difficult with Adam, you ran. When are you going to turn around and face your demons? Are you going to go on feeling like a victim for ever?'

I was stung. Now, *now*, he turns into Chatty Cathy, and it's so he can have a go at me.

'Thanks.'

'You see, you're being a victim now. Why are you thanking

me for saying something that obviously upsets you? If you don't like what I'm saying, tell me so. Tell me to fuck off. Don't hold back. I'm not going to run away.'

'Well, then, fuck off. Aren't you supposed to be supportive and sympathetic?'

'I'm supposed to help you. I'm not going to help you much by sitting here and saying, "There, there, poor you." Of course you deserve compassion and understanding, but, 'gnes, you have to look at the way you react to these events. There's no prince coming along to rescue you. You have to do it for yourself, so you can move on with your life.'

I couldn't speak. My chest was tight, but it wasn't because of the asthma. The box of tissues on the side table was wavering in front of my eyes, but I'd be fucked if I was going to give him the satisfaction of weeping. A little pink wisp of paper protruded gaily from the serrated oval mouth, taunting me. What a frivolous colour. How could he expect people to mop up their guts with a sheet of bubblegum-pink tissue?

'What do you suggest?' I said coldly.

'It's not my job to make suggestions. Ask yourself where you want to go and see if there is something you can do to take yourself there.'

'I can hardly force someone to talk to me if they don't want to. Is that what you want me to do?'

'I assume you mean Adam?'

I nodded.

'Is that what you want to do?'

Jesus, I was getting tired of this. It was like one of those games you play where you have to answer every question with another.

'Of course not. He knew where I was if he wanted to find me. He obviously didn't. When I saw him, he drove away.'

'You knew where he was. Look at it from his point of view. You'd been living there for – what – six months?'

'Seven.'

'Living there under an assumed name and he'd fallen in love

217

with you, or this person he thought you were, then pow – your supposedly dead husband walks in. Don't you think the onus was on you to make sure your voice, your explanations, your apologies, were heard?'

'He didn't want to hear.'

'You know that for sure?'

I swallowed, mentally hissed at the tissues to piss off and nodded again.

'Well, fine, so you just have to accept it and move on.'

Silence.

'What about your daughter? Are you going to treat her the same way? You know where to find her, but you've made no attempt to contact her. Do you see that she could be forgiven for making the same assumptions about you that you're making about Adam?'

'But it's true – I don't want to see her. I would rather eat my own liver than speak to her. I have absolutely nothing to say to her.' I was going to get this printed on cards and start handing it out to people. 'Anyway, there's nothing good I *can* say to her.'

'How do you work that one out?'

'I don't want to go over the past – I don't want to have to tell her about . . . all that old crap,' I finished weakly.

'You could start by telling me.'

I can't.

'Okay, when you're ready. But you could still think about seeing your daughter. You only have to say whatever you feel comfortable talking about. Just as you do here.'

'I suppose,' I said.

Yes, right, I thought.

I sniffed and looked back at the corner where the cobweb hung suspended from the ceiling like a loop of saliva. Maybe it was like one of those dream-catchers, but for misery. God knows the wallpaper looked saturated with the stuff.

'I don't think she's looking for me any more, so it doesn't really matter.'

I waited for his response. It was his turn, but there was nothing.

Silence expanded to fill the room like the brown-paper bags I used to blow up as a child just for the joy of hearing them bang when I slapped them. I felt as if I were suffocating, as if the quiet were absorbing all the oxygen in the room and then, at last, Irshad coughed, the bag burst, and I could breathe again.

'Excuse me,' he said, clearing his throat. He watched me very carefully, as if I might implode and leave nothing but a pile of scorched bones on his Eames chair. Maybe that's what the ashtray's for: incinerated patients that he's pushed too far.

'Obviously it matters or you wouldn't be here . . . What are you afraid of?'

'Letting it out and then not being able to push it back in again.' I sighed. 'You know, it's like I've been sitting on it all these years, hidden under a trapdoor, but if I stand up and move aside, it will just – erupt, uncontrollably.'

'And do you think you can go on suppressing it? This could be a safe place for you to examine these difficult feelings. Then you could walk out and leave them here. Pick them up again when you feel able.'

'That's the theory,' I said to him.

'That's the theory,' he agreed. 'You've been walking out and leaving things behind your whole life. Why not do it here, where it might actually help you?'

I stole a look at his face. He was still wearing his fire-extinguisher-at-the-ready expression.

And so I thought, oh what the hell, I might as well give him a controlled explosion.

I gripped the sides of the chair.

25

I didn't want to get out of the car, but he just stood there in the open doorway, beckoning. Kirsty had gone inside. So, eventually, I had no choice but to unglue myself from the back seat and follow.

My face throbbed with every step. I longed to go home. I couldn't care less about what sort of trouble I would get into. This was worse.

I stumbled across the threshold. There was a little porch, hardly big enough for the two of us to squeeze into. There was another internal door. He steered me through, with a pat that was almost a push, and then pulled the front door closed behind us.

Inside there were only a few pieces of furniture, but it was bright as day. A long fluorescent strip light was suspended from the ceiling, dripping coils of electric cable like fat white worms across the bare floorboards. The beams were exposed, sandwiched with wadding that spilled out like horsehair from an old sofa. The walls were bare. In some places there was striped wallpaper with dainty Dutch girls carrying milk pails at jaunty angles and clogging gaily up the Delft-blue bands; in others there was plaster, pink as new skin.

'I'm doing it up. It needs to be gutted, but I'll have to wait for the better weather before I do the structural stuff,' he said, smiling awkwardly at the strain of talking to us as though we were proper people, not kids at school, then urging us to sit down. 'I camped here in the summer, but now I've moved back into my flat. It's a bit basic for the cold weather.'

Kirsty was already comfortable on the couch with a perky look in her eyes. Gloss had been applied to her lips. She was combing her hair with her fingers – I noticed she had taken out her ponytail

– and had crossed her legs. She was bouncing the top one, pointing her toe.

That left me the armchair, which even in my bloodied, grimy state I hesitated to occupy. It was worn and greasy with continental stains across the arms and seat.

'Aye, sorry it's not the Ritz, girls,' he said.

I perched. He went into a lean-to at the back, and I heard water gushing out of a tap and hitting the aluminium of a kettle. Gas hissed, and he made tea, while, behind his back, I made worried faces at Kirsty. She gave me a shrug of impatience and told me to shut up havering. We'd have the tea and I could clean myself up, then we'd go home, she whispered. Her mother would be comatose by now. She'd never miss us.

'Mr Anderson,' she piped up, 'can Aggie use your bathroom?'

'Call me Bill,' he said. 'We're not at school now.'

'Bill!' mouthed Kirsty with delight.

In answer to her question Mr Anderson handed me a chipped enamel bowl full of steaming water.

'There isn't really a bathroom as such. At the back' – he gestured with his head – 'there's a toilet and a sink, but no hot water. You'll get a towel in there too.'

'Oh, Bill,' she giggled. 'That's my dad's name,' I heard Kirsty say as I opened first the wrong door, which led to some closeted stairs, and then the right one, leading to a tiny toilet.

'There's no light,' I called, flicking the switch uselessly.

'No, the place isn't all wired up yet,' he answered.

I washed as best as I could with the door ajar. My face looked like a butcher's block in the small cracked mirror that hung askew above the chipped sink. When I closed the door to pee, it was like being in a coffin. The window was bricked up and the only light came from the rim around the door frame.

Kirsty was drinking whisky from a floral mug when I came back. I knew she hated whisky. She was just showing off for the teacher.

'It's good for shock,' he said, offering me some.

'I don't like it, so no thanks.'

'Look, I'll put it in your tea, it'll do you good.' He spooned in a few sugars, no milk. I sipped it reluctantly. It tasted rancid, but it was sweet and warm. I drank it anyway. It was a bit like the drinks my mother made when I had a cold.

'So you've been out on the razzle, then,' he said. He was sitting next to Kirsty. A bit too close, I thought. His body was turned towards her, and she practically had to prise herself away in order to face him when she was speaking.

'Aye, Bill,' she said carefully through a pert little smile. 'Our Agnes here got in the middle of a gang fight in some lassie's house. Anything to be the centre of attention, eh, Ag?' She lifted her eyebrows the way you do when you're talking about a baby that's not very cute. But I didn't have time to respond. The tea was making me gag. I rushed back into the toilet and retched again.

'Shut the door, Agnes,' she yelped. 'That's chronic, listening to that puking.' When I didn't move, she got up and did it herself, leaving me in the dark, where I hung over the side of the bowl, threading my hair behind my ears.

I could hear their voices burbling through the door, but the banging in my head drowned them out.

The water was tepid. I used the last of it to wash my face. There was a sliver of Imperial Leather; the sharp deodorized smell of it clung to my skin. I even rinsed out the inside of my mouth, replacing the acid taste with the sour tang of soap. I spat bubbles into the sink.

I got halfway across the room before my knees hit the floor for the second time that evening.

'Has she been drinking?' asked the teacher. They both jumped up and tried to get me back on my feet, but I could hardly stand.

'Leave me,' I whimpered.

'Are you sure she hasn't been drinking?' he asked again.

'Maybe,' Kirsty said airily, though she knew I hadn't had more than a couple of swigs of cider.

'She needs to lie down,' he said. 'There's a bed upstairs. Come on, give me a hand to get her up there.'

'But I want to go home. I don't feel well.'

'You canny go back to my house like this, Agnes, so go and lie down until you feel better,' ordered Kirsty.

I managed to walk up the short flight of stairs and fell upon the bed. It was no more than a mattress with a pillow and tartan blanket on the top, but I closed my eyes gratefully. I couldn't fight the overwhelming desire to throw myself into the black.

I felt as if I had only just closed my eyes when Kirsty started pulling at me and pummelling my shoulders. It was as though there was a steel weight on my head. I could hardly lift it from the bed. Kirsty was shaking me and shaking me, her earlier arch flirtatiousness replaced by panic.

She was crouched over me on the mattress.

'Wake up, wake up, come awn . . . Agnes . . .' The toe of her boot kicked me hard on my hip. I squealed.

She reeked of whisky. I barked at her to leave me alone, but she just dug her fingers into my shoulders and shook harder, giving me another hard kick.

We were in the dark, but there was enough light from the single skylight window in the roof to light the room. I could see the rim of the moon and a few stars, like sparks from a fire.

'He's away and left us here,' she sobbed, throwing her soft, podgy arms around me and clinging to my chest through the blanket.

'How are we going to get home?'

I forced myself fully awake and told her not to worry. There was no problem, we could just walk. I told her that I was feeling better, which was a lie, but I would have said anything to reassure her. She was scaring me. Kirsty was supposed to be the one who knew everything and now she was carrying on like a daft bairn.

'But he's left us. I came up here to get you and then I heard his car. When I went back downstairs, it was all in darkness. He put the lights off. Why would he do that?' she whimpered in a small, needy voice.

'We'll put them back on. Come on.' I tried to push her arms away from me. It was like being in a straitjacket. 'Put the light on in here and we'll see what we're doing.'

'Dinnie be stupid, Agnes, there's no light.' She was almost screeching, but she was right. I looked around the room and saw no dangling cord, no light switch, only the burned-down stubs of a few candles, an ashtray – or at least a tobacco tin that had been used as an ashtray – and bits and pieces of timber and plaster-board, a tin of paint, some bales of roof insulation.

'Look, we'll light the candles, then. Where are your matches?'

'Downstairs, in my pocket.'

'Well, go and get them.'

'No, it's too dark, I'm feart. Come with me.'

I held her hand and raised myself up. The floor came up to meet me as I stood, but I took a few breaths and steadied my feet. 'Come on, we can see where we're going; let's get the matches, sort ourselves out and get out of here. What time is it?' I looked at my watch in the moonlight. It had stopped and the face was cracked, but I knew I must have been asleep for hours. I'd never been out this late in my life.

I picked up one of the candle stubs and led the way, holding Kirsty with one hand and feeling the way with the other as we descended down the dark pothole of the stairwell. The door at the bottom pushed open easily, but Kirsty wasn't exaggerating. It was pitch black.

I edged round the side of the room, probing until I felt curtains, which I tugged opened with a flourish, only to stand there perplexed when the room grew no brighter.

'There's no window,' I said.

Kirsty started sobbing again.

'Don't get into a paddy – calm yourself. Just stand for a minute and our eyes will get used to it. There's a wee bit of light coming in from the stairs.' I put my arm round her and sure enough after

224

a few seconds I could make out the dark humps of the furniture, then the outline of the table, littered with mugs and papers.

'Where did you leave your coat?'

'Over there,' she said, though I couldn't see where she was pointing. I walked over and flailed at the sofa.

'Why did you take it off, anyway? It's freezing in here.'

This sent her sobs into a crescendo. 'He made me. He yanked it off. He tried to get my jumper off as well. He's a dirty pig.'

'What?' I couldn't believe it. She probably stripped it off herself so she could flaunt her chest at him.

'He jumped on me. Tried to get his hands under my clothes and everything. I thought he was nice. I thought he liked me. I mean, he's a teacher. He's not supposed to be like *that*.' Her words degenerated into wails. 'That's when I came to get you, but you just wouldnie wake up and then I heard the door shutting.'

I had found a bundle that felt like her jacket and gave it a shake. I heard the welcome rattle of matches, pulled the box out of her pocket and sparked one.

The room flared into focus. 'Gimme the candle,' I said, and lit the stub. I sat down, holding it between my thumb and forefinger, yelping as hot wax ran over my hand.

The effort had tired me. My feet were cold. I realized I'd need my shoes before we could go. They must still be upstairs. I asked Kirsty to go up and get them, but she was afraid. She wouldn't leave me. Once again, we crocodiled up the narrow staircase, picked up my sandals and went back downstairs, where I wedged them on. They hurt. The straps pinched the blisters they had branded into my feet.

'Look, if I'm going to walk I'll need to do something about my feet. Give me a minute.' I started looking around downstairs for something I could wrap around the peeling skin, while Kirsty, gaining courage, let go of my hand.

'Put the big light on,' I instructed. She played at blind man's buff in the shadows and eventually found the light switch, but when she pressed it nothing happened. 'It doesnae work,' she said unnecessarily.

I was impatient. I stumbled over to the front door, listing three inches to the side with one sandal on, the other in my hand, and fumbled with the handle. 'Just open the fucking door then, and let the light in.'

But the handle didn't move.

'Shit, it's stuck.' I banged it with my hip, forgetting my bruises, and yelped with pain. 'Don't just stand there, help me push it.'

Her little face was like a torn piece of paper in the glow of the candlelight. 'Ha, you look like Caspar the scary ghost,' I said, trying to lighten the atmosphere, and it worked in as much as she snapped at me to fucking shut up. But pissed off was at least better than petrified.

I counted to three and we both leaned on the door. It didn't budge.

Kirsty's voice was like a spent match, just before the flame gutters out. 'I think he's locked us in,' she said.

'Give the girl a coconut,' I said under my breath.

I started shouting at her. 'Why did you let him leave and lock the bloody door? Where was your brain? You're always that busy showing off.'

'He was horrible to me. Called me names. I didn't know he was going to leave us here, did I?'

'What happened to "yes, Bill, no, Bill"?' I muttered. But there was no point in arguing. We would have to try to figure out what to do.

It was a long night. All the windows downstairs were boarded up. The ones in the kitchenette and the bathroom were filled with bricks. The skylight wouldn't open from the inside, and the door was locked. We found two new candles in a box in the kitchenette, but to save our meagre supply we sat upstairs huddled on the bed waiting for it to get light. We both slept on and off, our ears straining for the noise of a car, but when the sun turned its 40w lamp on in the morning there was still no sign of him.

We went downstairs to make tea. The stove worked on Calor gas, so we could at least have a hot drink, but Kirsty was frightened we would set fire to the place and not be able to get out, and she stood there watching the kettle boil with a bucket of water in her hands. I tried to rationalize that we were more likely to suffocate on the fumes than incinerate ourselves because there was nothing to set fire to, but she was teetering on the edge, even then.

We were starving. There was nothing to eat, and the day crawled backwards through the hours, but nobody came.

Maybe he was never coming back, said Kirsty, and we would die here, locked up for ever. But I told her not to be daft, that he wouldn't want two skeletons to explain away when his builders turned up to put on the new roof.

She didn't think it was funny. Neither did I. I didn't even think it was very likely. We could sit here and rot. He could dig a big hole and drop us into it and no one would be any the wiser. But when I thought like that, panic squeezed the air out of my lungs and stole my voice. Kirsty was freaking out enough for both of us.

When the sun went down, we sat there alone in the glow of a candle. And then it started to snow. That's when I felt the first waves of terror. With the snow covering our only source of natural light, we would be entombed inside the house. I kept tapping on the skylight, trying to stop it settling, until Kirsty told me to stop. If you break it we'll get the snow in here and freeze to death, she said.

Of course, then it occurred to us. We could knock the glass out and climb on to the roof.

'Not in six inches of snow, we couldn't; we'd slip and fall and be dead anyway,' said Kirsty. 'He'll come back; he probably forgot he locked us in and thinks we'll just put our coats on and leave when we're ready. He was a bit drunk; I bet he just wasn't thinking straight.'

I agreed. But I was supposed to have swimming practice with him today. He could hardly fail to notice that I was missing.

'But he'll just think you're not well.'

'My mother will be going mental,' I said, picturing her at home, wondering why I hadn't come back from Kirsty's house before it was dark and then going up to see where I was.

'My mother is mental anyway.'

'But she'll notice you're not there in the morning.'

'Aye, but what will she do? She'll try calling my dad, and he's away golfing.'

'But he'll come back when she tells him, won't he?'

'What the fuck do I know, Agnes? Anyway, she won't leave the house till he's back.'

'Surely she'll call the police?'

'Not without telling my dad first. She won't put the kettle on unless my dad okays it. She might think I got up and went out again.'

We sat on the bed drinking tea as the night filled with snow. We had just lit the second candle when we heard the hum of an engine. We nearly knocked each other over in our haste to get back downstairs, with Kirsty shouting at me, telling me not to drop it, not to start a fire.

Two keys turned in two locks, there was a click and then the light came on, almost blinding us. Another lock turned, and Mr Anderson walked into the room with a couple of bags. He stamped snow off his shoes, and said as coolly as if he had invited us for the weekend and we had turned up early: 'Ah, you're still here, then. I nearly couldn't get back. The snow has the road blocked and the ploughs don't do these wee back lanes till last.'

Kirsty shouted at him: 'We could hardly be anywhere else, could we? You fucking locked us in – in the dark.' She ran to the door, opened it and went into the porch, where she rattled uselessly on the outer door. 'You've locked it again. I'm going to get the police on you – you pervert. What do you think you're playing at? Let us go. My dad will kill you.'

'Sssh.' I held her arm, tried to hold her back when she started slapping at him. 'Calm down. He's hardly going to let us out if you start threatening him. Be nice,' I whispered into her hair. I stroked her arm through the coat and held her in a tight cuddle.

'Come on, we need to get home now, can you open the door, Mr Anderson? Our folks will be worried,' I said linking arms with Kirsty, both of us clutching our handbags.

'Girls, you're not going anywhere in this weather. You're snowed in,' he said, not lifting his eyes from the plastic bag that he was slowly unpacking in the back kitchen.

'No, we'll manage. They're probably out looking for us; just open the door.'

'Nobody's looking for you,' he said quietly.

Kirsty started crying, as she looked at me in horror.

So I tried a different tack. I begged. 'I promise that we'll say nothing. Just that we got lost and let ourselves in here out of the snow. Nobody even needs to know that you even saw us.'

'I'm telling. After what he tried to do to me.'

He laughed. 'Oh, you're telling,' he mimicked in a sing-song voice. 'Are you not a wee bit old to be running crying to your mummy and daddy? Do you think anybody's going to believe you? Two lassies looking like that –' he nodded at Kirsty's low-cut t-shirt – 'you're old enough to know what you're doing; you're not weans. What are you going to say to convince anyone different?'

'You locked us in – you attacked me.'

'Oh, did I? And how can you prove that? You've been throwing yourself at me for weeks – sitting down next to me at school in that little skimpy swimsuit – and now you're all coy. There're words for girls like you.'

'I never did,' she said.

'Oh, shut up,' I screamed at her. 'You're making it worse.' We were both crying, but for different reasons. She was mad. I was worried. I could see that he wasn't bothered either way. He was crouched on the sofa, having carried the contents of his Co-op bags into the sitting room. He'd brought a sliced loaf and cheese, a bottle of milk. There were biscuits. Some bananas. 'I thought

229

you might be hungry,' he said, smiling his funny smile. It was as if he didn't think he had done anything wrong. As if this was – well – normal.

I looked at the food. I was so desperate to eat something I would have done tricks for it, rolled over, played dead, given him a paw.

But Kirsty was defiant. She snarled that she wouldn't touch his filthy food, and neither would Agnes, daring me to say different. But I had my own ideas. 'I'm starving, thanks,' I said quietly, wiping away my tears. And I sat down next to him and folded two sheets of processed cheese into a soft slice of Mother's Pride and ate it. He poured milk into a mug, first throwing the inch of cold tea that was still in it on to the floorboards, where it soaked away in seconds. I hated milk, but I gulped it down. He looked questioningly at Kirsty, but she told him to go fuck himself.

'Okay, princess,' he said, 'suit yourself.' He poured himself a glass of whisky and started to roll a cigarette as he watched me eat. He took a couple of draws and passed it to me when I'd finished the sandwich. I puffed on it, and coughed. It tasted vile.

'No, don't blow the smoke out, keep it in your lungs. You don't get the effect otherwise.'

'I don't want any effect,' I replied, worried again.

'Don't smoke it, Agnes, it's wacky backy. He's trying to drug you.'

'Kirsty, sit down and shut up. Stop being so melodramatic,' I spluttered through a cough, but I passed the cigarette back to him and shook my head the next time he offered it.

'Now then,' he said, putting his hand on my trousers, which were filthy with mud and blood from my fall the night before, 'you go back up to your bed, hen. Me and the princess were having a nice wee chat last night, and we need to pick up where we left off.'

Kirsty begged me not to go. 'Don't leave me, Agnes, you promised.' He turned and gave me a look, then petted my cheek.

His eyes were a bit glassy. I thought – maybe he's stoned, maybe he'll fall asleep if he keeps drinking.

'It's all right, don't worry. I'll not go.' I turned towards him. 'Mr Anderson . . .' I began.

'Bill, darlin'. I keep telling you we're not at school now.'

'Okay, Bill.' His name tasted worse than the soap, worse than the cigarette, but it came out of my bruised lips like a kiss. 'Let Kirsty alone. Let her go up to her bed. I'll stay with you.'

Kirsty punched me on the arm. 'What are you doing? I told you what he was like with me.'

'Never mind, just go. I'll be fine. Don't worry about me – wait up the stairs.' I pushed her away. 'Go on. Go up and shut the door.'

'But it's dark up there,' she whimpered. 'I dinnae want to be up there by myself.'

'Go up the bloody stairs, Kirsty, and take the candles.'

This time she didn't argue, but started weeping and snivelling as she stumbled up the stairs. I could hear her heels clumping through the floor.

Though why she thought she had anything to girn about, I don't know. I wasn't upset. Everything was fine. There was absolutely no need to get myself in a state. Not after my lip started to bleed and he let me do something else.

Then all I had to do was lie there.

26

'Are you okay? Would you like a glass of water?' Irshad's skin has gone from ash to silver-birch. I think he's the one who needs a drink, not me.

I nod, defiantly.

Of course I'm okay, I want to snap at him. It's not the first time I've heard the story. I lived it.

'I'm afraid our time's up for today,' he said gently, as though he were calling in a pedal boat on a pleasure lake rather than stopping me halfway through my big finale. 'But we can talk more about this next time.' He pats me on the shoulder as he sees me out, and we walk past the other anonymous doors with their discreet brass plaques to the arthritic lift at the end of the hall.

Hurriedly, I replace the demon on a high shelf at the back of my mind, and leave it there to deal with later. It'll keep. It's kept this long.

'You know, 'gnes, if you feel you need to talk to me before we meet you can always call me. Leave a message, I check them regularly. I'll call you back. Any time, day or night,' he says as the lift arrives and I slide back the metal grid that threatens to snap off my fingers in its mesh teeth.

I look at him as though he's a bit slow and thinks I need a note pinned to my lapel to remind me where I live. 'I said I'm okay,' I snap, but inside I feel relief. I haven't had anyone to call on for a long while. I want to collapse against him, but I keep my head high and my spine rigid as the lift whirs and chatters manically and I sink through the floor.

I walk tall all the way up to Euston Road, where I buy a packet of gum and chew piece after piece, spitting each out on to the pavement the moment the sugar is gone. I buy a *Standard* that I don't read and stride on, perfectly composed, until I get to Baker Street. For some reason I always cry when I get to Baker Street Station. I don't know why. It's not the worst station on the Hammersmith and City Line. Royal Oak – now that's what I call a shit underground station. Westbourne Park's pretty dreadful as well, but – no – it's always Baker Street.

I wipe the tears as covertly as I can and stare at my reflection in the empty carriage window all the way to the Broadway. Every time the train lurches my face expands and contracts, my nostrils gaping like they've been devoured by some flesh-eating disease, my eyes and mouth converging into jagged lines on a television with bad vertical hold. There's another upside-down Agnes coming out of my head like a Siamese twin, who curls up across the roof until the glass stops her at chest height. Our hair stretches apart glutinously, as though the two heads have been stuck together with my chewed-out chewing gum, then flick back together into one broad forehead.

When I bend to rise out of my seat, I finally separate my head and pull away from her, leaving the reflection hanging there, ready to attach itself on to the next person.

27

Over the next weeks Jocelyn and I graduated to the intimacy of a shared mid-morning beverage, during which she read aloud articles from *Holistic Health* and I counted backwards from five hundred before excusing myself.

This morning I had returned from Jim Goldmann's surgery to find a brochure for the Royal Albert Hall laid out next to Jocelyn's plate of toast, the bread pocked and freckled with grain like an old man's back. My stomach sank when I saw its twin on my side of the table. The high polyunsaturated fat spread glooped ominously in a lake of jauntily coloured plastic.

I sat down while Jocelyn splashed hot water over the tea bag in my cup. I had lost the war on white bread, but I had won the battle of the PG Tips. There was a franked letter waiting for me from John, Singh & Choudry, which I regarded with some trepidation.

Irshad was right. I couldn't go on hiding for ever. When I called Francisco to tell him what to do with the few personal possessions I had left in storage at Balfour, he mentioned that the girl had rung him again, wondering if he had heard from me. He didn't like lying to her, he said, and so had given her the address of my solicitors. They had already had a letter from her. Whether I liked it or not, I was going to have to confront my past. I discussed it with Mr Singh, who reminded me that I wasn't under any obligation to meet with her if I didn't want to. He suggested that he should reply saying that, at this time, I did not wish to have any contact with her.

'It's brutal, but it's better to be clear,' he said in his toffee-flavoured voice, managing to make it sound as if I would be doing her a kindness.

I opened the envelope and shook out the enclosure. It was an invoice. I read the total at the bottom and tossed it aside with a deep sigh. Legal anonymity did not come cheap, but it was worth it. It was worth it to have this bloody thing settled once and for all. My attention focused on a stray cat hair curled in the sugar bowl.

I picked it out gingerly.

'It's frightfully bad for you, you know,' said Jocelyn, as, fully satisfied the sugar had been dehaired, I added a large spoonful of it to my tea.

'What, cat hair? I know. It's a terrible allergen.'

'No, *sugar*,' she said with distaste, as though she should be throwing salt over her shoulder to deflect bad luck, except that salt wasn't allowed either.

I made no comment, but kept on stirring, then separated the scalloped edges of the torn envelope and stared, over-attentively, at the enclosed letter.

'. . . really, little more than refined poison. It's the first thing I advise my clients against.' Jocelyn was driving home her point with a Black & Decker. 'Sugar *and* alcohol,' she added pointedly. 'Especially spirits.'

I began to wonder if I could get Mr Singh to threaten Jocelyn with a gagging order.

'Sugar, alcohol, caffeine, wheat, hydrogenated oil . . .' She completed her litany of toxins and began to examine her brochure. 'Mmn . . . oh' – a small squeak of pleasure – 'Shostakovich, *Suite on Poems* . . .' she murmured, placing a little tick in biro beside a column. 'That's on Thursday, 20 July. Would you like to go, Agnes? You could leave work early.'

Months away. Who was that organized? I consulted my empty mental diary and hurriedly shook my head. I didn't want to think much further ahead than the next appointment with Irshad, and about Shostakovich I didn't want to think at all.

'What about György Ligeti, that sounds interesting, don't you think? Monday, the 24th. That's a lunchtime concert. You could have a late start.'

Another tick was added.

I started to count, 499, 498, while dropping crumbs of bread on the floor for the cat, which was dozing under the table. They skipped, unseen, within inches of its nose.

We skipped, tick-less, through Mozart, Vivaldi and Haydn, which would have been more to my taste. I prodded the cat, trying to draw its opaque eyes to the food, but it was blind, not dim-witted. 483, 482, 481.

'Oh, silly me. I forgot to tell you. You had a phone call. Not more than half an hour ago.'

I looked up from the still somnolent cat. The telephone ban had also been relaxed of late, so that Irshad and I could keep in touch.

'It was a man. He left his number.'

'Was it Irshad changing a session?' I asked, slightly petulantly. I needed to know these things so I could prepare myself. I had grown used to the routine.

'It might have been, but it didn't *sound* like him.' Jocelyn looked around her, twitching her tiny nose, great fronds of dense curly hair undulating around her face like a giant sea sponge, then reached behind her to where a row of numerals was printed in minute, homoeopathic handwriting on the top sheet of her *Road Less Travelled* thought-for-the-day calendar that was still on the page for 17 February – *If an act is not one of work or courage, then it is not an act of love.*

It had been a long time since anyone had called either of us.

'Please use the phone. It's a local number.'

I took the opportunity to push a piece of toast into the waste disposal under the pretext of rinsing out my cup, then went into her sitting room, where I dutifully stooped to dial. Using the phone was one thing; sitting down on her ironed slip covers quite another.

I didn't recognize the area code, but Irshad practised all over London and had an office in the Tavistock, in north London. He might have been calling from there.

The phone rang three times before being answered, tersely, by a bored male voice that sounded nothing like Irshad, or his giddy Cockney secretary.

'Yup, Davenport, here. Can I help you?' the voice said, just as Jocelyn slipped her head around the door and whispered with the exaggerated mouth shapes of a signer for the deaf: 'I *think* he said his name was Adam.'

Meanwhile, in my ear, despite my overwhelming disbelief, Adam Davenport repeated his name and had growled hello, twice, increasingly crossly.

I was mute with astonishment, too surprised to register either excitement or dread.

'It's Agnes,' I finally croaked, before realizing my mistake. 'I mean, Edith,' I muttered after a cringing pause.

'Ah . . .' There was the muffled sound of a hand held over the receiver. Voices. Then more Adam. 'Sorry about that; someone in the office.'

'That's okay.'

I could hear him gulp while he obviously searched for something to say. 'Um, this is awkward,' he managed finally.

I began to answer and then realized I was holding my breath. I inhaled hurriedly. 'Yes,' I agreed. 'I hope I'm not disturbing you, but I had a message that you called. Maybe there was some mistake?'

'No, no mistake, I did call you, it's just, well, it's just, em, good of you to call back . . . You well?'

'Enough,' I answered, holding my breath again for the uncomfortably long second of throat clearing that followed on the other end of the line.

'Erm, Ed, Ag . . .' he began before abandoning all attempts to name me. 'I've . . . I've been meaning to get in touch, and I'm sorry it has taken me so long, it's just that I wanted to apologize. When I saw you last month on the street and I didn't stop . . . well, I couldn't stop. But, even so, it was shabby, really. Unforgivably rude.'

'No, not at all.'

'No, it was. No excuses, but it's only that it was the worst possible day of days, and I felt terrible about it . . . But then it was the London Book Fair and after that I went to South Africa, and the weeks *vanished*, and it seemed too late to contact you, but I decided I simply couldn't let any more time go past . . .' He took a breath, as did I. A long, fluttering sigh of relief.

'Look, do you think we could meet? It's better than discussing things on the phone.'

'Yes,' I agreed again.

'What about lunch today, tomorrow, any day this week? You could come here to South Ken, to the office. I mean, not *to* the office, but to Bibendum, or Quai St Pierre. Racine.' He was tossing restaurants all over the place like a card shark, trying to dazzle me. 'Anywhere you like.'

'I have to be at work at two o'clock.'

'Oh. Yes, of course, I wasn't thinking. Where are you? I mean, where do you work? Which part of London?'

'Chiswick,' I replied, postally promoting myself to a better area.

'Well, I shall come to you. Today okay? There's a very nice French place in Devonshire Road, La Trompette, do you know it?'

I didn't even know where Devonshire Road was, but if he had asked me to trek to Machu Picchu, I would have been there by half past twelve. I agreed, and he hung up.

I held the phone to my ear, listening to the dial tone, afraid to break the connection.

My knees were trembling uncontrollably. I pulled my old cardigan around my bones and sank on to the arm of the nearest chair, dislodging the cat, which had followed me in. A small flurry of dander puffed into the air, accompanied by furious mewling. I was still sitting there, wheezing, absent-mindedly, when Jocelyn came back, handed me my inhaler and led me, very gently, back into the kitchen, casting a wary eye over her hopelessly crumpled embroidered arm covers.

'I'll make you a nice cup of tea. Valerian tea,' she said. 'Very good for shock. Very soothing. Calms the nerves.' She put her arm around me and patted me. 'I hope it wasn't bad news, Agnes?' she inquired, handing me a cup of pale straw-coloured liquid.

'No, not at all,' I said, smiling.

The tea tasted like horse's pee. Very tranquil horse's pee, but I drank it gratefully.

And then I put my arms around her and kissed her.

28

Jeans. I had gone down a size. They fell to my hips. I shrugged, sticking a safety pin in the back of the waistband. Hipsters were fashionable.

Hair. There was nothing I could do about that except wash it, brush it or wear a hat. I didn't have a hat so I would have to put my faith in shampoo. I stuck my head under the tap and lathered up.

Shirt. It wasn't quite warm enough for short sleeves, being only early May. 'Never cast a clout till May is out' was my mother's old maxim, but she didn't have to go to lunch in a smart restaurant with a coat that threatened to hoist me aloft like a barrage balloon in a high wind. I put on a t-shirt, 99p from Tesco, and wore a short-sleeved Indian cotton shirt on top, which I tied under my bust to hide the fact that it was two sizes too large.

Sweater. I picked the bobbles off Gay's ancient cashmere jumper, used sticky tape to remove the cat hairs and looped it round my neck like a Ralph Lauren ad, Acton-style.

I was overly layered but at least it padded me out.

I shaved, I filed, I pumiced, I moisturized. I dried my hair flat and spat on the wand of a dried-up mascara to spike up my eyelashes, and then I walked to the restaurant, resisting the urge to run all the way there.

Even with three unnecessary detours and a visit to the building society to withdraw money, I arrived twenty minutes early, loitering in the small forecourt surrounded by bay trees and a knee-high box hedge, trying to look innocuous. The whole way there I thought of reasons why he should want to see me. I didn't dare to think it was of the 'I can't live without you' variety, but I allowed myself the luxury of an 'I thought we should clear the air'.

What I hadn't expected was 'I think you'll find this more or less covers what I owe you', accompanied by a cheque, pushed across the table in a discreet white envelope.

Adam had also arrived early and was, even then, sitting on a banquette on the far side of the restaurant, leafing through a manuscript. It was one of those aggressively smart places, all chrome and black leather, like a French housewife at an S & M party, with round white-swathed tables arranged in rigid lines in the middle of the room like holes on a board of solitaire. I pegged across the room towards him. He stood up as I approached but made no move to touch me. He looked ghastly. Ghastly and wonderful. His hair jumped in unruly curls from his forehead. His eyes squinted and blinked behind the magic-marker rectangles of his heavy-framed glasses, his beautiful smile was held at bay, pinned down by long lines, tethered from his nose to his chin.

I dragged my eyes from his face to the cheque, as though a reporter from the *News of the World* would appear with a flashbulb should I dare to touch it.

'You don't owe me anything. I'm not taking it.' I had sat down, but was still gripping my handbag in my lap with two hands, as if it were a boisterous dachshund awaiting only a moment's inattention to bound away.

'Well, it's yours. You left without your wages, and I should have paid you some notice. I left it blank because I didn't know who to make it out to.'

I picked it up and ripped it in two. 'Don't insult me. I feel sick about what happened. If there's any debt here, it's entirely mine.' My voice quavered like Jocelyn's version of Lotte Lenya in the shower. 'In any case, you didn't need to come and meet me for this. You could have sent it to me.'

'I didn't have your address.'

'You did. I sent you a note. In February.'

He shook his head. His curls bobbed frantically, like a sea of drowning swimmers. I longed to catch them, smooth them down. I couldn't take my eyes off his lips.

An unctuous waiter with a comedy French accent appeared and asked us if we wanted to order. The rough-trade menus, with steel studs bolted into their leather spines, clenched their secrets at the side of the table. We hadn't opened them.

'We'll wait,' Adam replied curtly. The waiter nodded and attempted to pour more water into our glasses before he noticed they were already brimming.

'I didn't get any note.'

'I sent it to the house. With my address in Acton and my telephone number.'

'I thought you said Chiswick.'

'It's Acton.'

He made a face that, right there, will tell you why people lie about their postcode. He unfurled and furled his napkin, leaving it like an unlicked Rizla on his side plate.

'I can't understand what happened to it. February, you said? There was only Lennie in the house. I got a new cleaner to come in a couple of days a week to keep an eye on her. But she wouldn't . . .'

I agreed. Lennie would be more likely to steam open the letter and read it than to throw it away. I knew who would, but there seemed little point in voicing it. It didn't matter.

'So how did you get my phone number?'

'From your husband.'

I was amazed. 'But I didn't tell him.' I had even given the practice as my address on the divorce papers so he wouldn't know where I had gone.

Adam looked shamefaced. 'I got Caroline to call him. She made some excuse about having borrowed something from you that she needed to return. But when I rang the number he gave her, a man answered the phone. An Indian chap, I think. I thought for one awful moment you were living with him. But then he said you worked there and gave me the number of the house.'

Fucking Krishna. I loved him.

'It was Caroline who told me you hadn't gone back to your husband. I assumed you had.'

'No, that wasn't ever going to happen. When I left him, it was for good.'

'Lennie and Ned both miss you. They kept asking me why you had left and wondered why you hadn't been in touch. I hope you don't mind, but I told them that you had had a family emergency, and had to go away very suddenly.'

I nodded my head in assent, the all too familiar lash of shame landing on my back.

'Lennie often talks about you. Asked me why I didn't go after you.'

Lennie. Unexpectedly, my heart softened, the way prunes do when you soak them in Armagnac.

'How is she?'

'She looks like a streetwalker, acts like a diva, sulks like a baby. Calls me "daddy fucking dearest". Even in front of my 79-year-old mother.'

I smiled. Yep, even steeped in fine French brandy, they're still prunes.

'That's nice.'

'What? That she curses in front of your mother?'

'No, that you're smiling.'

'I don't do it often. It's bad for the complexion. Gives you wrinkles. According to Lennie,' I added.

Inspector Clousseau returned, this time with tiny bread rolls and a pair of silver sugar tongs. We waved him away.

I asked about Ned. He was fine. There were a few football stories, something about a trip to Australia that Adam wasn't keen on him taking.

'Adam,' I began, when we had finished playing family Cluedo. 'I didn't get a chance to explain anything, to really tell you how sorry I am, how sorry I was.'

'I didn't let you, did I? Throwing you out in the middle of the night like some kind of Victorian tyrant. I did try to find you. I went through the dustbins looking for anything you might have left with an address on it, but everything was gone. I drove around London in the car half the day.'

'You did?'

'I did.'

'Anyway, you didn't throw me out. I left.'

'You have to have the last word, don't you?'

I smiled again.

'It's so fucking wonderful to see you. I can't believe you're really here. That day. It was nightmarish. Gay and I had been screaming at each other all morning. Then we had to put a bit of a face on it for Lennie – she went on a school trip to Chamonix, skiing – and then, after months of wishing, *praying*, that I would get the chance to see you again, there you were, like a vision, at the side of the road, and I couldn't stop. It was like the whole universe was conspiring against me.'

'I wanted to run after you, but then I saw Gay get into the car. I thought you were back together.'

'God, no. She's got a new chap. In television. Only thirty-two. Robert Frost – like the poet but no relation, I'm sure. He and Gay make quite the couple.'

He laughed easily. 'He does those reality talent show thingies that Lennie loves. She's delirious of course, thinks all her birthdays have come at once. He's also worth a fortune, but Gay still feels I should be subsidizing and satisfying her every whim. They were planning on hiring a yacht in Cannes for the film festival this summer, and she wanted me to pay half while Tricky Rickie paid the rest. So we were battling it out, all tight-lipped and heavy innuendo, then just straightforward yelling, and there you were. God, but I felt like a total bastard. You were crying. And you looked like shit.'

'Compliments, compliments. I can see why you're in publishing, you have such a way with words.' I laughed, or thought

I did, but tears began running down my face and into the hollow of my throat.

'Oh, don't cry, please, I'm sorry. You still don't look well. You've got so thin. You haven't been taking care of yourself. You look pretty, beautiful, fantastic, unfuckingbelievably wonderful, but not yourself. Don't cry.' He stroked my hand, leaving little burn marks under his fingertips.

'I've been ill. Nothing serious. Just flu. Bad flu. But you don't look so hot either. What's your excuse?' I held his hand for a second, then pulled it away when the temptation to press it to my face became too strong.

'Divorce. Bad divorce, but all better now.'

The waiter hovered again. 'Can I get you a glass of wine?' he asked.

'Wine?' Adam offered. I shook my head, giving my face a quick swipe with the napkin.

'I've had that too,' I said.

'What?'

'Divorce, but not a bad one. Very civil. Not unlike this, actually.' I nodded at the torn envelope. 'But I didn't rip his cheque up.'

'So it is over?'

'I'm just waiting for the absolute.'

'I'm glad. I mean, I . . . well, you know what I mean, don't you?'

I did.

His hand was lying flat on top of the menus, and he moved as though to pass me one, but I stopped him, laying my hand on his. I remembered the first time I touched him, in the kitchen at Holland Crescent. Our eyes met.

'There's such a lot to talk about, to tell you, to explain, I'm not even sure I can,' I said.

'Edie, I don't want to hear it. Not any of it. I don't care. I've missed you,' he said.

And I was back.

He was wearing a pale blue shirt and a tie, slightly loosened at the neck, a dark suit. Office clothes. The sort I used to peel off him, night after night. They would smell of his shower gel, and peppermint shaving cream, and other people's cigarettes. I couldn't stop myself from touching him. I moved my hand to his face, to his cheek, to his collar, stroked the knot of his tie, ran my fingers over the silky material.

'Are you really hungry?' I asked.

'I couldn't eat a thing.'

He reached for his wallet, from which he withdrew a fifty-pound note, tossing it on to the table.

'What about the manuscript?', I asked as we reached the door. It was still on the table, underneath the two halves of the envelope.

'Oh, forget it. I don't even know what it is. I haven't *had* to read a manuscript for work in years. I do admin, for God's sake, sales forecasts, flow fucking charts and spreadsheets. I just grabbed it off the slush pile so I would have something to hide behind.'

I should have felt some remorse for the unfortunate author. But, who am I kidding, I didn't give a damn.

29

Adam wanted me to move back into Holland Crescent immediately, but I was cautious. I kept my job at the practice, despite
failing to turn up for work at all that afternoon, but I stopped
working weekends.

I also said goodbye to Mr Goldmann, who gave me a box of
floss, a bottle of mouthwash and a year's supply of toothbrushes
as a farewell present. I don't quite know if he was trying to tell
me something, but I left with the offer of free check-ups for life,
so possibly I didn't have the full ring of confidence that I thought
I had.

In all other respects, my life went on pretty much as it had
done before, but with sex: glowing skin, scraps of underwear in
apricot silk bags (touchingly, two sizes too large for the more
luscious woman Adam thought me, rather than the wraith I had
become), white burgundy instead of vodka and *pesche al dolcetto*
from Carluccio's which we ate with our fingers in bed.

During the next week Adam picked me up every night after
work, purportedly to take me out for supper, though we never
once made it to a restaurant. When Lennie went to Paris with
her mother, we spent three days in the Mandarin Oriental in
Knightsbridge without getting out of bed except to answer the
door to a man with a tray in his hand, or to run a bath.

I had urged him not to tell his children that we were back
together. I didn't want them to know there was anything between
us until I was sure that there really was, but he insisted. And the
sky didn't fall, nor did the children do more than shrug with
possibly more embarrassment than they would have done if he'd
told them he had syphilis.

Irshad had spread his palms in an I-told-you-so fashion and

smiled as though he had arranged it all for me himself. I was gaining a little weight and my bones were padding out with contentment.

There wasn't a single cloud on my happy-ever-after horizon as I sauntered home on a Monday morning from Adam's house to drop my bag off at Jocelyn's before going in to work. A black cab dropped me at the end of the road, and I almost sang as I swept along the street. I was so carried away with my own remembered carnal pleasures, running blue movies through my head, that I had my key in my hand before I noticed that there was someone sitting on the doorstep.

It's funny how the weather can change from sun to storm in the blink of an eye.

A girl was leaning against Jocelyn's porch, stripping the withered, rust-ringed leaves from a rotting geranium in the pot by the door. Her two large feet, shod in clunky, all-terrain sandals that looked as though they should have had monster wheels, were planted on either side of the path.

She didn't need to introduce herself, but she did anyway. She leaped up at my approach, wiping the dust off her bottom with one hand and clutching a hefty knapsack with the other.

'Hello, I'm Cheryl, Cherry Dawson,' she said.

The demon had just climbed down from the shelf. Not the most fiendish of Satan's handmaidens, I thought at the time, but pretty hellish, nevertheless.

Of course I knew who she was. I would have recognized her anywhere. As Francisco had said, it was as if someone had drawn me on her face – but slightly off. She wasn't as skinny as I had been when I was her age, or indeed as I was now; nor did she have the same inbred undernourished look from centuries of bad diet and no sun. Her body was broader, bulkier, exercised; but she had the sharp nose, the papery McBride skin, only photocopied with too much ink. She was dark like Bill Anderson and toasted a hardy golden backpacker's brown. She also had his thick dark hair scrawled untidily around the flush of high colour on her cheeks, and his straight unwavering eyes, grey, like flints.

Those eyes made me shudder. It was like being kicked back in time.

'I couldn't wait to see you, so I just turned up. I spoke to your flatmate Jossy-something yesterday on the phone and said I was coming, but she doesn't seem to be in,' she said, as I stood there, wishing I could rewind the tape, get myself back to the end of the road and stop before I got to the garden gate.

'But . . .' Nothing else came out. It took all my resolve not to turn on my heel and flee. I thought of Irshad's words. Oh fuck off, I thought. Fuck off all of you.

'I know I should have written to you again. But I didn't think you'd mind.' She explained that the adoption agency had told her there was a procedure. They had warned her to be careful because some mothers don't want to be found; that they may have made new lives for themselves with partners and second families who had no idea of the child's existence.

'But that isn't us, is it? You wanted to see me, or you wouldn't have got in touch.'

'But I only got in touch to say that I wasn't ready to meet you yet,' I stammered. 'You did read the letter, didn't you?'

'Yeah, but *you* contacted *me*. It was only ever going to be a matter of time before we met.' The grey eyes held mine, daring me to contradict her. 'I've been looking for you for such a long time. I registered with the adoption people last year and got a copy of my real birth certificate before I went to India. It was like a dream come true when I finally got yours.'

'My solicitor's,' I corrected.

'And so I was sitting at work on Friday, thinking about it, and I said to myself, why wait, just get yourself on a train, Cheryl.'

She had a dry Yorkshire accent, her vowels so flat they could have been ironed by one of the huge industrial pressing machines I had threaded with sheets in the Earl's Court hotel.

'I just took myself off to the station early this morning and here I am.' She paused. 'And here you are. Finally,' she said delightedly, as though a royal herald were about to appear and sound the march triumphant

I supposed some form of welcome greeting was in order, but while I hesitated, trying to fashion my face into a rictus that could pass for an expression that wasn't horrified shock, she slapped two cobra arms around me and clapped my back, almost lifting me off my feet.

I felt as though she had assaulted me.

'I don't know what to say? I've imagined this moment for years, you know?'

All her sentences ended in question marks, whether or not they contained any inquiry, and for someone who claimed to be lost for words, she had suddenly hit the mother lode. They followed each other so rapidly that it was as if she were firing them from a nail gun.

She told me she had been travelling through 'Aja?' with her fiancé, 'having a bit of a *holiday*?', as though I might not have come across the concept before. She was a rower, which accounted for the steely grip she had in those arms, though what relevance it had to the Silk Trail I didn't know, and she was 'really glad to have finally caught up with me'.

Oh, yessir, Bob's your uncle and Agnes is your aunt; I most certainly felt caught.

I wrested myself from her embrace and hugged my overnight bag to my chest like the baby I never wanted so she would keep her distance.

'I must have written you like about a gazillion letters?'

'Yes,' I acknowledged doubtfully. 'I've been travelling around a bit myself. Life has been sort of difficult lately,' I said lamely, swaying the overnight bag to and fro.

Words were dripping out of her mouth, on and on like a tap with a faulty washer.

'I was worried that it might be a bad idea, you know, just coming here,' she said, while I reeled at the understatement. 'But I had this hunch, like, that it would all be fine?'

'It is a bit much to take in. Just springing yourself on me like this,' I protested.

'Oh.' She looked crestfallen. 'I thought you would be excited.'

'Excited,' I repeated in disbelief.

'I'm sorry about your husband and all. When I saw him in Oxford, he told me he didn't know where you were because you weren't together any more. I went there hoping I might find somebody who knew you at your old address, and luckily he was in,' she said blithely. 'I met his girlfriend too. She's a lovely woman?'

'Oh?' I could insert a mean question mark myself when it suited me. I waited to hear more about the 'great girlfriend' who had been around since last year. The thought burned through my stomach like battery acid despite the fact that I, myself, had been fucking like I was training for a sex marathon.

'She's from Argentina. That's where Lee and me, that's my fiancé, that's where we're going to go for our next big trip, after we're married. South America?'

She stopped babbling and looked at me expectantly, as though waiting for me to do a backward flip. So I did.

'Hey, why don't we go and have a cup of coffee?' I suggested, reversing out of the gate.

She was disappointed. 'Aren't you going to ask me in? It's just that this pack is really, really heavy. Couldn't I leave it inside, and wash my hands? I've been up since seven o'clock this morning. Who knew that Acton would be so far from the station? London's that big. You could get lost here.'

Oh no you fucking couldn't, I thought, as she chewed her lip, another gesture that had travelled from my mother's face, through mine and on to hers.

I couldn't take her into the house. Jocelyn might come back and then there would have to be explanations. I would never get rid of her: she'd be in my hair, crawling all over me, and I'd never be able to comb her out. It was only good luck that there wasn't anybody home that morning. Jesus, I cringed at the possibility of finding Cheryl sitting in the kitchen with a chirping Jocelyn. I certainly didn't want her comfortably settled with a cup of yarrow tea and an alfalfa carob muffin, spilling her guts to the homoeopath.

'Of course, leave your bag, what am I thinking of . . .' I lifted the haversack. It was heavy. I hoped she wasn't planning on staying. I took her inside and showed her where the bathroom was, then stood in the hall with my hand holding the door ajar until she returned. I told her that my landlady was a fussy old thing and that she didn't really like my having guests and asked if she minded walking up to Acton High Street to find a café. After looking pityingly around at the dusty hand-made pottery and grotty homespun tapestries from Jocelyn's various misguided attempts at arts-and-crafts evening classes, she agreed, walking beside me, looking at me out of the corner of her eye, as if she were going to describe me later for a photofit.

I glanced at her too, covertly, in the window of Supersave. She was half a head taller than me, and she made me feel small. The height and wide shoulders were Bill Anderson's legacy, and intimidated me; the reason I had never, until Adam, spent any significant period of time with a man I couldn't look in the eye in my stockinged feet. I had liked to maintain the fiction that, if it came to a fight, I could always knock them over. Though the idea of my fighting anyone was laughable. Hadn't I always just laid right on down for anyone who asked? She walked with a swagger, as though drunk, or recently disembarked after a long sea voyage, but then I realized her gait was caused by her repeatedly turning round to examine my face.

She pulled a strand of black hair out of her mouth, showing an uneven incisor, crossed as though for good luck over the tooth next to it. She had bony twiglet fingers, just like mine, and a diamond on the third finger of her left hand that was as tiny and as brilliant as a dust mote.

'You look almost as young as me,' she said approvingly, as I slid into the chair opposite her. 'We could be sisters. You're so young, compared to my mother. My other mother,' she corrected herself.

I twisted my lips into what was supposed to be a smile, wondering how much of my life I would have to rehash and serve up to her on a plate, but, as I sat at my end of a Formica table decorated with a round plastic tomato, I realized my function was to listen, not to inform.

I should be charging for this, I thought, as she rattled out her potted childhood, the trajectory of her romance with a boy called Lee, her mother's job, her father's job, the house they had in Emmerdale country, her training as a legal 'secetary'. On and on and on and on it went, while I nodded like a Japanese business-man. For the first time, it occurred to me that Irshad actually did earn his money. Listening was exhausting.

'Are you still in touch with my dad?' she asked, jolting me out of my fact-filled stupor.

'No.'

'It's not your husband, is it?'

'What?'

'Your husband isn't my dad?' asked Cheryl. 'He said he wasn't, though at first I thought he might be, 'cos he's dark like me, but he's a bit short to be related. Nice, though,' she added apologetically. 'Dead nice.'

'Dead?' I was startled until I realized it was just an expression. 'Yes, he's nice. But, no, he wasn't your father.'

'Who was, then?' She was squirming, as though the question were being wrung out of her through a mangle.

I laughed. I did a good job of it too, full teeth, lips, head tossed to the side. 'Oh, if I'd known the answer to that, life would have been a lot easier.'

She looked puzzled. 'You don't know?'

'I was a wild girl,' I said. 'It could have been anybody. I honestly don't have any idea who your dad was. It had been my birthday and . . .'

'Oh, when?' she interrupted.

'October the 31st.'

I waited for a Hallowe'en joke and instead got astrology.

'What's that, then? Libra?'

'Scorpio,' I answered automatically, though it had been decades since I had thought of myself in terms of star signs.

'I'm Leo, the sixth of August,' she said, then giggled faintly when she realized that I would know this already, having been there at the time. 'Sorry,' she added, 'you were saying?'

'So I had been to a big party, a weekender, in Glasgow. There were loads of people I didn't know there, and I got very drunk . . . speed, dope, mushrooms.' Listen to me, I thought, the most exotic mushroom I'd ever eaten was a cep. 'I couldn't even tell you what happened that weekend, let alone who I was with.'

She looked both dejected and queasy.

'I know, it's not pretty. It's not a story you really want to tell anyone,' I said ruefully, while thinking that it was *Little Women* compared to the real one.

'Oh, well,' she allowed eventually, 'you were just a lass. I mean, people do daft things when they're young and don't know any better.'

'But I did know better. I just didn't care back then.'

'Oh, I'd never get away with that sort of thing. My mum and dad are strict. I was brought up right.'

I asked about her family. Both grandparents were dead, she told me, and she was an only child. Her parents were quiet people, Salvation Army, though Cheryl had rebelled against that. But she didn't have many relatives, and no 'real, blood ones'. That's what made me so special, apparently, and explained why this big, cold-eyed Colossus was so desperate to reattach all the family bonds that I'd quite happily cut decades earlier.

'I went up to see your mother, I mean, in the home? But she didn't have a clue who I was. The nurses say she hardly ever recognizes anyone. It's a real shame.'

'Yes, it is,' I agreed and left it at that, while anxiety swirled round and round in my brain, picking up questions like a tornado wrenching parked cars from driveways. How had she found the home?

'Lee and I are getting married in the middle of August. After my birthday?'

I tried to look interested.

'I'd really like you to meet him before then. He's working in Leeds now. He's a chef.'

I shifted awkwardly in the chair, as though the inoffensive pine seat had suddenly pinched me. I'd rather meet Stalin, I thought. 'I'm not sure I'll be here then. I might be going to Italy with my . . . em . . . boyfriend.' How ridiculous, I thought. How can you call a middle-aged man a boyfriend?

She looked disappointed. She pursed her lips, pouting with uncertainty, then she thought of something else and smiled at me, as if preparing me for bad news that could be worse. She had better teeth than me, apart from that one crooked tooth at the side. Mr Goldmann would approve.

'Could I ask you something?' She was waiting for permission, so I nodded and waited for her to continue.

'Well, like, I know you were very young when you had me, but did you ever regret giving me up for adoption?'

I didn't know how to respond. Strangely, I hadn't anticipated this question. I think this was the moment I was supposed to say that I still had the baby bootees and a pile of unsent letters and birthday cards in a drawer that I'd been saving up since her birth, but I was rescued from the need to invent something by a pair of white mugs set down on the table together with a bowl of sugar sachets. Dear God, all this and we still had to drink the bloody coffee. It already seemed as if we had been sitting there long enough for dinosaurs to become extinct.

'Everything all right?' said the waitress, as though there were hidden nuances in the delivery of powdered instant coffee that she had, perhaps, overlooked. We both nodded our heads and tipped our chins in an identical gesture.

Undeterred she went on: 'My mother had three miscarriages

before she adopted me, and she used to talk about them as if they were still around, as if they had been born and were playing in the other room. She even had names for them – our Jack, our Richard, our Edward. She used to say she couldn't understand how anyone could give away a baby.'

There was an awkward silence; or at least a silence even more awkward than the already hugely awkward ones that were milling around us like people waiting for trains.

'You know, this isn't going to work, Cheryl,' I said, as she stirred and restirred her coffee.

'What isn't?'

'This. You and me,' I blurted out.

'I don't understand?'

'You asked me if I regretted having you adopted, and I'm sorry, but I didn't. There was nothing to regret. Adoption was the only option open to me at the time. As you said, I was far too young for the responsibility of a baby and then there was the scandal. My mother couldn't have stood the shame of it.'

'Scandal? What happened?' She looked offended. She was taking the shame as a personal affront. 'Was it really that bad, having a baby?'

I felt as though a blade had sliced through my head. It was hard to keep all these lies straight. I suddenly felt afraid that I had said too much. What if she went around digging up the past? What if she went back to the village and started asking questions?

'Oh, people were very small-minded. And I already had a "bad name" around the village. Getting pregnant was the last straw, as far as my mother was concerned. I was told to say nothing. I just vanished for a couple of months, had the baby adopted, and when I came back I was expected to pretend like nothing had happened.'

'Me, adopted,' she corrected, reminding me that this wasn't just a faceless baby, but the real-life grown-up person sitting beside me playing with her lips.

'It was what people did back then,' I said, not mentioning that it had suited me fine, that I just wanted the thing out of me and gone. That I never gave her another thought that wasn't filled with dread from that day to this.

What could I tell her? That I felt guilty? I didn't. I just wanted things to stay the same as they always had done: with this girl far away and out of sight, if not out of mind, living the life that had been stolen from me. I wanted her gone so that, every time I looked at her, I didn't have to remember what had happened to me.

'I'm not complaining that I was adopted, like,' she said. 'I've got a brilliant mum and dad, you'd like them. I wasn't really bothered until Lee and I decided to get married. Then I thought it would be good to know what you were like, in case I had brothers or sisters, or if we had illnesses in the family, anything catching, you know – for when I have my own kids.'

Fuck, she had a lot of questions. But some of these I could answer. 'Well, as for other brothers or sisters – you don't have any; and, as far as I know, there are no hereditary illnesses.'

She asked what my mother was like before she lost her marbles. 'Kind,' I said. 'Funny and attentive and good-natured and cheerful.'

'What about your father?'

'Over-indulgent, jolly, always telling jokes, light-hearted and helpful,' I said. Then I coloured in their golden haloes with stories of all their funny ways and amusing mannerisms and the dog we never had, and decorated my family with smiley faces, little gold stars and hearts all around the edges of the paper. The Pope would be calling any minute to sanctify them.

She asked about her birth. I wished I had suggested the pub instead of a café. But even I couldn't drink vodka at eleven o'clock in the morning. Then, I thought, why stop now? I was on a roll. So I gave her a rose-tinted, soft-focus, hand-held version, leaving out the twelve hours of solitary labour, followed by mastitis and the weeks walking around with bandages strapped round my bullet breasts to stop the milk. I didn't tell her that even when I was living in the youth hostel in Oxford, and my stretch marks had faded from ugly red to silvery snot, I could still squeeze drops of sweet, blue-white fluid out of my breasts. I left out the forceps, the stitches, the gas and air, and the pethidine.

I passed over all that and filed the birth plan for *Rebecca of Sunnybrook Farm* while the reality had been more like *Bleak House*.

I stayed at the nuns' hostel for nearly three weeks before the birth, though in pregnancy time five minutes can seem like months and adding nuns to the mix doesn't exactly speed things along.

As Irshad pointed out, teenagers have been having babies since the dawn of time, and there was a good representative sample of them at the hostel. There we spent the days having parenting lessons from a health visitor not much older than ourselves, who taught us how to bathe a stiff-limbed plastic doll in a bowl and instructed us on a variety of ways to pin nappies on to its unyielding asexual limbs.

Why, we dared not ask. Not one of us was planning on keeping her child. We knew there was a long line of baby-snatching parents with their gaze already fixed greedily on the nursery window, ready to whip our little cuckoos off and plant them in an instant, brand-new borrowed history that owed nothing to the circumstances of their birth. Nevertheless, we powdered plastic bottoms and winded plastic backs while little plastic eyes swivelled hither and thither, rattling in plastic faces that were permanently dimpled and never cried, giving them names, not all of them the sort of thing you would want to be calling out in the playground.

The girls and I cooked supper for each other under supervision from one of the sisters, and we slept all together in a dormitory where we swapped sob stories about fathers who wouldn't marry us, and, in one case, a father who was already married to the girl's mother. I was the youngest in the hostel and subject to a bit of babying myself. One or two left in the middle of the night clutching their stomachs as if they were being eaten from the inside by a starving animal, but they never came back to tell us how their story ended, though we all knew, more or less.

My aunt visited once a week. She had warned me about the pain. 'Don't let them give you any of that natural childbirth nonsense, be sure to ask for the injection or you'll be crying for your mother and begging them to put a gun to your head to save you from the pain.'

She was right about the drugs. But I didn't cry once for my mother.

'You be lucky,' the midwife said, as I screamed in tandem with the woman in the next room. 'You see, it all be over soon and it be like it never even happen.' She gave my cheek a pinch with her sharp West Indian fingers. 'Once you have that baby in your arm, Lord, you forget ev-er-y-ting.'

She was suffering from some selective memory loss herself. She had forgotten I wouldn't be keeping the baby; it was going straight to social services. The family were already assembling the cot, hanging the mobile, airing the baby clothes, buying tins of formula.

'Where the babydaddy be?' she asked me towards the end, but I was too busy keeping the gas mask over my face to say that he was out on remand.

'I feel the Holy Spirit wit'me, praise the Lord. God bless you,' she sang as she plopped the baby on my stomach. I didn't feel much like praising anything that didn't come at the end of a needle, but I held the baby for a few anaesthetized minutes. She looked like a grub, a bloody, purple-faced wax doll, her head dented from the prongs that had dragged her out of me, her eyes squeezed shut, then blinking, then drooping back to a drugged sleep, dopey from the same stuff in her bloodstream that was also in mine.

'What you going to call her?' asked the midwife, lifting her out of my arms and carrying her away to a Plexiglas box, where she peeled back the blanket, pressed a stethoscope to her flutter-ing chest and began to fill out a form.

'Girl,' I remember saying.

'Yes, I know it's a girl, but what's her name, darlin'?'

'Just Girl,' I repeated.

So she wrote, Baby Girl McBride, 06.08.74, 3.2 kg, and attached the tag to her wrist.

Well, it was better than Agnes anyway.

The midwife dressed her in the little nightdress my aunt and I had bought in Mothercare, and, without breaking either arm, expertly threaded her stringy limbs into the hand-made matinée jacket – my one and only attempt at knitting. It was a lurid shade of lime-green with gold flecks. My aunt had bought the wool in a sale – it would have been great for a disco.

'What you think you be havin', darlin' – a frog?' said the midwife, chuckling. She put a cotton hat on her head – she looked like she was going to a bar mitzvah.

I held her again, wrapped in a papoose of blue cellular blanket. Her little mouth opened and closed, and her tiny star-shaped hand wrapped itself around my finger, which was tipped with un-even purple sparkly nail varnish. How could I have a baby when I couldn't even get colour on my nails without smudging it?

'You can feed her if you like; I can show you how, darlin'.'

'No, I can't,' I said, stroking the little face, marvelling at the downy skin, soft like a peach.

'Course you can. It's the most natural thing in the world,' said the midwife, now all gap-toothed, pink-gummed smiles, but I asked her to take it away until the woman from social services arrived. I said I didn't want to see it again, and nobody ever insisted I did.

Until now.

How had she turned into this strangely familiar person in chain-store denim and a tracksuit top? Yes, her hair was lacklustre and black, her eyes fringed with lashes I would have, indeed almost had, killed for; but the thin, pointed chin, the cheekbones, the sharp bones at her narrow wrists, the collar bone like a coat hanger across the open neck of her t-shirt – it was like looking at myself, reversed in a mirror. But with Bill Anderson's eyes.

I couldn't stand it. I couldn't stand looking at her. I wound my feet round the legs of the chair to keep me anchored there.

'It must have been dead hard having a baby and being away from your family and all your friends? I'd be lost without my friends. My best mate, Pat, she's going to be my bridesmaid when we get married this August. We're that close, like sisters?'

I nodded.

'Who was your bridesmaid when you got married?'

The girl was gushing all over the place like a garden sprinkler. You never knew where the next jet was coming from.

'He was called Karl.'

'Carole?'

'No, Karl. It was a boy. I didn't have many girlfriends.'

'What, not one? A bloke for your best maid? That's different.'

'I suppose.'

'So who was Kirsty, then?'

I needed an air bag to protect me from these blows she kept raining down on me.

'Kirsty?' I repeated dumbly.

'The first letter I sent. To your old house. I wrote to them asking if anyone remembered you. I got a nice reply from the people living there. Old folk. They said they remembered you when you were a girl. You and your friend Kirsty. They didn't know where you'd gone, but they gave me your mum's new address. That one got forwarded to her nursing home?' Her voice went up more emphatically than usual, as if I might not remember where my own mother was, though given the rarity of my visits that would, at least, have been an excuse for my continued non-appearance at visiting times.

'So what happened to her?'

'I don't know.'

'You're really not a great one for keeping in touch, are you?'

I gave her a level look. Did she know what she was doing? Did she know more than she was letting on? I had no idea who was living in our old house, but what had they told her?

'No, you're right,' I said baldly. 'I don't believe in looking backwards.' I was running out of vocabulary. Clichés would have to do: 'You have to look forward. The past is the past.'

'So you have a new bloke, what did you say his name was?' Dear God, it was like having a conversation with a squash ball.

I looked at my watch. It was two minutes later than it had been the last time I looked.

I didn't answer. Instead I tried a question of my own. 'How did you find my address?' I asked. 'I didn't give it to you. I wrote to you through the solicitor.' I had this creeping feeling of strangulated panic that the girl had put some sort of homing device on me.

'Oh, that was easy. It's not a secret, is it? I told you I was a legal secetary. I just rang the solicitor from work and spoke to his secetary.'

Another missing *r*. Where do they all go, I wondered, moronically. Maybe there was a huge landfill somewhere with all her dropped *r*'s, Irshad's vowels and my *t*'s.

'I gave her the name of my firm in Harrogate and she told me your address. Sorted.'

She seemed to be expecting congratulations. I pictured the solicitor's bill and stripped off all the zeros after the first digit. Bloody Singh would be whistling for his money.

I could bear it no longer.

'I need to get going,' I said, scrabbling to my feet. 'Sorry, but I have to be at work by two.'

'But it's only half eleven,' she said.

'I know, I know, but I have a lot to do, and it's a long way away. I work on the other side of London; it takes me hours to get there. I didn't know you were coming, after all.'

I started to gather up my things before I realized I only had one bag. Instead I lifted the torn sugar packets and crumpled napkins, dropped them into the inch of coffee in her mug and carried them to counter.

'I took a few days off work. I was maybe going to stay for a while.'

'I don't think that's a good idea. I don't have time to see you. I have work,' I repeated.

'Well, I suppose . . . There's a train from King's Cross every hour. You're not going that way, are you?' she asked.

'Barnes,' I said, mentioning the first place that came into my head, which was less than a mile away on the other side of the river. Thank goodness she didn't know her way round London.

'But you'll keep in touch, won't you?' she asked apprehensively, as I struggled into my jacket.

Jesus, this is why they leave kids to die on a hillside in China. She wouldn't take the hint.

'I don't mean to be unkind, but, as I've already told you, I can't see you any more. The letter that solicitor sent said that I did not want to meet you. We've both got our own lives. It's better that we just leave things as they are.'

'What, not even a card at Christmas, just so I know your news?'

'I won't have much news' – I struggled to spit out the name – 'Cheryl. You're the one who's starting out in life, with all these plans to get married and travel. I'm not going to be doing anything very much different.'

'I could tell you my news?' she offered.

She still hadn't stood up. 'Look, I don't want to be harsh, but no.'

'But I would like to see you again,' she said querulously. 'Sometime, like if I had kids. Wouldn't you want to meet your grandchildren?'

'Well, we'll see. One day,' I finally conceded. By then I could tell her I'd emigrated to Zimbabwe or be 'dead busy', as she might put it, or even just plain dead.

We walked back to the house, which, mercifully, was still Jocelyn-free.

'Will you show me the way back to the tube station?' she asked.

Even better, I bundled her and her haversack swiftly into a black cab and gave the driver a tenner.

'Well, bye, then,' she said, looking pitiful as she prepared to climb into the purring taxi. I embraced my handbag like a life preserver to keep her from hugging me.

I felt like the woodcutter, abandoning his children in the middle of the forest without even a paper trail to enable them to find their way home. I had hated that story as a child. Now I understood it perfectly.

'It was nice to finally meet you,' she stammered awkwardly, as though it were a phrase that had been instilled in her since childhood, for birthday parties and visiting dignitaries.

I thought for one awful moment she was going to curtsy. 'Yes, wonderful.' I waved, and smiled, and waved, and smiled, and waved, and smiled, and finally, after my lips had stuck to my teeth as if superglued, the cab drew away from the kerb and lurched into the traffic.

Demon down. Buffy the Vampire-Slayer couldn't have done it better herself. I felt relieved and dizzily, kick-ass happy as I walked back to Jocelyn's. It was over. I had done it.

Unfortunately, I had forgotten to drive the stake right into her heart.

That girl wasn't vanquished. She was just gathering her strength for the next round.

30

'And that's just about it.'

'Really?'

Irshad is sceptical but trying to hide it.

He has been expecting that I would eventually feel relaxed enough to open up and tell him the rest of the story. He's been patient, week after week, while I have distracted him with the cat-and-mouse game I played with Cheryl, interspersed with selected chapters of *The Good Sex Guide*. But if he wants more, he's going to be disappointed.

'You don't feel there's anything else you'd like to bring to the space?'

I know what he means, but he's annoying me, so I look up from the tissue that I've been shredding and give him a baffled look. 'Space?' I say, pretending not to understand him.

'Here, in the analysis.'

'Oh, no. I don't think so.' I have a sudden picture of myself dragging my feet round a department store with my mother in her black cape trying to interest me in a serviceable fawn school coat that I don't have the courage to tell her I hate.

He chipped away: 'So how did things resolve themselves?'

'Oh, eventually we found a way to distract him and I managed to get away. I was lucky. A car picked me up at the first crossroads, and he called the police and took me to the hospital.'

'And Kirsty?'

'The police went back to get her. But she was in a bad way. Hysterical. He had slapped her around a lot too. I didn't see her again.'

'Ever?'

'Never. Her parents blamed me. Quite rightly. They felt I had abandoned her, said I had led her astray.'

'Why do you say "quite rightly"?'

'I was the one who got away first.'

'But it wasn't your idea to go with him into the house, it was Kirsty's. So why are you so ready to take the blame? How did your own parents react?'

'They didn't know what to believe. Kirsty and me . . . well, our stories didn't exactly match up.'

He waited.

'And it was our word against his, and he was a teacher. He said that we had thrown ourselves at him, that we had been hitch-hiking, and that he had only been trying to help us. He said we had begged him to give us a lift and then wouldn't go home because we were scared we would get in trouble with our parents. He made us sound like a pair of slags.'

'And what did you say?'

'I could hardly claim that we hadn't gone with him. And we had been hitching. We went willingly, didn't we?'

'I wouldn't describe it as "willing". You didn't know what lay ahead.'

'I suppose, but there were other problems.'

'I don't understand? You say that the two of you distracted him. You got away. You got her help. You saved her, in a manner of speaking.'

'I don't think anyone else saw it that way.'

'And was the man sentenced?'

'At first they charged him with rape, then with assault, but they couldn't make it stick. He'd hit Kirsty, threatened her with a knife, but she kept changing her mind about what happened. At first she said he did, then she claimed he hadn't touched her. She had all these old scars and a history of cutting herself. Not that I ever knew about that. It all came out later. They put my injuries down to being caught up in the fight at the party, and I couldn't say that he'd raped me.'

Irshad tried to protest, but I kept on talking. 'My parents didn't want me to press charges; they just wanted it dropped, especially when they knew I was pregnant. Kirsty's parents were furious with me; and then she got really ill. The police said they didn't have enough evidence to charge him without Kirsty's testimony. It all turned on its head. In the end he made it look like we'd entrapped him, the honest teacher. The Larksridge Lolitas, they called us.'

Irshad shook his head questioningly.

'That's the name of the village. Newspapers. They like alliteration. He came out of it the much maligned hero.'

'But surely you had a good case against him. Why couldn't Kirsty testify?'

'She wasn't there.'

'In what way?'

'I mean, at first she wasn't there because she zoned out. They had her in a psychiatric ward for a while, doped up, electric shocks. She wouldn't talk, apparently. Then, after a couple of months, they let her home and she *really* wasn't there.'

He waited.

I closed my eyes against the picture of the rickety train whooshing out of the tunnel at the golf course, reeling down the two-track line on the perimeter of our village: Edinburgh, Galashiels, Selkirk, Hawick, Langham, Carlisle. When we were small we used to stand on the links and wave. But this time Kirsty hadn't waved.

'I mean, she jumped in front of a train,' I said.

'My goodness.'

It wasn't often I got much of a reaction out of Irshad. 'I was in Scarborough by then,' I added quietly, as though to excuse myself from any blame, which was, of course, impossible.

'Did you get any counselling at the time?'

I raised my eyebrows: 'We're talking Scotland here . . . They give you a glass of Irn-Bru and tell you to pull yourself together. No, but I did see somebody after we got away. An old man in the same psychiatric hospital they banged Kirsty up in. I was supposed to go back to him, but by then I had been sent off to Scarborough.'

'That's a great pity.' He paused. 'Wouldn't the pregnancy have helped your case?'

'Nothing would have helped me by that point. I think it would have made it worse. I woke up every morning surprised to find that I wasn't the one on trial. Anyway I didn't tell anyone.'

'No one?'

'It was hard enough telling my mother.'

'It must have been so difficult, for you. Keeping it all inside. Then and now.'

I didn't respond. I realized I had shredded an awful lot of tissues. My lap was full of pink ribbons. I could see him looking at them. I waited for him to comment.

'What happened to the man, the teacher?'

'Anderson. *Mr.*' I imbued the word with some sarcasm. 'Anderson. He moved. Went to America as a sports coach for some school. My mother saw it in the paper years ago, before I was married: Fucker Fucks off to Florida, or something. Actually, I think it was Ohio or somewhere.'

'Is he still there?'

I shrugged.

'I wouldn't know. I'm not exactly going to seek him out, am I? I never think of him.'

'No?'

'No.'

Irshad looked meaningfully at my lap. I scraped the tissues into a pile and threw them into the bin. I missed and they tumbled over the carpet like party streamers.

I couldn't think of anything else I wanted to say. The silence was excruciating. I searched my mind, desperately, for something, anything, that would move the session closer to completion. The hands on the clock seemed frozen, with ten minutes still to go.

I swallowed loudly enough to hear my gulp echo off the walls. My stomach began to gnaw itself. Audibly.

Inevitably, it came: 'Have you had any dreams you want to share?'

Dreams. Share. Like they were fucking KitKats you could tear into fingers and pass round. And then, it came to me that I had had a dream.

I'm hiding in the shed at the back of our garden in Scotland where we used to keep the coal. It was our favourite place for hide-and-seek. I was there with my cousin, 'wee' Pamela – one of the lucky ones whose big sister got saddled with the A word. And this man comes, fully grown and sinister, but unknown to me, black-faced like the person who used to deliver the coal, and tries to pull me out. I wrestle myself away and tell him: don't take me, take Pamela. So then he reaches back in and grabs Pamela's arm, and pulls her out instead.

The dream popped into my head like a piece of mental toast. I figured I could spread butter on it for Irshad, just to pass the time, but it was too risky.

'Yes, actually, I dreamed about my mother . . .' I said instead.

He signalled that I should go on. 'I dreamed that she was dead.' Okay, so it was a very short dream.

I wait for his response.

'What do you think it means?'

'I know what it means.' I might be mad but I'm not stupid. 'It's guilt, isn't it?'

'And how did that make you feel?'

'In a way she's been dead for years. She's not the person she was; just this lost, pathetic shell.'

'You haven't answered my question.'

'Okay, well, actually, I was angry. Angry that she had removed herself before I had a chance to talk to her.'

'Interesting choice of words: "removed herself".'

I remained as mute as my mother used to when confronted with uncomfortable and leading questions.

'So what would you have said to her?'

I shrugged like a sulky teenager.

'You obviously have a lot of unresolved issues to explore,' he said, his face sweet with compassion.

I tutted impatiently. It all came back to bloody unresolved bloody issues and 'exploring' things.

'I don't want to *explore*.'

'Okay,' he said patiently, 'but, 'gnes, you have to learn to forgive yourself. And maybe that's something I can help you with . . .'

Oh, yes, and maybe you don't dye your hair, I thought.

'It'll be all right, you'll see, we can work through it together.'

That's what the police officer said when she came to take my statement. She gave me a hug when she got up to go. She said, 'Don't worry, hen, you're safe now. Everything's going to be all right.'

But I knew it never would be.

31

You know, I might not have a row of certificates from the University of Durban, but I was right about one thing. It doesn't go back into the box once you've let it out. Your past arranges itself in the here and now, like unpacking your possessions in a hotel room. When you arrive it's bland and anonymous – white sheets, clear surfaces, a white bathroom with the soap in a little wrapper – and then suddenly there's a hair in the sink and the pointy end of the toilet paper is flushed into the lavatory. You put your dressing gown behind the door, your nightdress under the pillow. That's what happens with the past – it draws up a chair in the present and sits down with its feet on the table. It finds a place and stays there, like the guest who won't leave.

The muscled bulk of Bill Anderson weighs down the other side of the bed when I climb into it at night. I feel the knotted string of the veins on his biceps pressing against my face and wake up, pushing tearfully at Adam's calming hands.

I've started to see him now and again, spreadeagled on the sofa when I watch television with my landlady; his eyes stare out at me from Adam's face while we're making love. I feel bruises on my arms. When I wake in the morning, Kirsty hunkers beside me on the floor, with a ratty tartan blanket over her shoulders. It's her cold bare feet that really get to me, the chipped polish. Moscow Mauve. My fingers seem to stink of nicotine. I've started to crave cigarettes again.

I'm not just being brave when I say it wasn't so bad. I did then what I did a hundred times later, with tens of different men. It never worried me. It was my choice. Irshad thinks I see myself as a helpless victim; he says that what happened to Kirsty wasn't my fault – but what does he know? Only what I tell him.

I told him about the girl just turning up out of the blue. I told him about the liberation of finally having got the meeting over with. I told him that I had finally faced my past in the present.

He was pleased with me. It was progress, he maintained.

It was a nice theory.

And then the phone calls started.

They came once or twice a week, and of course I ignored them. Each time she would leave a message wondering when she could see me, which Jocelyn printed out in microscopic capitals on Post-it notes and stuck on my bedroom door. I peeled them off, but two days later there would be another, and then another, until I felt as if I were being hounded by those damn yellow squares.

Meanwhile Adam and I had been dating like teenagers, going to the cinema and leaving halfway through to go home to bed. He went into work late so that we could sit around in our hastily donned pyjamas, reading the newspapers; we walked in the park and had candlelit picnics in the garden square in the evenings. But, fun though it was to play at Barbie and Ken, he was impatient for me to settle permanently into the Dream House.

The prospect was thrilling. The plan was that I would move in before we left for Italy at the end of July, and come back from holiday fully transformed from the bit on the side to the bit on the inside.

I imagined dissolving into Adam's life, my worries cushioned by money. I could empty my emotional handbag on Irshad's Eames chair until the leather moulded itself to my bum. I could spend my days in the kitchen being Fanny Craddock, burying my sins like chocolate chips in the double-fudge cookies, and my nights in the bedroom being Fanny Hill. He wanted to marry me. My divorce would be through by autumn. I could change my name again, this time legally, and fill Gay's bathroom, hell, fill *my* bathroom, with a smorgasbord of scented soaps. I could grow to tolerate Lennie, and even like Ned. In four years' time they would both be at university and it would be just Adam and myself, alone in Holland Crescent or wherever we chose to live.

I could be happy.

But how was I going to explain Cheryl to Adam without her book-marking herself into my future? I simply didn't know how best to handle the situation. And then the situation began to handle me.

She turned up again on a Saturday morning. I was just on my way out of the house to meet Adam and Lennie for breakfast in Ed's Diner. Lennie wanted me to take her for a haircut, and, God knows, I needed one myself. I was combing out my fringe with my fingers, examining my reflection in Jocelyn's hall mirror, trying to flatten out the kinks, when a broad-shouldered shadow on the other side of the frosted-glass door blotted out the light.

Cheryl stood on the doorstep holding a bunch of tulips wrapped in soggy paper, drooping like a joint that has been passed around a lot of people.

'What are you doing here?' I asked crossly, barring the door with angrily crossed arms and ignoring the outstretched tulips. 'You need to leave. I don't want to see you.' I half closed the door in her face and began to gather my things together, ramming stuff that I didn't really need into my handbag as a shorthand for I'm ignoring you, so fuck off. But she obviously needed it spelled out for her in joined-up writing because she didn't budge.

I reiterated what I had told her the last time. I explained that I couldn't give her the kind of relationship she wanted.

'But I only want to know a bit more about you,' she pleaded. 'It's my birthright. My history. It's not too much to ask after twenty-one years. You owe it to me.'

'I owe you nothing, Cheryl.' The name was getting easier to say. It flew out like an obscenity. 'All I want from you is to leave me alone.'

'I just want to know what your life is like.'

'I'll tell you what it's like,' I retorted. 'Hell. Now let me burn in it by myself.'

The flowers flopped petals down in her hands, and she laid

them across the doorstep like a wreath. If she had cried I wouldn't have been able to help myself – I would have relented and brought her inside to console her, but mercifully she grew irritated.

'But what about me?' she said in a raised voice, glowering.

'You have parents. You have a fiancé. You have a life. Go and live it,' I said. 'What part of "adopted" don't you understand?'

Her angry stare, her tight, bitter mouth, the black crow of her eyebrows, only made it easier to close the door.

I drew the bolt across and went upstairs to Jocelyn's bedroom, where I watched from the window until I saw her disappear round the corner at the end of the road.

My guts quaked and my legs shook, as if the carpet underfoot were heaving and buckling, but I still felt like a hard, heartless bitch as I watched the slow reluctant clump of her sandals up the street, and I could hardly bring myself to touch the discarded flowers, which I hastily threw in the neighbour's dustbin.

But then, the next day, she came back.

When I let myself into the house at five o'clock on Sunday, Jocelyn rushed to meet me in the hall wearing a delighted expression and an equally unusual apron, and whispered, as thrilled as a debutante at her first ball, that I had a couple of visitors waiting for me.

Outside in the garden, I found Cheryl in a striped deckchair with the cat on her lap, drinking coffee that I didn't even know we had and eating scones and jam that Jocelyn had actually gone out and bought for her.

This time she had brought her boyfriend. He was a raw, awkward, big-boned guy with blond leg hair and blue plasters on his fingers, intimating that he wasn't as expert with his chef knives as he should be.

My face drained of what little colour the sun had beaten into it as I apologized to Jocelyn for the intrusion and asked them both to go.

Poor Jocelyn didn't know what to do with herself. She had imagined she was being the perfect hostess and now I was marching her guests out the door. 'I'm sorry, I thought they were friends of yours,' she stammered, forlorn in her frilly apron, her cheeks, previously bright with excitement, now blotchy with embarrassment.

I patted her arm in apology and glared at Cheryl, willing her to leave with the poison darts I was shooting into her chest with my eyes.

But she merely rubbed her index finger under the chin of the cat, which closed its eyes in rapture. 'Sweet,' she said, making a kissy face and murmuring some sort of cat-lover's nonsense, and still made no move to rise from her chair.

'It's okay.' She attempted a smile but it came out like a smirk. 'I just wanted you to meet my fiancé. This is Lee,' she said, as the boy clambered to his feet, wiping crumbs off his blue-ringed hands, obviously unnerved by the drama unfolding around him.

'Come on, Cherry, love, we should go,' he said, flapping his arm as if he were fanning an already out-of-control fire.

Jocelyn glanced from my face to Cheryl's, then slowly scanned back to mine. It was like watching a slot machine roll through her eyes. I saw one bell fall. She caught my blind, animal-on-the-way-to-the-abattoir panic as the next bell spun and stopped.

'You know she's my mother, don't you?' said Cheryl, as the final bell racked up and ding, ding, ding; and not only did the penny drop but it paid out the whole bloody jackpot.

'I think Agnes is right. You had better leave,' Jocelyn said in a voice suddenly as steely as her hair.

Cheryl's boyfriend shuffled his feet. 'Come on now, love, you don't want to be making a scene.'

'You're not going to let my own mother throw me out?' asked Cheryl, her voice rattling like a box of little thumb tacks, spilling and skittering all over the ground; and me in bare feet, afraid to cross it. But Jocelyn was undeterred and escorted them out with a sharp jab of her finger in the direction of the front door, brooking no further discussion. 'I'm the one throwing you out. This is my house, and if I want you to go, then you go.'

I stammered some ineffectual thanks and a garbled explanation, but Jocelyn merely gathered me into her arms and held me in a vice-like grip that could have been marketed as a weight-loss system. 'Don't say another word, my dear, it's absolutely nothing to do with me,' she said, giving me a brisk pat on the back that almost knocked my glasses off; then, unbidden, she made me another cup of valerian tea.

Unbidden, I drank it.

I was even getting to like the taste.

However, though I could tolerate the tea, it didn't do anything to solve the problem of Cheryl. The girl was shit on my shoe, and I was never going to be able to scrape her off. What homoeopathic tincture was strong enough to get rid of her?

'Get a restraining order,' suggested Jocelyn. 'I had to do it once when I had a patient who wouldn't stop harassing me. Does Adam know about her?' she asked shrewdly.

I turned to her, shamefaced. 'No.'

'Well, I don't want to interfere, but you probably should tell him before she does.'

'She doesn't know anything about me.'

'She won't hear anything about him from me, but you need to be careful; she doesn't look like the sort of person who gives up easily.'

And she was right. Despite the solicitor's letter I sent threatening legal action if she contacted me again, a week later an embossed wedding invitation arrived, followed swiftly by a telephone call from her adoptive mother, hoping that I could find it in my heart to attend.

My heart?

Fucking hell.

I didn't even have the postcode for it.

32

Jocelyn and Irshad were singing from the same hymn sheet. He said I should think carefully about beginning a new relationship with another lie.

'It's not another lie; it's the same one,' I snapped.

He didn't even dignify that with an answer, but gave me a long, reproachful, pursed look and held me to six squirming minutes of silence before I conceded defeat and admitted he was right.

I knew that I would have to tell Adam that I had a daughter. She had me backed into a corner as surely as Bill Anderson ever had, and, once again, there was seemingly nothing I could do to escape. But I couldn't just produce Cheryl, then stand by while she picked away at me like icing on a cake, asking questions she had a right to have answered. I hadn't told Irshad everything, and, even if she stopped coming to see me, she would go to somebody else; and, as well as gossip, there would be records, newspaper archives.

I screwed my fists into my eye sockets to wipe out the vision and wondered if there might still be something she could find out. It depended on how determined she was. On impulse, I called the *Selkirk Courier* and asked them how far back their records went.

'We've got the last few years in the office,' said the woman who answered the phone. 'What year were you looking for?'

'Er, 1973 or thereabouts,' I said quietly, as though I might be overheard.

'Oh, you'll get those on microfiche at the library headquarters.'

I thanked her and prepared to hang up.

'It's the funniest thing, hen,' she said, 'but you're the second person this week to ask that exact same question.'

And so I surrendered to the inevitable. I did what Irshad suggested. Instead of evading the past, I embraced the future. I decided I would tell Adam about Cheryl when we were in Italy, when we were both relaxed and I could do it gently, and only divulge as much as I wanted to.

In the meantime, I would move in with him, and put some distance between Cheryl and myself. Jocelyn was sorry to lose me, but she agreed that I was doing the right thing. I needed to go someplace where the girl couldn't find me so that I could shake her off. I needed to get on with the business of living.

'I know you're going to be so happy. I'm glad for you,' she said, stroking the cat mechanically, sending clouds of hair into my face.

I sneezed, and pulled the last suitcase into the hall, where its wheels rocked to and fro on the Victorian tiles, sounding like a cricket with a sore throat. I had already taken most of my meagre possessions to Holland Crescent and unpacked the few boxes of bric-a-brac that I had left behind at Balfour.

Adam had found me a place on a copyediting course, and the basement sitting room had been cleared of teenage crap to serve as my study. A freshly photocopied manuscript sat on the new desk especially bought for the purpose, and every time I walked into the room, I twanged the elastic bands holding the pages together with the same relish as a pervert would a stocking top.

Instead of CDs and magazines the shelves held a motley collection of Colombian bowls, a painted wooden angel Francisco had bought me in El Salvador and a sheepish collection of photographs, embarrassed in their new frames, of Maisie and her kids, and Adam, Lennie and me, red-eyed and over-exposed, taken at the summer party in the communal garden. There was also a pot that Jocelyn had given me, which I had turned at an angle to hide the lack of symmetry, and a collection of matchbook altars from Brazil. The sofa had been recovered and was draped with a gay collection of magenta and bright orange woven cloths.

'Very north Oxford,' Adam had said approvingly when he saw it.

'Oh, no, very west London,' I corrected.

I couldn't wait to really make it my own and get down to work, but first we had three blissful weeks in Sorrento to enjoy.

'I'm going to miss you,' Jocelyn said, sniffing with what she claimed was a summer cold.

'I'll miss you too, Jocelyn,' I said, surprising myself with the truth of the statement. 'I don't know what I would have done without you. You've been so supportive.'

She went pink with pleasure. 'Don't be silly, dear. It was nothing.'

I draped Lennie's old duvet coat over my arm. I wouldn't need it, but I had grown too fond of it to send it to Oxfam.

Jocelyn enveloped me in the old aunts' scent of lavender and mothballs, and kissed my cheek. The cat mewled, crushed between us.

'We'll be lost without you at work. Particularly Krishna.'

'I'll come back and see you all after I get back from holiday. We can have lunch.'

'Yes, but it won't be the same as having you there every day.'

I heard the taxi trundling down the street, and I walked out to the side of the road where I stood, with my hand up like a kid with the right answer, until it stopped. Then, shouting over the crunching of gears and an urgent sports commentator on Five Live, I directed the driver to Holland Crescent and sat back watching the meter tick off the minutes in twenty-pence increments as he navigated the back roads up to Ladbroke Grove.

'Where do you want, love?' he asked through the intercom, as we turned into the street. I could hear the roar of an ecstatic crowd behind him.

'Just along here,' I answered, craning my neck as the houses repeated the two times table up to No. 22. 'This will do; just stop opposite the bus stop.'

He cut the engine and drew into a gap between two parked cars.

My stomach lurched and dived with merry excitement, as though I had ridden a roller coaster and was just now coming up for the biggest dip.

I could hardly contain myself from jumping out of the taxi and running up the steps, knowing that Adam was inside, waiting to welcome me home. I pictured myself weeks into the future, day after day after day of opening the door, dropping my bag on the floor and turning my head up for Adam's lips. I could smell the supper I would cook later, already bubbling on the stove, something with basil and garlic, I thought. I could taste the wine – crisp, Italian, maybe Prosecco, the bubbles tickling my nose – and see an armful of showy flowers waiting to be arranged in a vase. Adam's cheeks would crease into his little-boy smile; Lennie would be somewhere in the background, like white noise, laughing at something Ned had done; there would be gym kit spilled across the floor and biscuit crumbs. I could hear music playing in the dining room: the brand-new soundtrack of my brand-new life.

The taxi door unlocked with a click and the driver swivelled round to face me. 'Do you want a hand with the case?' he asked.

I dragged my rapt gaze away from the house where I had been placing myself, like one of those fuzzy felt figures, in a variety of fantasy panoramas: answering the door, weeding the window box that bloomed sedately with white geraniums I had planted the previous weekend, kissing Adam goodbye, kissing Adam hello.

'That would be terrific, since there seems to be no welcoming committee,' I said happily, a smile like a standing ovation on my lips, and a twenty-pound note in my hand; and then the words dried in my mouth.

At the bus shelter I saw a foot planted on the pavement. It wore a crude ugly sandal with a thick rubber sole and Day-Glo orange straps, and its similarly shod partner slowly tapped on the side of the bin. I leaned back, flattening myself against the leather seat. My skin stuck to the upholstery.

'No, wait a minute,' I said. 'Not here, could you keep going?

Just up to the end of the road. Slowly . . . Pull in at the corner, by the lights.'

He tutted and shook his head, as though women, capricious creatures, were something he would never be able to understand, revved the engine with a sound like loose change in a tin box and restarted the meter as he crawled down the street.

I glanced behind me as a figure emerged from behind the bus stop, and Cheryl stepped on to the road. She followed the cab as it drew away, perplexed that nobody had got out.

Fuck, fuck, fuck. What was she doing here? I ducked down, my skin making sucking sounds like a plaster being ripped off, till I was almost flat on the back seat, hoping she hadn't seen me.

'Is this all right, love?' the driver's voice interrupted me. His eyes met mine in the rear-view mirror. I could see he thought the nutter was in the back of his cab instead of standing in the middle of the road watching us. He stopped at the junction, though the lights said green.

I risked a glance out of the side window and saw Cheryl cross the street. She seemed to hesitate, then walked up the steps of No. 22 and pressed her palm to the bell.

'Twelve pounds and 20p,' said the driver.

'I've changed my mind,' I whispered as I saw the front door swing open.

He swore under his breath. 'Bleedin' women. Make your mind up, love. Where do you want to go now, then?'

'I don't know,' I answered. I craned my neck anxiously towards the house. Adam appeared on the top step. They exchanged a few words, then Cheryl shook his hand.

As a frown formed on Adam's face, she turned towards me, lifted her hand, pointed and waved.

'Oh, God. Just drive, please; anywhere,' I said, so softly I had to repeat it twice before he heard.

'Are you okay, love? You look like you've had a bit of a fright?' His voice came over the intercom, loud and tinny. Somebody, somewhere, scored.

I nodded in reply. I couldn't speak, and in any case my words would have been swept away by the tears running down my face.

Irshad would have told me to get out and confront her. He would have maintained that this was the ideal opportunity to tell Adam the truth. As far as Irshad was concerned, it was just a simple matter of filling in the details.

But that's where the Devil is. In the details.

And, as I said, I didn't tell him everything.

33

'You have to talk about it,' says Irshad. His cure makes confession the answer to every problem.

But some things are too great to admit, even to yourself

The hardest part was the night. Sitting awake for time that seemed to hang suspended in the suffocating darkness, after he'd locked us in again and gone. I had begged him to leave the light on, but it was almost worse sitting there in the harsh flickering glare of the fluorescent tube than it was in the dark. So we moved upstairs, with the door open, and squatted on the bed like two stray mutts, covered with our coats and the blanket. Kirsty wouldn't talk to me at first. She was disgusted that I had let him touch me, so disgusted that I didn't tell her what he'd made me do. I couldn't. She made me ashamed.

I assured her that it had been fine. I said it was nothing. I said that I didn't mind, which I hadn't. Not really. I told her I liked him. It made me feel less vulnerable. I was terrified of him, I might have said. Strangely, both were true. I couldn't understand why she, who had been the one who had droned on at length about how good-looking he was, how much she fancied him, was now revolted at the thought of touching him, and appalled at the idea of my touching him.

'Did it hurt?' she asked eventually.

'Nah. For a second – but my bones are sore from falling down. That hurt.'

'I've never done it. Not even with Dan. It was horrible. He tried to force me,' she spat, the emphasis on 'me'.

'He was going to force one of us – it was either me or you,' I reminded her.

'You didn't take a lot of persuasion,' she said, loftily. She maintained that she would rather be dead than do anything with him. I didn't point out that this was still a distinct possibility. After all, he hadn't let us go.

Kirsty was like my mother: she did it all for show. In her case, however, it wasn't the house she covered in ornaments; it was herself she put on the mantelpiece. She liked to flirt, she liked to display herself, but hadn't let either of her last two boyfriends have more than a furtive, fleeting grope of her breasts. Not even I had seen her naked. She hid herself in a big housecoat and long nighties whenever I visited, and was careful always to lock the bathroom door when she changed.

She was still a virgin. We had both been. But whereas Kirsty, at least, had the guide book for the world of sex, I hadn't even had a boyfriend. I'd hardly been kissed. There were things I had done that I hadn't even known existed.

Kirsty said she was saving herself. For what, I wondered. A shallow grave? I couldn't see how we were going to get out of this house alive except through persuasion.

I warned her that she would have to stop threatening him or he would never let us go. I told her to be sensible – why would he let us out if we were going to tell the police that he'd abducted us? That would get him into trouble. 'He's not going to let that happen, is he?' I said. I reminded her that she had got into the car, and that she had wanted to go to his house – that it had been her idea.

But no, it was my fault – I had got knocked out. I was the one who knew him, who had trusted him, who had let her believe he was safe. I was the one who had thrown myself at him. I was just a slag.

I slapped her.

She wept and I wept, and she wept more.

I told her to shut up or I would slap her again. I needed to think.

She snored and snuffled and took most of the blanket. I stared at the white felt rectangle on the roof and tried to think of a plan. To this day I don't like skylight windows.

I went through everything that he had done when he came in. He had unlocked two doors. I heard three bolts. He had put a big key in the inside pocket of his coat. I heard the metallic chink of it as it hit something else, but I hadn't seen him use another key. He hadn't taken his coat off, not even when he was on top of me.

Maybe I could sidetrack him next time; hit him on the head with one of the planks of timber. I could lock him in the toilet. But, no, it opened from the inside. So did the door from the stairs. I could smash the window, or the milk bottle, and stab him. But none of these would work. I knew that. He was huge. I couldn't overpower him, and any attempt to hurt him would only madden him and make it worse for us.

If I could persuade Kirsty to knock him out while he was on top of me, I thought. That might work. But, no, she was in no state to do anything. And then he might lose his temper and strangle me or something. He hadn't been too rough the night before, but he was strong. His arms were wider than my thighs. Anyway, I couldn't rely on Kirsty. She just whinged and rocked and cried and ranted at me.

The next morning when the sun shone through the rectangle of snow and lit up the room, I coaxed her down on to the sofa and made her some toast by holding it up to the Calor gas until it was brown. She wouldn't eat the first piece, which I had burned. I smashed banana on top of it with the heel of the milk bottle – there was no knife. I heated the milk and made her a cup of coffee. I'd torn up a dish towel and strapped a strip on to my blisters with masking tape, while Kirsty was still wearing her new boots. I persuaded her to remove them, telling her she'd be more comfortable without them digging into her flesh. She was reluctant, but I insisted, and eventually she peeled them off, the zips leaving long indentations on her chubby calves, her pink toes naked like small blind animals blinking in the light. She had a thin scab on the inside of her thigh, like a line of dead ants, and, beside it, a criss-cross of little lines, like snail trails but straight, almost geometric. She thumped me when I asked her what they were.

'None of your fucking business,' she snapped.

I thought she was embarrassed – perfect Kirsty with some sort of scabby rash.

She made some snide remark about my freckles and the mole on the back of my neck looking like a spider, which was supposed to shut me up.

It did.

After agreeing to keep a bucket of water by the fireplace in case the house burned down, I got together a broken picture frame and some splintered wood, rolled up some newspaper and lit a fire in the grate. I could see daylight up the chimney, so I hoped I wouldn't choke us out. Maybe someone would see the smoke and investigate.

I read her bits from three-month-old copies of the *Scottish Daily Record* to pass the time, but she wasn't listening. I did the crosswords with burned matches.

He didn't come back in the evening, although since snow was covering our only window we had just a sketchy idea of the time. It was either dark or it wasn't. And now it was.

As darkness fell and Anderson failed to arrive, Kirsty became alternately hysterical and catatonic. I fed the fire by jumping off the stairs on to planks of timber and breaking them into smaller pieces. It kept her warm. I fed her cheese on the crust of the loaf until the combination of the heat of the fire and the whisky I added to her tea put her to sleep. When she dropped off, I tried on her boots. Her feet were smaller than mine, and I had to struggle to get them on. They pinched my toes like pliers, but I decided that I could probably get them on, although the strips of cloth I had wound round my blisters would make it difficult.

I cuddled up on the sofa next to her and tried to warm myself so I could get some sleep, but she pushed me away.

It felt as though I had lived through three lifetimes by the time he came the next day. I'd just scraped the carbon off the toast I'd burned the day before and given it to Kirsty with the last of the cheese. He brought fish and chips this time, and lemonade and beer. I almost bit his hand off as he passed me the newspaper-wrapped parcel. I would have danced on my hands for them. The smell of vinegar was intoxicating. Kirsty said she didn't want any, but I put some on her knee, and she ate it in tiny bites without looking at him.

But he was jittery. I tried to appear unruffled, and asked if he would let us go home now, but he replied in an almost casually detached voice that, no – it was too late for that. His eyes darted all over the room as he told us that it had been on the news that we'd disappeared and not been seen since the party. Our picture had been on the TV, and was in the morning paper. The police had been to school that day and asked questions. They'd taken some boys who'd been at the party away for questioning.

'So there you go, then,' I said breezily, as if it was all a fuss about nothing. 'Nobody knows we're here. You said it yourself. Who would believe us? We'll say you haven't done anything wrong. If you could just not lock the door we could make our own way home,' I rationalized.

I swore that I wouldn't say anything – and that I would make sure Kirsty wouldn't either. I even told him that if anything came out, I would take the blame, say that I was the one who'd wanted to stay and that I'd forced her to remain. I'd say that he didn't even know we were in the house. I'd call her a liar if she said anything different, but he didn't respond. Instead, he paced.

'It's a problem, hen,' was all he said.

It was still snowing, his coat was flecked with it, and it was melting into little pools on the floor. Kirsty, roused by the food, began to threaten him again. She railed at him until he reached into his coat and produced a penknife, which he fanned out slowly until he found a hook to flick the top off his beer. The blades winked in the light as he bent them back into the sheath.

I watched him slip it back inside beside the key. Maybe I could get my hands on the knife, but first I had to force her to keep quiet for her own good. I sent her to the bedroom, forcibly ramming her up the stairs, pleading with her to shut her mouth and let me handle it.

'But, Agnes,' she whined, 'I don't like being up here without you. Don't leave me. You promised that you wouldn't leave me?'

'Yes, yes, shush, I promise, cross my heart. Where am I going to go? I'll be right here and I'll sort it out, okay?'

Then she wanted her boots back on. Her feet were cold, she whimpered. I took off my jacket and threw it after her. 'Wrap them in this – come on now – go away before he gets nasty.'

I waited until I heard the match fizz and saw the candlelight dance across the rafters, then I pulled the stair door closed. His eyes had followed me, but it wasn't me he wanted to see; it was Kirsty. Even after three days without a bath and with her hair tangled, she was beautiful. My shoulders shrank into two curls of defeat. It always came back to Kirsty.

I sat down next to him and smiled brightly, or as brightly as I could with a bruised eye and a bust lip. His eyes switched from me to the closed door. He still had his heavy outdoor coat on. I smoothed my hands over the lapels.

It was soaking. I said, 'Is it still snowing outside?'

'It's turning to sleet,' he answered. 'But it's going to freeze. The roads will be bad, and there's already a foot of snow out there. I don't know when I'll get back again.'

'Never mind,' I soothed. 'But your coat. You should take it off. The fire will dry it.'

In answer he looked at the grate and told me I shouldn't be burning any of this stuff.

'It was for Kirsty,' I replied. 'She was cold.'

'She's a lovely-looking girl, isn't she? What a figure. That hair.'

I agreed, though it felt like I was coughing up a knife.

He wanted to know everything about her. Where she was going when she left school, how old she was, where she lived, what her father did. I answered him but monosyllabically. I didn't want to get drawn into a Kirsty love fest when I was the one who had spent the day holding her hand, spooning food into her mouth and wiping her nose.

He smoked a joint. I pretended to smoke it too, but I held the smoke in my cheeks and puffed it out. I told him his coat was soaking me and making me cold, and he finally took it off and laid it on the back of the armchair. He got down beside me.

'You're really skinny, aren't you?' he said, looking at my ribs appraisingly. I crossed my arms protectively across my chest. 'Your bones are sharp.' He put his large, spade-like hand on my hip. 'You could use a bath,' he said.

'Aye, well, there's a shortage of towels in this hotel,' I replied.

Then he asked me about the boys the police had picked up. Was one of them Kirsty's boyfriend? I sighed. I was lying there spread open in front of him. He used me, but he didn't see me. I was just the stand-in, the inferior body double for the main star, who was upstairs, curled into a ball, sucking her sleeve.

'Oh, she has loads,' I said, puffing out my cheeks, though this time there was no smoke to pad them out.

'Really?'

'Ever since she was wee – her first boyfriend was seventeen and she had him when she was thirteen.'

'Hah, that's not the way she tells it. She's a bit of a stuck-up little cow, isn't she? Thinks she's something special. Mind you, she is something special.'

'She's spoiled. Her father gives her everything she wants – she's used to getting her own way with everybody. Especially boys. They all fawn over her.'

'So lots of boyfriends, you say?'

'Definitely,' I replied. 'She's always been a bit loose. Plays them off against each other. You don't want to believe the little miss prissy act. She's just having you on. Whose idea was it that we were walking home the other night? Why do you think we were even at that party?'

He went quiet, and so did I for a while. I had my eye on his coat. I was sure the key was in the pocket. I felt around his trousers; there was nothing there but some coins.

'You should go upstairs. Don't listen to her. All that shy stuff, it's all kid on.'

He sat up, lifted the bottle of whisky, unscrewed the cap and drank from the bottle.

He wiped the back of his mouth with his hand. I was bleeding again. I could see it on his cheek and on the tail of his shirt.

'Go on,' I whispered. 'I'll not say anything. She likes you. She used to fancy you. She told me. It was her who wanted to come here, wasn't it?'

Keeping a grip on the bottle, he stood and pulled his trousers together and, with barely a glance at me, walked towards the stairs. I held my breath, but then at the last minute he doubled back and picked up the coat.

Damn, damn, damn, I wailed. I was so tense I thought I was going to wet myself.

I sat on the sofa and wiped myself with newspaper. Then yanked my clothes back on as swiftly as I could.

The stair door was open. I could hear Kirsty telling him he was disgusting and to go away and leave her alone.

I darted around the room as quickly as I could. I grabbed Kirsty's boots, opened the porch and threw them inside.

Kirsty was roaring now. Crying and screaming at him to stop. 'Agnes,' she was shouting, 'Agnes, help me.' I heard the slap of a hand against something hard as I crept up the stairs, holding my breath. He was talking to her, telling her to be still, to hush, but she kept on struggling and fighting until there was another hard slap and then she just sobbed, in muffled gasps. He had his hand over her mouth.

I saw the coat: it was hanging over the little banister at the top of the stairs. The candle was guttering wildly as I stood on my tiptoes and tugged at the hem. Slowly, it slid into my arms, making a soft thunk as the collar landed on the wood. I froze, but the steady movement on the bed continued with Kirsty's strangled cries. I walked backwards, my feet feeling as though they were floating on air, but the minute I got back into the room I sprinted to the front porch, pulling the coat on to my shoulders. It was massive and kept slipping off.

My heart was beating so loudly that I could hear it above Kirsty's crying, while my hands raked through the deep pockets. I couldn't make my fingers work. There was no penknife, but I felt the key. There was only one – it was huge and old-fashioned, and I grabbed it tightly in my fist like a spear. I closed the porch door as slowly as I could bear, jammed the key into the lock and turned it. Please, God, he hadn't heard it. I shot a look at the wall. There was a fuse box with a big handle that I knew would put the house into darkness. I pulled it. That would hold him up a little longer. I drew the bolts, then I grabbed the boots, tossed them out into the snow and went out into the bitter black night, locking the outside door with the same key.

I sat for a minute tearing the wadded masking tape off my feet, pulling strips of skin that had bled and hardened, adhering to the cloth. My fingers were covered with bright scarlet blood. Then I screwed my feet into the boots and zipped them halfway up, where they jammed on the bunched-up material of my trousers. The zip pinched the bare skin of my leg, but I ignored it, stood up, and slipped and lurched across the driveway. The wheels of the car had compacted the snow into cursive loops, and scribbles, like a big mistake.

I looked inside his car, checking behind me to make sure there was nobody coming. There could be another way out of the house that we hadn't found. He'd left the car door unlocked and the keys in the ignition. I took them out and held them for a second in the palm of my hand. Then I threw them across the snow into a hedge.

Behind me there was a muted banging on a door coming from inside the house. Mr Anderson was yelling and swearing. 'You fucking bitch, I'll kill her if you don't come back, ya fucking bastard hooring fucking bitch.' I could hear Kirsty screaming my name, saying don't leave me, Agnes, don't leave me . . . but I didn't hesitate. Not for a second.

I pulled the coat together and never once looked behind me. I ran and ran and ran.

I ran, and I never stopped running.

Acknowledgements

Authors always offer profuse gratitude to their editors and agents, but anyone who has ever been involved in producing a book will know that this is more than a polite gesture. So a sincere thank you to Toby Mundy, who introduced me to George Capel, who, together with the enthusiastic Rosie Apponyi, tirelessly supported this book. Thanks also to Jenny Dean and her fellow Vikings at Penguin for plucking my story from the great wall of manuscripts that land on their desks every day, and patiently nursing me through the second whimpering infancy that is editing a book. Donna Poppy's painstaking copyediting must be praised for removing many of my glaring acts of idiocy, but those that have slipped through her net are mine and mine alone.

My children, the best part of my life, were probably grateful for the respite that writing gave them from my nagging, but were also fiercely supportive. Thank you, Nel, for being my perfect imaginary audience, and thanks also to Eduardo Posada-Carbó, who patiently helped me with some background details, though he cannot be blamed for my inaccuracies. Other friends – Maria, Julia, Sarah, Judith and Yvonna, especially, were great supporters. Finally, I want to thank Christopher MacLehose, whose kindness, interest and help, over and above the call of casual acquaintanceship, set me on the road from Don't Bother to Don't Give Up.

Getting a book published is the result of a long chain of random acts of encouragement and other people's good will. Editors who have commissioned me, readers who have responded to things I have written, people who have listened to my stories – all the great women at Atlantic Books and particularly Miranda – friends and family, past and present, and those loved and lost along the way, have all played their part. I'm only sad that some of them are not here to see the book.

He just wanted a decent book to read ...

Not too much to ask, is it? It was in 1935 when Allen Lane, Managing Director of Bodley Head Publishers, stood on a platform at Exeter railway station looking for something good to read on his journey back to London. His choice was limited to popular magazines and poor-quality paperbacks – the same choice faced every day by the vast majority of readers, few of whom could afford hardbacks. Lane's disappointment and subsequent anger at the range of books generally available led him to found a company – and change the world.

'We believed in the existence in this country of a vast reading public for intelligent books at a low price, and staked everything on it'
Sir Allen Lane, 1902–1970, founder of Penguin Books

The quality paperback had arrived – and not just in bookshops. Lane was adamant that his Penguins should appear in chain stores and tobacconists, and should cost no more than a packet of cigarettes.

Reading habits (and cigarette prices) have changed since 1935, but Penguin still believes in publishing the best books for everybody to enjoy. We still believe that good design costs no more than bad design, and we still believe that quality books published passionately and responsibly make the world a better place.

So wherever you see the little bird – whether it's on a piece of prize-winning literary fiction or a celebrity autobiography, political tour de force or historical masterpiece, a serial-killer thriller, reference book, world classic or a piece of pure escapism – you can bet that it represents the very best that the genre has to offer.

Whatever you like to read – trust Penguin.

read more
www.penguin.co.uk